CABIN FEVER

THE SEAMUS McCREE SERIES
BY JAMES M. JACKSON

NOVELS
Ant Farm
Bad Policy
Cabin Fever
Doubtful Relations
Empty Promises
False Bottom
Granite Oath
Hijacked Legacy

NOVELLAS
Furthermore
Low Tide at Tybee

NONFICTION
BY JIM JACKSON

*One Trick at a Time:
How to Start Winning at Bridge*

CABIN FEVER

James M. Jackson

Second Edition
Trade Paperback Edition: April 2017

Cover Design by Karen Phillips

Wolf's Echo Press
PO Box 54
Amasa, MI 49903
www.WolfsEchoPress.com

ISBN-13 Trade Paperback: 978-1-943166-08-4
ISBN-13 e-book: 978-1-943166-09-1
Library of Congress Control Number: 2017902392

Printed in the United States of America
1098765

DEDICATION

For three of the greatest animal friends I've ever had:

Orestes (1994-2008)
Electra (1994-2012)
Morgan le Fay (2000-2013)

ONE

FACING NORTH INTO A BRISK wind, I searched for signs of the aurora borealis but spotted only a front forming in the distance. *It's probably nothing.* The skies above were so clear the Milky Way seemed almost within reach. I never worried about getting lost on nights like this. As long as stars were shining, the reflective snow made it easy to follow my old tracks home.

I checked the northern Michigan sky again. *The stars are bright—stop making excuses, Seamus, and get crackin'.* With my breath crystalizing around me, turning my beard and mustache white, I strapped on snowshoes and began my trek, the snow squeaking in protest with each step.

I was six miles into an eight-mile loop when I exited the shelter of a cedar swamp. The evergreens had been holding much of the snow in their branches, making travel relatively easy. Deep in thought, I had paid only passing attention as snow-laden clouds from the north brought with them a howling February snowstorm that threatened to erase any trace of my tracks.

That was a stupid mistake for someone living all alone, miles from his nearest neighbor.

To the snare drum rattling of hardwood treetops, I climbed the rise from the frozen swamp to the head of the lake following faint indentations. At first, the trail headed the way I expected, but soon it veered off and I realized the tracks had drifted in. *No problem, I'll cut straight up the hill to the lake.* I pushed through the brush border at the lake's edge and met a fierce blast that tore my breath away. A thousand hypodermic snow needles jabbed my exposed face. I ducked my head into my parka, pulled ski goggles from my knapsack, and fastened them over my mink hat.

I could take the safer approach: go back down the hill and partially retrace my sheltered steps to a road that would eventually lead me home. Or I could move forward and strike directly over the lake toward my property. The wind on the lake would be terrible without cover. The wind also meant there would be less snow, and what there was would be hard-packed, allowing better footing. Walking up the middle of the lake would lop off considerable distance and time. Not wanting to retreat, I rationalized that if conditions worsened, I could cut over to the shoreline and follow it home.

I turned to consult Abigail, remembering in a flush of regret that she'd been gone for a month. To the wind I muttered, "Mad wolves and Irishmen go out in the dark winter storm."

Realizing I needed to stop channeling Noël Coward and get with the program, I strode onto the lake. After ten labored steps, I turned around to block the wind and wipe the snow from my goggles. The shore, a scant twenty-five feet away, was almost invisible. I could picture the headline in the *Iron County Reporter*: "Snowmobiler Finds 'Tourist' Frozen on Shank Lake." I retreated to the shoreline and followed it around toward my place.

An hour later, I located the gaps in the wild cherry bushes marking the start of the path leading past my guest cabin and up to my house. Sections of my dismantled dock stacked next to the path for winter served momentarily as a windbreak while I gathered my strength. I stuffed my mittens between my legs and fished a Petzl headlamp from my knapsack. Flipping the red filter down so I wouldn't lose night vision, I fastened it around my head. Almost home.

Halfway to the cabin, I entered a group of hemlocks blocking the wind. Not paying enough attention as I left the trees' shelter, the wind whipped a maple branch across my nose. Jerking away from the sting, I staggered a step into the unpacked snow and buried my left leg up to my crotch in powder. I threw both arms forward to cushion my fall, bucking as my sleeves filled with snow. It took me two tries to regain my balance. If coyotes were watching, they would howl for hours at my bipedal comedy. I wiped the snow from my nose with bare fingers, felt a dribble of warmth, and licked away the salty blood.

The guest cabin was rustic: no electricity, no plumbing. I periodically shoveled the stoop to allow access to the bookshelves my son and I had built years ago when it was the only building on the property. I dithered at stopping to get something new to read—I was almost through a Rex Stout collection—or getting to the main house to take care of my nose. The dithering itself was a sign I was overtired and not thinking clearly.

An arc of smoothed snow on the stoop formed a single angel wing.

Someone had recently opened the door to the screened porch. Squatting down, I flipped up the headlamp's red filter and spotted prints of bare feet.

Now I knew I was going nuts. Occasionally holding conversations with a disappeared Abigail was one thing, but phantom footprints meant my imagination was reaching a new level of desperation. *Get a grip, Seamus. No one walks around barefoot in this weather.* At the thought, my arms reminded me they were freezing from my nosedive into the snow. My teeth started chattering.

I knelt to inspect the tracks: all faced forward; no departures. Must be guys from one of the nearby camps playing a trick. Peering into the swirling snow, the track of partially filled footprints disappeared down the driveway.

A frisson of disquiet struck me. Although only sixty-five yards away, the house and garage were invisible with their lights off. What if it wasn't a joke? What if someone found this cabin and took refuge? I yanked open the screen door and tromped in, ignoring the scrape of snowshoe claws on the porch floor. I peered in the glass door to the cabin proper. No one had lit the fire preset in the wood stove.

A shiver running from my toes to the top of my head reminded me I needed warmth. A book could wait for morning. Turning from the door, I caught a flash of two bare legs dangling below the chair hammock attached to a porch rafter. I laughed so hard my sides ached and my lungs hurt from the frozen air.

In a place where winter lasts half the year, jokes and jokers get odd. The jerks must have stepped a blow-up doll onto my porch to make the footprints and posed it in the swinging chair. They had concealed their tracks well. In this dark, I couldn't figure out how they did it, but I'd find the evidence in daylight.

Fine. Like pink flamingos mysteriously congregating in front lawns of townies about to return from vacation, this babe was definitely going to show up in someone's sauna in the near future. *Might as well drag it to the house so it'll be close at hand for future revenge.* I grabbed the plastic legs to haul the thing from the chair.

The legs were real.

Two

Her breathing was shallow and slow. Her breath warm and odorless. Her pulse erratic. I moved her to the house using a fireman's carry. It felt about the same as lugging a couple of fifty-pound bags of sunflower seed to the basement so I could feed the birds all winter. After shucking my snowshoes, I deposited her in the tub and ran a tepid bath to defrost her.

First thing I thought of was drugs. Her body was athlete-thin. Her hands and feet were callused. She sported fresh scrapes on the bottom of her left heel, probably from walking barefoot. A chipped fingernail on her right hand added to my impression that her work was physical. A recovering hickey on her neck showed she had recently spent time with someone. Most disconcerting, fresh rope burns on her wrists and ankles had left them raw. I had never been interested in bondage games and these had to have hurt. No needle tracks.

Her cropped hair looked as though she'd run a beard trimmer over her scalp. Or maybe she had shaved her head and let it grow a few weeks. She had three holes in each ear, but no earrings. I found no other punctures, but she had a rose tattooed above her left breast and a Celtic braid on her right ankle. She was not wearing contacts.

I replaced cooled water with hot to return the bath to room temperature. After forty-five minutes her skin tone changed from milky white to mottled pink. I shifted her weight to check her pulse again and her eyes fluttered to consciousness. She jerked away from my hovering hand, cracking her head against the faucet. "Ouch." She closed her eyes and shook her head several times as though trying to shake out cobwebs. "Who . . . the fuck . . . are you?" Her voice rose. "Where the hell . . . am I?"

"I'm Seamus McCree." I slowly and clearly enunciated the "Shay-mus." Most people haven't heard the name and, if I say it too fast, they usually ask me to repeat it. "And you're . . . ?" I released her shoulders. She slipped into the water, caught herself, and raised her body on extended arms. Her face took on a quizzical expression. She looked at herself in the tub, then at the cathedral ceiling, and finally pinned me to the wall with her glare.

"I . . . don't remember . . . shit. Roofie? Why's this . . . bath so . . . damn cold?" She pointed to my outerwear left strewn on the bathroom floor. "Where are mine?"

She tried and failed to get out of the tub. "Too tired . . . to move. Cold."

"You were frostbitten," I said. "Doesn't look too bad. Only your fingers and toes appear chapped. The rest of you . . ." I realized I was about to say "looks pretty good," which she could easily take the wrong way. "The rest of you was preternaturally white. We can make the bath a little warmer, but not much or it will be really painful—at least that's what I remember from Boy Scouts. You don't remember anything?"

She closed her eyes and furrowed her brow. She was either concentrating intensely or putting on a great act. "No frostbite. I . . . was really . . . hot." In apparent frustration, she slapped the water, spraying me and the floor. "Where . . . am I?"

Hot made sense. People in the last stages of hypothermia sometimes think they're really hot and strip off their clothes. "You're at my camp on Shank Lake." No glimmer of recognition in her eyes. "It's in the northeast corner of Iron County."

Her eyes briefly widened. "Wisconsin?"

"The Upper Peninsula of Michigan."

"You don't sound like a Yooper."

"I wasn't born in the U.P. I found you on the screened porch of my guest cabin. I've been thawing you ever since. You still haven't told me your name."

"Want to . . . call the cops."

"I wish we could," I said, using what I hoped was a nonthreatening voice. "Problem is there's no cell phone coverage. Let me get you some clothes."

"I'm tired." She released a long sigh that appeared to back up her claim. "Need sleep . . . alone."

After lifting her out of the tub and holding her steady while she toweled off, I threw a ratty bathrobe around her. On my six feet two inches, the bathrobe nearly touched the ground; on her slight frame, the robe hung like an Elizabethan gown, fanning out on the floor around her. I led her to the main bedroom, which was next to the bathroom, and pulled back the down comforter. "I can put on fresh sheets if you want." She waved away the offer and crawled into bed still wearing the bathrobe. I tucked the comforter under her chin. From the bureau I pulled a pair of flannel pants with a tie string and a T-shirt advertising the Nature Conservancy's Pine Butte Guest Ranch. "These are way too large, but it's the best I can do."

"Leave them." She pointed to the chair. "My head hurts." She twisted her head back and forth. "Not a hangover. Flu or something. You got pain meds?"

I brought two Advils and a large glass of water. "It would be good if you drink it all. I think you get dehydrated with frostbite."

She downed the tablets and several slugs of water. "Maybe later." She placed the half-emptied glass on the nightstand. Her eyes narrowed. "How is it you're the only person in a thousand miles who uses 'preternaturally' in a sentence, but's too dumb to check my ID to find out who I am?"

I took the hint of humor and the compound sentence as a good sign. "I found you freezing to death on my porch," I said. "No clothes. No purse. Just you. I have no idea where you came from." I heard a testiness entering my voice. Why was that? I consciously lightened my tone. "You're probably suffering from shock. You want a nightlight in the bathroom?" I was talking to a sleeping woman.

I stood at the foot of the bed and watched the comforter rise and fall with her breathing. She looked nothing like Abigail, and yet the memories of standing helplessly next to her hospital bed buckled my knees. Abigail had been shot protecting me, and I almost lost her then. Now I had.

I left the bedroom door ajar, hung the wet towel above the bathtub, and plugged in the nightlight. The house elves were on strike. The fire in the great room stove had burned down to coals. The outside temperature had dropped to minus fifteen, and I needed to keep the fire going to maintain sixty-five indoors. I placed kindling and two logs into the wood stove. Distracted with worry, I cleaned the tub, mopped the melted snow I had tracked in, and returned the coat, snow bib, mittens, and extra socks to their assigned pegs.

Concern for her blurred into concern for myself. Her blurted accusation about roofies and what that implied left me wondering what kind of trouble I would be in if she didn't recover her memory. The cops sure weren't going to believe I found her *au naturel* on the cabin porch. Is that why I had started to lose my temper with her?

I poured a glass of red wine from my favorite box and curled into the chair next to the wood stove, trying to anticipate what tomorrow would bring. Whatever it was, it would wreak havoc on my normal routine. Where had she come from? The closest neighbors were miles away. Was she taking a late snowmobile ride and broke down? Riding by yourself midwinter was dangerous, but so was walking miles away from home, which I did both day and night. Maybe someone would follow whatever tracks the storm hadn't covered and show up here, saving me the trouble of sorting out what happened.

I didn't feel like making up the futon in the guest bedroom, so I laid my sleeping bag on top of the Oriental rug nearest the wood stove. From there, I could easily tend the fire and hear her if she called. Before I crawled into the bag, I tiptoed upstairs and listened at the open bedroom door: her breathing was regular, but raspy.

Stripping off my thermals, I snuggled into the sleeping bag and watched reflections from the wood stove dance on the pitched ceiling. Even if she seemed fully recovered tomorrow, she really should have a doctor examine her, and, depending on what had caused the restraint abrasions, she might need the cops. My next expected visitor was the supply man who came on Tuesdays, five days away. Not exactly timely. *Maybe I should have bought a snowmobile, after all.* Tomorrow I'd have to cross-country ski the eight miles to the permanent residences on Deer Lake and use someone's computer to request help. On that decision I fell asleep.

And awoke to someone shaking me.

Her strong fingers dug into my shoulders with the force of pliers. Sleep vanished. "I'm burning up," she said. Firelight twinkled in the glistening sweat covering her body. "I can't find the Advil."

My mother never gave me anything to reduce fevers. She said fevers are our body's way of burning out what ails us. I wasn't sure if that applied to someone recently frostbitten or, for that matter, why frostbite would cause a fever. Maybe her body was overreacting.

"Let's take your temperature and make sure what we're dealing with," I said. "Turn around and let me get some clothes on."

"I don't give a shit about your body. Just get me the drugs." She plopped down on the couch and braced her head on her hands.

I shucked off the sleeping bag, donned a pair of briefs, and rummaged in the closet containing medical supplies. Found a red thermometer with a pear-shaped tip, a rectal one from when Paddy was a tyke. I was not going to go there if I could avoid it, so kept searching for an oral thermometer, which should have a long, blue tip. Finally, in the medicine cabinet over the sink, I turned up one with numbers on a strip. Not perfect, but preferable.

She didn't open her eyes while I held the thermometer strip on her brow. To my hand she was steaming. I watched the tape's digits start with 94 and rapidly light up the 98.6, 100, 102 and finally settle somewhere between 104 and 105. Paddy, at around three, had a fever that high. Bad for a kid, terrible for an adult. I dressed while she sat up to choke down two more Advil—it had been almost four hours. She slumped onto the couch and coughed a long dry rattle. Pneumonia?

I gathered several self-help medical texts from the nonfiction library in the basement. All agreed I needed to cool her down. If she had viral pneumonia, there was nothing else to do. If bacterial, treat with antibiotics. What did I know about viral versus bacterial pneumonia, or if it was pneumonia at all? A doctor friend, learning Abigail and I were going to spend winter at my isolated camp and would only have someone come in once a week to bring supplies and mail, insisted I fill a prescription for erythromycin. The seal remained unbroken. The girl raised her head and took a dose. Better safe than sorry, as long as she wasn't allergic to the stuff.

"Back in the bathtub, kiddo," I said once she finished the water chaser to the drugs.

She looked at me with glassy eyes. I helped her upstairs and ran another tepid bath, making sure to point her feet at the faucet. She was sufficiently coherent to sit up this time, so I grabbed a washcloth and gave her a sponge bath, without soap and without any rubbing. I was still a little concerned about frostbite, although that didn't seem to be a problem. She had mentioned earlier she had been hot; I wondered if her fever had mitigated the frostbite.

I replaced her soaked sheets with a fresh set. She crawled into bed and quickly fell asleep. The bath had dropped her temperature to a hundred; how long before it spiked again, I didn't know. I added wood to the stove and turned off the two ceiling fans so more heat would stay upstairs. The best place to monitor her was the bedroom, so I scooted the rocking chair away from the bed and wrapped myself in a Hudson Bay blanket.

What am I going to do? I had been either sanguine or fatalistic about my chances living so far from help. Abigail maintained it was necessary for her as a bodyguard to either recognize that life could end at any time or to find another profession. I'm not sure she ever really accepted the philosophy as it pertained to living in the middle of nowhere, but that wasn't why she left me.

This situation, however, didn't affect my mortality. This woman needed medical attention. Unless her fever broke, I didn't think I could leave her for the time it would take to ski the eight miles to Deer Lake and my closest neighbor. If someone was around to snowmobile me back, it was one thing; but if they weren't—and I had to assume the worst—I'd also have to ski back. I could do it, but it would take several hours. I'd given her the Advil at four a.m.; she could have more at eight. By then it would be light enough to see. I closed my eyes.

From the depths of sleep I heard, "Mister, Mister. Snakes are all over the walls." Her forehead was again on fire. She drained the water from the glass I proffered. "No snakes," she said. "Just a bad dream."

Hallucinations, more likely. I gave her a second glass of water. "Drink while I draw a bath."

She latched onto my arms for support as we shuffled from bedroom to bath. She caught sight of herself in the mirror, fingered the hickey, and closed her eyes.

"Does that help you remember anything?" I asked.

Her eyes exhibited a series of flickers, as though she were in REM. She popped them open. Looking straight at me, she mumbled, "No."

The bath again dropped her temperature, and this time I wet her head to help keep her cooler longer. It was too soon to give her more medicine, which left me crossing my fingers. While she toweled off, I put my third and last set of sheets on the bed. Abigail had last washed this set, and the faint scent of the dryer sheets she used remained on them.

The woman placed a fresh glass of water on the end table and slid back into bed. Any thought of leaving her alone while I got help vanished with her renewed fever spikes. I threw the soaked sheets into the washing machine and plunked into the chair next to the wood stove. Gazing into the fire, I prayed for inspiration. Ideas were slow in coming. The most likely possibility was for snowmobilers to pass by. They would travel by road or lake; I needed to mark each route to alert passersby to the emergency and get them to stop.

Another possibility occurred to me. The previous week, a mining company had flown magnetic imagery runs somewhere west of here. I heard them all that day, running a series of parallel courses towing sensors designed to find places where the magnetic direction of the rock layers change, indicating a possible fault into which gold or copper may have flowed. To catch the attention of any planes flying nearby, I wanted to put a distress signal on the ice.

I turned on the radio to NPR. The world still existed, but the bad news/good news ratio was nineteen to one. The weather forecaster predicted an end to the snow by dawn, clearing by afternoon, and winds less than five miles an hour. Predawn slowly arrived. I flicked on an outside light—a whisper breeze juked a few flakes through the bright cone. My guest was sleeping again, so I put on snow gear and retrieved the can I used for ash from the wood stove.

Most people think the Northwoods are dark in winter. They're actually darker in the summer because the maple, birch, and aspen are fully leafed out. At its worst, we do have only eight hours of daylight. But by now in early February, we had around ten; I could easily work outside without a flashlight. The storm had increased our snow depth to more than three feet. Unlike in civilized areas where snow quickly turns dirty, ours would stay luminous white until it melted away in the spring thaw, better known as "mud season."

With snowshoes strapped over boots, I carted the ash bucket up the driveway to the road. The wind had smoothed away any evidence of civilization except for faint traces of one of my cross-country ski trails. A lone coyote had painted the snowy canvas with its characteristic track as it wandered down the middle of the road, occasionally checking something on the edge before returning to the center. For a moment, I forgot why I was standing in the road with an ash bucket in my hand. The air smelled fresh and clean and the silence was so complete that the only sound I heard was the whoosh of blood coursing near my ears. The tickle of a single snowflake reminded me I was outside for a reason.

I stamped HELP in block letters taking up the width of the road. It might work to stop a snowmobiler, but often they traveled forty, fifty, or more miles an hour. At those speeds the tramped area would be a blur. I darkened the letters with ash. Initially, the ash melted the snow with a hiss of steam; soon cooler ash from the can silently covered the bright snow. I stepped away to look at the completed project: it should stop any passing traffic.

Back inside, I checked on the girl—still sleeping—and despite the room smelling of a mixture of Abigail's shampoo and the dryer sheets, this woman was not Abigail, nor would she ever be. No one could be, and I missed her like crazy—maybe the reality was that I was crazy with the missing.

The road was only twelve feet or so across; the lake spanned three-eighths of a mile. Unless I guessed the right spot on the lake, a snowmobile could easily pass by my message, and I had to make it large enough to attract a pilot's attention from a long distance. From the garage I retrieved three blue tarps and cut them into footwide strips.

Light tinted the tips of the evergreens across the lake. Isolated patches of pale blue pockmarked the clouds, providing promise of a clearing sky and warming temperatures. I snowshoed onto the lake and, using the blue tarp swatches, displayed SOS in six-foot letters, finishing with an elongated arrow pointing to my house. The letters and arrow covered as much of the lake between my house and the opposite shore as possible. From the air, the message would be clear; I hoped a snowmobiler would notice at least a flash of blue tarp and slow down to figure out what was going on. I weighted down each letter's corners with packed snow. Without fresh snowfall, they should remain visible. I didn't expect enough sun to cause the tarp to act as a heat trap and melt snow beneath the letters, but, periodically, I'd have to make sure.

I checked on my guest—still sleeping, albeit more fitfully—and I returned outside to unbury my woods truck from the winter's accumulated snow. A serviceable Ford Ranger, I had pulled its battery shortly after Christmas once snow had closed the local roads for the duration of winter. To institute the third component of my plan, I reinstalled it and shattered the silence with three long horn blasts: the universal signal of distress. I figured the sound would travel at least a couple of miles since the leaves were off the trees and the wind had died to a gentle breeze. I planned to repeat the blasts every half hour.

I sent a silent message in all four directions asking someone, anyone, to find me before I had a dead woman on my hands.

Three

SHORTLY AFTER NINE IN THE morning, Jimmie Heitzmann arrived at Boss's rented cabin accompanied by the roar of a finely tuned snow machine. Attached to his canary-yellow Arctic Cat was a utility sleigh. He circled the camp and parked next to Brett's truck.

Jimmie dismounted and removed his helmet and black balaclava, exposing a clean-shaven face, squashed nose, eyes the color of a Caribbean bay, and a ruffled mess of mud-brown hair. He left the snow machine running and checked to make sure the long gun was still firmly bungee-corded to the sled. He patted the Ruger strapped to his side and followed his breath cloud to the front door.

Inside, his glance took in the nearly empty rum bottle on the table and the inert form under the quilts. He tiptoed to the bed, leaned down, and yelled as loudly as he could, "Wake-up, fuck face!"

Brett groaned and tugged the covers further over his head. Jimmie walked to the sink and started running cold water into a bucket. Took off one glove and tested the water. *Damn near to grabbing ice cubes.* He blew on his hand to warm it, and replaced the glove.

"I'm up, goddamn it. I'm up." Brett threw off the covers and heaved out of bed. "Don't you start with that water shit again. We got time for breakfast?"

"You drank it last night. We need to get tracking. Boss already filled me in. You got three minutes."

"It's freezing in here. What's the hurry? There wasn't hardly any gas in the snow machine she stole. That's why I was in town when she escaped— to get gas, y'know? She's frozen someplace not far. Alls we got to do is follow her tracks. She didn't have long anyway, her fever was way up there."

"Save your excuses for Boss. You did get rid of the guy, right?"

"He's anchored with concrete and feeding fishes." Brett finished dressing and opened the door to the wood stove.

"Leave it," Jimmie commanded. "Pipes won't freeze before we get back. We need to find the girl."

Brett pulled his first beer of the day from the refrigerator—"hair of the dog"— and downed it before they got to Jimmie's sled. Even with the new snowfall and the night's high winds, it took no skill to follow the girl's trail for several miles. Wind had drifted in the runner lines, but the packed center track was still visible. She had followed the main road west, then cut south, skirted a gate, and headed up a camp road.

Brett tapped Jimmie's shoulder and he slowed to a crawl. "This leads into a guy's camp on Long Lake. He wasn't up a few days ago when I got rid of Brandon." Jimmie dipped his head in understanding and sped off, shooting snow rooster tails behind him. They followed her trail to the camp, a two-story log edifice. The yard was a mess of tracks.

Jimmie stopped the machine and both men hopped off. With face masks up and gloves off, they studied the tracks and decided she had backtracked a hundred feet and followed a frozen lead down onto the lake where the track disappeared. "Now what the fuck do we do?" Brett said. "I didn't think there was that much gas in the sled."

"Keep your eyes peeled, asshole. If she ain't in the lake, she musta cut into the woods. We need to find where she came out. If I was her, I'd try the little log cabin across the lake."

They followed the shoreline down to the outlet and started back up the far side. In short order, Jimmie found the state's boat landing, which he remembered led to an old trail. They got off, walked up the bank, and saw recently disturbed dead ferns. *Gotcha, girlie.*

A distant automobile horn honked three times. "Fuck's that?" said Brett.

Jimmie held up his hand for silence. They waited a minute, but heard nothing other than chickadees and a red-breasted ass-up feeding in a gnarled yellow birch. Gunning the snowmobile, Jimmie followed the girl's trail around a bend and saw the stolen sled. She had run it smack under a chain running across the access to the smaller cabin. It must have knocked her ass over teakettle. The snow machine zoomed off without her and buried itself in a snowbank. Written in the snow was her struggle to extract the machine, but it was too stuck and too heavy for a small woman.

"Leave it for now," Jimmie said. "We'll get it on the way back. She can't have gone far in this snow without snowshoes." They remounted Jimmie's snow machine and slowly followed the occasional dimple in the snow that indicated her path. Wherever the woods opened up, everything drifted in and they had to guess which way she went. The problem became more acute once they entered a Plum Creek clear-cut. Whenever their first guess didn't quickly pan out, they strapped on snowshoes and walked arcs until they restruck her trail.

Fifteen minutes into the process, they hit a larger road and again followed the shuffling tracks south. Brett tapped Jimmie's shoulder and pointed to a blue knit hat hanging on a tree limb. Jimmie gave it a good sniff—smelled like the aloe in her shampoo—and pitched it into the sleigh's storage compartment. They soon discovered a glove decorating a bush.

Brett began to bounce up and down on the seat like he was five and about to get Jell-O with canned fruit for dessert. "Can't be much farther," he shouted over the engine. Jimmie ignored him, stared down the road, intent on glimpsing a spot of color or toe sticking up.

Her coat was next. Then her snow bib.

They entered another clear-cut and found her boots perched on a giant white pine stump, tops rising above the four-inch mound of snow, under which they discovered socks, long underwear, bra, and panties neatly folded.

A car honked. Three long blasts: still distant, but closer and in the direction they were heading.

"Fuck *is* that?" Brett asked using the whine that drove Jimmie bonkers. "Ah, man, with all these stumps and piles of snow, she could be lying dead anywhere."

Jimmie left Brett to check the immediate vicinity. He glided down the road searching for tracks. The more he considered those car horn blasts, the more he thought it unlikely they would find a body. At a fork, he followed the wider road to the left. Snow was heavier in this area, and he didn't find either a corpse or her tracks. The road teed at Shank Lake where he struck a well-traveled snowmobile route; nothing had passed by since the storm. Jimmie checked his plat book. There were several camps on this lake and more along the route into town. Taking a left onto Shank Lake Road, he followed it to the head of the lake, where Lukes Road, unmarked by snow machine tracks, came in from the right. He backtracked to the original fork and took the less-used direction. Thought he might have spotted a footprint or two, but never anything he could convince himself was a trail. No body. Hit Shank Lake again and stopped to consider his options.

Three blasts on a car horn. Closer this time. Exactly half an hour since the last three blasts. Jimmie now knew for certain that someone had already found her and that she was alive. He needed to execute Plan B.

He roared back to Brett, motioned for him to hop on, and buzzed their trail to Brett's snow machine that the girl had left stuck in the snowbank. Jimmie parked next to it and told Brett, "Fill 'er up with gas. Let's see if we can blast her out."

Brett hauled one of the gas cans to the trapped sled and poured. Jimmie followed, leaned close, and brought the Ruger an inch away from the hollow in the back of Brett's neck marking the spot where spine entered skull.

IF SOMEONE DIDN'T SHOW UP soon, I was screwed.

With a combination of Advil, erythromycin, and lukewarm sponge baths, I kept the woman's temperature under 102 for most of the day. She wasn't getting better; stabilized was the best I could convince myself about her condition. Before the end of each Advil cycle, her temperature spiked and her skin turned clammy. She spoke little. Each time she tried, a wracking cough doubled her up like a rag doll. She vomited breakfast of toast and jam. I had to hold down my gag reflex while I cleaned up the mess.

She tried to gargle, but it caused her to choke. I gave her a new toothbrush and from then on she smelled like Tom's of Maine's fennel toothpaste. Because she had felt worse the last time she ate, she refused solid food. Throughout the day I needed to coax her into slurping bouillon with its faint taste of chicken overwhelmed by sharp brine. I did get her to drink three glasses of water.

Early in the morning, I thought I heard a snowmobile's buzz, but it never came close. Back inside, I tuned the radio to "Telephone Time" on WIKB in hopes someone would call the talk show to report a missing woman. No luck and nothing on their hourly news report either. A plane flew past shortly after noon, but was probably too far away to spot my signal. I mostly sat outside the bedroom and worried.

I would feel terrible if the woman died on me. It would be one more person I had let down. Besides, I had no doubt the police would suspect me of something— unlawful imprisonment at the least. *Come on, girl. You've got to get better.*

I set an alarm to remind myself to honk the horn every half hour. At the start of the three-thirty routine, she was sleeping soundly. After hitting the truck horn three times, I snowshoed up to the guest cabin to see if I could follow her tracks. The snow and wind had done a fine job of filling in any footprints, although close to the cabin I could pick out what appeared to be a small indentation here and there. Unfortunately, a light breeze was dumping the remaining snow from the trees, producing a minicrater with each plop of snow. I gave up before I got to the end of the driveway. I'd been away no more than ten minutes, but it was enough time for the woman to reprise her Lady Godiva act: walking up the driveway wearing only a hat from the hook by the kitchen door and a pair of work gloves I had left on a nearby counter. I corralled her and asked what she was doing. "Brandon honked for me," she said. "I'm late for school again."

She did remember who I was; she didn't remember how she got here; she didn't remember who she was. She couldn't tell me who Brandon was or whether he was responsible for the hickey or the rope burns. Yet she was not without memory. Propped into a sitting position in the bed by several pillows, an hour before dark she spotted a mature bald eagle cruising the lake, head and tail as pure white as fresh snow. "Size marks her as female," she said. "She's shopping for carrion." She coughed, finally controlled it, took several long glugs of water, and whispered, "If I don't make it, just haul me to the middle of the lake. Everybody out there's a little hungry this time of year."

I protested. She raised her hand to cut me off. "Joke," she whispered. "Just a joke." Minutes later she was asleep.

Her pulse remained strong, but her breathing was increasingly labored and featured a wheeze that sounded like someone sucking air through the wrong end of a reed instrument. I worried that if her fever spiked and I wasn't around, she might hallucinate and walk away, as she had earlier looking for Brandon. Equally treacherous, she might go into convulsions.

With time on my hands and not daring to go out to ski or snowshoe to burn off all the nervous energy, I polished off the Rex Stout. The thought of reading another mystery didn't feel right—I was living a mystery. I pulled a John McPhee from the nonfiction shelf in the basement, thinking that would occupy my brain. Nope.

I reread the letter from Paddy that Owen had delivered earlier in the month along with the weekly supplies. Paddy, a natural networker unlike his dad, packed the letter with news of friends and acquaintances. He filled me in on what his girlfriend, TV investigative reporter Cindy Nelson, was working on. My eyes stuck on his passing mention that while he and Cindy were in a Chicago nightclub they ran across Abigail. *Who was she with? Was it for business or pleasure? Did she at least say hi?* The printed note gave no hint.

I tried journaling about the last few days, but lost focus. Writing about the woman's rope burns got me thinking about the body police had found in my Cincinnati home the previous spring, and how that had touched off a series of events leading to all kinds of things I didn't want to remember.

One lesson from that experience certainly applied here: police were predisposed to focus on the initial suspect long past the point when other evidence—evidence that they didn't find because they weren't looking for it—should have directed them toward the real perpetrator. If she died at my home, how could I prove I had done nothing wrong? With such an improbable story, why would cops spend much time trying to find alternative suspects?

It was Friday, and I had half-convinced myself that one of the locals with a camp on the lake would come out after work to spend the weekend ice fishing and drinking. If so, I'd hear their snowmobile roar down the lake after dark and could risk leaving her for the short time it would take to ski to their camp.

It didn't happen that way.

FOUR

THE SUN HAD SET AND the wall thermometer read minus four by the time Jimmie finished at Boss's rented camp. He was surprised how good he felt. In the movies, they showed a first-time killer getting wobbly knees and puking his guts out. Bullshit. This was easier than putting down his old hunting dog. He'd loved Bomber; Brett was a pain. Besides, no one paid him for putting down Bomber, whereas Brett was worth decent bucks.

He kept his gloves on except to wash the dishes. He dried those and neatly hung the dishtowel on the rack by the sink. After draining the water lines, he cleaned the wood stove of ash—good thing dumbass Brett had let the fire die—stripped all the linens, and shut off the propane. Brett's gear piled on the sleigh provided cover for the girl's stuff underneath. Camo tarps served as wrappers for foodstuffs, which he also tied down on the sleigh.

Using rubbing alcohol and shop rags from a box, he wiped down every surface where fingerprints could be found. Always liked the smell, maybe because it reminded him of cleaning guns? Although, thinking about it, he concluded gun oil smelled heavier. He let the rags air dry and stuffed them in his parka pocket to toss into his home burn barrel. Using a million-candle torch, he checked the cabin and grounds one last time. Satisfied, he padlocked the cabin and generator shed, pulling on the locks to make sure they were secure even after hearing the satisfying click of the lock engaging. He then used Brett's shotgun to blow off the door hasp, leaving the lock burnished by twenty-gauge shot and buried in the snow.

The shot brought a pair of gray jays from the woods to investigate, their conversation alerting Jimmie of their presence. "Nothing for you camp robbers today," he told them. "Gonna be slim pickings around here for a piece."

Eight long hours after he had dispatched Brett, Jimmie pulled his snow machine and sleigh onto the trailer he'd attached to Brett's truck and left the camp. His stomach protested the lack of food. His only break had been to force down cold pasties, which tasted like shoe leather when they weren't warm. Twenty minutes later, he had cell coverage and called Boss. "She's still missing, but I think I know where. Everything else is cool."

"Meet me tomorrow at eleven," Boss said. "Sooner we solve that problem, the better."

NEITHER THE WOMAN NOR I slept much during the night. Her fever held steady at around a hundred degrees, so maybe the drugs were helping keep it down. The dry wheeze of her cough morphed into a wet rattle. Those episodes occurred more frequently, each one lasting longer. After one particularly long and violent coughing jag she waved me to her. "Am I going to die?"

"Of course not," I said too loudly to fool myself with the false confidence.

"I think someone already has, but I just can't remember. Will you hold me? I need someone to hold me and my mother isn't here." Talking sparked another long coughing spree. "Please?"

I kicked off my shoes and got in the other side of the bed, sliding over to spoon against her muscled back, laying my arm around her warm shoulders. Again, the scent of Abigail surprised me, even though I was the one who had washed her with Abigail's lavender soap.

"Thank you," she whispered into the pillow.

She calmed down and slept. I didn't. Wrapped against her, I measured every shallow breath she took against the previous one, worrying she was getting worse. Despair grew as I held this nameless woman and recognized I had no clue what to do. All my years of education, all my years in business, all my years as a parent, provided no preparation for this moment.

Who was Brandon? What did she mean by someone already died? Did that relate to her rope burns? I wished for so very many reasons that Abigail were still here. If she hadn't left, one of us could have stayed and the other gone for help. This woman would be in a hospital, getting real care.

And I missed Abigail. I'd screwed it up again and lost her for good.

"Do the best you can, and let go of the results," my mother had often told me when I was fussing over something I couldn't control. Had I done my best for the woman today? What did I need to do tomorrow? The dueling calls of barred owls outside interrupted my contemplation. Even if hunting was tough for them with so much snow on the ground, they had it comparatively easy, worrying only about food and sex. Just two days ago, I had stood at the window for the better part of an hour watching a snowshoe hare inspect the clearing around my house. That once-idyllic life now seemed a fantasy.

Lying on my back, I marked the passage of the nearly full moon as it slunk toward its setting an hour before official sunrise. My guest was wasting away. If I didn't get her medical attention, I might justly be accused of letting her die. I had no choice but to act, but what if I made the wrong choice?

JIMMIE FIGURED BOSS HAD ALREADY arrived for the meeting: a curl of white smoke drifted into the bluing sky from the single-wide trailer set on top of the hill. He checked for company—no traffic on Rock Crusher Road in either direction—and pulled into the plowed gravel driveway around the single-wide and into the second stall of a pole barn building at the rear of the clearing. In typical Yooper fashion, the pole barn was quadruple the size of the trailer home.

He left his keys in the Chevy Blazer, walked to the edge of the trailer, and listened for traffic. Still nothing, so he slipped around to the front and let himself in. He pulled off his gloves and hat, but left his coat on. The propane furnace was clacking away, but it had some work to do to raise the temperature from fifty—Boss's setting while away—to something comfortable. He grabbed a mug from a tree—they all advertised Hematite National Bank, no surprise there—and poured coffee from the pot left cooking on the hotplate. He liked it plain and black, no mochaccino crap for him. Maxwell House "good to the last drop" was still best in his book. As the boss said, "The closer to diesel fuel, the better." The warmth tumbled down his gullet and into his stomach.

Boss emerged from the bedroom. "Prompt as always, Jimmie. I appreciate that. Set your ass down." Boss waved toward the gawd-awful orange plaid couch in the living room and plunked down in the La-Z-Boy. "Tell me what transpired with Brett."

Typical. Flaunts that college degree using words like "transpired" when "happened" would have done just as well. Well, Jimmie knew all those words too; he just didn't use 'em. He took a couple slurps of the coffee, sagged into the couch feeling it envelop his hips as the springs stretched with pings and pops. Once everything settled, he related the previous day's activities.

"Couldn't you make it look like a hunting accident? Shot himself?"

"Didn't you ever read that book, *The Sweater Letter*? They'd never buy it. I made it look like a drug buy gone bad. Left a stash of blow in a baggie in the tank of his snow machine." He added, in case Boss thought he was asking for more money, "Part of my full-service package." Tried a smile, got nothing back, and plowed on. "Here's the thing. I'm pretty sure someone around Shank Lake found the girl. Every half hour, some guy's nailing his horn three long honks."

"Distress signal, sure as shit."

Boss rustled around in the bookcase and opened an Iron County plat book. "Lukes Road comes in from US 141. That's the only other way in other than up The Grade from Amasa. There are only a few camps on Shank—forty-acre zoning. We hold the mortgages on a couple. Thing I can't get my head around is why they were honking their horn instead of packing her into town."

Jimmie tried out his theory. "What if the girl's alive and somebody staying by theirselves didn't figure he could leave her to get help?"

Boss looked up sharply. "I kinda figured maybe you were gold digging me with your suggestion she was alive, her walking around naked in below zero temps and all. But now I hear you telling it, well, shit, you might be right." Boss tapped the plat book. "Looking at that section, I seem to recall something about a guy name of McCree planning to overwinter, and I see a McCree family trust owns an eighty. Neither of those biologists ever laid eyes on you, right?"

"Even so, if I rode into someone's camp, it might tie me to them. If I found only one guy with the girl, which is what I'm now thinking is the case, I could take care of both of them. But I didn't think of that at the time, and if it was a group up for the weekend, I'd have been totally fucked. Besides, you told me if the girl escaped, I had to take care of Brett . . ."

Boss nodded a few times, which led to a hacking fit. Boss pulled out a handkerchief and coughed something into it Jimmie was clearly not supposed to see or ask about. Supposedly the lung cancer was taken care of, but maybe it was back? Jimmie pretended to concentrate on the plat book, noting it smelled a bit musty.

"Point taken," Boss said. "By now if she were a stiff, she'd be parked in some funeral home and 'Telephone Time' would be chatting away helping the cops figure out who she was—and there wasn't a peep. You've taken care of Brett's stuff?"

"And the girl's. Burned everything except his truck. That's a cube of crushed metal sitting in a recycler's lot in Duluth. He ships the stuff to China. I've never heard of anyone named McCree."

"Tourist, not a local. You've done a good job, Jimmie, but we're not finished by a long shot. You and I need to check the Shank Lake camps. We'll start with McCree. I got an extra sled you can take. You got a choice of weapons." Boss pointed to a gun rack lining one wall of the living room. "You got your snowmobile duds in the truck, right? Let me get changed while you prepare the sleds. Gas is stored in the pole barn."

Jimmie realized he was jazzed—like before playing a high school football game. How would it go down when their two snow machines drove into McCree's camp? He chugged the last swallow of coffee, cleaned his cup, and hung it on the tree, making sure to wipe off his prints in the process. Never can be too careful.

THE SUN BACKLIT THE EASTERN hill, and I had finally reached the crap-or-get-off-the-pot point regarding how to handle the woman. My style had always been to take in as much data as I could and put off making a decision for as long as possible—but not a moment longer. The good news was that her fever had abated overnight. The bad news was her cough was much, much worse. I needed to get her help, but I needed to minimize the chances she would wander off while I was gone.

My strategy was to tire her out so completely that she would sleep until I returned. I bundled the woman in warm clothes, sleeves and pant legs bunched to the right length with elastic bands. A binder clip cinched in the waist of the old snow pants I had managed to wrestle over pajama bottoms that kept riding up her limp legs. My feet were seven thousand sizes larger than hers, so I stuffed newspaper in the toe boxes and around the heels of the boots.

By the time I finished dressing her, she reminded me of some children in the winter that are clothed in so many layers they can't move—all they can do is stand or fall. I carried her outside and settled her onto my son's old wooden Flexible Flyer, which I towed down to the lake. Across the way, a pair of ravens entertained us with an aerial show and the accompanying soundtrack of raucous croaks before flying away. With the exception of a couple of small snowdrifts I had to dust off, the blue SOS was still okay.

I dragged the sled from the lake to the road and inspected the HELP sign. The dark ashes had absorbed some of yesterday's wan sunlight and caused the message to melt a bit, but it would do for another day.

The house seemed stuffy after our hour-long outing. I cracked open a couple of windows and fixed lunch of split-pea soup laced with chunks of salty bacon. She ate tentatively at first. Once she decided it wouldn't come back up, she wolfed down a bowl and, after a terrible coughing spell, asked for more.

Fortunately, the cold air and warm soup did the trick, and she soon fell asleep. Praying her slumber would last until my return, I attached a note to the back door: "Gone for help. If you get here first, please take the woman to the hospital in Iron River. VERY HIGH fever and possible pneumonia." I strapped on cross-country skis and took off.

At the edge of my property, an old logging road meanders toward a clear-cut. A snowmobile had come down the road and turned around at that intersection. They had been so close; if only they had made it onto my road they would have seen the HELP sign and the woman would be in treatment. My Irish luck was on holiday, probably in a warmer clime.

Birds, normally active feeding in the brief daylight hours, became silent at my approach, no doubt wondering at the intrusion. Only the swish of skis cutting through fresh snow marred the woods' silence. Ice crystals stuck to my mustache and beard and coated the long wool hat that wicked sweat and heat away from my head. After a mile, I was in a zone, having found a strong, easy rhythm that ate up the distance.

The sun was as high in the sky as it was going to get. Even through yellow-tinged goggles, snow sparkled as though laced with diamond chips. Trees lining the road cast blue shadows, giving form to the otherwise smooth landscape. Several camps had access from these roads, but only deer, coyote, and wolf tracks marred the palette of whites.

Skiing through new snow tired me more than I expected, but the thought of the woman waking up with no one around spurred me on. At first, I sensed a ticking clock in my head, but that morphed into an hourglass leaking sand from the realm of the living to the dead. I pressed forward as fast as I could. Trucks had plowed the last two miles of my trip and I didn't have to break trail. I glided around the final corner and spotted both a blue car and red truck parked in a cleared driveway I knew belonged to a couple who lived year-round on Deer Lake. Relief caused a chill to run across my skin with the tingle of a weak electrical current. I'd lucked out; they were home.

I pounded on the door and the woman, dressed in sweats and a heavy wool sweater, informed me her husband had taken off on their snowmobile and was ice fishing with his buddies. She used her satellite internet and tried to find an email address for the Iron County Sheriff's office in Crystal Falls. No go. She promised to drive the ten miles to Amasa, the nearest town, and call them.

My hourglass was leaking faster. Thoughts of the woman waking up and spacing out drove me to maintain a punishing pace toward home. Reusing tracks I'd made coming to Deer Lake helped speed my return since I didn't have to fight new snow, but my age was starting to tell. I huffed and puffed with the look and sound of an old steam locomotive. For an old fart, I was in outstanding shape, but this exertion proved there was no way I could ever be a professional soccer player again.

Turning onto the A Grade, I discovered snowmobiles had obliterated my path. Their tracks followed mine onto Shank Lake Road, and I gained extra energy from the sense of relief. The cops must have already been in the vicinity when the Deer Lake woman contacted them. By now they were certainly taking care of the woman.

Unless it wasn't them.

I pressed on at top speed. At the head of the lake the snowmobile tracks took Lukes Road instead of staying on my side of the lake. They hadn't made it to my house. My mood crashed and drained my energy.

The steepest hills in the entire eight miles were on my property. By the time I reached them, my legs were whipped; I had to herringbone up them. From the top of the last hill I glided down to my driveway, turned in, and spotted two snowmobiles I didn't recognize parked outside my house.

FIVE

Iron County Sergeant Lon Bartelle thought about the story the character sitting on the opposite side of the table had told him. It sounded practiced, bored, too cool, too calm for a guy who had spent the better part of the afternoon and into the evening answering questions from his deputies. "Here's what I don't get," he said, curling his left arm over his head and scratching his gray crew cut. "Instead of relying on some pilot calling us because he sees your SOS on the lake, why didn't you bring her out yourself?"

"Like I told your cohorts," McCree said, "I don't have a snowmobile. I don't have a snow plow. I have an ATV, but that's an All Terrain Vehicle, not an All Snow Vehicle. With three feet of snow my ATV wouldn't make it much past the garage. What did you want me to do, sprout fairy wings and fly?" He puffed out an exclamation of air. "I've been patient and answered the same questions about six times now. I'm tired. I'm hungry. The sun vanished hours ago. I want to go home. Who's my ride?"

"When a sled's free," Bartelle lied with accomplished practice, "we'll take you back. Might be a while, though. Be better if we could do that in the morning. How about we get you a meal and put you up in town?" Bartelle cocked his head, as though he was interested in the response.

"If you're waiting for a search warrant, that's not an issue. I'll grant the county, the state, and/or the DNR full access to my land and buildings and vehicles and anything else you want to look at. Heck, I'll even throw in the Animal Control Officer. Just give me something to sign."

Time to play dumb. Bartelle put on his quizzical expression. "Huh?"

McCree gave him the open-handed "what do you want from me" gesture and said, "I've been cooling my heels for hours since I volunteered," he drew finger quotes around the word volunteered, "to accompany you to town. I told your people everything I know. The questions haven't changed. You think I held her prisoner—I saw the rope burns on her wrists and ankles—and you think I've done who knows what to her over an unknown period of time. Of course I'm a suspect. Problem is I've already told you everything I know."

"Fair enough." Bartelle slapped his hand on the table, stinging his palm. *Dumb.* He heaved up from the chair, walked to the dirty window, and stared out. "Truth: we don't want you alone cleaning the place, and we'd prefer to do the search in daylight. We can arrest you on suspicion and provide a cell for accommodations, or I can treat you to dinner at Mr. T's and put you up at the AmericInn, which will cost the county a whole lot less than the OT. Either way, going home is not one of your options."

MR. T'S FAMILY RESTAURANT WAS nothing fancy: a half-dozen booths and a scattering of Formica tables. Years ago, the place smelled like a burning cigarette pack; now the day's cooking provided the perfume. He judged it had been a big fried onions day. An hour before closing, and without a liquor license, the place was quiet and Bartelle led McCree to a booth. Unasked, the waitress brought Bartelle a diet cola, handed McCree a menu, and said to the Sergeant, "The usual?"

McCree leaned back and locked his fingers behind his head. "So, he's in here so often he has a usual?"

"He claims he's teaching himself how to cook, but I don't see no evidence of it. He's got him a couple different breakfasts, but for dinner—"

"Stop telling all my secrets, Agnes"

A hint of a smile attached itself to McCree's face. "Does he insist on *the usual* for his suspects or will he let me order on my own?"

"You're a suspect?"

He grinned. "The good sergeant seems to think so. I'm not armed, but he still believes I'm dangerous. I'm looking for an independent opinion. Do I look dangerous to you?"

"Only if you're married."

"Divorced for years, but not currently on the market either."

She grinned right back at him. "Well Lon, you put me on the stand, and I'm taking the fifth. Now, sugar, what are we having today?"

"Since you have breakfast all day, I'll take the cheese omelet, breakfast potatoes, and some OJ, please."

"You want that in a four, six, ten, or sixteen-ounce glass?"

"Well, I'm a guest of Iron County, and I don't want my taxes going any higher, so I think I'll stick with the ten ounce. Thank you very much."

The waitress bustled off with the orders.

The interaction between McCree and Agnes, who had to be sixty if she was a day, and not exactly a looker, amazed Bartelle. When had a suspect ever admitted to the first stranger he met that he was one? Never that Bartelle could remember. Was McCree slick or just friendly? He thought it best to ease into the conversation. "Seamus isn't a very common first name," he said. "Family name or just a parental favorite?"

"My father's first name was Seamus, although he went by his middle name. I grew up in an Irish neighborhood so I didn't have to get into too many fights over my name."

"My neighborhood was Italian and everyone wanted to know why we didn't spell Bartelle with an 'i' at the end instead of the final 'e.' Poor penmanship. At Ellis Island the 'i' lost its dot and was kind of loopy. The immigration papers said 'e' and grandpop just wanted in." The pleather seats creaked as Bartelle shifted his weight. "I'd be interested in hearing why you're wintering out in God's country."

McCree seemed to weigh his words carefully. *Too bad, he's not going to be a loquacious bastard who tells me more than he realizes.* Bartelle waited him out.

"Last year, my house in Cincinnati was broken into. My . . ." He paused. *To make sure he used the right word?* "My . . . then girlfriend was nearly killed. A real mess, very traumatic. After she recovered, we spent some time traveling and decided it would be interesting to spend winter at my camp.

"I made arrangements with a guy from Amasa—maybe you know him, Owen Lyndstrom—to bring in supplies once we got snowed in. He comes on Tuesdays. Brings mail, groceries, whatever else I might need as long as I can think of it a week in advance. It's worked pretty well."

"I take it the girlfriend isn't there anymore?"

"Shipped herself out the Tuesday after New Year's. She loved the house, loved the outdoors, loved not having three thousand cable channels. Loved everything except not seeing or talking to people. Snow came early this year, and after three weeks she couldn't hack it. I still had some things to work out, so I stayed." He lifted his hands, which Bartelle interpreted as, "And that's the story."

Bartelle tried waiting him out again while making notes on a pad he kept in his lap. McCree showed no signs of speaking further. The only sound was the scritch of Bartelle's pen. *The problem with McCree is that he doesn't seem to have any problem with silence.* "This girlfriend have a name and address?

"Abigail Hancock." McCree provided an address in Chicago. "But I don't know if she's there. Her work takes her all over. She's a bodyguard."

Bartelle caught himself rubbing his scalp again, left arm crooked over his head like a human Cape Cod. Thought about the gesture for a second and continued to scratch. *I ain't trying to impress anyone, and it feels so good.* He struggled to place this guy's accent. Not from here—didn't use "eh?" to end every third sentence. No way was it Midwestern flat. Reminded him of those presidential candidates from Massachusetts who always got their asses whipped. That was it, like John Kerry or that short guy who looked stupid in the tank, what was his name? This guy dressed like a Yooper, nothing matched, but his clothes were neat without holes or patches. To fill the growing silence, Bartelle asked, "Get laid off, or something? Collecting unemployment?"

The waitress delivered the food, determined neither man needed anything else, and removed the ketchup McCree said he wouldn't need because he didn't spoil his breakfast potatoes with the stuff. She turned to leave, but must have changed her mind because she swung back.

"What does he suspect you of doing?"

"That's a very perceptive question," McCree said. "How about you answer that, Sergeant Bartelle. Two of us are interested."

Mary, Mother of God, how did he turn the tables? "Agnes, you know I can't say anything about an open investigation."

"For Pete's sake why not, Lon? It will be all over town by morning."

McCree laughed. "Just so you know, my name's Seamus McCree." He stuck out his hand. "I'm pleased to meet you, Agnes."

Agnes left with a self-satisfied smile on her face, and McCree picked up his fork and shoveled more food into his mouth. Bartelle decided McCree was using the food to avoid answering his last question. Fine. They would eat in silence, and after McCree put down his fork, he'd ask again.

But McCree surprised him.

"Actually, I retired several years ago."

Bartelle raised his eyebrows to express interest without taking McCree off the hook to continue speaking. He concentrated on chewing the grilled cheese sandwich, letting the sharp taste of the cheddar satisfy him.

"Long ago and far away, I analyzed bank stocks for a Wall Street firm that no longer exists. Quit after someone tried to change one of my reports. Caused a big stink, but that's ancient history."

Bartelle considered the information. McCree couldn't even be a young fifty. Full head of hair, raggedy black beard with a dusting of red highlights. Probably been going native since he left paved-road life and jumped into the woods. Obviously in good shape. No broken blood vessels in his nose, so probably not a drinker. Eyes clear. *In fact, the blue sometimes feels uncomfortably piercing, as though he's looking straight through me.* It reminded Bartelle of a wolf who'd just as soon ignore you and go his own way but, when you pressed, would not back down regardless of the odds— or consequences. "You help make up them Collateralized Mortgage Obligations that got everyone in trouble?"

"Few years ago, no one knew what CMOs were; now everyone's an expert on them and derivatives and a bunch of other fancy financial terms." McCree smiled, like he was remembering something interesting. "I wasn't smart enough to invent new stuff. I told people which bank stocks to buy and which to sell."

"And I suppose you predicted the mess they got themselves in?" Bartelle knew his voice dripped with sarcasm. Didn't want it to; couldn't help it and, underneath the table, he dug his fingernails into his palms to punish himself for the lack of control.

The subject physically tightened after that jab in a way Bartelle couldn't define. McCree used a long sip of water to regain control and replaced a smile on his face. "You caught me," he said. "It's all my fault. That's why I'm in hiding."

Bartelle dug his nails in again to regain concentration. *Shit, I blew that.* Everyone wanted to ring a Wall Streeter's neck after the mess they got us in, but I'm supposed to get this guy to talk. He matched McCree's water drinking trick, put on his own smile, and said, "I'm not buying the *mea culpa*, Mr. McCree. I have a feeling there's a different reason why you quit."

McCree snapped up the bait. "Call me Seamus. My bosses changed a report I wrote that recommended downgrading a now-failed bank's stock because they were early participants in the subprime mortgage market, and I believed their liabilities were understated. The bank was a major client of the firm and making a buck was more important to management than accurate predictions. If they had released the report I wrote, the bank would have taken their business elsewhere. You scratch my back and I'll scratch yours was the corporate style." He tilted his head back and blew a puff of air at the ceiling. "Fact is, I was right, but that was a long time ago. I quit in protest, but it didn't help the world avoid the debacle."

"You get another job, or just take it easy?" Bartelle asked and motioned to Agnes for more diet soda.

"Ever hear of Criminal Investigations Group?"

Bartelle nodded. "I worked with them on a case down in the Mitten before— Mitten's what we call—"

"I know what the Mitten is," McCree interjected, showing Bartelle his left palm. "In lower Michigan they point to their mitten to show where they live. Fact is, we Yoopers refer to people from Lower Michigan as trolls since they live below the Mackinac Bridge."

"I was happy to move somewhere I still had family," Bartelle snapped. He'd intentionally tried a bit of one-upmanship, and McCree had turned it against him, managing to nail his hot button about not being accepted by the locals as a true Yooper. He forced a laugh. "So, yeah, I was a troll before I hired on up here. Anyway, CIG provided computer expertise on that case to help us crack a fencing operation out of one of the big GM plants. Can't remember who we worked with. What do you do with them?"

"About a year after I quit Wall Street, the guy who runs CIG convinced me to set up a group to tackle international financial crimes. Took a couple of years to get all the people in place. It's been successful both here and abroad, and from time to time they ask me to give them a hand. I guess you could say I'm a forensic accountant, or you could think of it as a financial crimes investigator—or at least I will be again once I return to civilization."

Bartelle was pleased. McCree had become animated once he started talking about CIG. "You're an interesting fellow, Seamus. Got any family?"

"A son. Lives and works in Evanston, Illinois." McCree centered the glass on a napkin. "I've been doing all the talking. What brought you to this neck of the woods if you're from the Lower Peninsula?"

Dinner finished with meaningless chit chat, during which Bartelle found himself liking McCree. His mind was so quick, like the way he twisted the Mitten thing back on Bartelle. He was an interesting mixture of big city sophisticate and blue collar regular guy: working in New York City, but son of a Boston cop. Bartelle got no sense that McCree was anything but genuinely interested in Agnes when he was talking with her. He had to remind himself that any really good salesman had that same trick—but if it was a trick, what was McCree selling? Innocence?

When McCree saw him put down a fifteen percent tip, he added a couple of bucks to it. "We're the only ones still in here," McCree said. "And she's living off tips."

While Bartelle checked McCree in at the AmericInn, McCree chatted up the night clerk and discovered the kid was working nights and taking courses at Bay College in Iron Mountain—stuff Bartelle had not known.

"Before you lock me in for the night," McCree said. "Can you ask the hospital how the woman is?"

"That reminds me," Bartelle said, "I've been meaning to ask. Why did you say you'll pay for her medical costs?"

"Because the seventy-ninth time the admitting nurse asked, 'Who's going to pay for this?' I got annoyed. To shut her up I said I would. Okay?" He lowered his voice. "As you can tell, it *still* pisses me off."

Bartelle called the hospital, and the benign feelings he had been developing toward McCree vanished. She had pneumonia, severe dehydration, a fever had spiked to 103 before they could control it. Doctors were clueless as to what she had. He reported all this to McCree, who seemed to take it in stride. One thing Bartelle did not want was a relaxed suspect.

Bartelle checked McCree into his room and left a parting shot, "You better pray she lives."

Six

As expected, I played host to much of the Iron County Sheriff's Department on Sunday. Their search warrant allowed them full access to my land and possessions. They removed ropes from the garage, took dirty bedclothes from the bedroom, and bagged ashes from my burn barrel. They even took the chair hammock I had found the woman in. Two deputies worked outside trying to make sense of the tracks on the property, their task made harder by the three inches of wet overnight snowfall.

From the snatches of conversation I overheard, they were clearly skeptical of my story, but found nothing to contradict it. Their parting words before roaring away on snowmobiles were that I should not leave the area without letting the sheriff's office know. They forgot to say please and thank you. I forgot to tell them that I knew I could go anywhere I damned well pleased until they arrested me.

I went to bed early, too exhausted by the tension of having strangers paw through my belongings to start cleaning up after their search. Returning everything to its proper place took most of Monday. After all the excitement, I appreciated the quiet. Deer returned to the salt lick I had placed between the house and cabin, and the loudest noise I had to put up with was the scolding of a red squirrel when I stuck my head outside.

Tuesday broke sunny and warm. WIKB proclaimed a heat wave: temperatures would reach forty in town, might break freezing around my place and start to reduce the snow pack. Owen Lyndstrom arrived to find me having given up trying to understand the geology in McPhee's book and instead pretending to reread Asimov's *Foundation* series. Still wondering how the girl was doing and fretting about what the police were thinking, I couldn't concentrate on anything for more than fifteen seconds.

Owen was a Northwoods jack-of-all-trades; he had mostly mastered them too. He had cut wood, walked the woods as a timber spotter, worked excavating equipment, graded roads, driven a logging truck, loaded logs onto railcars, plowed snow three seasons of the year, and trapped during the winter of '70–71 when there was no work. He had made more money off an illegal cougar pelt that year than from a whole winter's worth of legal beaver, muskrat, coyote, and snowshoe hare. Although the cougar was the only other witness to the confrontation, I had no reason to doubt Owen when he said he had backtracked it after it jumped him and discovered the cougar had been stalking him for half a day. The DNR didn't fess up to cougars returning to the U.P. until forty years later, so as far as they were concerned, the incident never happened.

He had worked some construction, was handy with hammer and saw, could mix concrete by hand—not the Quickrete stuff either. Liked to keep his feet on the ground, thought any building more than a story high was putting on airs. Hired out as a guide for a year, but couldn't stand having to listen to a bunch of rich folks who "didn't know their dicks from a garter snake." He proudly proclaimed that he'd been no farther from the U.P. than the northern counties of Wisconsin. Never been north to visit "them Canucks," nor as far west as Minnesota.

When it came to talking, Owen was a contradiction. In the woods, Owen could go weeks without uttering a word. Wasn't one of those guys who had to sing or whistle or have the radio blasting so as not to go stir crazy. "Cain't hear what the woods is tellin ya if alls you do is gab."

Yet put a piece of gossip within thirty miles of his elephant ears, and guaranteed before nightfall it was part of the unofficial male grapevine from Copper Harbor to Ironwood to Sault Ste. Marie and all points in between.

Each Tuesday, he'd arrive around noon, we'd unpack the supplies, and then he'd slip in his false teeth. For lunch, I provided soup and he shared some of the sharpest tasting jerky I ever sampled. Between slurps he'd dish the week's news and I'd pump him about his jobs, and the woods, and anything else I could think to ask him. Two weeks ago, I had surprised him with birthday cupcakes to celebrate his eighty-second birthday. Owen was my model for what I wanted to be as an octogenarian—in fact, if I could be half as active and half as interesting as Owen, I would be more than satisfied. I liked the old coot a ton and a half.

For the last two days, I'd listened to WIKB's news and funeral reports and heard squat about my unexpected guest. This week, I was actually looking forward to the gossipy part of Owen's visit.

Owen hardly got his teeth in place before he asked if I'd heard about "that Janie Doe person brought to the hospital."

His face fell when I told him I had.

"I seen from tracks you had all kinds of company. They musta beat me to the story, eh? My Cousin Molly's daughter-in-law—the second one, not the first—she works down there at the hospital. Smarter than a trout, that one. Just this mornin she was tellin me that poor girl is alive, but sicker than a dog chowin down on skunk cabbage. Don't nobody know who she is. Folks sayin some perv kept her tied up somewhere. Had a change in heart when she got sick. Me? I'm leanin toward a sugar daddy. Molly was sayin this guy's payin for her medical expenses. Wish I knew me that feller. Medical expenses are outrageous. You know how much her stay's gonna cost? Geez, I'm thinkin maybe ten grand. She stays in there long enough, could even be twenty. Thank God for the VA, that's all I can say." He cackled at his humor.

If she was uninsured, the stay would cost a lot more than Owen's estimate. Without a competitive market to keep costs in check for the uninsured, hospitals can jack up their prices. They don't have to deal with any insurance companies. It's like allowing a hotel to charge the rates they post on the back of the room's door, which are probably there for some legal reason, but I suspect mostly to make people feel good about how little they paid in comparison.

His rant gave me the idea to talk to an insurance company CEO I knew to see if he could cut me a deal to insure the woman. I'd pay them administrative expenses and reimburse them for all her expenses, but with insurance, the hospital would charge only the insurance company's negotiated rates. It wasn't strictly cricket, but no one would be harmed.

I shoved down anger at an unjust system and used Owen's pause to relate my version of the truth about "Janie Doe." Owen cupped his hands to his ears to make sure he didn't miss a bit. "Nekkid. Well don't that beat all, eh? Say, you hear about the brawl in Gaastra?"

He left quicker than usual, possibly because I was not holding up my end of the conversation, not remembering to ask about his week or about one of his past jobs. Or maybe he left because I gave him the inside scoop on the hottest story of the week.

It would be a week before Owen returned, and I would miss his company, but I had the feeling it would not be a week of solitude. Some say we Irish are superstitious. I say it ain't paranoia if it's true.

* * *

BOSS FIRST HEARD SEAMUS MCCREE'S name mentioned by someone else during the gabbing before a Wednesday morning prayer meeting. Heard the name twice more in the bank before lunch, with more or less the same story attached to it. Jimmie had led the two of them right to the McCree family trust's eighty acres on Shank Lake. Unfortunately, Iron County deputies had beaten them to the scene. Each time Boss heard "McCree," the disappointment of coming to the top of McCree's driveway and seeing the two Iron County snow machines parked at his house reappeared.

For whatever reason, that triggered Boss to hum the opening line from Carole King's "So Far Away." Boss hated songs getting stuck in a loop, replaying over and over until finally the mind's disk jockey replaced it with some other tune. Only thing Boss hated worse right then was the coughing jag the humming triggered, which caused back spasms sharp enough to double over a Greek god.

"You okay, Boss?" the executive secretary called in.

"Fine." *As fine as you can be with stage IV lung cancer and three months left on the year the doc gave me.* Of course, the year had assumed no more cigarettes and no more drinking, and that last part was not going to happen. Boss threw on overclothes and headed outside to think-walk. Wandering up Superior Avenue toward the Iron County Courthouse, Boss picked up the weekly Iron County Reporter. The article on page two took four column-inches to say the unidentified woman had entered the hospital Saturday afternoon, and at press time her condition was still critical. If anyone had information, blah, blah, blah.

Boss checked the rag from stem to stern. Still no news about Brett's murder. The longer it took to find him, the less evidence would remain. At the foot of the courthouse steps, Boss turned around and gazed at the far hills past Crystal Falls, willing a threatening cough to be still. Whispering to stave off the cough, Boss recited the first two verses of the sixth Psalm. "Lord, rebuke me not in thine anger, neither chasten me in thy hot displeasure. Have mercy upon me, O Lord; for I am weak: O Lord, heal me; for my bones are vexed." Boss could still picture the 1875 family Bible all these years after memorizing the complete Book of Psalms in fourth grade from it and winning the Sunday school's Student of the Year Award.

Lost in the reminiscences, but feeling calmer, Boss damn near got bowled over by Sergeant Bartelle. The hairy ape was yapping a mile a minute into his cell phone. He flipped his phone shut, doffed his hat, and pardoned himself up and down, which Boss saw as a natural perk of funding the Democratic ticket in the county; people did tend to bow and scrape.

"What brings you to the courthouse today, Boss?"

Boss glared at the hireling. *Damn his curiosity. We never should have brought him up from the Mitten.* "Care to set me straight on these rumors I hear about that girl down in the hospital, Lon?" Boss vaguely nodded west toward Iron River.

"Open investigation. You know I can't comment, but I will say the rumors are just rumors."

"You saying this McCree guy didn't find her?"

"You know McCree?"

"We had a mortgage on that parcel twenty, thirty years ago, back before it was split up."

Bartelle ignored his cell phone's ringtone version of "God Bless America."

"Well, I've heard a lot of things in the last twenty-four hours and none of them have come from witnesses." Bartelle replaced his hat. "How's the banking business holding up these days? You weren't looking at deeds to foreclose, were you?"

Boss relaxed. Bartelle had provided a perfect excuse for this courthouse visit. "I know deputies hate serving eviction notices. So do I, I'll tell you. Storm's passed, thank goodness. Property's not rising yet, but it's stopped falling. Fortunately, we don't have many foreclosures coming up. Can't say what's happening at the other banks."

Conversation complete, they do-si-doed around each other. Boss decided not to return to the bank, going instead to the single-wide outside of town and toward the passion few living people knew about.

Seven

Thursday morning, a northwest breeze stirred snow devils on Shank Lake, bringing with it a hint of wood smoke: probably someone burning slash from a winter logging operation. The brilliant sun in a clear Paul Newman blue sky hurt my eyes. I decided to combine my normal morning cross-country ski and my evening snowshoe ramble into one long backwoods workout. Skiing is all about rhythm: getting into it and staying in it. You don't feel your legs and arms move. The effortless rhythm is perfect for contemplation; it allows your mind free rein to sort through all the facts, possibilities, impossibilities and perhaps arrive at a "eureka" moment. I had been stirring that pot for well over forty days and forty nights with my twice-daily exercise.

My thinking had come this far: in psychospeak, I had a few issues. My father died when I was young. My mother chose to bury her sorrow in silence; with the exception of five words spoken while under extreme duress, she had not uttered a word for decades. My wife dumped me after I quit Wall Street.

Although I had dated some, I had been skittish about new commitments. I don't blame anyone else; the problems are mine. Abigail told me I was a closed book and took too much responsibility for problems that weren't mine. Every day while we were together, we spent time talking about my issues—our issues. I thought we were making a lot of progress. I really, really wanted us to work out, so I was trying hard—but she left anyway.

Friends I could make—even good women friends. Something was preventing me from staying in a loving relationship. Either I needed to do something differently or admit I was not cut out for "we" life.

On these daily excursions into the woods, I had parsed all of my actions, all of my words and come up with . . . more questions and no answers. I hoped, as I had hoped every other day, that today I would have an epiphany. While concentrating on keeping rhythm and picking lint off the dark blanket of my thoughts, I missed a turn and found myself in new territory. The vegetation began to clog the road, constricting it into a narrow, winding path. The young firs underneath the snow grabbed the poles and jerked me backwards if I strode forward before working them free. My shoulders ached from the repeated evergreen abuse. Skiing became impossible.

Obviously this was not the day for enlightenment-through-skiing. The wrong turn instead offered me the gift of exploring new territory. I shoved the skis into a snowdrift to await the return trip and strapped on snowshoes.

Soon I ran into a second problem, much larger than the first. Literally. A cow moose and her calf blocked the path. They looked at me. I looked at them. Moose can be patient buggers. Five minutes later, they ambled into the tag alder thicket. I took it as a sign that I should turn around. Today was just not my day, period.

By the time I reached the home stretch on Shank Lake Road, I was plumb tuckered out. I concentrated on sliding one sore leg in front of the other without crossing ski tips. It took some time before the distant burr of a snowmobile barreling up the road intruded on my consciousness.

They were either coming to visit me at the house, which was only a quarter mile away, or they would blast on by. Most Yoopers don't expect to see anyone skiing in the middle of "their" road, and I moved to the edge to avoid looking like Wile E. Coyote after a truck ran him over.

The roar diminished and then the woods returned to silence. *Visitors. There might be something to Irish intuition—or paranoia.*

I caught Sergeant Lon Bartelle peering into the house from the screened porch. Another parka-clad figure huddled over a snowmobile in the driveway, removing what looked like fishing tackle boxes. I pulled off my gloves and shook hands with Bartelle. His hands were cold. "Forget something?" I bent down to unclasp my skis.

"Sorry we're here so late in the day. We planned to be here much earlier but something else grabbed us first. Got some more paperwork for you." He handed me a search warrant.

I skimmed it. "Water?"

"We're interested in pathogens, actually, but they'd come from your water. Beautiful day, but I'm freezing . . . Shall we?" He stamped his feet for emphasis.

We shed our gear in the mud room and Bartelle introduced me to the technician, who walked with a hitch in his giddyup. I immediately forgot his name and thought of him as Tex. "Can you give him a tour so he can determine where he needs to take his samples?"

"You guys want to start up or down?"

Tex said, "Basement. That's where the water comes in, eh?"

"My drilled well goes to the pressure tank. It has hard water with some iron, so I installed a prefilter and water softener. Water heater operates off the furnace. Do you care about the heating system?"

"Don't think so," Tex said. "Water at the little cabin where you found the Jane Doe?"

"The little guest cabin? My rustic retreat? No electricity and no running water unless I sprint with a bucket from the lake."

No one cracked a smile at my weak attempt to be funny. After the tour, Tex hauled his tackle cases containing empty sample vials and testing chemicals into the basement.

Bartelle pulled a pocket notebook from his shirt, flipped a few pages, rubbed his head. "While he's working, I got a few follow-up questions—assuming you don't mind? Did the Jane Doe ever take a shower here?"

"Only baths, trying to get her fever down. Why?" I refilled the wood stove and settled him on the chair in the great room that faced the wall of windows.

"This is a great view you've got, McCree. I can see why you love it here."

My stomach growled its discontent with emptiness. "Do I dare offer you my water to drink? Or I've got soda in the cold room downstairs if you want. I assume beer and wine are out? I need to grab something to eat. Want anything?"

"I'll take a rain check. What guns do you keep here?"

"As you know from your search, I don't have any guns. Never owned one."

He rubbed his scalp, leaving his crooked arm resting on the top of his head. "Now that's what confuses me. In the U.P. we've got more guns than people. You're living here all by your lonesome. Some real weirdos out in the woods sometimes and you don't have a gun. Make sense to you?"

I don't answer rhetorical questions.

After another scalp massage he continued, "Here's what else tickles my curiosity: last Sunday, one of the guys found four nine-millimeter jackets in the woods across the road. Care to explain?"

"Abigail set up a little range facing the swamp. Used it to practice with her Sig Sauer. Why the interest in guns?"

"Miss Hancock have any .22s?"

"Sergeant, you have me totally baffled. Tex is sampling my water for pathogens. You're asking about firearms. I assume this has to do with the woman, but I'll be darned if I can understand how."

"Tex?"

I explained my reasons for the name.

"Suits him. By the way, Lieutenant Hastings from the Cincinnati Police said to tell you she's real sorry you and Miss Hancock didn't work out. You're supposed to give her a call when you're back there."

To stall for time while I considered the implications of Hastings' message, I knocked down the damper on the fire, brought water from the kitchen, and filled the Delft porcelain humidifier on top of the wood stove. Obviously, he had researched me, looking for arrests, and found those relating to the killing at my Cincinnati house the previous year. The thought of the dead man lying there caused me to flash back to that scene. I shook it off. Bartelle would also know the prosecutor had dropped all the charges because the guys had broken in, were armed, and had shot Abigail.

He wouldn't know that I still suffered nightmares that caused me to wake up with a racing heart and a deep black knowledge that I had failed to protect Abigail in my house. I switched my thoughts to Lieutenant Hastings, who was the head of Cincinnati's Homicide Unit and a friend. Another not-to-be relationship. I had once been interested in her, but she then hooked up with a Cincinnati Bengal. After the football player dumped her, "for a first-round cheerleader pick"—her words, not mine—she made a move, but by then, Abigail was in the picture. Two ships passing . . .

Taking a cop's perspective, I figured Bartelle probably thought any person who had killed once—like me—was more likely to get into trouble than the average bear. All well and good, but how did any of this relate to the woman?

"How's she doing?" I asked after I finished my domestic duties. "The woman . . ."

"Docs have her stabilized. They're keeping her in the hospital. She still claims not to know who she is, where she came from, how she got to your place or what she did here, or before. Doc says high fevers can wipe all that stuff out, but it's usually temporary. Don't worry, we'll get the real story."

"And in the meantime, here you are, looking at your one and only suspect."

Tex stomped up the basement steps, and I found myself counting each percussive step. From the kitchen he called, "If you filter and soften your water, how come you also use a Brita filter?"

"I liked the taste of my water before conditioning, but it stained everything. Hence the softener. With the softener, the water tastes salty, so I filter it."

"You say so. Ever melt snow or anything?"

"Only when I stayed at the cabin and the lake was frozen so deep I couldn't chop a hole through. But that was several years ago, before I built the house."

"Shoulda used an ice auger," Tex laughed. "As a kid we used to ice fish this lake. Got lots of perch and some good northerns too. I'm about done here, just need to pack everything up. Oh hey, is that water you got on the stove?" He walked to the humidifier. "Yes. Look at those crystals." He pumped his fist in celebration. "Sometimes the stove gets so hot the water boils and then the crystals precipitate out. Hot dog!"

He filled two vials with water from the humidifier, then donned fire gloves I kept on the hearth and carried the humidifier to the sink. After dumping the water he scraped samples of the residue clinging to the inside of the vessel. "Perfect," he said. "Let me pack and we'll be out of your hair."

"We'll be back," Bartelle promised.

EIGHT

BOSS STOOD TO ONE SIDE OF the tellers, antennae extended, to gather facts and rumors about the murder up by Long Lake. Everyone agreed some guy snowmobiling from Witch Lake with his son had seen three eagles on the far side of Long Lake. In winter, eagles are primarily carrion eaters, and the kid wanted to see what had died. They discovered an abandoned snowmobile and portions of a frozen corpse, which in the conversations only Boss seemed to know was Brett Aho's carcass. Boss chose not to share that information. Wolves and coyotes had scattered bones over a large area and eagles were picking over the leftovers. The father stayed to keep the eagles away from the evidence, while his son scooted into Amasa to the nearest phone. He was so shaken up by the time he reached the Tall Pines general store and gas station that the clerk had to make the 911 call.

The medical examiner, looking like one of his cadavers, popped in around noon to cash a check. Boss maneuvered across the ME's path on his departure from the teller and cast a line in front of him. "Heard tell the sheriff caught an ugly one."

The ME eased to a stop and extended his head like a turtle reaching for a tasty morsel. "Yep, got ourselves an old-fashioned murder," he rasped through a voice box scarred by a three-pack-a-day habit. "Everybody's been asking if we know who it is."

Boss waited for the ME to continue, but the old man seemed to be enjoying some kind of power game, standing there, bobbing his head at the information he knew but had not yet shared. Boss knew how to play those kinds of games. "And?" Boss stretched the vowel.

"We'll probably have to rely on dental records." The ME eased back on his heels.

"Because?" Boss again drew it out.

"Bartelle would have ordered the state boys to run the prints, 'cept some animal decided they were finger-lickin' good." The ME coughed and grimaced at the pain.

Boss didn't give the ME the satisfaction of groaning at the joke; it would only encourage him. And Boss didn't want to comment on the ME's pained look, which would only lead to a discussion about how the docs had removed one of his lungs and part of the other, but cancer had still spread to his bones. Better to ask another question and avoid any reciprocal health questions. "Bartelle's running the investigation?"

"Caught a real break there. Seems the sergeant was in the area on the Jane Doe matter. Nobody's got more experience than Bartelle at running a grid. He met the lad at Tall Pines a few minutes after the call came in. Settled him down until the rest of the sheriff's boys showed. Everyone followed the kid to the murder scene. They searched for pieces and eventually the state crime scene boys from Marquette arrived."

"They find anything useful?" Boss asked.

He leaned in, bringing with him the hint of death. "I pulled a .22 slug from the deceased's brain pan. Think about it. Everyone knows a .22 is a girl's weapon. Gotta go, probably said too much already." The ME tipped his hat.

"Yeah, woman for sure." Boss said, knowing they were barking up the wrong tree. Watching the ME hobble out the door, Boss thought, "I will not let my cancer do that to me. I'm going out with a bang, not a whimper."

TWO WEEKS AFTER THE GIRL first appeared, Sergeant Lon Bartelle sat at his desk, feet up, arm wrapped around his head, drawing blood from worrying a scab. He stared at the toxicological tests from McCree's house that Tex—thanks to McCree, he couldn't think of him as anything else— had dumped on his desk.

"All negative?" Bartelle felt his face glow with the heat of disappointment. Tex stood mute before him.

Bartelle choked down his anger. No sense shooting the proverbial messenger. "Sheriff know yet?" Bartelle asked.

"Figured you'd be the one to tell him," Tex said. "Anything new on Jane?"

"You figured that, did you?" Bartelle tried a smile to get Tex to relax, but the effort died through lack of practice. "With this, I have exactly nothing I want to tell him. The woman still claims no memory."

"But she's remembering the current stuff."

"Not good enough," Bartelle growled. "Add in the stellar work we've done so far on the murder vic. We got him narrowed down to about one hundred and sixty million possible males. We have no clue who owned the Polaris we found at the murder scene. I wasted four man days of department time looking for spent brass nearby. They turned up a junkyard full of iron, but nothing useful." Bartelle slapped his forehead hard enough to produce a loud thwack. "I know why you're still standing there. You got something useful from your DEA contacts? Please tell me I'm right."

Tex leaned back against the doorframe. "Love to, Sarge, but I wouldn't want to do anything to spoil your mood. They heard nothing about a buy gone bad. All I can tell you is the victim's hair showed no drug use. Don't know about alcohol because his organs were already recycled. You still figure the murder and the Jane Doe are related?"

"Don't you? It's only two miles from the murder site on Long Lake to McCree's camp on Shank Lake where the Jane Doe pops up at approximately the same time. She's a suspect for the murder by proximity alone. Unfortunately, the sheriff and DA want proof, and the distance between me having no doubts and giving them proof looks about as big as the Grand Canyon. McCree has got to be lying—unless he's telling the truth."

"Glad you got that clear," Tex said and gimped through the doorway.

THE SNOWMOBILE'S WHINE ANNOUNCED OWEN'S weekly visit. I threw on a jacket— the temperature was already above freezing—picked up a pair of work gloves and got as far as the back porch before I realized he had a passenger. She placed her helmet on the snowmobile seat and shrugged out of a one-piece snowsuit, which she folded and placed next to the helmet. Her shoulders rose and fell in a huge sigh. Spinning around, she caught me staring at her and flashed a smile. Jane Doe.

I uprooted my feet and helped unload my week's supplies. With three pairs of hands it went quickly, especially since no one chose to break the uncomfortable silence.

Owen disappeared behind the pole barn to pee—he maintained it was a waste of water to use a toilet—and left the woman in the kitchen shifting from foot to foot. I gathered an extra placemat and cloth napkin from the Indiana cupboard. "All recovered?" I asked.

"They've released me." She approached me. "I came to thank you for saving my life."

I slipped around her and grabbed a soup bowl and spoon. "That really wasn't necessary."

"I've got my own questions, but those can wait. The doctors told me that if you hadn't given me the antibiotics and brought my fever down, I would never have made it. Somehow I contracted Legionnaires' disease—don't worry, it's not catching. That's worth at least a thank-you and a hug—saving my life, not the disease."

She wrapped her arms around me and squeezed hard. At least I now knew what Tex was looking for with his pathological sampling. I stood there, arms raised, wondering what to do with them as her body pressed to mine. I could picture her in the bath and it was making me uncomfortable. Owen walked in and barked a short cough. She applied a last bit of pressure and released me. "Soup smells homey," she said. "What kind?"

While I used the bathroom, she served the lentil soup. I returned to hear Owen chuckling. He saw me, choked down the chuckle, and said, "No problem."

Owen had already installed his teeth and between slurps of soup, he jumped to the gossip. "You hear they identified the guy was killed?"

I hadn't, so Owen enthusiastically took the bit. "Lived in Trout Creek or Ewen, 'round there. Went by the name of Brett Aho. Not related to the Ahos in Iron County, I don't think. Had a weekly meet-up with some floozy. Guess it had been two, three years he was seein her for their lay-zon. When he missed and she couldn't contact him, she got to worryin, remembered hearin about the murder, and called the state police.

"Took 'em some time to find his dentist. Geezer was winterin in Arizona. Had enough teeth on the jawbone to match his X-rays. Hear tell there's a sister somewhere. Ain't claimed the body yet. Course there ain't much to claim, neither. More soup?"

I served Owen seconds and motioned to the woman, who shook her head in refusal. I poured a ladleful into my bowl and passed the bread. "What kind of work did he do?" I sucked in a spoonful of soup and burned the inside of my mouth.

"Trucker I heard this from didn't know no more than what I told ya.

You all hear the DNR is looking for some jerk who shot hisself a wolf over by Cable Lake?"

The woman dropped her spoon and it clattered into the bowl, splashing drops of soup onto the table. "Where's that?" She dabbed at the spill with her cloth napkin.

Owen waved toward the wall of windows. "Other side of One-Forty-One and a little bit south. Ten, twelve miles maybe. DNR used to think the Cable Lake pack and the one up arounds here was the same ones. I kept tellin them they was separate. Finally, they got radio collars on the alpha pair and proved it was two different packs. Listened to me they could have saved money and used it on somethin useful, like stockin the lakes. The radio signal didn't move no more and the local DNR found the bitch gut shot. I ain't got much good to say about wolves, but shootin 'em like that is lower than snake shit in Death Valley."

The woman flinched when he mentioned the gut shot and looked as though she would be sick.

Owen must have noticed her discomfort as well. "Pardon my French. I ain't used to polite company."

Owen's apology brought a smile to her face and caused me to remember her colorful language when she first came out of her stupor. Whatever had caused her discomfort, it wasn't Owen's swearing.

Owen nattered on about other local happenings, finished his soup, patted his beard and mustache with his napkin, belched to proclaim it had been good, and announced he needed to see a man about a dog—his way of indicating he was going outside to pee again.

Owen had painted the silence with his gossip; now I wondered how to broach the topic of her lost memories. I gave up on clever. "Any luck with your memory?"

"Nothing worthwhile. You're still looking at Jane Doe. I decided on the ride out I was going to adopt a temporary name. I'm feeling like a Niki today. N-I-K-I. What do you think?"

"Isn't it usually with two 'k's?"

"I don't want to be greedy with the consonants. One's all I need."

"Niki's good. Staying with Doe or moving to Smith or Johnson, or something a little more unique?"

"I'll be one of those single-named people. You know, like Madonna or Rihanna."

Outside the snowmobile sputtered to life. "I guess you'd best catch your ride. Miss it and you'll be stranded for a week."

She rose from the table and gathered the dishes. "There's no hurry. I'll wash these."

In the midst of our friendly argument about whether or not she should wash the dishes, the snowmobile engine roared, and through the mudroom window I watched Owen speed up the driveway. "What the . . . ?"

"I guess now would be a good time to fess up," she said from behind me. I spun around and she greeted me with a crooked smile. "Before lunch . . . while you were in the bathroom, I told him you had agreed to let me stay here until I figured out who I was."

NINE

Jimmie had to pass by Boss's place the first time. A logging truck was coming the other way, and he'd agreed that no one should see him here. He pulled as far to the right as he dared and gave the Yooper wave—four fingers raised from the steering wheel while the thumb still steered—as the logging truck rumbled past. "Bastards think they own the damn road," Jimmie grumbled through clenched teeth. He continued moseying down Rock Crusher until he hit the Enstrom Cutoff, where he executed a three-point turn.

Boss's vehicle wasn't in the pole barn. Jimmie parked in the same place he had before, kicked some accumulated snow from around his tires, and entered the unlocked single-wide. He boosted the thermostat to sixty-eight. Figuring Boss would want coffee, maybe even with a drop of brandy being as it was the end of the day, he ran water into a kettle and put it on the hotplate to boil.

Jimmie drummed his fingers on the table, warming them to the rhythm of some Sousa march. The kettle soon whistled. He hunted for the Maxwell House; found it in the same cupboard containing powdered milk and rat poison. Paused to think about that for a moment, then dumped a heaping teaspoon of coffee into the mug. Nothing worse than weak coffee. Jimmie stirred in boiling water, snorting the steam to capture the smell of freshly made instant. He rotated the mug to look at the Hematite National Bank logo and wondered if they shouldn't update their graphic from a miner with a pick to giant earthmovers and three-story dump trucks.

The first mug of coffee warmed Jimmie's insides; the second he carried as a hand warmer while he searched the main room for something to read. Found an ancient *Playboy* stuffed under the couch, checked the centerfold, and read the "Advisor" column before tucking it back where he had found it. He'd never entered the bedroom. Still no sound of Boss, so what the hell.

He set the mug on the table, pulled his sleeves over his fingers, and pushed the door open. Blackout curtains covered the window and he flicked on the overhead light. Except for the bed in the corner, it looked like the reading room of a library: cherry keyhole desk in the middle with a Herman Miller Aeron chair, bookcases on three walls, a locked gun safe in the other corner. Three-by-five cards with Boss's back-slanted printing labeled the sections. He read the cards tacked onto the bookshelves on the left wall: Constitution, Police State, Militia.

The row at eye level contained the last few volumes of "Police State" and ran into the "Militia" section. He perused the spines with titles like *Waste in Waco* and *Your Rights After an Unauthorized Search and Seizure.* Sitting open on the desk was *Life and Hard Times of Mark Koernke: Radio's Voice of Truth.* Huh! He had never heard Boss speak one word about the militia. At the crunch of tires coming up the driveway, he knocked the light switch down with his elbow and, with his sleeve again covering his hand, shut the door.

Boss shucked the parka onto the couch. "Been waiting long? Must have been. Feels decent in here and smells like you made coffee. More water in the pot?"

With a brandy-fortified coffee in hand, Boss asked, "You hungry? I bought some pasties for later, but I can heat one up."

At the mention of food Jimmie realized he was hungry. Breakfast was a long time ago, but he felt a little skittish, and the tour of the bedroom hadn't eased his concern. Boss was one part Chamber of Commerce, one part backroom pol, one part church deacon, and one part certified. "I'm good for now," he said.

"Tell me I was right." Boss settled on the couch.

"As always," Jimmie said, plastering a genuine thousand-watt smile on his face. "I seen that old coot pick her up at the hospital just like you figured. Trailed along until they got to his place in Amasa, then I parked by where the snowmobile trail cuts the highway near Tall Pines and unloaded my snow machine from the trailer. Took off ahead of them, hid my sled in a stand of hemlocks off that back road we seen from the plat book was on McCree's property. Had on my white camo suit. Snuck up on 'em so's they never seen me peeking over the hill spying on 'em."

"Just the two of them?"

"She rode in behind him. While old hairy ears and McCree bring the first bags into the house, she takes the knapsack you give her and stores it inside the woodshed sticking off McCree's pole barn. Then she quick-like grabs some groceries and helps unload the goods."

Jimmie stopped his recital while Boss made another spiked coffee. "Could you hear them?"

"Not then. Later. They was in the house for a good long time. Probably et something. Finally the old coot comes out, steps behind the pole barn, and takes a second leak. Then he cranks up his machine and takes off. Leaves the girl behind."

"You're messing with me, Jimmie."

Jimmie leaned back, held his hands up in the universal I'm-only-telling-the-truth gesture. "I stuck around and a few minutes later the two of them—McCree and the girl—come out the door. She says, 'I put my stuff out here,' and gets her knapsack from the woodshed. He follows her and says—and you can tell he's totally pissed— he says, 'Look Nikki, I'm not going to make you walk to town, but tomorrow first thing . . . ' She kind of shrugs," Jimmie exaggerated a shrug, raising his shoulders almost to his ears, "and walks past him and inside the house. McCree takes off on cross-country skis going lickety-split. We ain't talked about whether you still want her kilt, so I slipped away."

Boss got up and patted Jimmie on the shoulder. "You've done well. You sure you heard McCree call the girl Nikki?"

"Yep." Jimmie had been feeling pretty good about the pats on the shoulder, but now he wasn't so sure.

Boss paced the room two circuits, paused to look out the window, then made a third circuit. Jimmie waited, feeling the vibrations of each step reverberate through the single-wide's floor. Boss faced him. "Good call on leaving the girl alone. Last I heard, she still wasn't remembering anything, and if I'm not mistaken, by now Owen is eating high off the hog on his story about the girl shacking up with McCree." Boss chuckled and Jimmie figured it was good policy to join in. "The cops were wondering about the two of them being in cahoots before. This should frost that cake. She is a cute thing and McCree's been holed up there without any companionship. Too bad we don't have the place wired for video."

Jimmie waited for instructions while Boss slurped down the dregs of the coffee, washed the mugs, and hung them on the tree. Boss tucked the dishtowel over the rack. "I'll keep an ear to the ground in town. You stay away from there until I get back atcha."

* * *

THE GIRL'S NAME WAS NOT Nikki. Boss thought back again to the two people selected from more than a hundred who submitted applications to the foundation—a foundation existing only as a downstate Michigan corporation with a postal drop that forwarded mail to another postal drop that was nearer to Boss's home, but not too near. Bethany and Brandon: if those weren't monikers representing white Americans born in the eighties, what were?

Both postdoctoral students, both orphans without close family, both loners, both able to leave everything behind and give their all on a six-month project. Despite assurances to Jimmie that he had done well, Boss worried about Bethany still being alive. A secondary question was whether Seamus McCree also posed an unacceptable risk. If the girl was calling herself Nikki, she obviously didn't know who she was. Nikki wasn't her mother or grandmother or former roommate's name either. Not even close.

If Bethany didn't get her memory of past events back in the five-plus weeks before April Fool's Day, then she could cause no harm to the plans. It seemed, however, too long a time. Since no one knew where the girl came from, if she went missing from the Northwoods without a trace, the cops might decide her disappearance was further proof she had killed Brett Aho—or that McCree had killed them both. Either result was acceptable. So, let Jimmie clean up the loose end once everyone decided McCree and the girl were romantically involved.

Let McCree choose his own fate: either he booted the girl out or he didn't. If he didn't, and Jimmie couldn't catch Bethany alone, McCree would become collateral damage. If Jimmie struck right after Owen Lyndstrom's next Tuesday supply run, it might not be until Owen's visit the following week that someone would discover the bodies.

If McCree ditched the girl, then he could live. If the girl returned to town, it would be harder to kill her, but fortunately Boss had been one of the deacons from the Presbyterian Church who organized the new red knapsack filled with donated clothing to keep her going until she figured out who she was. The fact they had already met might make it easier to lure the girl away when the time was right.

Eschewing more coffee, Boss filled a juice glass with brandy and took it to the office. Moving the Koernke book aside, Boss retrieved an archaic Dell Inspiron 2500 from a cardboard box stored in the office closet. Slower than making toast by solar heat in December, the computer eventually did the trick. Checking email was a four-step process: attach the laptop to the phone line; wait for the dial-up connection to take; download email from NuWrldYooper@gmail.com, an account only a few people knew; delete email. Two messages:

Congratulations on test results. Two out of two healthy students is great! Just think what this will do to old damaged goods.

Cysteine levels remaining sufficiently high and sodium levels now under control. Should be concentrated in three weeks or less.

Boss took a celebratory slug of the brandy and felt the liquor burn a path from throat to stomach. Time to sing a psalm. Interesting when you thought of it: in the Bible, the psalms came immediately after the afflictions of Job. To everything its time and place—Ecclesiastes was two books after the Psalms, leaving room for Proverbs in between.

Boss drained the whiskey and thought of a favorite proverb: "When pride cometh, then cometh shame: but with the lowly is wisdom." Boss put away the laptop and pulled a folder from the drawer and spread its contents on the desk.

Ten

MY CHASE DREAM THAT NIGHT took its typical form: unknown people were after me, and I knew that if they caught me, they'd kill me. I awoke wondering if people who died in their sleep had also suffered chase dreams, and if, in their terminal dream, their demons finally did reach them.

The house was silent except for the metronome ticks from the grandmother clock hanging on the wall. My feet didn't recoil from the cold floor as they usually do. The house was warm. I threw on fresh clothes, tiptoed from the bedroom to the loft and stopped at the sight of Niki downstairs, facing the lakeside wall of windows, performing yoga's Salute to the Sun. Dressed in a tank top, boy shorts, and slouch socks, the glow from the wood stove fire painted her skin a warm orange. She was as supple as I was stiff.

Trying unsuccessfully to ignore her scanty attire, I waited until she had run through the poses before I continued down the stairs.

"I've figured it out," she said at my entry. "I'll stay in your guest cabin. There's plenty of split wood, and I already lit the fire. It'll take all day before it's comfortable for sitting, but it should be fine for sleeping tonight. You've got enough cooking utensils over there for me to take care of my breakfast and lunches, but it would be nice if we could share dinner?" She slipped into blue jeans and a T-shirt with the names of all the Forest Park Trojans football players. "I can only pay you with labor, but you're not exactly domestic. Have you ever washed these windows? Wood heat isn't clean, you know. I can—"

"You hatched this plan this morning, did you?" My voice dripped with skepticism. I had to give her credit. She didn't turn away, didn't look down. She didn't plead or shout. She continued her conversational tone.

"Coyotes yipping and yapping woke me around three. I couldn't get back to sleep, so I borrowed your headlamp and restoked the stove since the fire had burned down. Then I walked on the lake. You missed the northern lights. The borealis showed for maybe twenty minutes. Not exactly bright, just green sheets in the northern sky." She pointed high on the cathedral ceiling on the north side. "While I was walking, I thought about everything you said yesterday. You know, about needing your space and everything. Then I remembered the cabin, so I checked it out."

She grabbed my arm, pulled me to the nearest window, and ran her finger over the window sill. "See this dust? I'd hate to think what it looks like under your refrigerator."

I pulled my arm away. "I appreciate your—"

"I know I'm costing you food, a little extra propane maybe, and wood. I'll replace the wood I use. If I cook and clean, would that compensate for the food?"

I didn't know what to say, so I temporized and poured a glass of water, drank it, and poured another. From the corner of my eye, I watched her follow my movements. "I'm not expressing myself well this morning," I said. "Yesterday's concerns still hold. I appreciate your not wanting to be a financial burden. Believe me, that is the least of it. I need space and . . ." *And what exactly did I need?*

She nodded as though she read my mind. "Here's the thing, Seamus. I don't exactly know who or what I am. I kind of think I'm a loner. The thought of staying at your cabin appeals to me. How about a week's trial? You don't throw me out until Owen returns next Tuesday. What have you got to lose?"

Any hope the cops won't think I'm involved with this person, that's what. With Owen undoubtedly letting the world know she's here, though, I guess that ship has sailed.

She pulled her earlobe a couple of times. "Your house will be clean. I'll leave you alone except we'll eat dinner together? You've got a couple of dead maples on the other side of your cabin. I'll take them down and work them up to replace the wood I use."

"You know how to use a chainsaw?" The inane question leapt from my mouth.

"How hard can it be? Please, Seamus. One week."

Once, in my corporate days, we underwent a Myers–Briggs personality test. I was an INTP. The *P*, which stands for perceiving, came into full play. *P*s like to take in information for as long as possible before they have to make a decision. I didn't have to make a decision this moment. If she had pouted or batted her eyes or tried any other stereotypical female ploy, I think I would have tossed her out. My normal morning routine was to stretch for thirty minutes, then cook oatmeal for breakfast and journal for an hour or so before cross-country skiing the rest of the morning and often into the afternoon. If I decided after journaling to ski to Deer Lake and arrange transportation for Niki, nothing would stand in my way. In the meantime, I might learn something about her.

I moved the footstool to make room for my stretches and started with easy back rocks. "What did the doctors tell you about your memory?" I asked.

"Full recovery," she said with a confident voice. "They're not sure of the timing or whether it will return in bits and pieces or all at once."

I shifted into a one-legged stand and caught her eye as I changed positions.

"Well, that's not exactly right," she answered, the assurance gone. "They're not sure. I could quite possibly never remember whatever happened while I had the high fever, but they gave me, like, a ninety percent chance of remembering all the rest of the stuff."

"What do you know about yourself?" I said in the midst of touching my toes—well, that's what they call the exercise—I was three inches short of the objective.

She paced the great room, careful to avoid interrupting my stretches. A series of emotions played across her face until she regained control of a blank expression. "I have certain . . . competencies. I don't know anything factual about myself. I'm like a scientific puzzle. You know, they find the bones of a new animal and try to determine what it looked like, how it lived, what it ate, who ate it? That's how I feel. I've figured out some things are easy for me and some are hard."

She effortlessly flowed from a standing position to a handstand, legs straight, her shirt falling down past her chest to cover her face, exposing an arched back and the tight body accented by the rose tattoo above her breast I remembered from the sponge baths. She bent her elbows, popped herself to standing, and pulled her shirt into place. "Like that. I knew I could do it, although I haven't tried it. But I don't know if I was a gymnast or I'm just a show-off. I go outside and my spirits lift, but I don't know why."

My next stretch was a shoulder stand. I had never done a hand stand, except with a wall nearby to lean into if I lost balance. I considered skipping that position and then figured, what the heck? I wasn't trying to impress her with my flexibility, I was trying to stretch. "What else," I mumbled with my chin tucked into my chest.

"God," she said. "You are skinny. Don't you eat enough?"

Most people abhor silence and find it necessary in a conversation to fill in the empty space when I leave one. She was no different. Ten seconds and she cracked. "What else? I've got tattoos. Not exactly news to you, is it?" She gave a nervous chuckle. "Unfortunately, they don't tell me shit about anything. Oh, I swear like a sailor, so I'm probably not a funda-mentalist anything. I like to read and I seem to have an eclectic taste—as do you, assuming all the books you have around here are yours?"

"All mine." I lay on my back with my arms stretched overhead, feeling my shoulder muscles slowly release their tension. "You know, with your tattoo, I'm surprised you didn't decide to call yourself Rose."

"Really!" She laughed with a Joni Mitchell leap of octaves.

"I haven't always been slim. I put on a lot of extra weight after my divorce. Eating and drinking too much, and exercising too little. My son eventually called me 'Blubber Man,' which forced me to see what I was doing to myself."

"Depression can do that." She stepped over to my stretched frame and pulled my feet out while pushing my rear in. "That's better balance. Yep, depression makes you fat or skinny. Hard to find someone with depression who weighs what they should."

While I finished stretching, she continued to pace, her socks sounding like two cloth brooms sweeping the wood floor. As I did my final stretch she said, "I gotta tell you, Seamus. I'm not afraid of what I will find, I'm afraid I'll never find out. Then what do I do?" She stared out the windows toward the snow-covered lake. "You know, you're tight because of your hamstrings. I can show you some stretches that are really good for that. Some of them need a second person, and while I'm here . . . But you haven't exactly decided whether to throw me out, have you?"

I banged around in the kitchen. "You want oatmeal?"

"Sure, can I help?"

"No," I said. "I can boil water all on my own." Harsh. She didn't deserve my anger. Anger at what exactly? "I'm sorry. That was rude. You can set the table. Napkins and placemats are in the Indiana cupboard. If you want coffee, filters and stuff are there too."

"Don't you drink coffee?"

"Never took it up. Don't do tea either, but I stock it, in case. So, help yourself." My mother would approve of my hospitality. Now, why had

Niki's presence caused me to bubble with anger? Yes, she had tricked me into housing her for a night. She should have been honest and asked—but I would have refused. Taking her at her word, she was homeless, penniless, and nameless. I had arguably saved her life, and it surely wasn't the cost of feeding her I objected to. Was it as simple as I didn't want the inconvenience of having to worry about someone other than myself? Had I become that self-centered—or depressed, as she had suggested?

"The water's boiling," she said so softly the words airbrushed my consciousness.

Once I stirred in brown sugar and added the oatmeal, I turned down the heat and checked the clock to know when six minutes passed. Who in my position didn't have the right to be a little depressed? My lover was now an ex; my home in Cincinnati was just a repaired building after everything of sentimental value had been burned. I was bored with the recent cases Criminal Investigations Group had assigned me.

Why shouldn't I enjoy the great outdoors and my freedom to do whatever I wanted, whenever I wanted? My son was well-launched with his anti-computer-hacking startup. Of course I needed new challenges, but those could wait until spring break-up when I returned to civilization. Or so I kept telling myself.

We ate in silence. Every few bites, her chair would squeak as she shifted position to sneak a glance in my direction. She clearly wanted to talk. *Well, let her stew. Nobody asked her here.* On the other hand, I had to admit to myself that breakfast tasted better accompanied by the smells of fresh coffee and slightly burned toast, even though I didn't partake of either.

She poured a second cup of coffee, took a sip, and said, "I've never had oatmeal with brown sugar stirred into the water first. I think I like my brown sugar and raisins on the top. Did you learn that from your parents?"

"Self-taught. I don't like the cardboard taste of plain oatmeal. This solves the problem."

"I add more sugar." Her eyes smiled. "How did the police discover me here?"

"Huh?"

"The doctors told me you saved me and everything. But if the only contact you have is with Owen on Tuesdays, how did the cops pick me up on a Sunday?"

I related how I had unsuccessfully honked the horn to get someone's attention. How I had finally decided to ski for help and how an amateur pilot flying from Marquette to Ironwood had spotted the blue tarp SOS. He called the coordinates in to the airport, who called 911. Iron County Sheriff's officers responded. End of story.

An impish smile played on her face. "Did you hear about the hunter who was lost in the woods and used the three-shot signal like you tried?"

"Nope." I took another spoonful of oatmeal.

"Well, this guy gets all turned around chasing a deer. He knows enough to stop moving and signal his distress with three shots so his buddies, who should be nearby, can find him. He fires his three shots toward the east and waits on a downed log. Nothing. An hour goes by and he fires off three more shots, this time facing south. Still nothing. Later, three more shots to the north. He's getting cold, and it's going to be dark soon. He only has enough for three more shots, but decides to use them, so he faces the setting sun, pulls the last three arrows from his quiver and lets loose."

I burst out laughing, nearly snorting oatmeal out my nose. The laughter surprised me. It was a sound I had not heard since Abigail left.

A smile flickered across her features, but then she became solemn, scratched her head a few times. "Please give it a week, Seamus. Somewhere nearby is the answer to who I am. I know you're taking a risk. I could be faking all this. I could be a cold-blooded killer. The police think maybe I am. Of course, they think maybe you are too." A grin briefly glimmered and retreated. "It's not like I'm exactly hiding or anything. I got the impression over lunch with Owen that he'll be gabbing to the entire world that I'm here.

"I could use your skis if you are snowshoeing or vice versa. And I meant what I said about cleaning this place and . . ." She wiped her eyes with the back of her hands. "I swore I wasn't going to cry."

I dumped the dishes into the sink—a darned good thing they weren't glass—and turned on the hot water. "Alright, a week. I've got extra snowshoes and skis and poles and stuff I bought for Abigail. She's taller than you, so size might be something of a problem."

"Thanks, Seamus. You won't regret it." She threw her arms around me, squeezed hard, and planted a wet kiss on the back of my neck.

I hoped she was right.

Eleven

TWO DAYS LATER, NIKI AWOKE in the middle of the night to the ululations of a wolf pack. Tingles ran up and down her back as she lay in the log cabin's bed listening to the haunting calls. Starlight from the moonless night illuminated the room. She added logs to restore the fire and slipped on every layer of clothes she had.

Standing underneath the sugar maple trees, she gazed at the Milky Way arched overhead, a sparkling promenade for the angels. She followed the path from the cabin to the house to get an unobstructed view of the sky from the yard, startling a deer from the salt lick as she passed. Orion hung above the lake: left shoulder the bright reddish star Betelgeuse that kids in her Girl Scout troop called Beetlejuice; belt—Alnilam, Alnitak, Mintaka—bold as a spit-shined biker's pride; sword—two stars and a nebula—pulsing with 1,500-year-old light from the birth of new stars.

Past Orion's right shoulder shone the Pleiades, the Seven Sisters, except it was so clear Niki could distinguish all nine of the major stars, the first time that had ever happened.

Above her, the sliding door from Seamus's bedroom opened and he stepped onto the small deck dressed in a T-shirt and Jockeys, his head covered by a fur hat. "Get some clothes on, ya dumb fuck" she yelled. "It's five below!" A sympathetic shiver caused her arms and legs to twitch.

He started. "What are *you* doing?"

"Those poor bastards in town never get to see this magnificent sight. I'm heading to the lake to get a better view."

"Hang on. I'll be right down."

For several hours they walked up and down the lake, watched stars wheel across the sky, caught brief glimpses of the northern lights, and eventually witnessed the stars fade away as the sun ascended into the sky. She spent the last hour trying to ignore the cold, but with the last star gone, the cold won. "I'm heading in."

He touched her arm. "Don't leave yet. Watching the sunrise from here is something you need to experience at least once."

She oriented herself to see its first direct light gathering behind the eastern hills.

"The other way." He took her shoulders and pointed her toward the western shore. The sun first gilded the tops of the trees, then as the brilliant orb moved higher into the sky, its light worked down the trees and onto the lake.

It was just a sunrise, but somehow it seemed like magic. Even as a wisp of a breeze brushed her exposed skin and reminded her how cold she was, she remained on the ice feeling . . . what? Excitement? She'd seen sunrises before. Were these the first stirrings of lust? A twinge rocked her at the thought. She fingered her neck where the hickey had once been. Whose lips had branded her? What promises? Dark thoughts returned. What trauma was implied by the rope burns? She closed her eyes and willed the memories to return.

Once inside, she convinced him to let her fix breakfast. She whipped up pancakes only to discover he didn't have maple syrup. Rooting around in the freezer, she discovered frozen cranberries, which she made into a sauce. He devoured the pancakes.

An internal voice said, *the way to a man's heart is through his stomach.* Whose voice, and why think of that now? He was certainly easy to look at. Lanky with a nicely rounded ass. With a razor and a comb he'd clean up right well. She announced her decision. "I think today is the day."

"Um?" he mumbled through a mouthful of pancakes.

She bit her lip. "You've had two days of solitudenous—is that a word?—forays. Today, I want you to take me to explore where that guy was murdered. Maybe I killed him."

He carefully put down his fork. She gnawed on the inside of her cheek. Maybe being blunt wasn't such a good idea. "Jiminy, maybe you did it! What the hell do I know? I could be a moth drawn to flame, but you know the country around here . . ."

He crossed his arms over his chest. "You know my routine—"

"And I know you won't go into cardiac arrest if you don't follow it for one single day. Take a walk on the wild side, Seamus. Explore with me first, then I'll go to the cabin and you can stretch and journal to your heart's content." That did not come out as she had intended. She brushed a nonexistent tear from the corner of her eye. "Give it a try. Please? Just this once?"

* * *

I MENTALLY KICKED MYSELF ALL the way to the murder site. *Where am I going to draw the line? Despite my protests, she insists on cooking breakfast. Then she convinces me to throw my daily routine in the garbage and pretend to be Sherlock Holmes. Next she's going to tell me to trim my beard. Five days.* I counted five snowshoe steps. *And then she's gone for good.*

At the murder site, it was apparent we hadn't been the only voyeurs. Snowmobile tracks crisscrossed the trails around Long Lake. A herd of snowshoed bipeds had trampled the area, packing down the snow. By the expression on Niki's face, I didn't think she recognized the site. We brushed snow from two roadside boulders to serve as seats while we snacked on gorp.

Between mouthfuls she asked, "Do you know they call this stuff 'scroggin' in New Zealand?"

"You've been to New Zealand?"

She closed her eyes in concentration. "Don't know. Maybe it's just a factoid I picked up. Here, you finish the bag. You need to put on weight. You may have been—what did your son call you?—'Blubber' or whatever once, but you're anorexic now. You need to work through your grief in better ways than eating disorders."

"Grief?"

"Yeah. You know, love's labor lost—the mythical Abigail whose stuff I don't fit into." She sprang to her feet. "Let's head down the lake and see if anything looks familiar."

We found evidence of ice fishing as we skied the length of the lake: circular holes had been drilled into the ice with battery-powered augers and were now refrozen. Near the outlet, we skirted a weird-looking patch of ice: not clear like most of the lake, but opaque with flecks of rotting leaves. We paused to speculate what might have happened and decided someone had broken through the ice with their snowmobile and stirred up the bottom.

On the lake's far shore, we explored a two-story log cabin up a short rise from the ice. I sat down on the porch stoop. Niki walked all around the house, peered into the windows, wandered down the entrance road. "I don't recognize anything," she announced, "but I'd like to determine where that road goes."

"Probably to the A Grade," I said. "It's about a mile away."

She whacked me on the shoulder with a mitten. "That's not what I meant."

At the A Grade, she headed away from Amasa and at the Camp Ten switch picked up the Cut-Across Road. At Camp Ten Creek, we stopped and drank half the water we carried. The day remained crystal clear and the sun had warmed the temperature to the teens. I pulled off my hat to let heat escape. From a snowbank at the edge of the marshy area surrounding the creek, an ermine periscoped his head and chirped. It ran in bursts to a rock outcropping where it dived into the surrounding snow. Periodically, its head reappeared. Sometimes we'd glimpse the entire body; mostly we caught sight of only its black-tipped tail as the weasel punched another hole in the snow to pursue dinner.

"I didn't realize how tired I was until we stopped," Niki said.

We had no sooner started back than we had to hustle out of the road to avoid a canary-yellow snowmobile with flaming red hotrod stripes roaring past us. Its operator returned our waves. Niki stared at its tracks.

"Not too ostentatious, is it?" I said.

"Seamus, I'm not exactly sure . . . but I may have seen it before."

TWELVE

I LAY ON THE COUCH reading a book, partly listening to Niki humming to herself as she stirred the Senate bean soup she was preparing for Owen's Tuesday visit. "You can't put off the decision any longer, Seamus. If you won't let me stay, I need to pack before Owen arrives."

Put-up or shut-up, as my father used to say. The house was clean, but not obsessively so. She had taken over the cooking. She knew how to use spices, so her meals were more varied and better tasting than mine. She was interesting to talk with, but didn't mind quiet. She stayed out of my way when I preferred to be alone. Mostly. We shared a love of the outdoors.

It came down to this: fate threw her on my doorstep, and I felt the responsibility to help. I leaned over the pot and inhaled, the steam clouding my glasses. "Smells great." Stepping back to give her access to the soup I added, "You can stay, I'll—"

She yelped with glee, pulled my head down, and planted her lips on mine. The kiss took me by surprise and into my opened lips she slipped her tongue. Without thinking, I replied in kind, even while my arms remained limply at my sides. She released my head and stepped away.

"Thanks," she said. Her smile preceded a rollicking laugh. My face heated with embarrassment at her laughing at me.

She controlled her laugh sufficiently to sputter, "I forgot I was holding the spoon and splattered your head with soup."

Owen zoomed into the yard while I cleaned up. I towel-dried my hair and helped him bring in the supplies—he had doubled the quantities on my supply list to account for Niki. Before taking in the last load, Owen handed me a small paper bag.

"What's this?" I hefted it to check its weight—light.

He looked down at the ground. "Don't know what kind you like, so I . . ." He motioned at the bag.

Inside was a package of condoms. "It's not like that." My voice rose an octave in protest.

"You don't know nothin about that girl's history. You gotta . . . well, you're old enough to know what you gotta do. You get in there. I need to see a man about a horse." He stomped off around the pole barn.

I tucked the condoms in my pocket. "She's not dangerous," I said to his back. *Is that true?*

Owen reappeared, pulled me by the arm to where his gun was strapped to the snowmobile. In a stage whisper he said, "Don't look at nothin but me. Somebody's spyin on you."

I thought back to the kiss Niki and I had shared and blushed like a teenager caught necking on the couch by his parents.

"I was about to pee when I caught a flash from a scope or somethin. He's dressed in white camo up on the hill between here and the cabin. Don't know how long he's been there. I seen fresh tracks from the road headin in that direction. Shoulda realized they wouldn't be yourn."

To give the impression we were talking about Owen's machine, I projected my voice. "I don't see anything wrong with it either." Under my breath I added, "We might be able to see from the bedroom window."

We removed our boots in the mud room and slipped by Niki, who was putting away the provisions. As Owen passed her, she grabbed his arm and planted a smooch on his cheek. "What lovely produce you brought. From Angeli's?"

Owen's blush made my earlier one pale in comparison. He mumbled a reply and I jumped in. "We'll be back in a minute. I want to show Owen something upstairs."

None of the windows provided a view of the watcher. "We might see from the balcony," I said and dragged Owen into the master bedroom where I stuck the condoms in my sock drawer.

"He could've taken us out while we was bringin in the groceries, so maybe we got ourselves some time. Either way, lettin him know we know ain't a good idea."

"So what do you suggest?"

Owen removed his choppers from his pocket and placed them into his mouth. "It'd be a durnblasted shame to waste the soup."

"So you figure he's interested in Niki?"

"Who's interested in Niki?"

Owen and I spun around to find her standing in the doorway.

"What? You two come in toting a gun and sashay upstairs and what—

I'm supposed to be the good little woman slaving away in the kitchen?" She fisted her hands on her hips. "Not likely."

We told her of the spy.

"Let them look," Niki said stomping to the door onto the balcony. "I've got nothing to hide." She pulled her shirt up to her chin. "It's Mardi Gras. He owes me some beads." She let her shirt drop.

"Don't think no voyeur is gonna come out here to look at your tits."

Niki pushed off the doorframe and again placed her hands on her hips, thrusting out her chest.

"I'm not sayin—not that they ain't worth lookin at—not that I'd know. Ah hell, a fellow got killed a couple of miles from here. I think you need to worry about that."

"And you think he's interested in me? Why don't we invite him in for soup and ask his intentions?" Before either Owen or I realized her plan, Niki slid open the door to the bedroom balcony a crack and yelled, "Hey Tom Peeper. Come on in and have lunch with us." To us she said, "Get downstairs and sit before my soup gets cold."

Owen led the way to the table, pulled out his chair and sat. He tucked a napkin into his shirt and looked up expectantly.

"Niki, the guy's in camo," I said. "With a scope."

"He's looking. He's not shooting. Besides, now that he knows we saw him, he's gone." Niki placed a bowl of soup in front of Owen and patted his arm. "I'd give you another kiss for protecting us, but it might cause you or our peeper to faint." She giggled and finished serving the soup. "Where was he, Owen? Sit, Seamus."

Good boy that I am, I sat.

We were almost finished eating when the roar of a snowmobile shooting down the driveway announced a visitor.

Owen grabbed the rifle and quick-walked into the downstairs bedroom where he could cover the rider. "Don't answer the door or go near a window until you know who it is. If he comes to your door, give me a few secs to slip out the side and cover him."

Niki and I ran upstairs to view the visitor from the upstairs window where we could stay low and peek over the sills. The driver eased around the pole barn, momentarily disappearing from our sight, pulled beside Owen's machine, and killed the engine. He stepped off his machine and pulled off his gloves and helmet.

* * *

Sergeant Bartelle dismounted from the snow machine and before he could even say hello to Seamus McCree or Owen Lyndstrom, the geezer asked, "Is the spy still there?"

Bartelle gave Owen a look that said, "What the hell are you talking about?"

"The tracks comin in from the road, a third of the way from the driveway to the cabin. Didn't you see them? Clear as blaze orange at noon. There was a guy up on the hill spyin on these folks."

"How are you, Owen?" Bartelle drawled, his voice quiet. "That why you're carrying your rifle?" He gave McCree a wink. "He always has it, but the DNR's never caught him doing anything illegal. Now, Seamus, we're going to play act a little. I want you to wave your arms around a lot and tell me to get off your property. I'll take my sled up to where Owen saw the tracks and follow them in. You and Owen go back inside like nothing's happening. Got it?"

In response, McCree turned in an Oscar-winning performance.

"Fine, then," Bartelle yelled in response. "I'll be back with your bleeping warrant." Bartelle slammed his helmet on his head and roared up the driveway. He found the tracks Owen mentioned, but it was clear someone had recently exited in a hurry. Bartelle dismounted and checked the spot the spy had used.

On his return, Bartelle found Jane Doe standing on the stoop. "So, it's true," he said. "You are here." He peeled off his outer layers and she hung them on a hook. They gathered around the wood stove, melting the snow off everyone's boots. The smell of drying wool perfumed the air.

"Well?" Lyndstrom asked Bartelle.

"Rabbited, but probably a good thing I arrived when I did."

McCree shifted from foot to foot and finally said, "No warrants today, Sergeant Bartelle?"

Bartelle felt heat burn on his neck. "You keep telling me you have nothing to hide and I can search anytime for anything. That changed?"

"Boys, boys," Niki's voice came from the kitchen. "I'll get a tape measure if you really want to find out who has the biggest dick. Care for some soup, Sergeant?"

Bartelle waved the idea aside. "Any idea who your visitor was?" To a chorus of "nos" Owen added, "What did you find?"

Time to remind them who was police and who was not. "What did you see, Owen?" Bartelle took a pen and spiral notebook from his flannel shirt pocket and recorded the description of white camo and maybe a scope. Matched what he saw on the hill, except based on the multiple trails in and out, it probably wasn't the first time someone had been there. He discovered the woman watching from the kitchen. "What are you doing here, anyway?"

"Washing dishes. Dishtowel's hanging on the stove if you want to dry."

Bartelle gave her his patented hard stare. It had turned many a knee weak, but had no visible effect on her. He scratched his head, bringing relief that would soon become pain if he kept at it. He forced his arm down to his side. "Owen, how about you git on home so I can chat in private with these two. I don't need to hear a verbatim transcript next time I'm in town."

"I can keep secrets," Lyndstrom looked miffed. "I only started gabbin after Vinnie, my wife, passed. Auto accident. We was married forty-seven years, and I was lonely. Bein with people, and tellin stories come natural to me. Been sixteen years last September." He turned away, but not before Bartelle spotted a tear leaking down his cheek.

"I'm sorry," Bartelle said. "It is official business."

"Before you go," the woman said, "I've got a couple of extra items to add to Seamus's shopping list."

Lyndstrom glanced at the paper she handed him and turned beet red. The woman let loose with a high birdsong laugh and gave him a peck on the cheek. Bartelle tamped down his curiosity and grabbed a dishtowel to start drying. Lyndstrom shrugged into his snowmobile suit and waved goodbye.

"Lyndstrom forgot his gun."

"We're keeping it," McCree said. "You and Niki need privacy?"

Bartelle mentally congratulated himself for not dropping a dish in his excitement. "You remember your name?" He put the plate away, but kept a sharp focus on her reaction.

Her shoulders slumped. "I didn't want to be called Jane Doe any longer."

Disappointment plopped in his stomach. "Sorry to hear that. What did you write on the list that got Lyndstrom to light up like a firecracker?"

She laughed. "Tampons."

Bartelle kept the smile off his face and put on his serious-talk expression.

"I decided to come up here and personally warn each of you. Either one of you could be a killer—unless you're in cahoots and did it together." Pointing at McCree he asked, "You notice anything about her that will help us figure out who she is?"

"Nothing useful," McCree said. "You know anything about someone spying on us? A fellow officer, maybe?"

"I guarantee it's not us. Maybe you should consider coming into town where it's easier to give you protection. Owen's gun won't work if they kill you with the first shot. So, neither of you has anything new to tell me?"

Why did they look at each other first before shaking their heads? Bartelle delayed. He inspected the last bowl, flipping it this way and that before drying and putting it away. "Then I'll move to the second reason I'm here. This is personal. Has nothing to do with any investigation. My research confirms you were a big player for a major New York investment bank. You're good with financial stuff?"

McCree led him to the living room seating. "Some. Why?"

"Know anything about viatical settlements?"

Niki said, "If you two don't need me, I'll head outside." In silence, the men watched her pull outer garments from pegs and leave.

"I know what viatical settlements are," McCree said. "You're not considering investing in them are you? There are all kinds of scams."

"A local company wants to buy my aunt's life insurance policy. She's in a nursing home. She has a few problems, but she's still pretty with it. Anyway, this company is trying to sign up everyone at the nursing home who has life insurance. They're coming by, like, every day or two."

McCree indicated with his hands for him to continue.

"She thinks she's going to live longer than they seem to think. Anything past how to balance a checkbook is beyond me. The truth is I barely even manage that. My antennas are twitching on this deal, and I got to thinking that I was investigating someone who did understand more about finance than how to balance a checking account."

Bartelle pointed at McCree, looked at his finger, and realized how crooked it was. "Can you take a look at this and tell me what you think?" He reached into his jacket and brought out a wrinkled manila envelope, unfolded the flap and shook the contents into his lap.

"I'm not licensed to give financial advice in Michigan."

"I'm just looking for your opinion."

"A viatical assignment is a security. You really should talk to someone who can give you an expert opinion."

"I'm not trying to make a federal crime over it. I'm just trying to help my aunt."

"What has she told you?"

Bartelle hung his left arm over his head and scratched behind his right ear. "They want to pay her $170,000 now if she'll sign over her $200,000 life insurance to them. They claim to have a letter of credit from Hematite Bank to guarantee the check. My aunt says she can earn five percent on her money and, as long as she lives three and a half years, she's ahead of the game. She's healthy as a horse except she's confined to a wheelchair and needs help going to the bathroom, taking showers, that stuff. What do you think?"

"What kind of a policy is it? Whole life? Does it have a cash surrender value or is it term? Is she still paying premiums? How old—"

Bartelle held up both hands. "I give. I don't have a clue what you're asking. I brought all the stuff. She gave it to me to look at, but what do I know, eh? She's seventy-seven, which is pretty darn young these days."

McCree took the file from Bartelle and leafed through it, mumbling about declarations pages and such. Concentration etched his face. "When do you need this?

"They want her to sign by the end of next week. I can come back whenever it's convenient for you. I assume you're not planning any trips to town?"

"Thursday will work. I should warn you, I could end up with more questions than answers. But I'm not writing anything down. It's just a couple of guys talking. Right?"

"I appreciate it. Sure I can't convince you to bring the girl to town?" Bartelle cocked his head and squinted through one eye.

"She would stay where and do what?"

"I don't have a clue what she would do, but we got a female deputy who could give her a room."

"Thanks for the offer. I don't think she wants to be under your microscope, and I can't say I blame her. Thursday, say before noon?"

"I still think you're taking your life in your hands—either with Niki or whoever was hiding on your hill."

* * *

Owen SHOWED UP AT MY place the next afternoon with a friend whose mouth looked like it came from a nineteenth-century picture: puckered and toothless. "This here's Badger," Owen said. "Got him this snow machine he's hankerin to sell. Runs good so long as you don't mind the color scheme. I got to thinkin you needed to get yourself some snow transportation in case you ever need to get out of here."

I didn't want a snowmobile. They had two big strikes in my book: they were mechanical and noisy. Abigail and I had talked about getting one and had decided we could do without. Besides, this was Yooper ugly. Its right side was blue and the left side Creamsicle orange.

Owen must have read my look. "Think about what you could have done if you had this when that girl showed up, eh? At least give it a try before you say no."

Badger handed me his helmet and said "Try 'er out. She's a real workhorse."

They showed me the throttle, brake, and where to stick my feet. Owen slapped the helmet hard. "Remember to let go of the throttle if you start to tip. Oh, and you ain't got no reverse."

I settled onto the cracked seat, jockeyed around, pinching my butt on a gator-toothed crack, and found a comfortable position for my arms. I arranged my feet and pressed the throttle with my thumb. With a vroom, the sled leapt forward nearly pitching me off the back. The sled and I skidded to a halt after my thumb slipped off the throttle. *Easy does it, Seamus.*

With a lighter touch I engaged the throttle again and crawled up the driveway. Once on the road, I gradually increased the speed. It operated like an ATV, except it was much louder. I began to feel comfortable. Then I made a sharp turn and flipped it. My head rattled around in the too-big helmet, but I didn't see stars. Before extracting myself from the snow, I mentally checked for broken bones and found myself humming the ditty about the ankle bone connected to the leg bone . . .

I righted the machine and it started up without problem. No harm, no foul. On the way back, I inched up the speed and realized it was darned cold creating my own wind. My hands nearly froze solid before I got back. I waited too long to start braking and avoided crashing into Owen's machine by pure luck. "I guess you're right, Owen. I trust your opinion if you think this one will work."

I haggled with Badger over the price, chiefly because Badger expected me to. Owen slapped me on the back once the negotiations concluded. "We'll make you a real Yooper yet, eh? Cain't do nothin about that Tourist accent of yourn though. Open your mouth and everyone knows right off you're an implant."

Transplant. I bit my tongue to avoid correcting him.

"Gonna need you a helmet and some gloves. Dependin on what you got, maybe a bib and jacket too," Owen said. "We'll need a real store." Owen craned his head. "Where's the little woman?"

"Snowshoeing. I'll need to get warmer stuff for her too. Logistics are going to be a real problem. I need to get it registered, notify my insurance company. You willing to be our chauffeur, Owen? I'll pay for the gas and an hourly rate, including getting us from here to your car."

Owen and Badger agreed to return Friday with spare helmets. They'd take us to Owen's place. I'd give Badger the check and get the registration transfer papers, and then Owen would take us into Iron Mountain to get gear and take care of business with the motor vehicle department.

"Almost forgot," Owen said. He handed me a box of shells for the rifle. "Ain't had time to get you a gun, so you keep mine 'til Friday. We can buy you one in town, since we're goin in. Unless'n I scout up a used one afore then."

I made a mental note to recharge my cell phone so I could arrange insurance and give my son a call. The real question was whether I should also call Abigail.

Thirteen

Boss parked the Lexus Hybrid SUV in a visitor's space, screwed on a smile, and prepared to finalize four sales, bringing the total to eighteen—seven short of the goal. Five more might agree today, and the others were still considering. Onward and upward.

The Crystal Falls brick building had originally housed a hospital. With the expansion of the hospital in Iron River this facility had been vacant for years, and after several false starts was rehabbed into a private senior care center. A local contest named the place the Laughing Loon Senior Care Facility. The logo was a black and white loon floating on water with its head thrown back, beak open and pointed at the moon. Talk about loony.

One really good thing about this place, Boss reflected, it was privately owned and didn't take Medicaid patients. These folks had money, and money meant opportunity. Boss scribbled an illegible signature in the registration book, greeted a couple who passed by, and paused at the elevator to check the green spiral notebook for the first appointment's name and room number.

A blast of heat assaulted Boss as Mrs. Pirhonen opened her door. The rattling of an overworked radiator sounded from inside.

"Hello, Mrs. Pirhonen," Boss said brightly in the too-loud voice one needed to use around here. "I've got the check ready. Just need your signature on a few forms. You all set?"

"K.C., do come in. I've got everything ready right here." She patted a pile of paper on the end table next to her rocking chair. "Pull up a chair and we'll get this done. I can't tell you how much I appreciate your bringing this opportunity to my attention."

Boss pressed down hard on the back of a chair, probably the remains of an ancient dining room set, to make sure it was sturdy enough and brought it to face Mrs. Pirhonen. "Still healthy as a horse?" Boss asked. "Haven't had any setbacks since we last met?"

Mrs. Pirhonen's face cratered with worry and her rocking ground to a halt.

"I only ask because if you have learned some bad news about your health we might have to redo the numbers. We don't want to cheat you. The check I brought assumes you're planning to live for a good long time."

Mrs. Pirhonen smiled and resumed rocking. "Arthritis is still kicking up, but that won't kill me," she said, presenting her twisted hands for Boss to inspect. Then she flipped through the items in her stack. "The birth certificate proves I'm five years older than I tell everyone, but you promised not to let anyone know." She giggled at Boss's nodded agreement to the little lie. "Got the life insurance certificate right here with a note from my agent showing I paid all the premiums. Next one ain't due for a few months."

She shuffled through the papers. "This here's the contract you left and once you hand me the check, I'll sign 'er on the dotted line, eh?"

"As promised, it's certified," Boss said. "Hematite guarantees it in the amount of $65,000."

"And if anyone should know about Hematite's guarantees, it's you." Mrs. Pirhonen inspected the check. "All us girls getting checks today are taking the shuttle to the bank to deposit them this afternoon."

"A very smart idea," Boss said. "Maybe I'll see you there. Now if you'll sign right here," Boss pointed to the contract's signature line, "I'll get out of your hair—speaking of which, I like your new 'do, and is that a new perfume I smell?" Boss made a big deal of inhaling. "Citrus?"

Mrs. Pirhonen glowed. "It's called 'Tangerine Vert.' My granddaughter gave it to me for my birthday. You say 'hi' to your son when you talk to him."

Boss put up with several more minutes of chitchat, returned the chair to its normal position against the far wall, and proceeded to the next crone on the list.

Several hours later, with only Mrs. Ricci left, Boss's mood had picked up. The coterie of women in this place had coalesced around how good the deal was, eventually pressuring the holdouts to sign; even two crotchety guys Boss had previously written off accepted offers.

Boss knocked on the open door. "Mrs. Ricci, is now a good time to talk?"

"Hello, K.C. Didn't we agree I'd get back to you at the end of next week? I still need time to make my decision."

Boss walked in a step and stopped. Mrs. Ricci did not back her wheelchair up or offer a seat. "Is there any additional information I can provide you with?" Boss made sure to use a neutral tone.

"I've given the papers to my nephew. I expect to see him Sunday."

Boss didn't feel comfortable maintaining eye contact with a cripple and so looked over her head. *What the hell did the old prune know anyway? It was a good deal, as anyone with half a brain could see.* Boss mentally counted to three. "Your nephew a financial advisor?"

"I thought you knew. He's the sergeant with the Iron County Sheriff's Department. He told me he would ask an expert." She looked at her watch. "Imagine that, it's gotten so late . . . if you'll excuse me?" She spun around with the squeak of rubber on linoleum and briskly pushed herself into her kitchenette.

Boss turned away from the door, angry enough to punch out the bitch, or at least tip over her damn wheelchair. *So much for the good mood. So Sergeant Bartelle, the damn wop, was sticking his nose into the deal. Well, Bartelle's expert wouldn't find a damn thing wrong because there wasn't a damn thing wrong—at least not with the viatical settlements.*

Boss signed out of the Laughing Loon, held the door for a biddy smelling like day-old piss and bent over her walker making an inchworm look like a roadster. *How can people live like that? Here's a pleasant thought: it's only four weeks to D-day—not Debarkation-day, but Death-day. Well, in fairness, the deaths would come after April 1st, but the mechanism would be in place that day.*

Then we can buy more than enough weapons to take down the high and mighty in Washington who are bankrupting our country.

THURSDAY AFTER LUNCH, I WORKED on the generator: changed the oil and filter, which I had to do every one hundred hours the generator ran. The day showed promise of warming past thirty-two. Despite some unsuccessful attempts in the last two weeks, it would be the first time since mid-November—sixteen weeks ago—that temperatures would be above freezing. Before I left the generator shed, I checked the inverter; the solar panels were charging the batteries at the rate of twelve amps.

Mud season would soon be upon us if it remained this mild. For those three or four weeks of mud each year, activity in the U.P. woods nearly comes to a standstill. The roads change from frozen solid to a goop deep enough and thick enough to swallow a car or truck at least to the floorboards. On unpaved roads, only ATVs work, and both of mine were currently inoperable.

I had brought the ATV batteries inside to avoid draining them in the minus forty temperatures of deep winter. With Niki off snowshoeing across the lake to spot a moose I'd seen browsing in a nearby swamp, I had time to reinstall the batteries and get my two ATVs into working order. Not knowing if we would be faced with more snow or immediate mud, it would be safest to have both the snowmobile and the ATVs tuned and ready to go. With that thought in mind, I left the generator shed and was surprised by a deep rumble coming from the direction of Amasa. I walked into the side yard to get a better fix on the sound. Heavy equipment was moving somewhere nearby. Probably loggers bringing equipment for an early spring cutting, beating the coming restrictions that prohibited anything heavier than a pickup from traveling these roads once thaws started.

Paying the ruckus no more attention, I installed the batteries, gassed the ATVs, and cranked them up. They both started like champs. I left them warming up and figured I might as well put the battery in the skid steer as long as I was in the mood. By the time I left the garage to get its battery, the low rumble had come much closer. The skid steer could wait while I satisfied my curiosity. I donned cross-country ski shoes, hooked the toes into the binding, and hurried toward the noise.

Immediately past the driveway to my cabin I stopped. Had someone taken a video, I suppose they would have caught my jaw bouncing off the snow pack. Lumbering up the hill was a caravan consisting of a Caterpillar D-9 pushing snow to one side, a smaller loader cleaning up after the D-9, and a police car bringing up the rear.

A CLEARED ROAD WAS NOT my idea of an improvement. I kept my trap shut while Bartelle uncharacteristically nattered on. "I got the county probation officer to let these two fine, upstanding citizens, who forgot it isn't legal to drive with blood alcohol levels in excess of point three, work off some of their community service time," he inclined his head in their direction. "Getting double credit since they're using their own equipment."

He noticed my less-than-enthusiastic frown. "Don't express your apprec-iation all at once now."

"Needed to get in to arrest me?"

"Not currently. I'm tired of snowmobiling out here. Actually, I thought it might be a way of saying thanks for looking at the stuff for my aunt." He scratched his head in the arm-curled-over-his-head way I had grown accustomed to seeing. "Doesn't seem like I guessed right. Well, no matter. If you run into some trouble, now you can get out, or at least it will be easier for us to get in. Speaking of which, any more visitors? Where is the Jane—uh, the woman?"

"I am unaware of any visitors," I said. "Niki's searching for a moose. We've seen their sign across the lake, and I saw a cow and yearling nearby."

"She'll be back soon?"

I shrugged and realized the muscles on my neck had tightened up. "You married, Bartelle?"

"Nuh-uh. Why do you ask?"

"Didn't think so. You're married to the job and I'm divorced. I don't think either of us can claim to predict what a woman is going to do next."

"You learn anything more about her?"

"I'm not your spy. You'll have to ask her. Your trip's not wasted, though. I've studied your aunt's issue."

We settled into the chairs near the wood stove, scooching them close to the fire to warm our toes. "I changed my mind and typed my observations so you can give them to your aunt and not rely on memory. I agree with her: the deal seems to be too good—even with the historically low interest rates we have now—assuming your aunt is an average seventy-seven-year-old woman." Bartelle's eyebrows arched at the word average. "Average in a medical sense. This is a great deal. I'd take it, as long as the payment is guaranteed, which appears to be the case."

He sipped a Diet Pepsi and flipped through my calculations and conclusions. "Numbers were never my strong point. You'd take it?"

"I would and I'd wonder if I could get some more life insurance to sell. You should back up a truck and take away as much of this as you can . . . which to me is worrisome. You know the old saw: 'if it looks too good to be true, it probably is'? These aren't the hardest numbers in the world to crunch. If they're buying policies from most of the Laughing Loon residents, you're talking serious money."

"So where's the problem? You mentioned viatical settlement scams?" He clicked his ballpoint a few times while I considered how to answer.

"Most scams involve suckering people who invest in the viaticals," I said. "But this is going the other way. We know your aunt is not the crook, which eliminates a bunch of other malfeasance. So, how can someone cheat your aunt? Number one, she signs over the insurance policy and doesn't get the promised money. Easy to solve: have a third party hold the endorsed policy until the check clears."

"Got it," he said. "What else?"

"They know something about your aunt's health that you don't."

He scratched his head. "How could they?"

"They could be in cahoots with, say, a local doctor. But since they're offering everyone there similar deals, that can't be it. They could plan to change the mortality table."

His face bunched into a question mark. "I'm just a Yooper Trooper. Want to put that into English?"

"Someone hurries their deaths. With enough policies, it wouldn't even have to be by much. A nurse's aide could give too much or too little of a medicine or swap real pills for sugar." A possibility occurred to me that sent a shill up my spine. "In fact, if they make the deaths appear to be from an accident and the policies include accidental death and dismemberment benefits, like your aunt's does, they really make out because they get paid twice the face value."

I popped out of my chair and busied myself with adding a stick of wood to the fire. "Do the residents go on bus outings? Most senior citizen homes have trips to casinos or to something like the Pine Mountain Music Festival in the summer. If they tampered with the brakes on the bus or . . ."

Bartelle had stopped writing and was studying me as though I had grown a second head. Into the silence, broken only by the ticking of my grandmother clock, he finally said, "That would take one sick fuck. Pardon the expression."

"Well, from my experience, if money's involved, there are a lot of sick fucks, and they're not all on Wall Street."

Fourteen

FINDING THE ROAD PLOWED WAS the first piss-poor surprise in Jimmie's day. A couple of miles from McCree's place, he met the D-9 and loader returning, widening the cleared road as they went. He quickly slid onto an old skidder road and pulled far enough into the woods so the operators wouldn't have much of a look at him or his sled.

The cleared road ended at McCree's driveway, where he paused to take a peek and received a second shock: an Iron County Sheriff's cruiser sat in the driveway. He was not about to stick around and have some cop wonder why he was in the neighborhood.

Jimmie zipped the sled down the road to its end at the Net River, realized he had trapped himself if anyone was following and worked his way to a deer camp a couple guys he knew maintained about halfway back to McCree's place. There he keyed off the sled, listened to the *dee-dee-dees* of a feeding flock of chickadees working over a stand of white spruce, and considered his options.

Boss wanted him to observe and if the opportunity arose, "put down the girl." Facing Boss and again reporting failure was not something he looked forward to. Unlike boozer Brett, he hadn't screwed up, but Jimmie wasn't sure Boss would see it that way. He remembered the casual shrug Boss had given before ordering Brett's "regrettable termination."

Ah, Christ. He released a long sigh he recognized as resignation. No help for it but to wait out the police and do the girl. If McCree's there, bop him too. He'd tell Boss it was unavoidable. Then cash Boss's bonus and spend mud season in Florida.

Plopping onto a wood plank bench tucked far enough under the eaves to be free of snow, he turned his face to the sun, closed his eyes. Warmth bathed his face and he drifted into a dreamless nap.

JIMMIE AWOKE TO THE SUN perching two fingers above the horizon: thirty minutes to sunset. To the steady *drip, drip, drip* of snow melting from the roof, he firmed up a plan: drive the snowmobile down McCree's driveway, pop whoever came out to greet him, and then pop the other one. If they barricaded themselves in the house, he'd burn them out. No subtlety needed: just two bodies.

At the top of McCree's driveway, he stopped and surveyed the scene. The cop was gone, but two sets of tire tracks now emerged from the driveway. A smile dimpled his cheeks. Maybe McCree had driven into town and left the girl behind? He stuffed the Ruger under his coat and cruised down the driveway, followed it around the pole barn, and parked facing up the driveway, his sled hidden from the house by the outbuilding. He turned off the snowmobile and listened to the tinkling of wind chimes. A solitary red squirrel, a bird wannabe, was gorging on sunflower seeds under one of McCree's many feeders.

He dismounted, removed his gloves and helmet and balanced them on the seat, bent down as though to inspect something on the snowmobile, and waited for the sound of a door opening or the crunch of footsteps on the freshly plowed snow. Nothing. The adrenaline rush was working overtime, and Jimmie knew he wanted to get this done now. Still no movement inside the house.

He swiped at his nose with his hand. Now what? He walked toward the back door. At the corner of the house, invisible from anyone inside, he removed the Ruger from his coat. He rapped on the door with his left hand, stood away from the door's outward swing, and held the revolver behind his back. Nothing.

No footsteps; no call to wait a minute; no whispered conversation from inside. Thirty seconds, a minute. He rapped a second time, using the window instead of the wood to make a sharper sound. Still nothing. He propped open the storm door with his foot and tested the metal door. Unlocked. Had the cop taken them in? Wouldn't it be fucking rich if the cops nailed the girl and McCree for Brett's murder?

Jimmie knocked once more, opened the door, and called, "Hello. Anyone home?" He stepped into the laundry room, gun now leading the way. Boss would want a complete report, so he took his time developing a mental picture of the house. In the laundry room he spotted two empty pegs where their overcoats should be. On the shoe mat was space for two pairs of boots. Should he wait for their return?

Unlike Brett who would have looked for booze, Jimmie concentrated on weapons. No gun safe and no rifle to match a new box of .30–06 shells he discovered under the sink in the upstairs bathroom. Returning to the front room, he appreciated the spectacular winter view from the wall of windows. This place was way nicer than any hunting camp. If he couldn't catch them outside, he'd need to find a good firing position to target the house. After dark, once lights were on inside, he'd have a clear forty-yard backlit shot from the lake edge if someone stepped close to the windows. With the sky clouding over to block the moon, he could get an even closer shot from the woods.

He considered staying. The refrigerator held plenty of food. He could hide the sled and walk in. Problem was, if the cop returned with McCree and the girl, it would get complicated, and he would be the one trapped inside if anything went wrong. Best to head into Amasa, get dinner at the Rusty Saw Blade, and fuel up for some primate hunting tonight.

Decision made, Jimmie hustled from the house, donned his helmet and gloves, and sped toward town. About a mile before the new sawmill, he caught up to an old Ford Ranger. He couldn't see into the cab, but a bumper sticker proclaiming, "AMASA—it's not just a place, it's a state of mind" indicated it was locals. He stuck up a hand in greeting as he blasted past.

NIKI POINTED TO THE SNOWMOBILE whizzing by Seamus's truck. "You know him? He's waving."

McCree held two hands on the steering wheel. "Looks like the same one we saw up past Long Lake. You want dinner in Amasa or wait until we get to the megalopolis of Marquette? Great pizza at the Rusty Saw Blade. Either way we need to make a quick stop at Owen's and let him know we don't need to borrow his truck."

Niki felt anxious, not hungry. She now knew who she was. She knew she needed to make a phone call without McCree's knowledge. She had regained her memory, except for what happened the last few days before she showed up naked at McCree's cabin. "The excitement of getting to the *big city* has killed my appetite." Well, that sure came out sarcastic. McCree didn't seem to notice. However, with McCree, not seeming to notice and not noticing were two different things. She needed to be careful around him. He was scary smart.

"Okay," he said. "Marquette it is. We'll decide on type of food after your appetite returns. We need to make a list so we don't forget anything. Might be a while before we hit the stores again."

"Which brings me to a question that's been bothering me," Niki said. "I was pretty skeptical at the hospital when they told me some guy was picking up my tab. I mean, who believes in fairy tales where the prince finds the beautiful girl lost in the woods, gives her the kiss of life, and they live happily ever after? Did you know the cops did a rape kit on me? Did they ask you for a DNA sample?"

She raked her fingers through her hair. "I'm rambling all over the place and not getting to the point. The point is, why the fuck are you helping me? You haven't made any moves. You've covered my hospital bill. Now you're taking me to buy clothes to replace the crap the church guild gave me. What do you get out of this? That's the question, Seamus McCree: What do you get out of this?"

Niki evaluated her performance. She had started out being argumentative, but by the time she asked the last question, it arrived in a whisper.

McCree glanced over and saw her swipe tears from her eyes. "You okay?"

"Of course I'm not okay. Do you realize today is our one-month anniversary?" She blew her nose, looked around for somewhere to store the dirty tissue, and, finding nothing, crammed it into her pocket. "For a month, I haven't known who I am, why I'm here. No one seems to know me. I'm like the twenty-first century version of *Stranger in a Strange Land*—like I got raised on Mars and dropped into the primordial soup of Michigan's Upper Peninsula. Sergeant Bartelle offered to take me off your hands so he could keep me a virtual prisoner until he found out what I know. Did you agree to take me in so you could control me if my memory came back?"

Niki wished she could get a straight answer from McCree. He was layers deep and could do silence like a monk. She stared out the window. After a few minutes she fiddled with the radio dials and settled on a hard rock station. They passed through Covington, then Michigamme, and were approaching Ishpeming before McCree spoke.

"Last year I killed a man. For a while it looked like I was going to have to defend that action in court, so I hired a top-notch criminal lawyer. Guy named Leroy Patterson. I asked him much the same question you're asking me. Why did he do what he did? He told me he was the guy with the white hat who gets the girl in the final reel."

Is he opening up? Niki turned off the radio.

"He clearly had a vision of his role in the judicial system," he continued. "He had earned enough money to be choosy and now only defends people he thinks were wronged by the system. And what, you wonder, does this have to do with you?"

Niki bowed her head and gently waved her hand in a please-proceed-if-you-would-be-so-kind gesture.

"You've heard bits and pieces about my background from my answers to Bartelle's questions. I made a pile of money understanding what made banks tick. I could tell you which bank was overvalued and which was undervalued, and they paid me handsomely. Information is power in Wall Street. To please a humongous client, my bosses changed a negative report I wrote.

"I discovered the chicanery a week before they paid bonuses and quit, giving up a big six-figure payment. After the dust settled, my wife left me. Any successful marriage has to overcome shocks along the way. She was furious that I was no longer the hard-driving winner she had used to cloak her own insecurities. I know it's not PC to say, but many women still determine their own value by their husband's job. In my opinion, most are selling themselves short. She certainly was. That was years ago and if I don't speed this story up, we'll be in Marquette before I get to the present."

Niki reached over and patted his hand, "Take your time." She returned her hand to her lap to join the other one.

"The one good thing remaining from my marriage is my wonderful son, whom I'm going to call while you're shopping. When we're young, we expect to save the world. Unfortunately, it's only a question of time before we discover that saving the entire world is beyond our capabilities. Anyway, footing your hospital bill and buying you a few clothes so you don't have to do laundry three times a week isn't going to cause me any monetary problems. So maybe the answer is I took an opportunity to try on the white hat and see if it still fits."

Niki rocked and wondered if he was also faking it. If so, he deserved an "A."

"And the girl in the final reel?"

"Well," he pulled his lips tightly together, "I guess I didn't think the comparison all the way through. Besides, if my current streak continues, the only way I'll have the girl in the final reel is if I steal all the reels after the one in which the girl and I fall head-over-heels in love. So how about you? No wedding ring, not that that means a whole lot these days, but someone was responsible for the hickey you sported."

She caught herself pulling at the hair around her ears and realized she was trying to block a question she didn't want to answer. She dropped her traitorous hands back into her lap and glanced out the window, all the while deciding how much truth to intersperse with the lies. "Here's what's so freakin' frustrating: I can't remember my name or how I came to pose as the ice queen on your porch hammock. I can't remember anything for at least the last six months and only a few earlier bits and pieces. I can remember everything since I woke up in your bathtub . . ." She tossed him a quizzical look. "Or at least I think I can. Who's to say, I guess? I don't know my name. I don't know who my parents are. I don't know where I grew up.

"But I can tell you the name of my best friend in second grade. I can tell you who the first boy I kissed playing spin the bottle was. He was chewing gum—ick. I know all sorts of stuff like that, but I can't tell you where I went to college, though I'm sure I did. I have no idea what kind of work I do, but I have a feeling it has something to do with the out-of-doors. I have no idea who gave me the hickey."

"I'm sure someday a switch will flip and it will all come back to you."

Well, it wasn't quite a flick of a switch.

"I didn't realize you had memories of the past. With what you remember, I'll bet Paddy could figure out who you are. Will you talk to him and tell him everything you remember?"

"And Paddy is who?"

"My son, the computer whiz, king of databases and, I hope, reformed hacker. He and some friends started a company to help banks keep their IT structure safe from hackers. But to hear him talk, the twenty-first century is all about networking, and I'm sure he can discover who you are."

She quickly faced the window and tugged her short hair hard enough to cause tears to form. *Oh Jesus, what have I done now?*

"Don't you want to know who you are?"

"Of course I do." She slapped her thigh for effect. "But I'm afraid I'll discover I'm wanted, or I abandoned four kids under the age of two or . . ."

Thankfully, he let her hanging question hang. They pulled into the Gander Mountain parking lot at the outskirts of Marquette. She waited until he killed the engine and pulled the parking brake before she faced him, tears streaking both cheeks. "What if I don't like who I am?"

He sat there like a lump, staring at her. Niki turned her gaze toward her hands folded in her lap, but looked up when he cleared his throat.

"If it were me—or is it *if it were I?*—whatever. I'd want to know. And I think you do as well. While you're shopping, I'll call Paddy."

She looked up and damn if he didn't snap her picture with his cell phone. Why hadn't she anticipated that? At least with this butch haircut she didn't look like herself.

"I'll fill him in, and if he agrees to help, you can decide whether to talk with him or not. Fair enough?"

Niki knew she had no choice. She hated that.

Fifteen

WATCHING NIKI WALK INTO THE store was like witnessing Atlas shouldering the weight of the world. She would signal me when it was time for me to pay. I dialed Paddy's cell phone and sent a prayer down the line that he would answer.

"Dad," he asked as salutation, "you okay? I didn't expect to hear from you for several more weeks."

My initial shock at his recognizing me before I spoke faded quickly away—his cell phone displayed my name. "A father can't call his son without causing concern? Before we hang up, I have a favor to ask."

We covered his girlfriend (still together), business (going fine) and cats (why didn't I get some?) for several minutes before he said, "You sound distracted, Dad. What's the favor?"

I related Niki's mysterious appearance at the cabin, the Brett Aho murder, the attentions I received from the police and from whoever was spying on me. "Can you help figure out who she is?"

"Should be a piece of cake. Why can't the cops do it?"

"When we were last together, you extolled the virtues of networking. The cops are old fashioned like me. They rely on fingerprints, and hers aren't in any database. They aren't going to spend the time posting information on social websites and sifting through lots of false leads or trolling through information databases to find people who match the bits and pieces of information she remembers about herself. Not unless they decide she killed Brett Aho. Then they'll go all out. So I was thinking, if you set it up as a kind of game—I could post a reward—you could get the whole networked generation helping to solve the problem."

"You thought of this all by yourself?"

I felt my shoulders hunch into my neck as my body tightened to protect me from the expected blow of rejection. "What am I missing?"

"It's a really good idea. Not the game part of it—that's a little hokey— but the idea of getting everyone working on it together. If we get the known facts along with a recent picture out to all the right spots of the blogosphere, I bet we have her name in a couple of days—max."

I smiled at his enthusiasm. He was in charge of sales for his company with good reason. "Your first job is going to be to convince her to do it," I said. "She's not sure she'll like her past and might prefer a fresh start. Shall I have her call you?"

"I can't imagine what it must be like to be cut off from all your friends and family. I know, before you point it out: I'm the extrovert, you're the introvert and often wish you could be done with all of us."

"Well . . ."

"Don't deny it. It's why you stayed in the woods even after Abigail left."

His mention of Abigail brought me back to his cryptic note about seeing her in a club and I missed the next few words he said.

". . .sales meetings tomorrow and the first part of next week. I need part of the weekend to prepare for them, so I won't be able to spend one hundred percent of my time on this. And I want to make sure when we hit with this, it's with a big bang."

He trailed off, mumbling to himself about timing and critical mass. I let him ramble and took the time to reflect on how much I appreciated this adult version of my son. His mother and I divorced while he was in grammar school. Paddy in junior high exhibited all the obnoxiousness of a smart preteen boy combined with a need to act out and garner attention from his parents.

By his sophomore year in high school, he had his act together—or so I thought until I received a visit from the FBI accusing me of hacking into a Defense Department website and posting online the expense reports of top department officials. Paddy's resulting juvenile record has supposedly been expunged, but in today's electronic environment, I'm sure it resides in a computer somewhere like the sword of Damocles hanging by a horse hair over his life.

"So you'll have her call me?" Paddy's voice brought me back to the present.

I couldn't bring myself to ask him about Abigail. We disconnected and I sent him Niki's picture.

The gnawing in my stomach was not hunger.

I checked my phone for messages. Before we had headed into the woods for winter, I told everyone I thought important what our plans were, and so there were only a few messages, several of which were wrong numbers.

A part of me knew Abigail wouldn't call because we had agreed she wouldn't. Another part of me hoped she had missed me enough that she had called anyway. That part was disappointed.

With no sign of Niki, I opened the phone's address list and scrolled down to Abigail. I looked again for Niki's appearance to delay my decision to call. Still shopping. I screwed up my courage, pressed the button to connect, and listened to the first ring.

DURING DINNER, I BRIBED NIKI to call Paddy by offering her the first ride on the snowmobile tomorrow after we completed the purchase, registered it, and arranged insurance. Once she understood I intended to accomplish everything the next morning, all reticence she had about finding out who she was seemed to disappear. After dinner and the rest of our shopping, she took my cell phone into her room and returned it an hour later. I checked the logs: she and Paddy had talked for about forty-five minutes; she had made no other calls; she had received no calls.

Nor had I. What I didn't know, and what caused a restless night, was whether Abigail was on assignment and hadn't heard the message I left, or whether she had chosen not to call me back.

At breakfast, as Niki chattered away, I put on my "isn't everything wonderful" smile, but felt like a pumpkin the day after Halloween: a carved smile fixed on my face, hollowed out insides covered with soot from a burned down candle, and a lump of melted wax in the pit of my stomach. I did notice and comment on her perfume— something fresh with a light, fruity touch. She didn't reveal the brand. Fair enough. Everyone has secrets.

I ordered pancakes because they had been tasty the last time I was here. Niki ordered the lumberjack special and polished off the three pancakes, a three-egg omelet, three pieces each of sausage links and rye toast, and a side of hashbrowns. My pancakes tasted like cardboard, but I knew the problem was not the cook. I was in a funk.

Acquiring the snowmobile with its attendant paperwork went off without a hitch. Owen and Badger had the beast ready when we arrived at Owen's. Niki changed into her new snowmobiling outfit. I followed her home in the truck. Actually, she left me in the dust as she roared off.

By the time I arrived home, she was pacing next to the snowmobile.

"Get on your snowmobiling clothes," she said with an urgency I had not previously detected. "We're going to try to find where I was imprisoned. I say 'we' to be inclusive. Fact is, I've got the key." She dangled it from her finger. "You can come or not."

I turned away so she couldn't see my smile. The real reason I had agreed to buy a snowmobile was so we could continue our search past the range of skis and snowshoes.

Sitting on the saddle, I snuggled against her back. It felt like I was cuddling the Michelin man given all the insulation and padding. I'd seen the speed at which she took off from Owen's so I wrapped both arms tightly around her waist. She zipped up the driveway, but once we got off my property, she slowed to walking speed. Over her shoulder she shouted, "Look for anything unusual. You see a squirrel squatting to pee, give me a good slap on the shoulder. Understand?"

While giving commands, her voice downshifted into a lower register, the one I found incredibly sexy. I reached in front of her facemask and gave the okay sign. We worked our way toward the spot where Brett Aho had been murdered. A couple of hundred yards before we got there, she stopped and plucked a glove from underneath a bush whose leaf buds had swelled but not yet turned red. Spring was coming.

She returned with her prize and tried it on. Her hands were small and this glove fit. She turned off the engine and yanked off her helmet. I followed suit.

"This is mine. See this small tear?" She held the thumb and first finger apart and revealed a ragged gash in the material. A tuft of insulation stuck out. "Cut it on barbed wire. Meant to slap some duct tape on it. Don't know why I didn't."

The uneasy feeling I'd had that she had somehow been involved with the murdered person began to spread. It was too coincidental. *Lover? Associate? Killer?* I offered up the possibility that it happened while she was sick.

"Could be. Let's see if any of my other stuff is around here."

No luck. Maybe we would find something else after the snow melted more. We briefly stopped at Brett Aho's murder site, but the melting snow had exposed nothing new. I directed Niki across Long Lake to the place where we had previously found numerous snowmobile tracks.

"It's starting to come back to me," she said after we stopped in the yard.

"I drove all around that cabin hoping to find someone home. Then I drove onto the lake. Remember when we saw that yellow snowmobile while we skied? Can you get us back to where the places started looking familiar to me?"

Several miles later Niki leaned back against me and shouted, "I think we're almost there. Just around the bend." She gave my leg a good slap.

"What's just around the bend?"

"Don't know, but we'll soon see."

JIMMIE WAS IN A BIND. He had broken into a camp across the lake from McCree's place and had spent the night there. It was cozy enough and with the binoculars he could observe any comings and goings at McCree's. By the time he realized it was the girl who had arrived on the grungy snow machine, McCree returned in the truck he remembered passing the night before on the way to Amasa. He planned to wait for dark before dealing with them; he had plenty of food. But instead of staying put as he expected them to, McCree joined the woman on the snow machine.

He followed their tracks; unless they veered off, they were heading straight to the rented camp where Brett had kept the two human guinea pigs. Like a homing pigeon, the girl was returning to her roost.

According to Boss, "The girl don't know shit about shit."

Had her memory come back? If so, he wasn't in immediate danger since she had never seen him. Problem was, no matter how well he had cleaned the camp, a CSI routine might find a partial fingerprint or two and maybe his DNA somewhere.

He felt the thump of his heartbeat slow to normal. *The girl can't tie me to the camp or to Brett. The camp is the immediate danger. Its forensic evidence might do the implicating without human testimony. Eliminate the camp, eliminate the problem.* He'd take care of Boss's problem with the girl and McCree later.

He parked the snow machine in a cedar grove a half mile from the camp, took the binocs and rifle, and trekked in. Still a quarter mile away, he steadied the binocs on a tree limb and scanned the area around the cabin. They were peering in windows. The girl gesticulated and he heard indistinct but excited words.

She knows.

He thought about shooting them, sticking their bodies in the cabin, and burning it down. Unfortunately, he had never been the best of shots. If he missed . . .

Jimmie watched them circle the cabin to the front door. He had made sure the door was inviting—actually hoped some kids would find it and muck-up the crime scene. McCree reached for the door, but the girl pulled him away. If they had gone in, he might have been able to get close enough to gun them down when they came back out. They circled the cabin again and then inspected the wood shed, carport, and sauna. He thought about his own activities while here. He had never gone into the shed or sauna, but he had been in the carport, which would also have to go. A few minutes later they took off on their machine. Whether they were going to get the cops or heading to Shank Lake didn't much matter, he had work to do before anyone returned.

After the sound of their machine died away, only a gentle breeze stirring the cedars remained. He skirted around the hill and picked up the road, rutted with frozen tracks from Brett's truck. He walked in one track, careful to avoid any soft area, and arrived at the camp without leaving footprints. He found gas containers neatly stacked in the carport and thought about opening the cabin and spreading the gas inside, but figured it would be harder for the cops to get any clues about the arsonist if he did everything from the outside. He scattered enough gasoline around the carport to make sure it would burn completely. He broke all the cabin windows to create a good draft and poured the gas inside. Fumes made him want to puke. With the remnants of the final container, he soaked one end of a cedar stick.

He used a firestarter he found next to the grill to turn the stick into a torch. The carport was handy so he lit it first, and then from as far away as he dared, he tossed the torch inside the cabin and hotfooted it back up the frozen track. He had expected the house would explode, but it didn't. The gasoline caught with a polite little whoosh. Eventually, flames did the work he had intended. He didn't think anyone was nearby, but there was no reason to take chances just to watch a building burn. He wasn't some sick firebug; this was business and his was done here.

Atop the last hill from which he could see the cabin, Jimmie looked backward. Black smoke billowed from the carport—probably chainsaw or motor oil. All the snow on the cabin roof had melted—he hadn't considered the water effect of snow— but yellow flames danced on the near eave. The cabin was history. Now he could take care of McCree and the girl.

He drove a circuitous route of little-used logging trails to the camp he had broken into across the lake from McCree and settled in to await their arrival. A current of warm air shimmered from McCree's chimney, heat from a played-out fire in the woodstove. Their snow machine was not in evidence and he concluded they had not yet returned. This time he was not leaving until McCree and the girl were dead.

Maybe he should walk across the lake and be there to welcome them.

SIXTEEN

SERGEANT BARTELLE WASN'T SURE EXACTLY what he felt. Ever since he received the call from McCree and the Jane Doe—he refused to think of her as Niki—his emotions had been on a rollercoaster. His first reaction to McCree's call from Amasa demanding he and "Tex," the lab technician, get their asses in gear to investigate the camp where she claimed she'd stayed, was relief that the woman had found her memory. Then on the trip out he asked himself why she took McCree there before contacting him. Anger soon blossomed, especially as he considered that they had surely sullied evidence at the scene.

The first acrid smells from the burnt cabin reached him a couple miles away from the site, further fueling his anger. By the time he arrived, it had grown into a boiling rage. High blood pressure ran in his family and he tried to tamp down his feelings so he wouldn't blow a gasket, but all it did was give him a splitting headache.

McCree and Jane Doe swore up and down someone had burned the place after they left. The woman remembered only suspiciously selective information. He didn't put it past them to have torched the place, but then why bring him to the scene?

He ordered Tex and two other Iron County deputies to collect fingerprints and bag whatever evidence they found. They must have sensed his mood because they exchanged only muted conversation as they worked. Bartelle separated the suspects and spoke first with McCree, who cooperated fully, answering his questions no matter how many different ways he asked the same thing. Whenever Bartelle's question required a memory, McCree's eyes shifted to the right, as the Reid Method of Interrogation said they should as a suspect accesses memory. And every time he asked a speculative question, McCree would pause, his eyes shifting upward, marking cognitive thinking. Bartelle would swear McCree wasn't lying— well, almost swear, 'cause what do you really know for sure?

Jane Doe, on the other hand, was not forthcoming. Everything was measured with her. Each question elicited a short silence during which her eyes twitched leftward or upward before she provided an answer. He'd be willing to swear on the proverbial stack of Bibles that she was lying.

"Hey, Sarge," Tex called. "Come lookee here."

The three of them hustled to Tex, who pointed to a fresh set of two-way footprints several hundred yards away from the burned cabin.

"What do you make of them?" Bartelle asked the woman and watched her eyes. Pause. Left flick. "Made today, you can still see the sole pattern. They're a guy's boots, or some honking female Sasquatch. If the three of us make some parallel steps, we can gauge how much he weighed . . . well, assuming he wasn't carrying anything."

Interesting analysis, she clearly knew something about tracking. "Where do these lead?" Bartelle asked as though she should know the answer.

Pause. Right eye flick. "There's a bunch of evergreens on the other side of the hill. I'll bet he parked a sled and walked in."

Bartelle thanked Tex for the find and sent him scouting for any other trails. The three of them followed the boot prints to a cedar grove where they gave way to snow machine tracks.

"All right!" Jane Doe pumped her fist. "Now we're getting somewhere. Let's follow this sucker."

She was glowing; McCree's face showed neutral. If McCree knew about these tracks before, Bartelle figured he should never play poker with the guy. Aloud he said, "The tracks aren't going to disappear. I'll have the boys run them down after they finish collecting samples." He indicated an inclusive circle with his arm. "This spot bring anything else to mind? Jar any memories?"

Left flick. "Not really."

"But you've obviously been here before. When? Why?" Bartelle asked for the thousandth time.

She shrugged and began walking toward the burned cabin.

Bartelle caught McCree's arm. "She tell you anything she hasn't told me?"

"Nope. You figure she's lying, but now you trust me?"

Bartelle was so attuned to eye movement that he felt his own eyes click left while he considered his answer. "She is lying. You—" He waggled his fingers. "My suspicion is we're going to find that the snow machine followed you. Might be safer for all concerned if you bring her into town to stay."

McCree went into his silent mode.

"I've got way more questions than answers," Bartelle said. "Was someone following you to see what you knew and, once you found this place, burned it down? Or were they following you because they didn't know where the place was, and once you led them to it, they burned it down?

"Or was he following you because your 'Niki' told him where you were going? When she used your phone in Marquette to call your son she could have called someone else."

"I checked the logs. No calls other than to my son."

Bartelle made a note to subpoena McCree's phone records as soon as he got to town.

BARTELLE FINALLY RELENTED AND LET Niki and me return home. She again took the driver's seat. Fine by me; I'd rather think than worry about driving. Bartelle clearly suspected Niki of something, and I had to agree: her answers were less than convincing. *Should I use the excuse of the coming mud season to move us into town?*

Once we were out of sight of the cops, she slowed down. "What's up?" I yelled into her ear.

"If I can find where our tail cut off and circled around to the back of that camp, I can follow his tracks."

"Bartelle specifically told us they would do it."

"You scared?"

Was I? I probably should be, but, strangely, that wasn't it. My feelings could be better described as cautious. "I suppose a little," I said. "I'm thinking about the dog that finally caught the car and then wondered what to do with it. I'm not against tracking the guy, but it'll be dark soon and I don't know what we'll find. Besides, we'd screw up the tracks for the cops. They might arrest us for obstruction."

She tilted her head and measured the sun's progress. "Crap. First thing tomorrow then."

She damn near dumped me off the back with her acceleration. I wrapped my arms so tightly around her I could count her ribs through the padded material. By the time we got home, the first stars twinkled in a cloud-free night. It would be a cold one. She zoomed down the driveway and parked behind the garage, close to the path to the cabin.

"I'm going to go change," she said. "Then I'll cook supper. Pasta good?"

"Perfect. I'll work on getting some heat."

I rounded the side of the garage and froze. Lights shone from inside the house, which I hadn't noticed as we passed it because my head was buried into Niki's back to avoid the wind. I was sure we hadn't left any lights on when we drove off the day before. I returned to the snowmobile and grabbed the rifle, then raced up the snowpacked path to the cabin, burst through the door and caught Niki midway through changing.

Backlit by the kerosene lamp hung from a rafter, she turned, surprise painted on her face. "If you were looking for a free show, all you—"

"Someone's in the house. The lights are on."

She stopped mid-motion, arms thrust into a sweater, ready to pull it over her head. "I told you to lock the doors." She pulled the sweater on. "Did you see movement inside?"

"I did lock the doors."

"Sure you did. I'll take the rifle. You take the flashlight. Let's circle around the woods to look in from the front. Don't use the flashlight—we'll let our eyes adjust to the starlight."

It was slow work without snowshoes. With the warmer weather, some snow had melted and packed down, but cooler temperatures had returned and thin ice crusted the snow. Each step I took broke through the crust, chafing my ankles with the rim of ice. With snow past my knee, I had to take baby steps, providing a compacted path Niki easily followed. As the ridge played out, I slipped into a little basin that would soon hold a vernal pond, staying close to its edge. We crawled the rest of the way. After what seemed like ten hours but was probably only a couple of minutes, we lay in position to watch movement through the large windows on that side of the house.

In whispered consultation we agreed lights were on in the kitchen, main room, and upstairs loft. No movement. No sound. The wind had tamped down to dead stillness. The silhouette of a man slid from the kitchen around a corner and down the stairs into the basement, where a light turned on. From our position all we could see was the light spilling onto the snow.

"Anyone familiar?" Niki asked.

"Never got a view of his face," I said. "Seemed pretty tall, but it's hard to tell from this angle."

We waited. I was still in snowmobile attire and didn't feel the cold, but I could hear Niki's teeth rattling.

"Better give me the gun," I said. "You won't be able to hit anything."

"Don't kid yourself," she whispered in a steel tone. "Hopping on one foot, whistling Dixie, I'd still be a better shot than you."

The guy turned off the basement light and I knew he would soon come up the stairs. With quick steps he appeared in the light, giving me full view of his face before he disappeared into the kitchen.

"How the hell did he get here?" I asked.

JIMMIE EXPERIENCED A QUICK FLASH of guilt as he entered the house across the lake from McCree's. He paused to consider what had caused it. Certainly it wasn't breaking into the house. A smile crept onto his face as he looked down at his boots. He was feeling guilty because he had tracked snow into the house. "Take your boots off, Jimmie. This ain't no barn." His mother yelled those words each time he had raced into the house to tell her what he had found in the woods. She would ruffle his hair and make him clean up his mess.

Her number one rule was "Make a mess—clean it up. Your mess—your fix." Worked then; worked now. Jimmie had a plan for cleaning up this mess, but it required waiting for dark.

Two hours later the buzz of a distant snowmobile caught his attention. Through the rifle scope he watched the old geezer, Owen Whateverhisname, drop off someone with a backpack and then zoom away. Not McCree. Not the girl. Who the hell was this guy and what was he doing there? Ah, crap. One more complication.

Anxiety triggered hunger pangs, and he was thirsty. He thought about grabbing a beer from the stocked cold room he had discovered in the basement. He slapped himself upside the head. Drinking beer on an empty stomach was not the best idea. In his excitement he had forgotten to eat.

Across the way, the guy checked all the doors and discovered them locked—Jimmie's fault; he'd unintentionally locked the door when he left. The guy retrieved an extension ladder from behind the garage and scurried up to the balcony off the master bedroom. A few minutes later, the guy exited from the side door and returned the ladder to the garage.

Either he knew the balcony sliding door was unlocked, or he had broken in through that door on the theory no one would notice until it was too late, which was a decent idea Jimmie would keep in mind should the need arise.

A stream of smoke rising from the chimney across the way soon caught Jimmie's attention. Whoever it was had relit the fire. McCree must have told him about the balcony entrance—a fatal mistake. Bullets were cheap.

The day folded to a close. Shadows stretched across the lake toward McCree's place—narrow, reaching fingers first touching the shore and then climbing the trees on the other side as the sun sank lower. Jimmie strained his eyes reading in the deepening darkness. Patience, he counseled himself, patience. It may be too dark to read, but it wasn't dark enough to venture onto the lake.

Anticipation worked in mysterious ways, even if he hadn't eaten or drunk anything. While he was outside watering a tree, he heard a second snowmobile buzz. Peering through the scope he scanned the opposite shore. A snowmobile zipped down the driveway. Two people. Probably McCree and the girl, but in the deepening dusk, he couldn't tell. A cheerleaders' chant from high school football ran through his head: *Victory, victory is our cry. V-I-C-T-O-R-Y.*

A smile creased his face. In an hour the darkness would be complete and he could walk across the lake unseen. The people inside the house, whoever they were, would be backlit like a shooting gallery. *Pop. Pop. Pop.*

SEVENTEEN

JIMMIE MOVED DELIBERATELY CROSSING THE lake, stopping a hundred and fifty feet from McCree's place. He spotted three people by the dining room table. Because McCree had a walk-out basement, the main floor was about nine feet above ground level, and the slope from the lake to the house added another fifteen feet. The large deck hanging off the front blocked his view of the main part of the living space. The dining area was framed on the side by three big windows, and that side had the best cover. Now he had to get into position without being seen.

From hunting, he knew that people look straight ahead to see, but catch movement using peripheral vision. Rather than risk being spotted by moving laterally on the lake, he retreated until he was several hundred yards away from the shore and then shifted ninety degrees and trotted at a half-crouch up the lake, cutting back to land only when he was sure he was out of sight. He came ashore where McCree kept his dock sections stacked neatly on land beyond the cedars lining the shore. One path stayed by the shoreline. Another headed toward the log cabin. He picked the third, which seemed to head toward the house, and was pleasantly surprised to come upon fresh tracks apparently made by McCree and the girl sneaking up on the house.

He inched forward. With no time pressure, the last thing he wanted was to pitch forward into the snow and foul his rifle. He covered the three hundred yards in about fifteen minutes and found the swale he had scouted earlier in the day. A large boulder provided cover and a steady support for the rifle. He was within a hundred feet of McCree's house, which was lit like a black box theater.

The girl and unknown guy sat side-by-side at the dining room table with their backs to him. McCree moved in and out of the frame made by the oversized windows, delivering food to the table. Jimmie wanted all three sitting down before he struck, but McCree was not cooperating. Time to prepare. He screwed in earplugs and replaced the glove on his right hand with a thin latex one. Cold air worked through the plastic, causing his hand to tense. He sent a mental picture of a warm fire to his fingers and focused on the dining room.

Boss wanted the girl stiff, so she was the primary shot. He visualized the action: squeeze the trigger and send one bullet spiraling toward the woman's torso. With a tiny rotation to the left he could nail the other guy, whose reaction to the first shot would probably be to rise, not drop. Even if he decided to drop, he was tall and it would take longer for him to get below the window sill than for Jimmie to aim and fire. Leaving McCree. Chances were he would also rise, unless the shock of seeing the other two killed froze him. In any event, Jimmie should have a clear shot. After all three were down, he'd make sure they were dead.

McCree was not cooperating. The girl and the new guy were eating; McCree was still screwing around in the kitchen, off and on bringing something else to the table. Jimmie felt an adrenaline surge about to come on. If his aim was going to be rock solid, he needed to squeeze the trigger before the surge arrived. He altered his plan and focused the scope on the middle of her back, barely putting pressure on the trigger. As soon as McCree returned to the dining room, he would shoot.

The girl laughed, rocking back and forth in her chair. The target he had mentally painted on her back stayed in the bull's eye. From the far end of the dining room, he sensed something that hadn't been there before and added pressure to the trigger. In a rapid, graceful motion he performed the choreography: squeezed the trigger, rotated, squeezed the trigger, rotated; squeezed the trigger. *Pop. Pop. Pop.*

NIKI TURNED TO MCCREE WHO was slightly lower than she was in the swale and hissed, "How the hell did who get here?"

"My son's wandering around inside." McCree began to stand up, but she grabbed his arm and yanked him down.

"How did he get here?" she asked. "You're positive it's him?"

"Positive." McCree stared at her. "I certainly didn't expect him. Maybe he's figured out your identity?"

Her fears exactly. In a calm, flat voice she said, "So soon? Let's make sure he's alone."

"You can freeze your ass if you want. I'm going in," McCree said. One by one he pried her fingers off his arm. *Nothing to do but follow the fool.*

McCree opened the unlocked door, stepped into the mud room, and called Paddy's name.

No response.

Niki stood beside him, pointing the gun down at a thirty-degree angle. She whispered, "Why didn't he come to greet us?"

McCree yelled louder, "Hey Paddy. We're here. Where are you?"

Still no response. The hairs at the back of Niki's neck tingled. She tried to restrain McCree but he again broke her grip and walked through the kitchen into the dining area of the great room. She followed, panning the space with the gun barrel.

Heavy steps sounded, coming up from the basement. Niki separated herself from McCree and covered the steps with the rifle.

A twenty-something with the same general build and looks as McCree loped up the steps, bopping to the beat of his iPod. He was halfway up before he saw his father and broke into a wide smile, which vanished when he saw Niki pointing the rifle at him. He stopped and removed the earbuds. Some unidentifiable hip-hop flowed into the room.

"Hey, Dad, welcome home." He faced Niki and said, "You can put the gun down, Agent Pendergast. I come in peace." He raised his right hand in the peace symbol, flashed a toothy smile, and continued up the stairs.

His words struck her like a kidney punch. She wanted to double over and wretch. The faint beat of the music and the off-beat slap of the kid's shoes on the stair treads filled the silence. McCree's mouth moved, but no sound came out. Niki lowered her rifle and watched the young man reach the head of the stairs.

She fixed him with a stare. "What did you call me?"

He reached into his pocket and shut off the iPod, walked to her and stuck out his hand. "Pleased to meet you, Agent Pendergast. I'm Patrick McCree. Dad, you've been harboring Agent Ashley Pendergast, undercover FBI working on a cross-jurisdictional task force with Homeland Security. Niki, by the way, is the name of the pet poodle she had growing up in Missoula, Montana."

Niki shook Patrick's muscular hand, willing her brain to assess the damage. "Who else knows?"

"Only one other person and I've sworn her to secrecy." Patrick paused.

"For now, anyway." To his father he added, "Cindy wanted me to give you a kiss from her, but I think I'll just pass on the sentiment. She would have come, but she's in the middle of a probe into the Cook County building inspectors. I brought up a bottle of red wine." He held it up for us to see. "Care to join me in a glass and some conversation?"

Niki rotated her gaze between the two men. Patrick continued to wear an "aw shucks" grin. Seamus glowed with a father's pride. "An excellent suggestion," Seamus said. "We have lots to discuss. Speaking of which, where's your car?"

"After what you'd written about Owen, I wanted to meet the guy and stopped in. He's awesome! Wanted to know all about me. I told him I was coming to check on your guest. He thought that was a *very good* idea. Then he took a look at my tires and suggested that it would be faster and safer if he brought me out on his snow machine. But the roads are fine—I could have made it out easy enough."

Seamus laughed. "He just wanted to see what happened when you surprised me."

"You may be right. He looked at the tracks as we turned into the driveway and said you guys were off somewhere. I just had him drop me off 'cause I was sure I knew where you kept a spare key. I ended up having to drag up a ladder to the balcony."

She watched the two in action. The son struggled with the corkscrew—clearly not an oenophile. The father moved at half-speed gathering glasses from the cabinet and setting them on the table. Niki leaned the rifle against the wall and sat down at the dining room table, back to the windows so she could observe them as they talked.

"You prefer to be called Patrick?" Niki asked.

Patrick extracted the cork with a pop. "I've tried converting my father, but he's too old to change his stripes. Should we call you Agent Pendergast, or Ashley, or are you sticking with Niki? Based on your reaction, you have your memory back. Had you ever lost it?"

"Use Niki," she said. "It's safer. How did you figure this out?"

"I refuse to answer on the grounds it might incriminate me." He poured the wine. "The big clue was the number you dialed from Dad's cell phone. Nice touch wiping the phone's memory for just that one call, but that does not wipe out the record." He faced me. "And yes, Dad, I do have access to your cell phone records. And no, I didn't hack the FBI's computer system.

Although I can't answer for some associates who helped me." He distributed the wine glasses.

"Associates? Who knows about me?" Niki asked. Her knee began bouncing underneath the table, trying to burn off excess energy. She willed herself to appear calm.

Seamus putzed around in the kitchen. Patrick took a seat next to Niki. "Okay, here's the scoop. The only people who know the whole story are me, my partner, Cindy, and now Dad. Some other people know your name but have no idea why I wanted the information. They could probably figure out more but don't have any reason to. They aren't the sort of folks who are going to show off what they know, if you get my meaning."

Maybe true, maybe not. Hackers aren't the most reliable group of people. "Who's this Cindy person?"

"We live together. She's an investigative reporter for a Chicago TV station. She's super curious about what's happening here. She and Dad have worked together in the past—in fact I met her through Dad, but that's beside the point. The point regarding Cindy is: she wants the story, but she's not about to endanger whatever you're doing. Dad can vouchsafe her. It's not my intention to screw you up either, which is why I came in person instead of calling or leaving a message or whatever. Also, I wanted to make sure Dad was safe.

"The FBI may be able to protect its undercover agents by getting their fingerprints removed from databases other police have access to, but it doesn't have the best reputation for avoiding collateral damage. Your turn to talk." He flashed his smile and took a sip of wine.

To stall, Niki said, "Let me think about this for a minute."

"I'll fix supper," Seamus said. "Pasta good, Paddy? I can make a meatless sauce."

"Perfect," Paddy said. "You want help?"

"I'm good."

Niki finished her internal debate. "I want to talk with you later about how you uncovered my identity." Patrick stiffened and she quickly continued, "Only to understand the holes in our security. We'll get the lawyers to give you and your . . . associates . . . whatever immunity is necessary." Her leg was bouncing so badly she started to get up, then forced herself back into the chair, and took a sip of wine.

"For now you should continue to call me Niki. The amnesia was real. I picked Niki because it was a name with good feelings. At the time, I didn't remember she was my dog and when I did, I had to laugh at myself since I told your father I was going to be one of those people known only by their first name. The dog, of course, went only by her first name."

She took another sip of wine, barely tasting it, and pressed both hands onto the table, her fingertips turning white.

"My alias is Bethany Palmer. The real Bethany Palmer had qualified for the job here. I took her place and we arranged for her to study the near extinction of wolves in parts of China. I have a field biology degree, experience with rustic living in cold winters, and no family to worry about not hearing from me for months at a time. It was my first—and now probably last—undercover assignment."

Seamus put a plate of cheese and crackers on the table between them. "Something to tide you over until I get dinner ready."

"If it hadn't been for your father, I would have died. The Legionnaires' disease fevers wiped out all my memory. I didn't know who I was, where I was, what I was. Nothing. Your dad is such a mensch. I can't believe how lucky I was to stumble upon him. When they released me from the hospital, I still had no memory. If Seamus hadn't taken me in . . . well, I don't know."

"He tries to show how tough he is," Patrick said. "But everyone knows he's Mr. Softie inside that rough Irish exterior. When did you remember who you really were?"

Niki released her death grip on the table. "Stuff came back in bits and pieces, all scattered. One of the first things I remembered was who Niki really was." She ruffed up both sides of her scalp and smiled at the recollection.

"I won't string this out. Bits of my childhood came back first. Later, I got more recent stuff like what I was doing out in the woods. But I knew that wasn't the full story. A few days ago, everything clicked into place. I tried to figure out a way to get to town to make contact with the Bureau, without success. Sergeant Bartelle—" At the questioning look from Patrick she explained, "Iron County Sheriff's Department. He had the road plowed, and your generous father offered to take me into town to buy new clothes."

She held up a finger to tell Patrick to hold his thought and turned toward Seamus. "My insurance will cover the hospital costs. I'll write you a check for the clothes once I return to being Ashley. I hope the delay won't be too much of a problem."

Seamus waved away her concern with the spoon he was using to stir the sauce, chuckled when he realized what he'd just done, and got a cloth to clean up the Jackson Pollock he'd painted on the stovetop.

"So what are you investigating?" Patrick asked.

"Your father figured out some of it. There's a paramilitary operation in this neck of the U.P., but I'm not allowed to tell you much." She shrugged. "I like you guys, but rules are rules, and the FBI is nothing without rules. Infiltrating the organization isn't our biggest concern. We need to determine how they're funding it."

"So you already have someone inside?" Patrick asked. "Anyone besides me want another glass of wine?"

Niki shook her head both to refuse the wine and to remind herself the kid was as sharp as the father; she needed to be careful what she did and didn't say.

"We know the master organization has placed a monstrous weapons order to be delivered and paid for this summer. Sources implied the U.P. contingent is not only taking delivery, probably smuggled in from Canada, but are also generating the funds. This wolf research project Bethany was hired for seemed like a possible cover for a drug smuggling operation, which is why the government finagled my switch with her."

"More cheese anyone?" McCree asked. "Dinner's still fifteen minutes away. I'm planning on a garden salad to go with it." With no takers, Seamus began chopping lettuce, carrots, and tomatoes for a simple salad, the whack of the knife punctuating the conversation.

"Listening to your tone of voice," Patrick said, "I have the impression you didn't have much success in unraveling the puzzle."

"Worse. Not only did the yahoo who was our local *guide* not seem to know anything about the militia, there was another researcher, Brandon Newhouse." She began to massage her neck in the spot the hickey had once been. "He got sick before I did. I'm afraid he's dead. The Iron County cops didn't find anything at the camp to indicate he had been there, so I figure they hid his body somewhere. I think we were onto something, though. Our guide, Brett Aho, was murdered not too far from here. Given the timing, I've got to assume it was because I escaped."

"Did you meet anyone other than Aho?" McCree asked.

"Just him. He picked us up at the 'Soo' airport, told us there was a change in plans, and drove us to the camp. Someone else brought in provisions while we were gone. We never saw him or her or them."

Seamus grabbed the empty cheese plate, washed it at the sink, and stood staring at the side yard.

"See something?" Niki asked.

Patrick answered. "Probably deer at the salt lick. There's a real good view from that window." Niki shifted in her seat. "Slowly," Patrick said, "or you'll scare it off."

"Paddy's right, except the deer is staring at something in the swale." Seamus tossed the dishtowel over his shoulder, ducked down and slipped into the dining area and played owl, shifting his head back and forth to try to give shape and substance to whatever it was.

Niki hated having something going on behind her. "What do you see, Seamus?" She slowly rotated her position.

"It's near the big rock at the edge of the vernal pond. Near where we hid. There's a shape—oh, the deer just took off. There's some kind of reflection. Gun!"

Niki ducked and felt a crushing blow strike her back.

Eighteen

Jimmie removed the earplugs and listened for movement in the house. Nothing. No shadows. No one turned off lights, which would be expected if someone was trying to even the odds. His heartbeat sounded a little fast in his ear. Adrenaline at work. He took two deep breaths to regain control.

No one turned on lights anywhere else in the house. He heard no windows or doors open. From this position, he could only see two sides of the house and he briefly considered moving, but decided he was in a good spot for now. He could cover anyone who tried to escape using the laundry room door, the front deck, or the basement door. He couldn't see the screened porch on the other side, but they couldn't get far from there. He'd spot them if they crossed in front of the house toward the lake, and he'd see them if they tried to get to the truck or the snow machine.

Everyone knew that if you met a black bear in the woods you were safe as long as you didn't get between a sow and her cubs—unless it was injured. A wounded bear was unpredictable and dangerous. Jimmie didn't know the condition of the people inside, but it would be pure luck if he had killed all three of them. They had a gun, so there was no reason to rush in. *Time is on my side; yes it is.* He ducked behind the rock and reloaded. Never can be too careful.

If there had only been two people in there, the odds would be much better for sneaking in, maybe through a porch door, and finishing them off. His uncle told him about entering Viet Cong tunnels so narrow in places only one person at a time could squeeze through. Jimmie wasn't sure if he had big enough balls for that. Of course, maybe those guys were juiced up on potent Southeast Asian weed. He gave himself a head slap. *No tunnels. No Cong. No platoon to watch his back. Just him, McCree, the girl, and the new guy. He was the wolf; they were the three little pigs. This time the wolf was winning.*

A vision of roaring flames crossed his mind. Fire had solved one problem today; maybe it would work again. He realized he was warming to the idea and chuckled at the pun. This place had a metal roof, so the thing to do was set the fire low in the house and smoke the vermin out. Any Yooper with gas-sucking toys had to have extra gas cans around—probably in his pole barn.

He backed away from the house and cut around the generator shed to the rear of the garage. The snow machine ignition key glinted in the moonlight. He pocketed the key—should have done that earlier. Did they leave a key in the truck as well? The only doors to the garage were on the house side and putting himself in a box canyon by going in the front wasn't a brilliant move. The extension ladder the new guy had used to climb to the balcony and enter the house hung on a pair of hooks attached to the rear of the garage. Jimmie considered it for about a quarter second. Talk about setting yourself up—halfway up an exposed ladder. The ladder did have another good use, though.

He set it against the garage, climbed three rungs, and smashed the window above the lock with the rifle butt. He unlocked the window and pried it open. In seconds he was standing on a workbench inside the garage. He fastened on his headlamp and explored, pocketing both ATV keys. No key in the truck ignition. He popped the hood and wiggled a cable off the battery and shut the hood. If they escaped the house, at least they would be on foot.

He tossed two five-gallon billycans of diesel, plus a full five-gallon and a partially filled two-gallon can of gasoline, out the garage window onto the snow. As he climbed out, he considered the thousand-gallon propane pig McCree had behind the garage. Would the pig explode with a shot through its innards? With how big an explosion? It worked for 007. Okay, first he'd go with fire; if necessary, he'd try the propane tank.

Another thought occurred to him: maybe he should cut the power to the house. Then if he saw any lights, he would know someone was about with a flashlight. He slipped into the generator shed, found the master switch, and plunged the house into darkness. Walking to the edge of the garage where he could watch the house without showing himself, he waited. No lights. No shadows moving in the moonlight filtering into the house. No sounds except for a pair of distant barred owls trading their hooted, "Who cooks for you? Who cooks for you all?"

One problem with carrying a rifle was it only left one hand for carrying anything else, which meant taking all the diesel and gasoline would require four trips. Jimmie decided the gasoline was sufficient for the task if he made Molotov cocktails and pitched them through a window.

Back inside the garage, he found a recycling bin filled with plastic soda bottles. Those wouldn't do; the bottle needed to break upon contact so the gasoline could spread rapidly. Rooting around in the garage he found another trash can filled with glass and extracted a balsamic vinegar bottle and two of some fancy-Dan extra virgin olive oil. How something became extra virgin he had no clue, but the bottles would do. Once he got a fire started, the dry wood of McCree's house would do the rest. If someone was alive and mobile, they would surely rush to extinguish the fire and become a perfect target. If they ran from the house, he'd have them in the open, which was a fine alternative. If everyone stayed inside—crispy critters.

Jimmie found a funnel near where the gas canisters were stored, tossed the bottles and funnel into the snow. Now he needed something to make a wick. Nothing cloth was on the shelves. He checked McCree's truck and came up with a heavy rag wrapped around a tire iron and realized cloth was not the big issue; the big issue was how to light the rag. McCree might have a lighter inside the house, but that wasn't going to do him any good. He searched the pole barn again and discovered a propane torch and sparker on a shelf, answering his prayers.

The torch lit like a charm. He touched the flame to the rag and it lit, giving off a putrid oily smoke. Dropping the rag on the floor, he ground it into the dirt and extinguished the fire. He stuffed the cloth and clicker in his back pocket and pitched the propane torch out the window. Returning to his post behind the garage he reconnoitered. No lights. No movement. Even the barred owls were quiet.

He stuck the bottles upright in the snow and filled them using the funnel, leaving an inch of room at the top. He tore the rag—had to use his teeth to start the tear— and soaked each wick in gas, then twisted the wicks into the necks so they blocked the openings. From across the lake, a coyote gave a quick bark, which was joined by what sounded like dozens more, although Jimmie knew there were probably fewer than ten in the pack and more likely only five or six.

Back at the edge of the garage for another look-see after the coyotes finished their caterwauling, Jimmie heard, saw, and felt nothing. Could anyone alive keep this quiet for so long? *Not likely.* He considered for the briefest moment sneaking up to look in the windows and make sure those inside were dead. No reason to take a chance; Molotov cocktails were less risky. *Now, which windows do I throw the cocktails through?* All the windows were double-paned, and he didn't want the bottle to break on the outside of the house. If he used an unbroken window, he'd need to shoot it out first, and then get close enough to make sure he pitched the bottle inside.

Best would be to use one of the windows he had already destroyed. Plenty of room under them so he could reach up and toss the gas bombs in. Getting underneath the windows involved either crossing the exposed side yard or working his way around the house using the woods in front. Someone in the basement would see the maneuver, and he'd find himself in the wrong end of a shooting gallery. The porch screens would deflect the bottle. The lakeside windows were too high. Leaving only the windows on the driveway side—if he could get to them safely.

Jimmie scooted around the garage and up the hill behind it to his original observation post where the geezer had spotted him. Seemed a lifetime ago. From there, he could slip below the ridge line and come out opposite the house. Less than one hundred feet away, it would be the best place to start launching the bottles like hand grenades.

He screwed in his earplugs, took aim, and blasted both windows in the downstairs bedroom. He slid down the bank behind the garage, listened at the edge of the garage, and blasted another big window in the dining area. Give 'em something to think about. He calmed himself, removed the earplugs, and listened. A breeze had arisen and maple tree tops softly rattled together like wooden wind chimes. Still no movement or light from inside. Nothing out of place outside. Time to reload, just in case.

He carted the three Molotov cocktails back up the hill and screwed the bottles into the snow so nothing would spill. He placed them enough apart so one wouldn't catch from another. On the second trip he carted the torch and sparker to the attack point.

Wait. Look. Listen.

Houston, all systems are go.

Jimmie leaned the rifle against a tree, opened the valve on the torch, flicked the sparker, and, with a whoosh, the torch burst into life. He brought the torch to a steady flame and screwed it carefully into the snow, well away from the bottles. He slipped on his right-hand glove to give those fingers much-needed extra warmth, and squatted in the snow, just under the ridge line. From that position he practiced the grenade-throwing maneuver. Bulky clothing inhibited smooth motion, so he peeled off his snow jacket. He might be cold for a few minutes, but soon he could warm himself around a very large campfire.

He knelt on the jacket and practiced throwing again. He visualized a perfect arc from his hand straight through the window and brought the first bottle to the torch.

A blue flame danced along the rag. He reached back and launched the bottle.

Time for a cocktail party.

Jimmie watched the bottle with its blue-fire tail arc through the night and explode on the driveway short of the house.

Bummer.

He lit one of the extra virgin olive oil bottles. He'd have to run down the hill to make sure he got the next one into the house. Fortunately, the hill faced the house and had only light snow cover, so it would be easy to run. The flames and smoke from the first cocktail screened him from anyone inside the house. He got up, and started running.

NINETEEN

I REGAINED CONSCIOUSNESS IN STAGES. Colored light appeared at the edge of my vision. I knew I had been unconscious, and blinking my eyes open, I expected to see a circle of teammates staring down at me, saying things like, "You okay, man?" and "How many fingers do I have up?" No faces, no noise.

With eyes closed, I ran a mental check of my body, starting with my toes. Wait. Where were my soccer cleats? I wore . . . socks? Jerking my eyes open, I stared at a ceiling twenty-eight feet above me. *Ah, camp.* Had I taken a spill? My body responded to the inventory with a sharp current of pain in my left thigh. I reached to rub the sore spot and stopped short: a splinter had entered my leg and stuck out eight-inches. Hoping it wasn't in too deeply, I gave it a tug. *Oh, man, don't try that again.*

I carefully patted the other side of my leg: no wood sticking through. Cavalry troops routinely left arrows in their legs until they got to a surgeon. They knew that if they pulled them out, they might bleed to death.

In a burst of recall, I remembered talking with Paddy and Niki, saw a gun barrel glint in the faint moonlight, and slammed into them to knock them to the floor.

I gingerly rolled onto my side. Paddy lay near where I last saw him in an aureole of blood shimmering in light. I rose on one elbow and peered past him. Niki was gone. Whoever had shot us had taken her. I crawled to Paddy and checked his pulse: slow, about forty-eight beats a minute. But steady.

I gently ran my fingers over his body. No compound fractures, so I risked rolling him over. His perfect nose was at an angle; a mixture of snot and blood covered the lower part of his face. Despite looking like something out of a horror movie, he was breathing regularly through his mouth. I ran fingers across his skull to find the source of the blood and discovered a groove in the top of his head, as though someone had lunged at him with a spinning drill bit and created a shallow canal. I gently parted his hair and examined the wound. Through the warm blood I couldn't find any skull or brains peeking through. I exhaled; I had been holding my breath the entire time. He wasn't going to die from anything I had found so far, but he was unconscious and I needed to get him to the hospital in Iron River.

"Paddy," I said, "Can you hear me?"

A low, urgent "shh," came from the other side of the room. Almost as though I dreamed it, I heard a whisper. "The shooter's still out there. Be absolutely quiet."

I spun toward the voice and a galaxy of stars flashed before me. Once the dizziness passed, I saw Niki crawling toward me. Her right arm was bound to her chest in a sling concocted from her shirt. She left a smear of blood in her wake. In her left hand she carried a cleaver from the kitchen. I slid away from the table to meet her partway, making sure to do nothing to snag the wood embedded in my leg.

Niki cupped my ear in her hand and whispered, "Talk this way and he can't hear us."

"How bad?" I whispered into her ear.

"Me? Just a flesh wound, broken clavicle and maybe a cracked rib or two. Nothing major. You accidentally gave Patrick the most vicious head butt I've ever seen. Knocked you both out. His nose may need a surgeon, but the head wound's a scratch. He might need to part his hair differently, is all. Glad you're with it."

"His heartbeat is so slow."

She laughed silently. "Your son is in serious shape. His heartbeat is elevated . . . I bet normal resting it's less than forty bpm."

Took me a moment to convert bpm to beats per minute. Paddy had been the captain of the crew team his last year in college, and after moving to Evanston to work, he'd joined a local Chicago rowing team for exercise.

"That's not our problem," she said. "Our problem is our gun's busted up from a lucky shot. I've heard noises from outside. I hid in the laundry room thinking he might come in that door and I could catch him from behind." She waved the meat cleaver. "With two of us, we've got more options."

"You can stay inside and I can sneak out and try to catch—"

"No can do, hero. He catches you outside, you're dead, and where does that leave me . . . or your son? No, we need him to come to us, but we need to know where and when so we can catch him by surprise. Here's my plan—"

The house plunged into darkness. "Generator shed," I said.

She grabbed my arm and worked her fingers down to my hand. "Take this. Stay below the window line and get behind the laundry room door." She shoved the handle of the meat cleaver into my hand. I went to move, but she held me back. "If he comes in, yell like a banshee and go for his trunk. I'm taking the porch."

I stayed low and again gave wide berth to anything that could snag the splinter in my leg. Without light, my progress was slow, but I reached the laundry room without blundering into anything. As my eyes grew accustomed to the dark, I realized the moon high in the sky provided ample light. What time was it? I peered around the entryway to check the time on the stove clock—which, of course, was dark.

Muffled sounds came from, I thought, the garage. A pair of barred owls called several times from across the lake. I shifted weight from foot to foot only once. Putting extra weight on the injured leg was not a good idea. Half my mind tuned for movement outside, the other half was sending positive energy to Paddy.

Sometime later, it could have been five minutes, it could have been thirty, Niki appeared like a wraith beside me. I bent my head down and she cupped my ear with her hand. "Your son's starting to stir. I don't want to move him, but I'm worried he'll start making noise. I don't know what the hell's going on outside. Obviously cutting off the electricity wasn't in preparation for an immediate attack. I think maybe he's planning to wait us out."

"We can't keep Paddy quiet. If we gag him, he'll struggle." Frustration had me whispering with force. "We can't wait any longer in here for an attack. There's only one of him and two of us. We've got to go after him."

"Just because we haven't been rushed doesn't mean there's only one person out there. Could be three of them, how would we know?"

Good point. "Should we intentionally make noise and entice them to attack?"

I sensed her shrug. "I'll stay here by the door. You get to your son. If he comes to, try to make him lie still and remain quiet. That's our biggest risk right—"

Shots rang and windows shattered in the guest bedroom. The remaining dining room window was next. Niki silently slid away from me. I remained still, willing my senses to bring me information. Finally, I heard a whoosh followed by the sound of breaking glass. Light poured into windows on the driveway side.

I ran past Niki, making no effort to mask my noise. Through the bathroom window I glimpsed a wall of flames. I yanked open the door to the screened porch and, keeping as close to the house as I could, sidestepped to the end of the porch on the driveway side. I peeked around the edge of the screening.

A wall of flame fifteen feet from the house lit up the night. Recognition leapt to mind: Molotov cocktail. I couldn't see through the blaze and, with now-ruined night vision, tried to spot movement on either side of the flames.

A spot of light appeared to the left of the burning and then quickly disappeared behind the hill. I edged toward the door from the porch, hiding my one hundred and seventy pounds behind four-by-four supports. The spot reappeared, and after a moment, began moving down the hill.

I pushed open the screen door, ran down the ramp to the driveway, and realized I would not get to him before he launched his second Molotov cocktail. With all my might I threw the cleaver at the figure slipping and sliding down the snowy embankment.

The man brought the flaming bomb behind him in preparation for his throw. The flame disappeared behind his body and his arm started forward. The cleaver reached the top of its arc, lazily rotating handle over blade. The flame reappeared from behind him moving upward at a rapid pace. The cleaver was on target but would not get there in time.

I screamed at the top of my lungs as the resulting fireball lit the night.

FRIDAY NIGHT AT CAMP, AND Boss was marking time. Jimmie hadn't reported in last night as expected, and the deadline for him to turn up didn't allow time for visiting the neighbors with a six-pack to shoot the breeze.

The viatical settlements had long passed the go/no-go mark. In fact, there were only two left to sign. It would be nice to get a hundred percent of the residents with the right kind of life insurance, but to worry about that now would be greedy. Boss was never greedy. Focused? Yes. Greedy? No. Pa often quoted the Wall Street ditty, "You can make money as a bull.

You can make money as a bear. You get slaughtered if you're a hog." Boss decided not to bother contacting the other two holdouts again. They knew the number to call if they wanted to get in on the action; although damn if it wouldn't be nice to include that old bag Mrs. Ricci and flip Sergeant Bartelle the bird after the old coot croaked in a month or two. Of course, she was probably going to die whether or not she signed the agreement.

The second hand on the clock made another full revolution and the deadline passed. Jimmie's failure to report was now officially a threat to Boss's plans. Time was of the essence. No way was Boss going to have a lung and a half removed, so days were counting down quickly—less than a hundred, if the doc's prediction was right.

This gig was to be Boss's legacy: a gift to allow the nation to get back on track. With the weapons and explosives they would amass, it should be possible to take out at least the majority of the senators and congressmen on the same day. Then America could elect representatives who would work for the people, not the corporations. Wouldn't the local Chamber of Commerce folks be surprised if they knew Boss's thinking?

Time for some outside resources. Boss opened the cooler, extracted a Bud, and held it as a salute. "Bye, Jimmie. It was kicks."

Retrieving a cell phone from a false-bottom drawer in the desk, Boss speed-dialed twenty-six—Michigan was the twenty-sixth state of the union. On the second ring, Boss heard the click of an open connection.

"Got me some varmints," Boss said.

TWENTY

Bartelle paced the hospital corridors, his nose twitching at the antiseptic smell. He had waited for hours for the doctors to release someone, anyone, for questioning. He checked his watch for the umpteenth time: nearly midnight. A nurse exited the emergency room door and held it open as Seamus McCree hobbled out on crutches. What an ungodly mess he looked: left pant leg cut off like short shorts, gauze bandage wrapped around his thigh, blackened right eye. Bartelle released a puff of air, put on his neutral face, and approached the pair.

"I wish you could have seen the other guy," McCree said once Bartelle was in range.

Bartelle shook McCree's hand, making sure not to bump the crutches. "You saying he looked worse than you?"

"I meant it literally. Someone with training may have noticed something worthwhile. The only thing I can tell you is he was male and somewhat shorter than I."

Bartelle fixed the nurse with his stare. "You're done with him, eh?"

"No rodeo for a few days, otherwise he's all set. Now Mr. McCree, you make sure to fill the script at the pharmacy. Your leg's going to be real sensitive for a few days. You want to stay ahead of the pain."

McCree indicated he would and thanked the nurse. Said he'd stick around until they finished with the other two.

"I'll bet anything the doctors will keep your son overnight for observation."

"And Niki?" McCree asked.

"Almost done."

McCree shuffled in a half-circle to face the nurse and extended his hand. "I appreciate your help. All of you guys are terrific."

The nurse beamed. Bartelle shepherded McCree to the empty waiting room. This wasn't an ideal interview spot, but it was convenient and the nurse would be able to find McCree to let him know the second she heard anything about his son, which might make it easier for him to concentrate on answering questions.

"Let's work backward, okay?" Bartelle asked. McCree didn't respond. "Last I knew, you didn't get cell service at your place. Who called the incident in?"

"Paddy brought a satellite phone."

Huh, at least someone in the family has sense. "Come to think of it, why didn't you have one?"

"Yeah, it would have been nice when Niki showed up. Put it down to either I'm too cheap, or I wanted to avoid contact with the rest of the world."

Bartelle scratched his head. Felt good. "Why didn't you drive yourself in?"

"Truck didn't start. Wouldn't catch."

"Hmph. Give me your impressions of the guy. I'm recording this, okay? You said he was smaller than you. White?"

"At first I only saw him as an outline through the flames. Really all I saw was a dark blob and the burning wick on his Molotov cocktail."

McCree related the details, starting with when he and Niki left the burned-out camp. McCree, even with half or more of his mind worried about his kid, and maybe the woman, gave a coherent, detailed description of the events up to the point where he'd charged out of the house.

"I don't get it," Bartelle said. "What possessed you to risk your life like that? You bucking to be some kind of hero?"

"It was pretty stupid if you think about it. I mentioned the last case I worked on in Cincinnati? Well, part of the reason I stayed up north this winter was because some asshole damn near burned down my house in Cincinnati, so something inside me snapped when the guy threw the first Molotov cocktail and it landed short. I was damned if I would let anyone burn this house down."

He reached down and, using both hands, tenderly shifted his injured leg. His face scrunched with the pain.

"The tree trunk was already jammed in your leg?"

"Sliver—well, maybe a small piece of kindling." He flashed a half-smile. "I didn't think about anything. Not my leg. Not what I was doing. Not about Paddy being unconscious. Not about Niki being hurt." He lifted and dropped his shoulder, exhaling a long sigh through his nose. "It was not a rational decision, okay? I lost it."

"I get that. I watched a World War II documentary about Medal of Honors winners. Every one of them a real hero. The interviewer asked one guy what he had been thinking at the time. The guy said, 'If I had been thinking, I wouldn't have done it.' So what happened after you left the house?"

"He started running down the hill—it was slow motion because of the snow. Even so, I wasn't going to get there in time to prevent him from heaving the second bomb. I was so pissed. I wanted to split him from stem to stern and I threw the meat cleaver at him. The cleaver had other ideas: it smashed into the bottle midflight and produced a fireball in the air between the guy and me. I think maybe some of the gasoline landed on him because over my yelling—the Irish know how to yell—I heard him scream, too."

McCree hung his head. Bartelle couldn't tell if McCree was dejected or tired. He placed what he hoped would be a comforting hand on McCree's shoulder. Felt the hard muscle and bone. "Then what happened?"

"Dummy that I am, I kept charging him. I was lucky he didn't have a weapon. He took off down the hill at a slant heading away from me toward the side yard. I veered to head him off. At first, I had the advantage. He was in snow and I was on the plowed driveway. Problem was, I was running around in socks."

Bartelle checked McCree's footwear. Boots.

McCree followed the glance. "We were sitting around gabbing away. I was fixing dinner. I had taken my boots off and never thought to put them on again. Another of my less bright decisions. He escaped because I tripped. Drove the splinter right through my thigh. I gimped to the snowmobile with thoughts of running him down, but he had stolen the key. Pretty much as soon as I discovered that, my leg refused to take any more weight."

"Try an experiment for me," Bartelle said. "Close your eyes and go back to the moment when the meat cleaver hit the bottle. Freeze it there and run the movie forward one frame at a time. Let me know if you see anything different."

McCree's eyeballs twitched as he progressed the movie frame by frame. Many people go through the motions but can't do it. McCree was working hard. At one point, he crossed two fingers on the right hand and later crossed two on the left.

"Definitely white. Wasn't wearing a coat. Had on a long-sleeved checked shirt. Carhartt, maybe?" McCree undid one set of crossed fingers. "He must have had a snowmobile at Spruce Point." McCree released his other digital reminder. "Soon after, a snowmobile started up across the lake and headed up their driveway."

"Spruce Point?" Bartelle prompted.

"Camp across the lake from me. Owned by some Chicagoans."

Bartelle made a quick note to check that camp as well. So much for a weekend off. "Think about the Carhartt plaid. The temperatures were what, in the twenties. Why do you think it was a shirt and not a wool jacket, maybe even a quilted jacket?"

McCree squeezed his eyes closed. "Long shirt tails. Coats are squared off, maybe have a flap in the back. Running, his shirttails flared away. Definitely a shirt."

Which led to the obvious question: what had the attacker done with his snowmobile jacket? The emergency room opened and the nurse held the door for the woman calling herself Niki. Bartelle checked his watch, already after one in the morning. She wore a figure-eight sling to immobilize her arm. Her face was pale and drawn, yet, like a feral cat, her eyes took everything in. Every time he saw her, Bartelle's gut told him something was not right, but he was clueless how to convert feeling to fact.

The accompanying nurse addressed McCree, "They will keep your son overnight for observation. The doctors can give you the details, and I'm probably not supposed to be talking, but when did that ever stop me. Right, Lon?"

She didn't wait for Bartelle to respond but chattered without pause. "He's one very lucky guy. The bullet took off a few layers of skin—quarter inch lower . . ." She shook her head. "His two shiners will last a couple of weeks. His nose should heal well, but I see you know something about broken noses." She touched McCree on the bridge of the nose. "Curiosity killed the cat. Your son won't tell us. How did he break it?"

"Head butt," McCree said. "I caught a glint from a gun barrel and dove into Paddy to knock him down. I misjudged and nailed his nose."

"Saved our lives," Niki said. "Seamus's quick action put both Patrick and me on the floor. The bullet clipped me instead of taking out my heart. He's a hero. While I dithered around, he's the one who took charge and drove off the killer."

She kept talking, but Bartelle was more interested in the look McCree had given her as she said she had dithered around: McCree wasn't buying her story, but didn't want to correct her in front of an audience.

The nurse finally broke in. "You two are ready to be discharged. I understand Mr. McCree is on the hook for both of you?" McCree agreed. "Then I'll take you to billing so they can finish their paperwork. I'll get your overcoats and stuff and bring them down there. Questions?"

"Can I see Paddy before we go?"

"He's sleeping." The nurse patted his hand. "Assuming everything is okay, he'll be released between ten and eleven tomorrow morning. You can call in about nine-thirty. We'll know by then."

McCree shot Bartelle a look that said, "That going to be a problem?"

Bartelle had already planned tomorrow, which included getting a subpoena for McCree's phone. "Will this be okay with you, Seamus? Rooms are available at the AmericInn. Stay there. I'll pick you and Niki up in the lobby at five-fifteen? I know it's not much sleep, but we'll get to your place at sunrise. After we go over the scene with you, you can drive back here in plenty of time to pick up your son. Right now, I need to ask Niki some questions while the incident is still fresh."

She laughed at Bartelle. "You mean before I talk with Seamus. No one is fresh this late at night, including you, Sergeant." She walked to Bartelle and slipped her good arm in his and said in a husky voice. "Take me to your interrogation room."

He didn't trust her a lick, but he couldn't help laughing. Yanking his flashlight from his belt, he shone it into her eyes and said in a Dragnet voice, "Where were you on the night of—" Couldn't finish for his giggles and knew he was overly tired. "Take care of the bill, McCree. We'll be here when you're done."

NIKI CONVINCED ME THAT WITH less than three hours before Bartelle picked us up, it was a waste of money to get two rooms at the AmericInn, especially since she had to sleep sitting up because of her arm. The room had a king-sized bed and a sleeper couch. If the county tongue-waggers needed proof we were coupling, they'd have it now. I was too tired to care.

The room was warm, so I gave Niki the blanket and quilt off the bed to make a cocoon; the sheet would be plenty for me. Once we turned the lights off, we acted like two kids on an overnight: instead of trying to sleep, we compared notes from Bartelle's questioning. We agreed Bartelle had no idea who was behind it.

"You need to call in?" I asked.

"You don't have your cell phone, and Bartelle will check the motel phone logs to see if we called out. I'll check in tomorrow after Bartelle finishes with us. Besides . . ."

I waited for her to continue, but the silence lengthened. "Besides what?"

"It can wait for tomorrow."

"It is tomorrow. Besides what?"

From across the room, I heard a long sigh. "I'm sorry. You can't stay in your house. Even if they release it as a crime scene, you've got all those shot-up windows. I'm beating around the bush. Your son was right. I clearly endangered both you and him. I didn't think I would. You have to believe me. There's no way you can be safe there until this whole thing gets resolved. And after tonight I've got to get distance from you guys. I'm too dangerous. Maybe if you don't want to go all the way to Cincinnati you can stay with your son in Chicago?"

She was right. I couldn't stay in the house until I got it fixed up, but I had the cabin. Remembering the broken windows gave me something else to think about: my backup heating system would be trying to heat the entire world to the thermostat setting of forty-five degrees. Fortunately, it would keep the pipes from freezing tonight, but it meant I had to drain the water system tomorrow. It was going to be a busy day.

Earlier in the evening, before all the fireworks, Paddy had implied I was a teddy bear, which I supposed was partly true. But, if someone tells me what I can't do, I tend to get my Irish up—it's not just an expression. Being unable to stay on my property was not an option I was willing to accept. Abigail had wanted me to own guns for my protection. She trained me at a range, and even though I was a good shot, I never agreed to buy any weapons. Owen had lent me a gun, which I didn't want. However, if the price for staying on my property was to have a gun, I was willing to arm myself. I felt a tiny piece of my soul detach and drift into the Michigan night. I couldn't grab it back; but if I didn't stay, I would lose much more.

Deep into my self-talk, I heard Niki offer another "I'm sorry."

"For what?" More heat filled my voice than I intended. "Look, I understand your position, but here's mine: once I can get Paddy to safety,

I'm staying at camp. You can decide for yourself where you want to be. We'd have to share the cabin until I get the house habitable. Hopefully, it shouldn't take too long. My mother used to tell me, 'It's better to run away and live to fight another day,' to which my father would append, 'But if it's going to be the same fight, might as well make it today.'"

"Put yourself in my position," she said. "What happens if I agree and it goes wrong and you're killed? What then? What do I say to your son? What if your son says the same to you? 'Fine, Dad. If you're staying, I'm staying.' What will you do then?"

"I'll bluster and shout and order him home, and if he tells me to stuff it, I'll remember I raised him to make his own decisions. I invited you into my home because I wanted to. If someone had told me what would happen because of my invitation, I'd still do it. That's just who I am. Some things I am unwilling to change." I slapped my open palm onto the bed. "That's hard for people to take, which is why I'm divorced and Abigail is who-knows-where. In that unbending way, we're alike, I think. So screw you, Agent Pendergast, and screw your FBI. I won't blow your undercover operation, but I'm not about to have you tell me what to do."

From the chair came rustling noises, but no words of argument, or of agreement. "Let's get some shut-eye," I said. "We're going to need it."

The bed shifted under her weight as she sat down beside me. "I understand. I'd like to stay, but I have to follow orders. They're going to pull me. You say all your tough-guy words. Beneath them, I hear the Seamus who lost his father, and the divorced Seamus who lost his wife, and the current Seamus who lost his lover." Her fingers brushed my cheek. "I hear the Seamus who wonders if he is loveable. If you listened to your son this evening, you should know you are. I know you are."

Lightly caressing my chest with her good hand, she leaned down and kissed my lips. "With this wing, I'll have to be on top. Okay, tough guy?"

Twenty-One

NIKI AND I WERE WAITING for Bartelle in the AmericInn lobby at the appointed time. He arrived carrying two coffees and a bag with cream and sugar. He pointedly looked at my naked bandaged leg and chuckled. "Love the fashion statement. We'll turn the heat up high for the ride."

Once in the car, I handed my cup to Niki—I couldn't remember when I last drank the stuff. Tex drove: he had had more sleep than Bartelle, Niki, and I combined. Bartelle rode shotgun. On US 141, potentially suicidal deer grazed along the edge. Once we hit the gravel roads, the vegetation grew closer in and deer were less visible, but we knew they were there, waiting to spook into our path. With a predawn rose glowing in the east, we crested a hill and Tex slowed down.

"Well looky what we got."

Niki and I nearly bumped heads as we leaned forward to peer between the front seats. A large male wolf, his black coloration flecked with cinnamon-tipped fur, loped down the road. He peered at us, huffed out a breath of warm air, and continued like a Cadillac—owning the middle of the road.

"DNR hasn't gotten to him," Niki said. "No radio collar and no ear tags." Bartelle shot her a quick look and returned his gaze to the wolf, which reached an area where the left snowbank was only four feet high. The wolf gathered itself in two quick steps and, in a graceful bound, jumped the mound. Five seconds later, we had lost it to the woods.

Bartelle spoke the words I had been thinking: "Sights like that are why I love being in the woods."

Several sheriff's deputies had already set up my screened porch as a staging area. Dawn had officially arrived, but the hill behind the house still hid the sun. They had turned on all the house and garage lights, which, combined with the furnace trying to heat the planet, had the generator running at full buzz. We donned blue booties and entered the house. After throwing on sweatpants, my first stop was the basement so I could flip the furnace circuit breaker. Tex followed me as I laboriously picked my way down the stairs.

"Later, we can all help drain the house," he said. "Pipes won't freeze before Bartelle's done with you."

"Thanks," I said, "but I have to winterize every year, so the house is designed for it. Draining the water heater is the longest part. Everything else is easy, although the biggest pain is the toilets. My bigger concern is figuring out what's wrong with my truck. It was working fine before. The guy must have done something to it."

We found Bartelle and Niki examining the southern wall in the dining room. A freshening breeze pushed air through the broken windows. "Once we've got enough light," Bartelle said, "we'll walk the grid. For now, take me through exactly what happened."

He recorded a lot of stuff in his notebook, even though we'd told him all of it before. While they used little flags to mark every exogenous item for photographing and bagging, Niki remained on the porch. I joined her after I completed draining the water from the house. Tex came trotting over.

"You were right. The guy messed with your truck's battery cable. I dusted everything for prints, but I'm not too hopeful. Anyway, I reconnected the battery for you, so you're good to get to your son in town."

"Thank you. This part of the kinder, gentler Iron County Sheriff's Department?" I joked.

He blushed. "More like the sergeant wants you out of here as quick as possible." He included Niki in his gaze. "You too, miss."

I caught Niki raising her eyebrows and sliding me a sideways glance—probably to see how I reacted. I consciously released my tightened shoulders. "Thanks for all your help." I shook his hand. "Let me grab my cell phone, keys, and Paddy's stuff and we'll head out."

Niki waited only long enough for me to steer the truck onto Shank Lake Road before saying, "I'm surprised you didn't take Tex's head off when he told you Bartelle wanted us gone."

"First, he was only the messenger. Second, you had prepared me, so I was ready and could handle it without a kneejerk reaction. Anyway, I do need to check on Paddy, and you," I handed her the cell phone, "need to call your superior. There was no reason to make a stink . . . yet. If Paddy has to remain in town, then I'll stay with him. As soon as I get him to Chicago, I'm back here."

To accommodate an approaching full-size truck towing an enclosed trailer, I pulled so far to the right that I scraped the side of my truck on tag alders. I sucked in my stomach as they approached. The trailer wasn't one of those specialized ones for carrying snowmobiles, but I figured that was what was inside. Every Saturday, town guys drove freshly plowed roads as far as possible and then offloaded their snowmobiles and explored the country. The truck eased to a stop and lowered its window as did I in the rural tradition of never letting an opportunity pass to discover who was out in the woods and why.

A grizzled bear stuck out his head. "You McCree?" I admitted I was. "Owen apologizes he couldn't be here hisself. Had to go down to the VA in Green Bay, but he sent me and my brothers to cover them windows was shot out with OSB?"

I knew he meant the OSB was to cover the windows, but I couldn't help smiling at the image of someone shooting the plywood equivalent through my windows. I didn't offer him a grammar lesson.

"We wasn't sure what you had for tools up to your camp, so we brung all we needed." He tilted his head toward the trailer. "Sorry we're so late. Had to wait for the lumber store to open to get the OSB. Owen said there was four or five big windows shot out. We brought twice as much stuff as we thought we needed, so we should be hunky dory."

I stammered my thanks and wondered once again at both the efficiency of the local grapevine and the willingness of folks to pitch in to help others. Eventually our conversation informed me they were third cousins once removed to Owen. I think. Owen had roused them at six o'clock. Only God, Owen, and his source knew how he found out about the ambush. After we'd chatted long enough that I wouldn't be considered rude, I mentioned we were headed to Iron River to hopefully check Paddy out of the hospital.

"You got plenty of time. Heard tell the doc would discharge him about eleven. They still got big northern in the lake? Back thirty, forty years ago . . ."

Took twenty more minutes before we disengaged to his parting words, "We'll keep an eye out 'til you get back."

Niki craned her neck looking back at the guys. "More examples of not judging a book by its cover. Sweethearts, aren't they? How come you didn't at least offer to reimburse them?"

"Yoopers may not have much money, but they're rightly proud of taking care of people in the community. I'll find out from Owen the best way to handle things so I don't accidentally insult anyone."

* * *

At exactly ten o'clock, Boss met Spider and Digger on a quarter-section of land Hematite Bank had recently foreclosed near the Michigamme Reservoir. Boss thought of them as the Mitten Men, given they came from that part of the state. Everyone stood around making small talk, stamping their feet to keep warm in the mid-morning chill, and slurping the coffee Boss had brought in thermoses.

Boss had no trouble guessing which one was Spider. Wearing a T-shirt and a sheepskin vest, his left arm sported the tattoo of a giant web with a black widow ready to pounce from his bicep. He looked like a spider too—drug-addict skinny, all arms, and legs with a little pot belly. Smelled like an ashtray. The look might have worried Boss, except these two came highly recommended. Digger looked like a fire hydrant: short, squat, and his face burned red. "Caught me frying on a beach in Florida," he said by way of explanation. "Looking forward to going back as soon as this is done. Who are the targets?"

Using the cell phone display, Boss brought up several pictures of the still-missing Jimmie, and one of Jane Doe taken in the hospital. "Take as much time as you want to memorize these faces. I don't want any printouts, nothing anyone could use to tie us together. Best for all our sakes."

Boss paid attention to their eyes, which revealed their skepticism. They knew it was one-way protection, but it didn't seem to bother them. Spider took one look at each picture, proclaimed he "got it," and handed the phone to Digger. Digger stared at a picture, closed his eyes, and described the picture in minute detail. Boss was impressed, but the proof would be in the pudding.

"Before my bank acquired this property, I checked it out. There's lots of coyote sign. Let's get acquainted while we do a little tracking and maybe get us some varmints. Tonight, you can start hunting some other varmints."

Digger brayed loudly at the joke. Spider laughed without sound. Boss did not want to be around these two for long. They were scary *hombres*.

* * *

It was a bit after noon by the time Niki returned to the hospital waiting room. She found Seamus reading a month-old issue of *The Economist*. "I thought you and your son would be impatiently waiting for me. Sorry I took so long." She plopped on the bench next to Seamus.

"Now you get to wait." He checked his watch. "One last doctor has to sign off on Paddy's release, but I hear he's stitching up a chainsaw accident."

Niki absentmindedly pawed through the magazines scattered on the coffee table: People, Woman's Day, Parents, Field & Stream, Sports Illustrated, North American Whitetail. "Where'd you get that one?"

"Guy was in earlier waiting on his wife. Retired anthropology prof, of all things. Anyway, we got to talking. When his wife came out, he handed it to me—he'd brought it from home. I'm almost done if you want it."

Only Seamus could walk into a podunk hospital, find an anthropologist to talk to, and come out with an Economist *magazine.*

Niki expected Seamus to drill her with questions, but he went back to reading. *This isn't going to get any easier with the waiting.* "Well," she slapped her good hand on her knee, "I just had the best time. I got to talk to my direct supervisor, then he conferenced in the guy he reports to, and finally that guy added in the AIC—Agent in Charge." She checked to make sure he was paying attention. "I'm supposed to provide whatever information I can to Sergeant Bartelle and then disappear. No one, not even Bartelle gets to know my real name. I'm Niki—one name—single 'k.'"

She tried a quick smile, but couldn't make it stick. "You're supposed to talk with the AIC."

"About?"

She dialed the number, pushed the speakerphone button, and handed Seamus the phone. AIC Cooper answered by grunting his name. Seamus introduced himself.

"Listen McCree, this is what you're going to do. First you're going to—" Seamus frowned at the phone and disconnected the call.

"Did you just hang up on him?"

Seamus removed the battery from the phone. "If Agent-in-Charge Cooper conjures a way to contact me and asks politely, I'll consider whatever request he had in mind. Otherwise . . ."

She had sat with her sling next to Seamus. A quick check showed no one was in the area. She danced around him and sat on his other side, leaned in and gave him a good, hard kiss. She closed her eyes and remembered last night. "He is a prick, and you . . . you are something else."

She leaned in for another kiss, but Seamus ducked away. She punched him lightly on the arm.

"One word is obstreperous," Patrick said. "What did Dad do this time? I only heard the last part as they wheeled me down the hall."

Oh, that's why Seamus avoided kissing me. She turned toward the voice. Patrick looked horrible: his swollen face featured a nose even Jimmy Durante would disown. His eyes presented a mixture of black, green, and putrid yellow. White bandages wound around the top of his head. He shifted his weight to get up from the wheelchair but the nurse restrained him with a hand on his shoulder. "Not until you're officially released."

Patrick slumped down, "Can't be too soon. Shall we?" He motioned with a grand sweep of his arm toward the exit. The nurse unlocked the brakes and we followed them out the door. Seamus brought the car around. The nurse reminded Patrick of his instructions about icing everything swollen and making sure he had his prescriptions for pain medication.

No sooner had Patrick shut the passenger door than he inquired about lunch, claiming breakfast was a year ago and he was starved. At the mention of food, Niki felt her stomach grumble.

Patrick grinned and pointed at her. "You're outvoted, Dad. How about Scott's Subs? Leave room for the ice cream. So who did you blow off?"

"FBI. They—"

"Not another word until we know we're alone," Niki said. "People can read lips better than we think. How bad does it hurt, Patrick?"

"Let me put it this way: next time Dad decides to head butt me, I need to remember he used to head a ball half the length of a soccer pitch—and get the hell out of the way." He poked his father in the ribs, causing Seamus to startle. "Were you jealous of my perfect nose and decided I needed to have the new McCree model with a crook?"

Seamus fingered his own crooked nose. "The ladies will love it, right Niki?"

"Oh yes. We swoon at the manly exhibition of broken noses. And if you add a chipped tooth or two . . ."

During lunch, Niki observed the interplay between the two McCrees. The playful banter showed a clear mutual appreciation. Underneath, however, she could feel tension. Seamus was probably contemplating how to convince Patrick to go to Chicago. She guessed Patrick was working on how to protect his old man. Maybe she could broker a deal to keep them all safe and not make either one lose face—to each other or to themselves.

After lunch, Seamus drove to the Wolf Track Trail at the nearby George Young Recreational Complex. The day had warmed to the lower forties with a light southwestern breeze. Most of the snow was gone and, although the trail was slushy, it had the advantage of being deserted.

Patrick asked, "Are you still Niki or Agent Pendergast?"

"Stick with Niki. I'm to inform Sergeant Bartelle about my undercover operation and provide whatever information might help his murder investigation. Then I am to leave, and I quote, 'on the first available flight.'" She added, emphasizing each word, "Oh, by gosh and by golly, can you believe—" She threw up her hands like a fundamentalist Christian. "—that I accidentally left a few things in your Dad's cabin? No? Well, fancy that."

She gave them her most mischievous smile. "I checked the flights." She rotated her attention to Seamus. "Even if I catch Bartelle before he leaves your place, I won't be able to get to either Iron Mountain or Marquette in time. So, you're stuck with me for one more night . . . unless you don't want to be. You heading down to Chicago today, Patrick? We can drop you off at Owen's to pick up your car."

"What makes you think I'm leaving?" Patrick stopped walking and forced Niki and Seamus to turn around. Niki shrugged at Seamus to say she had given it her best try.

Seamus may not have seen the gesture, but Patrick did. "You two in cahoots? I knew something was going on."

Niki didn't dare look at Seamus. She felt a flush reach from the roots of her hair down to her toenails. She hoped it didn't show.

"Like father, like son," she said. "No one's going to tell you what to do. Patrick, you showed how smart you were to deliver the news about who I am in person. There's nothing else for you to do here. Tell you what: when this is all over, I'll give your investigative reporter girlfriend, Cindy is it? I'll give her a ton of 'anonymous source' background for her story."

"Now I know I'm staying." Patrick glared at her. Seamus looked like he wanted to shoot her.

What a fucking mess she had created.

Twenty-Two

WE DROPPED PADDY OFF AT Owen's to get his car. He wanted to grocery shop for fresh fruits and veggies to fill his vegetarian needs. Niki and I kept to ourselves on the drive home. I was lost in thought and not paying much attention to the scenery, but as we crossed the intersection to Long Lake, I realized someone had recently plowed a one-lane path through the drifts. The tracks of a number of vehicles were visible in the melting snow. "In a hurry to get home?" I asked.

At Long Lake, we discovered hordes of uniforms: Iron County deputies, the State Police crime scene unit, and rescue squads from Amasa and Crystal Falls. We joined a group of snowmobilers standing behind yellow tape strung between two trees close enough to the shore to see what was happening on the lake, but sufficiently removed to stay out of the way. Bartelle stood on the ice about fifteen feet away from a watery hole. Niki wandered to the tallest of the snowmobilers and asked what was going on.

"On the police band, they said a snow machine broke through the ice. Got us a camp yonder." He waved toward Michigamme. "Course the problem is they can't get no machines out on the ice, so they had to wait for guys in dry suits. Ain't seen no body yet, but see there?" He pointed toward the near shore. "They snaked a couple hundred feet of towline across the ice and winched out the yellow Arctic Cat with the flaming red stripes. Belongs to Jimmie Heitzmann. Got him a camp around Witch Lake."

Niki and I followed his pointed finger and shared a glance of agreement. We had met that snowmobile the first day we explored this area. Now I was sure that a couple of days ago it had zipped by us on The Grade near Amasa.

"Divers just went in?" Niki asked.

With a *pffft*, the guy ejected a stream of tobacco juice from between his two front teeth. "Only one. Body probably drifted under the ice toward the outlet."

The diver popped up and summoned Bartelle. We were too far away to hear the words, but Bartelle ordered a deputy to slide the towline across the ice again. What else was down there?

The diver hauled the line under the water and popped up a minute later. Bartelle signaled to the guy running the winch, who cranked up the loud gasoline-powered motor. After ten feet of line, Bartelle gave the stop sign. From the water, the diver pushed two concrete blocks onto the ice.

Niki pulled my head toward her so she could whisper into my ear. "I got a bad feeling there's a body attached to those blocks."

I realized what had happened. The spot on Long Lake I had originally thought was a large ice fishing hole wasn't. Someone had chopped through the ice and dumped a body weighted with cement blocks. A shiver ran up my spine as I wondered if the person had been dropped into the lake dead or alive.

The diver ducked under the water and Bartelle reached into the hole and between them they lifted a body onto the ice. From Niki I heard a great intake of air.

"It's Brandon."

Another mystery solved. I had no doubt that if Niki had not escaped, she would have worn her own set of cement blocks.

Two cops laid the body on a tarp and carried it to shore. The police photographer scurried around taking pictures. Other than waterlogged, the body looked in good shape; yet if my supposition was correct, it had been in the lake a month or more.

As if reading my mind, Niki said, "Very cold water slows decomposition. They need to take pictures immediately because once exposed to the air, the corpse will quickly deteriorate. The diver's going back in. Are there more?" She faced the group of guys and asked, "Anyone got a pencil and paper I can use?"

She wrote a short note to Bartelle and handed it to the officer assigned to make sure none of the civilians got too close. After one look at Niki's note, he called another officer over to take it to Bartelle, who read the message and shoved it in his coat pocket. I later caught him frowning at Niki.

After a quarter hour, the diver surfaced. From the reaction of the cops, I surmised he had found something else. The police soon carted a second body to shore. This one was dressed for snowmobiling with helmet, gloves, a heavy wool shirt layered over insulated coveralls, but no coat. He was our fire bomber and justice had been served. He must have been half-frozen driving the snowmobile without a coat. Embarrassed by my pleased reaction, I hoped he'd died of an immediate heart attack when he hit the water rather than the more cruel death by drowning.

The loquacious tobacco expectorator speculated on whether the body was Heitzmann. Too tough to tell with the helmet still on, but he seemed to have the right height and build. The police photographer gave a signal, and one of the cops removed the victim's helmet. With the cops standing around, it took a while before we could catch a decent look at his face.

Next to us, twin jets of brown juice stained the snow. "Hey, I know that guy," he yelled. A smile lit his face. To us, he said, "That *is* Jimmie. Just wait till I tell the missus."

An officer took him aside, notepad in hand, pen at the ready. Bartelle motioned Niki to meet him away from listening ears. I tagged along.

"What's so important that it can't wait?" Bartelle asked.

"Two things. The guy with the concrete weights is Brandon Newhouse." Bartelle put on his steely stare. "What's the second?"

Niki shook her head. "Can't tell you here, but you need to hear it. We're staying at Seamus's cabin. Stop by when you're done."

Bartelle nodded agreement to Niki and jabbed a hard finger into my chest, setting me on my heels. "You're playing with fire, McCree. I hope you have insurance."

BARTELLE SAW THE THREE PAIRS of boots parked outside the sliding door on the screened porch of McCree's cabin. Inside, McCree, his son, and the woman who called herself Niki sat around a table playing cards by the light and hiss of propane lamps. He stamped off the snow—he didn't trust them enough to go shoeless. Warm air rushed out as he opened the door. Quickly getting inside, he shrugged off his jacket.

"Have a seat," McCree said. "Can we get you something to eat? Drink?" He pulled a chair from the wall and added it to the table. "You've had a long day."

Bartelle noticed the clock hung from a nail on the wall. *Jeez-o-Pete, how had it gotten to be nine o'clock already?* He could have sworn it was only about an hour after sunset. What had happened to the time? Had he zoned out? He needed sleep, for sure. While McCree settled the chair into place, he automatically scoped out the cabin: single room, adequate wood stove with a blazing fire. Wet wool scenting the air from a nearby drying rack. Three propane lamps hissed and added to the warmth. A double bed, the table he sat down at, and a chest of drawers furnished the room, which he gauged was a cozy fifteen by twenty-five.

He took the offered chair. "You made sure I came here tonight instead of getting some much-needed rest. Although come to think of it, you've had as little sleep as me."

"Sure you don't want anything?" Patrick asked. "I've got stew ready to warm up." Bartelle looked around and didn't see any pot of stew. "We do the cooking on the porch. All I have to do is light the burner."

"It's tasty, but vegetarian," Seamus said.

Mention of the food triggered his stomach, which growled at its emptiness.

"One vote for stew," Patrick said. Everyone laughed as though it was an inside joke and to Bartelle's surprise, he found himself laughing as well. "Coming right up."

McCree poured him a glass of water from a gallon jug. Bartelle drained it, and McCree poured another. Bartelle tipped the glass toward the woman. "Just start talking. I'll ask questions if something isn't clear. I'm recording it." He pressed the start button on the digital recorder, set it on the table, and announced the date, time, place, and persons present.

McCree interrupted. "It's actually eight-ten. Technically we're in Central Time, but I keep the camp on Eastern Time since we're only a mile south of the Eastern Time Zone."

That at least explained why he thought he'd lost an hour.

"I want to formally introduce myself," the woman said. "I'm an agent for the FBI working undercover, using the name Bethany Palmer. The FBI has not authorized me to provide you with my real name as it may jeopardize national security. I will give you my AIC's name and number and you or the sheriff can hash it out with him."

Bartelle felt a thousand emotions rip through him. He was pretty sure none of them showed on his face. He felt vindicated: he hadn't bought the woman's story. He was ticked off: he hadn't figured her as an undercover agent. He was doubly ticked off: he had forgotten to check on the results of his subpoena of McCree's phone records. He was ticked off squared: a fellow officer had been lying to him all along, preventing him from doing his job.

His anger soon changed to a combination of discouraged and enraged. He was finally making progress on the case—cases—even if he did end the day with two more bodies than he had started with. And now the FBI was going to hijack all the work. He'd be the kid at the candy store pressing his nose against the window.

"Proceed, Agent X." She appeared to ignore his sarcasm, assuming she had even realized it for what it was.

"Brandon Newhouse and Bethany Palmer," she said, "were research biologists hired to study wolves by an outfit we believe has ties to possible domestic terrorist groups. Homeland Security thinks they're funding their operation smuggling stuff in through Canada. I replaced Bethany. You pulled Brandon's body from the lake. He got sick before I did, but I must have been out of it when he died. My AIC can give you Brandon's contact information and pretty much anything else you want to know about him. We researched him thoroughly.

"The project Bethany and Brandon signed up for was supposed to take place near Sault Ste. Marie, which is, of course, a major border crossing with Canada. Brandon and I flew there and Brett Aho picked us up. On the drive to the base camp, he told us plans had changed: they had gotten permits from Michigan DNR to trap and track wolves in the central U.P., so he was taking us there.

"I never saw any contraband: no drugs, no weapons, nothing at Brett's camp— the one someone torched. He's the only person we saw. Someone provisioned the place while we were out tracking wolves. The only thing that really tells me we're onto something is the effort someone made to try to kill me—and they had no idea I was an agent."

"Unless," McCree said, "you said something while you were delirious with fever." Agent X blanched. Patrick came in from the porch, placed a steaming bowl of stew on the table, and handed Bartelle a blue-checked cloth napkin and a soupspoon. Bartelle wafted the stew's aroma like he was some kind of professional taster. He noted a variety of spices he couldn't quite name, so he dug in. Tasted as wonderful as it smelled. Looked like it was simple enough to make. Maybe he should get the recipe.

"There's a little more if you want it," Patrick said. "And be careful of the bay leaf." Bartelle used the cover of eating the excellent stew to formulate his questions. The propane lamp above the table started to lose its full glow, and soon the only light and hiss came from the other two lamps in the room. No one made a move to switch lamps.

"End of story," Agent X said. "Anything from Brandon's body give you a clue about his death?"

"The ME didn't think there was water in his lungs, so he was dead before he was dumped into the lake. Cement was probably to make sure the body didn't float once the ice broke up. Second guy probably drowned. Neither of you recognized him?"

They hadn't, but they told him about recognizing the snowmobile. An uncomfortable silence filled the cabin. Bartelle finished the bowl of stew, pronounced it delicious, and threw the elephant on the table. "FBI bringing in a team tomorrow?"

Agent X gave him a big smile. "Nope. In fact, my orders are to get out of Dodge. We respectfully request that you destroy the recording and notes of this conversation to protect our investigation. It should be easy for your people to 'discover' all this information now you know what to look for." She air-quoted with her fingers. "We expect the mystery of Niki will remain unsolved."

Bartelle could tell that everyone was waiting for his reaction. He slowly drank the remaining water in his glass and leaned back in the chair. He patted his lips with the napkin and carefully folded it along the creased lines. "All well and good for the FBI," Bartelle said. "But, that is one decision that will not be mine."

TWENTY-THREE

SHORTLY AFTER BARTELLE LEFT, I used the outhouse. Upon my exit, I spotted Owen Lyndstrom walking up the drive with two guys dressed head to foot in camo. The camo was summer–fall, shades of greens and browns; the first leaf wouldn't arrive for two months. Owen left the two outside "to stand guard" and lugged three semi-automatic rifles inside. From a canvas bag slung over his shoulder, he produced boxes of ammunition, which he thunked on the table.

"Me and the boys are takin these here woods back startin right now."

"What do you mean?" I said.

"What I mean is these woods are for huntin and fishin and trappin and for breathin free air, and every man's got a right to live out here if he wants to. Me and the boys are puttin on a . . . what's they call it? . . . a 24/7 operation. We ain't allowin anyone to harass you again. Shootin up someone's place. Tryin to burn them out. No sir. That shit's over and done with. Pardon my French, ma'am." Owen doffed his cap in Niki's direction.

"We got two guys stationed at the head of the lake where Lukes Road splits from Shank Lake, and these two," he pointed through the window toward the Camo Boys, "will watch the road where it comes into your property in case someone tries a back way in. We tried walkie-talkies but they aren't workin so good in the woods, so I'll ride the road between 'em. That should do 'er. Oh, I almost forgot: the password for tonight is 'Nessie'—you know, the Loch Ness Monster? Think you can remember?"

I had picked a bad time for a gulp of water. Hearing "Nessie" I snorted, which caused a coughing jag, which I tried to end by slapping my thigh. The instantaneous bolt of pain from my injured leg immediately ended the coughing. They should have that cure in the medical texts. Fortunately, anyone seeing tears in my eyes would assume laughter, not pain was the cause.

I was concerned the boys would be more likely to shoot each other than prevent another attack, so although I was pretty sure arguing with Owen wasn't going to do any good, I needed to try. "Didn't you hear the guy who tried to kill us drowned in Long Lake?"

Niki put her arm around Owen's shoulders. "That's so sweet of you. Wouldn't it be easier if we packed our stuff and stayed in town?"

Owen squirmed away from Niki, stood by the door, hands on his hips—a picture of exasperation. I knew Niki's well-intentioned gambit was about to backfire.

"We don't run from trouble up here. We don't look for it, neither, but if it comes . . . well, we take her on." He turned from Niki and spoke to me. "Jimmie Heitzmann— the drowned guy? Something went wrong with that boy over in Iraq. He was a grunt, not a general. He didn't get no idea himself to kill you. Somebody pointed him, and whoever that asshole is—sorry, ma'am—he's still around and maybe he's already got him another Jimmie Heitzmann. You see what I'm sayin?"

Owen's glare shifted between Niki and me. Paddy looked up from the laptop he had been pecking away on. "What my father forgot to say was 'thank you.' He thinks he can do everything himself, and he's reluctant to ask for help. I hope your trip to the VA wasn't anything serious?"

Owen's countenance smoothed out. "That warn't for me. Guy from the VFW got readmitted last week. He and I both had a little colon cancer a few years ago." He must have seen the concern on our faces. "Me, they just gotta check the exhaust pipe once a year. He ain't been that lucky. Youse folks need anythin else? Otherwise we'll get out of yer hair. You remember the password, right?"

"Nessie," we said simultaneously.

Owen smiled approval. "And load them guns before you get to yackin."

"Speaking of thank-yous," I said. "Who can I pay for the work your cousins did on closing up the house?"

"Them boys don't want nothin. They was happy to do it. It'd be right nice if you could pay them for the supplies. I'll let you know how much it was."

Owen and the Camo Boys drove away. Paddy took one of the guns and loaded ammunition while Niki watched, an approving expression on her face.

"Where did you learn that?" I asked.

"From someone else who doesn't look for trouble but is ready if it comes." At my confused expression he added, "Abigail taught me." He confirmed the safety was on before setting the first gun in a corner and grabbing the second one.

When had that happened? It wasn't while I was around, but since Abigail lived near Paddy maybe . . . The mention of Abigail's name changed the warm stew to a chunk of iron ore in my stomach. The time with Niki had been fine, but she wasn't Abigail. No one else could be. I shook my head, then realized Paddy and Niki were watching me. I'd have to ask about his seeing her when we were alone. "We're going to have to figure some way to get Owen and the other guys to give up this guard duty. I'm afraid one of them will get hurt."

"Let me get this right," Niki said. "You're willing to risk your life—you who would prefer never to touch a gun. You're willing to risk Patrick's life—your only child. But you don't want those guys out there helping protect you and yours because they might get hurt? That about it?"

Paddy laughed. "He may be a math guy, but that doesn't mean he's logical. He is Irish, after all."

BOSS FLICKED ON A LIGHT in the camp to hold back the onset of night. The Mitten Men were off reconnoitering McCree and the girl. They had shown themselves to be excellent trackers and marksmen, each drilling a coyote. Boss planned to give them the pelts as souvenirs from the mission. Late in the afternoon, Boss had wandered through town and gathered the news trickling in from the woods. It was damned ironic: Jimmie killed Brett, and Brett's dropping Brandon through the ice after he died of the Legionnaires' disease had ultimately killed Jimmie when Jimmie drove through the thin ice over Brett's hole. Evened out their karma and saved the Mitten Men the task of tracking down Jimmie and eliminating that loose end. What really cranked Boss's engine tonight was McCree and the girl still staying out in the woods. It would make their removal much easier and that was worth celebrating.

Boss got up, retrieved another beer from the kitchen, and returned to the couch. Sitting down triggered a coughing fit. Two, three, four minutes, Boss kept hacking away. Chest felt like it was in a vice. Thought it was under control and started hacking again. The April Fools' plan was still three long weeks away. According to the doctor's timetable, the lung cancer wouldn't win for another three months. Boss kicked the coffee table. *I will get this done.*

Boss hooked the Inspiron 2500 into the phone line, went through the painfully slow dial-up routine, and downloaded a message from NuWrldYooper@gmail.com.

Short and sweet: "Magic potion concentration working great. Sufficient supplies ready by March 13. Delivery on Sunday the 15th?"

The Ides of March was a week from tomorrow. Boss typed a one-word reply: "Yes."

The excitement kicked off another hacking spree. Maybe they should push up the original timetable. April Fools' had a cachet to it any other date lacked; but really, who would get the joke? Signing up the Loonies at the retirement home had gone better than expected. Maybe an incentive would get Laughing Loon's management to push up the work? Boss imagined the pitch to get management to move the date when they did their annual HVAC maintenance: "We're trying to keep all our people busy and this is a slack time of the year, so if you . . ."

Or should I make it an all-of-a-sudden thing? "Another client went bankrupt and so it frees up some time . . ."

A truck crunched into the driveway. Moments later, the Mitten Men were inside. "Looks like five guards," Spider said. "Two got them a checkpoint at the top of the lake. Got two more stationed closer to McCree's place, maybe three-eighths of a mile away. Fifth guy is driving a truck up and down the roads. Going real slow."

"Can you take them?" Boss asked.

Digger grabbed a beer from the fridge without asking, which Boss didn't like, but didn't make a fuss about. Spider answered, "They're sitting ducks, but we'll need one more person. Those trophies on the wall yours or did they come with this place?"

Boss took umbrage but didn't let it show. "What's the plan?"

"We could avoid the guards altogether and get into McCree's place, but killing them will generate a lot of noise. We don't want to have to shoot our way past five alert guys getting out, which means we take care of them first. Supposed to be bad weather tomorrow night, which should help."

"Why not tonight?" Boss asked.

"To get here, we've been up most of the last twenty-four hours. With all those guards we need some planning. We'll do this tomorrow. Relax. A day isn't going to kill you."

Spider waited until Digger downed the beer before continuing. "When the truck driving between the two checkpoints reaches the head of the lake, we have three of them in the same spot. Your job will be to take care of those three. Problem is, when you hose the three down, the other two guards will be alerted. So I'll take care of the other two at the same time."

"Still leaves the targets," Boss said, seeing the hole in the plan.

"Digger'll wait for them and cut 'em down if they leave the house. If they stay barricaded inside, I'll join him for the turkey shoot. Once you take care of your three, hoof it to our truck, and pick us up."

"Why your truck, not mine?"

"Locals know your truck and our plates aren't traceable."

They spent an hour and a couple of beers discussing contingency plans: what they would do if there were more guys the next night; how they would handle it if anyone got hurt unexpectedly. After planning petered out, the conversation turned to politics, and Boss got into a stump speech. "There is not a lick of difference between the Democrats and the Republicans when it comes to anything that really matters. Big corporations bought them both. Damned regulations nearly killed my bank, but they spend billions to save people who should be in jail. We need to start fresh."

Spider shot Digger a sideways glance; stillbirthed whatever Digger had planned to say. "I mostly agree," Spider said in a neutral voice, "but in our neck of the woods, we all would have been hurting big time if the government hadn't given the automakers a helping hand."

Boss grew red in the face. "Government Motors, you mean? Would have been better off if we let them die. Anybody can't run a profitable business deserves to go bankrupt. This country was founded by individuals for individuals. Nobody told Daniel Boone where and when he could hunt."

Digger stormed outside, which cut Boss's rant short. "What's his problem?"

"Four generations of his family worked for Chrysler. Sometimes that skews his perspective on what government should and shouldn't do. Best we get going."

Boss saw Spider out and popped one last beer to chase down the painkillers before going to bed. It would have been interesting to debate the Mitten Men on the federal government. Didn't matter, though, because in a few months, once the militia eliminated most of the incumbents, they'd see the light. Tomorrow was going to be an interesting day. Boss's last decision before falling asleep was to go ahead and accelerate the schedule at the Laughing Loon.

OWEN'S SOLDIERS HAD CONSTRUCTED A makeshift roadblock using brush and downed trees. I rolled down the window as they opened the path. "We're heading to the Iron Mountain airport. Here's one of the guns. There'll just be the two of us now."

"New password for today," one of the guys said, "Snuffleupagus." Everyone got a good laugh.

At the airport, Niki retrieved a package containing her ID. I assumed the FBI sent it and when I asked, she answered by waggling her eyebrows.

While we waited, she put on a full-court press to convince us to leave the U.P. until this imbroglio played itself out. "You two have nothing to prove to anyone," she summarized.

Paddy crossed his arms. "Except ourselves."

Niki hugged Paddy, gave me a quick peck, and proceeded through the screening. Paddy and I watched from the parking lot as her plane took off, plugging our ears at the jet's blast. As soon as we pulled our fingers from our ears, he said. "We've got a stop to make on the way back."

I gave him my patented sideways look.

"Rita Pirhonen lives at the Laughing Loon Senior Care Center in Crystal Falls. She and Jimmie Heitzmann have been talking on the phone a lot over the last few months. Maybe he told her something that might help."

Myriad thoughts roiled my mind. How had Paddy developed this connection? Having never heard of the Laughing Loon Senior Care Center until I looked at the viatical settlement for Bartelle's aunt who lived there, now it had come up a second time.

"Fill in the blanks," I said.

"You found the guy's gun leaning against a tree with his coat? His cell phone was in the coat pocket and I checked his call logs—only one number. I used the internet to get the owner's name and—"

"We don't have internet."

"When Owen showed up last night, I was working on my laptop, which has satellite internet. The number belongs to Rita Pirhonen, who resides at Laughing Loon."

I could only hope he had obtained all the information legally, but the fact that he didn't discuss this until Niki, also known as Federal Agent Pendergast, was no longer around, left me wondering.

TWENTY-FOUR

IN THE LAUGHING LOON VESTIBULE, we shook the rain off our coats and signed the guest register. After getting lost in the hallways reeking of disinfectant, we eventually arrived at Rita Pirhonen's room. She held out her hand first to Paddy and then to me. The strength in her arthritic hands surprised me.

"You're the fella that took in the lady with amnesia?" she asked after we introduced ourselves. She settled us on a couple of rickety dining room chairs and offered something to wet our whistle, all the while sneaking peeks at Paddy's battered face, his head still wrapped in white. I'd gotten used to it and hadn't considered the effect it would have on others. "How awful that someone tried to shoot you folks. The radio says they found the person drowned?"

"Did you hear who the person was?" I asked.

She scratched her head. "Yes, but I don't remember the name."

"Jimmie Heitzmann?" Paddy offered.

She placed her hand in her lap and looked openly at Paddy. "Could be . . . yes, that does sound right. Why did he do it?"

She gave no indication of recognizing the name. This was not what I'd anticipated. "I know this will sound like a weird question, but please bear with me." I flashed her a smile, which I hoped looked comforting. "Did you happen to loan your cell phone to anyone?"

"Oh, dear no. I used to have one. My daughter made me get it when I still lived at home. She insisted I have it in case I fell down, so that I could call for help. Now we have these gadgets." She retrieved a small electrical device attached to a chain around her neck and held it out for us to see. We leaned in to get a good look. "No matter where I am on the property, all I have to do is press the button and the staff can locate me. Now who was I talking with? It seems so long ago. Was it that nice lady they have here . . . what do they call her? . . . the ombudsman. Yes, I think so. The ombudsman. If I never used the cell phone, she said I should turn it in and cancel the contract."

"When was that?" I asked.

Her hands fluttered in front of her and settled again on her lap. "I'm sorry, I don't remember. You young fellas can't imagine how hard it is when you can't remember everything like you used to. Last year sometime?"

Paddy cleared his throat. "Did you return the phone?"

"It had to go to Iron Mountain where I got it. Of course I have no way to do that. One of the deacons from church took it. They have a collection box for old cell phones and another one for eyeglasses. I don't get bills for it, so I'm sure everything's okay."

I traded glances with Paddy. He had tucked his bottom lip under his teeth, a thinking gesture someone once pointed out he had inherited from me.

"Which church?" I asked. "Those church ladies can be such a comfort, can't they?"

"Oh, my yes, they can," she said. "It's the Presbyterian Church here in town. Young man, I'm sorry to be nosy, but it's a privilege of my age. Does it still hurt?"

Leaving Mrs. Pirhonen and Paddy to chat, I used the facilities, which consisted of a commode, shower stall, and pedestal sink. Grab bars decorated all the walls. This wasn't a hospital, but I still made sure to thoroughly wash my hands with antibacterial soap. While I waited for the hot water to get reasonably warm—it never did get hot—I snooped through her medicine cabinet. TV detectives always find something interesting in people's bathrooms. Maybe they know what to look for; I didn't see anything unusual.

FIFTEEN MINUTES BEFORE SUNSET, PADDY and I reached the roadblock. "Snuffleupagus," I said through the opened truck window. "Owen, who came up with these passwords?"

"Grandkids. Oldest one is into dinosaurs and saw a TV special on the Loch Ness Monster. He wants to check all the lakes around here, see if he can find him his own Nessie. Youngest is into Sesame Street. Loves Snuffy."

"You got any other grandchildren?" I asked.

"Not yet. One in the oven, though. We turned some visitors away.

Claimed they come to talk to you. Flashed FBI badges, but wouldn't leave no card. I told them they was on private property and, unless they had a warrant, they wasn't gettin no further. They said they was gonna wait until you returned." Owen indicated with a bob of his head one of the guys who, in response, ejected a stream of tobacco juice through the gap where his front teeth should have been.

The guy towered over Owen, and I realized I'd met him at Long Lake when they pulled out the bodies. "Nice seeing you again," I said.

"You know Bruce?" Owen sounded almost offended that something had happened without his knowing about it. "Bruce started lettin air out of their tire to make sure they stayed. They hightailed it. I'm not sure they were legit. I didn't think them Hoover guys were supposed to swear."

Everyone laughed. I kind of felt bad for whomever Special Agent Whatshisname had ordered up, probably as a response to my hanging up on him. I felt confident I'd see them again.

"Startin tonight," Owen said, penetrating my fog, "we're leaving our trucks down by the Amasa mill and four-wheelin in. Town's already closed their roads to heavy traffic for the duration. The frost is coming up real early with this rain and warm temperatures. Muck'll get so bad on these roads you'll get sucked in up to the runnin boards. Usually gets cold enough for a few days so's the roads freeze at night and you can get out 'fore sunrise. Course, you ain't gonna get in again with anythin bigger than four-wheelers, and not towin no trailer neither. Then, I won't be able to bring in no new supplies. You'll have ta consider headin into town soon."

PADDY PREPARED DINNER WHILE WE still had light on the cabin porch. I restoked the wood stove. My original plans with Abigail had been to stay the winter and leave before mud season. Well, mud season was here with a vengeance, and it was time to "act my age" as my mother would say. My stubborn Irish pride that refused to let me accept help was not a mature response, as evidenced both by Niki's direct arguments and Owen's gentle suggestion.

"Paddy?" I yelled over the knife slapping the cutting board as he chopped carrots for the salad. He jutted out his chin in acknowledgement that he'd heard. "With the roads turning to goop, there's nothing we can do out here. I'm thinking we should head into town. I can arrange for repairs to the house. If we leave early tomorrow while the road's frozen, Owen's guards can follow us out and get back to their lives. We've proved our point."

He deliberately laid the knife on the cutting board. "You trying to get me out of here?"

He'd nailed part of my thinking, but I wasn't going to admit it. "You can stay with me in town if you want, but there's nothing really for you to do."

He picked up the knife and drummed the blade on the table. "Maybe you should hook the trailer to the truck and haul out the ATVs."

"Good idea. Just in case we want to get back in before the roads dry up. Owen will let me store them at his place. He won't even notice they're there with all the junkers decorating his yard."

In the waning light, I donned a headlamp, hooked up the trailer, and discovered Jimmie Heitzmann had stolen the ATV keys the night he tried to kill us.

To avoid breaking the police tape, I used Paddy's method of entering the house and scrambled up the ladder I propped against the railing of the master bedroom deck. The unlocked sliding door yielded to my tug. Besides getting spare keys, I wanted to make sure the repairs were holding with all the rain we'd been having.

The upstairs was unaffected by the attack, but as I walked down the staircase, my legs felt leaden. I crunched broken glass with every step. A broom leaned against the couch next to a small cleared area. One of the workmen had probably started to clean up and the police stopped him. Owen's workers had removed the double-hung windows and stacked them in the kitchen. They cut the OSB to fit into the window frames and, on closer inspection, I realized they had siliconed the heck out of them. They had even filled in the bullet holes on the other side of the house with silicone. Water was not going to get through their repairs.

I grabbed keys from their pegs by the back door and stuck them in my pocket. Sometime later, I found myself slumped in a chair staring at the lake through the wall of windows. Tears streaked my cheeks. I had designed this house, and it was like a child to me. Everything here could be fixed, but its pureness was corrupted. Telling myself it was "only camp" didn't help. I gave into the sobs, realizing the tears were not solely for the losses I had suffered, but for the kindness of strangers. Owen, the old cuss, had gone out of his way to rally his friends to fix my house and now act as guards.

I left the house the way I had come in and replaced the ladder on its hooks behind the garage. After dinner, Paddy worked on his computer. I curled next to the wood stove and read to the sounds of rain pounding on the roof and the hiss of propane lamps. Having made the decision to leave, I felt relaxed. When the book slipped from my hand and clunked to the floor, I called it a day and set the alarm for five a.m.

ALL DAY, BOSS EXPERIENCED AS much anticipation as an elephant in the twenty-second month of pregnancy. It took every scintilla of effort to seem natural on the outside. Whatever the pastor said at church had gone in one ear and out the other. The social hour afterwards had been interminable, with everyone talking about spring breakup coming early this year, maybe winter was over, and wouldn't that be just great, and did Boss know Linda Cather slipped getting out of the bathtub and chipped her elbow, and *blah, blah, blah.*

On the way out the door, Boss learned the cops hadn't let McCree back into his house, which meant they were using the cabin. Digger needed to watch the right structure. Boss begged off lunch, headed straight to camp, and prepared a real Sunday dinner: half a chicken breast, mashed potatoes with gravy, and canned sweet corn. With the meal consumed, dishes washed up and put away, it left plenty of time for a nap that lasted most of the afternoon.

The Mitten Men showed up around ten p.m. and everyone napped again after finalizing the plan with Boss's new information. They scheduled departure for one in the morning so the attack would begin between three-thirty and four, when the guards should be least alert.

The dirt roads were holding up fairly well despite the rain, which had recently morphed to a steady drizzle. At two twenty-five a.m., Spider backed the truck into an old skidder trail a hundred yards past the turn off to Shank Lake. The three warriors, as Boss thought of the group, put on winter camo, donned white packs and, with their assigned weapons, slipped into the woods.

Their GPS allowed them to parallel the road while remaining hidden from it. Twenty-five minutes later, they reached Boss's assigned ambush location. They observed two guards shuffling around behind a makeshift barricade. A whiff of cigarette smoke reached Boss, setting up a desire so strong that the only way to fight it off required clamped teeth, clenched hands, and curled toes. Boss had quit cold turkey, but now wondered why.

Seven minutes later, a four-wheeler *putt-putted* in from the direction of McCree's place. Boss shot Spider a look saying "Where's the truck?"

Spider shrugged. "Swapped the truck for an ATV," he whispered.

The driver made a three-point turn, stopped long enough to steal a cigarette—driving Boss crazy once again—and slowly drove off.

The three synchronized their watches. In whispered consultation they set the assault for as soon after three forty-five as the four-wheeler reappeared. Boss leaned against a tree, taking comfort in its solid feel, and watched the Mitten Men follow their GPS toward McCree's place.

TWENTY-FIVE

Percussive blasts of nearby gunfire woke me from a comfortable sleep next to the wood stove.

"Paddy," I called across the room to the lump still sleeping on the bed, "Get up! No, stay down! Keep below the windows. We need to get out of here."

Squirming loose of the sleeping bag, I reached for my glasses and knocked them skittering across the floor. Ominously, the shooting stopped. I pulled on a T-shirt and felt the tag sticking into my Adam's apple—backwards—left it, and slipped on a wool shirt. Patting the floor softly in front of me, I crawled around until I found the glasses against the far wall.

Paddy tossed me a coat and slithered on the floor to the back window. "Get rifles, Dad." He raised a window and forced the screen, shattering the quiet with the screech of metal on metal. He tumbled outside. I handed him the two rifles and, favoring my injured leg, climbed through the window headfirst.

"Where to?" he whispered.

I patted my pocket and felt relieved at the hard outlines of the keys I had retrieved from the house. "ATVs are our best bet."

We cut down the hill behind the cabin to a small ravine where we came to the head of an old trail we had created years ago. We followed it along a ridge running between the cabin and the house and came out near the vernal pond, which was now filling with snowmelt.

I didn't see anybody near the house. "You cover me and then I'll cover you. I'll run to the corner of the garage. As soon as I get there, you go. Okay?"

He shot me a thumbs-up, stuck his right glove in his pocket, and released the gun's safety. I mirrored his actions.

Mentally counting to three, I took off across the open yard. Fifty feet had never felt farther. With each step, pain shot from my left thigh down to the sole of my foot and up my back to my neck. To avoid screaming once I stopped at the side of the building, I shoved the glove from my pocket into my mouth and bit down hard. The taste and smell of oil and grease nearly caused me to gag, but had the analgesic effect of making me forget about the pain. Around the material I panted quick breaths and waved Paddy on. He kept low to the ground and covered the distance in a fraction of my time.

In a whispered exchange, I insisted I could handle one of the ATVs—my left leg had nothing to do once we were riding. Riding single, we could go faster and, if something happened to one ATV, we had a spare. He agreed, and since I was more adept with the Honda's manual shift; Paddy took the Polaris with its automatic transmission. We slung the rifles over our shoulders and entered the garage.

I was glad I hadn't had time to drive the ATVs onto the trailer. The moment we cranked the ignitions we would give away our position. Maneuvering the ATVs off the trailer would have taken way too much time. Using my left hand's fingers to count down from five, we both cranked the engines when I curled my last finger. The Honda caught immediately, but the Polaris cranked like it wasn't getting gas. I leaned over and pulled out its choke. It burst to life. "Go. Go. Go!" I yelled and off he went.

Roaring up the driveway, I shifted into second, then third. At the turn onto the road, I heard the close-by triple bark of a rifle. From the corner of my eye, I saw muzzle flashes from the intersection of the road and the cabin driveway. As I roared away, I heard two more bursts, and felt something tug my jacket, nearly knocking me off the ride.

BOSS FELT JAUNTY ON THE walk to the truck, sucking on a cigarette stolen from one of the corpses, celebrating the successful attack. As planned, the first burst caught the guy on the four-wheeler. The second got one of the guards before he figured out what had happened. The third target took off like a rabbit. In the night scope, he showed up fine. The third burst nailed him mid-stride, but wasn't a clean kill. Boss walked to the prostrate form, forgot to change from three-shot burst to single shot for the *coup de grâce*, and blew off the back of his head. He was the one with the cigarettes and clearly couldn't use them in whatever afterlife there was.

Once at the truck, Boss locked down the four-wheel-drive mechanism and, before taking off, mumbled a mantra to remember to keep moving through any mud patches, especially since the Mitten Men's tires didn't have aggressive treads. Stop in the wrong spot and they'd be walking out.

The truck slid sideways before trenching through one soft spot. Otherwise, the road held. The truck's headlights caught Digger approaching on a stolen ATV. Boss didn't dare stop the truck in the low area and kept plowing forward. Digger veered off at the last minute, barely avoiding a collision. Dismounting, he ran hell-bent for leather to Boss's side of the truck, yanked open the door, and yelled something Boss could barely hear.

Digger motioned for Boss to remove the earplugs.

"I said, two of 'em got away on ATVs. Spider took one of these yokel's wheels," he inclined his head toward the bodies sprawled under a hemlock, "and is following them." He waved toward the woods away from the lake. "He says you're to drive to where we hid the truck and block the intersection. Nothing gets by you, hear? Hose down anything that gets there before we do. *Comprendé?*"

"What happened?" Boss asked, keeping the exasperation at bay.

"They snuck out the back while I was watching the front. I winged the one. Spider's on their tail. I'll loop around the top and close the trap. Don't sit there like shit on a stick. Git and be useful." Digger ran to the four-wheeler, spun it in a tight circle spitting mud all over Boss, and took off.

Boss's hands shook. One winged; two untouched. This was not what was supposed to happen. All the way to the intersection, Boss muttered threats at Digger and Spider for not getting their job done and killing all three of the people in the cabin. Boss seethed at the insult of being told what to do, not to mention the indignity of the mud shower from Digger.

Boss lost traction and spun wheels going through the trenched-up area, thought the truck was stuck, then felt first one, then two wheels gain traction and pull the truck out. At the intersection, Boss jockeyed the truck perpendicular to the main road on the Amasa side of the junction with Shank Lake Road. Nothing could get by without stopping, and all roads to Amasa went through the intersection Boss now controlled.

From the east came the first hint of dawn.

* * *

I ACCELERATED THE ATV AND tried to catch Paddy. Shank Lake Road came to a dead end at the Net River, and we needed to avoid any traps. In a mile was a cutoff to the other side of the lake. But from there, the only exit not returning us to this side was Lukes Road, which a beaver had flooded last fall. Between the beaver and the current thaw, we had no hope escaping that way. Our only possibility was to outrun them or outfox them by doubling back, because there was no way to successfully cover our tracks. The one advantage I figured I had was a mental map developed over the years of every abandoned road, skidder trail, and path in the vicinity wide enough for an ATV. I caught up to Paddy shortly before an old logging road pushed into the forest. It was our best chance. I motioned for him to take a right.

I had no sooner congratulated myself on picking well when my engine hiccupped. Sounded like a fuel problem. I was sure I had filled both ATV tanks earlier in the week but, leaving nothing to chance, I reached down on the left side and quickly switched the fuel tank to reserve, tapping the bottom gallon of the tank. The engine immediately perked up.

The trail twisted to follow the high ground and, with better suspension on his ATV, Paddy pulled ahead of me. I lost sight of him in the curves and only caught glimpses of him on long straightaways, hunched low to reduce wind resistance. Soon we would come to a T intersection. I sent Paddy a mental image of turning left.

Lowering my head against the wind, I accelerated to catch him and lost ground when I nailed a hole deeper than I anticipated and rooster-tailed through a puddle. Water sprayed the engine and with a hiss, steam bathed both of my legs, warming them well past the point of comfort. Regaining control, I pressed on.

The engine sputtered as though it was running on fumes—much too soon to have depleted the reserve. Was the fuel filter clogged? I used the choke to try to blast out whatever was causing the fuel malfunction and stalled the ATV. It coasted to a stop around a bend. I tried to restart it. And tried again. And again.

No go.

Ahead of me, Paddy roared away.

Behind me, another ATV. Getting closer.

I hopped off my ride and pushed it back into the bend I had just passed. It wasn't much of a plan, but if I could position it at the point where the pursuing ATV would still be going fast, maybe he would run into it or lose control as he swerved to avoid it. Even if he momentarily lost his concentration, I might get the upper hand. I twisted the ATV sideways across the path so it took up more space and looked for a hiding place. In jerking the ATV around, I smelled gas and realized the gas tank had sprung a leak. I cut the lights and removed the gun from the ATV rack. With no night vision, I stumbled around looking for the right place to hide.

This part of the forest consisted mostly of maple, selectively cut maybe twenty years ago, leaving no big trees. No close evergreens to hide in. No big rocks to use as a shield. The best I could do was position myself on the inside of the curve, away from where the pursuer would be looking as he rounded the bend. I closed my eyes to help redevelop night vision and listened to the oncoming ATV.

The simplest thing would be to shoot whoever followed me. The thought of pulling the trigger brought a flashback of the man I had killed when he and an accomplice invaded my Cincinnati house. I did not need more nightmares. I knew I would kill if it was the only way; but maybe I could use the rifle as a club and knock him out before he realized what was happening. If they were riding tandem . . .

Something in the sound of the various ATVs caught my attention. The one chasing me was still coming on. Paddy's was also growing louder as he headed back toward me. I judged the sounds of Paddy's machine and the guy following us—it was going to be close who would get to me first.

Paddy did. He screeched on his brakes and stopped a few feet short of hitting my stalled ATV. "Dad?" he yelled.

"Turn around. I'll hop on," I yelled.

I remained in ambush until he finished maneuvering. The other ATV was almost on us. I grabbed my rifle, limped to Paddy and struggled onto his machine. My left leg now ached with any movement. Before I settled in, Paddy accelerated, slamming my butt onto the ATV and jarring the rifle loose from my grip.

Paddy returned to the intersection where I had hoped he would turn left; his tracks went right. So much for father–son telepathy. I tapped him on the arm and pointed left. This could work to our advantage: if our pursuer wasn't a tracker, he might waste time following the wrong tracks until he discovered Paddy had turned around. At the next intersection, I motioned for Paddy to stop. With his ATV idling, I tried to determine if we were still being followed. No clue; we were too loud. I gave Paddy's shoulder another pat and off we went deeper into the woods.

Wherever we had choices, I pointed Paddy toward the direction I wanted, mentally tracking where we were. I tried for the roughest possible trails while avoiding dead ends. Most of the time, we traveled less than fifteen miles an hour over rock-strewn trails. Although predawn lightened the woods, Paddy continued to steer by the high-beam headlamp.

We finally reached a Y from which we could take the offensive. A mix of pine, hemlock, and balsam grew close to the trail. The evergreens dampened sound, blocked light, and provided a secure hiding place. The two old skidder trails bowed away from each other for three-quarters of a mile before hitting a decent gravel road. From here we could run down one path to the gravel road and cut back on the second trail. We'd ditch the ATV about a quarter mile in and walk through the woods to the first path to set an ambush—assuming he had crashed into my disabled ATV and was far enough behind so we could implement the plan. Once we disabled him, we could make a mad dash down the main road to Amasa and get help.

Time was of the essence. I pointed in the direction I wanted Paddy to take and yelled in his ear, "Goose it!"

Twenty-Six

WE HUDDLED NEXT TO A steep, rocky section of the trail—a place where our pursuer would have to go slowly. Young balsam firs grew densely and hid us from sight. If either Paddy or I had MacGyver's skills, we could have constructed some device to unseat our pursuer as he ATVed by. Without those talents, we ended up in a whispered shouting match, which sounds like an oxymoron, but isn't. We gesticulated, our faces turned red, we said things I later wished we hadn't, and finally I uttered a parent's last resort: *because I said so.* I briefly wondered if those were Custer's last words.

"Fine," Paddy fiercely whispered after I had laid down my parental trump card. "We won't shoot him as he drives by." He yanked the stout branch I had found away from me and ran to the ambush site. I limped behind, each step accompanied by pain sharp enough to take my breath away. When I finally caught up to him he said, "With your leg, you have no prayer of running up and knocking him off his ATV as he goes by. If that's our so-called plan, then I'll do it." He held out his rifle. "If that doesn't work, are you going to be able to pull the trigger?"

Once I caught my breath, I replied. "I already told you. Of course I can . . . and will, if I have to. This isn't like some video game, Paddy. There's no reset button to resurrect the dead."

"I got the point," he said. "Just make sure you hit the right one of us. Here he comes."

The oncoming ATV downshifted at the base of the hill, its engine whining as he maneuvered around and over the rocks in a series of short bursts. Paddy grasped the four-foot-long stave at the end, flexing his fingers like a baseball player waiting for the pitcher to read the signal from the catcher.

Through the trees, I saw a hint of green as the ATV canted toward us while climbing a particularly large rock. Paddy sprang from our hiding place and with a yell modeled on *Braveheart,* swung the limb at the pursuer's exposed neck. A last rock raised the ATV and the blow caught our attacker high on his right shoulder with a muffled thud. Combined with the rider's lean to the left, it was sufficient to knock him off the four-wheeler.

Paddy was right about my leg; it nearly collapsed as I rose to cover them with the rifle. The good news was the guy was unarmed; his rifle was still strapped to the ATV. The bad news was the guy was agile. He came off the ground, and entered a crouch, holding a long blade low, as knife fighters do. So much for being unarmed. I aimed the rifle, but Paddy was moving quickly and I couldn't be sure whom I would hit. I pointed the barrel away from both of them and fired a shot.

Paddy knew I had a gun. He flinched but continued his attack. The shot startled the guy for a fraction of a second—enough for Paddy to start a second swing with the tree limb. The guy leaned away from the blow, but Paddy's actual target was the guy's knife hand. Like a batter tracking a curveball, Paddy adjusted his swing and nailed the hand with a sickening smack. Paddy's follow-through pulled him off balance.

The knife spun into the mud. The guy howled. Instead of grabbing his injured hand he sprang forward and knocked Paddy down, sat on top of him and pounded Paddy's head with his good hand. I grabbed the rifle by the barrel and slammed the stock into his back below his shoulder blades.

Even though his winter coat lessened the impact, the blow reverberated in my arms. As I brought the rifle back for a second try, he turned his head and his mouth formed a perfect "O." If he made any sound, I didn't hear it. I swung again, aiming for the same spot. Paddy heaved to shake off his opponent, and the gunstock slammed into the small of the guy's back, knocking him to the ground.

I brought the rifle above my head to slam it down on the man's knee if he moved, but he didn't. His face showed a frozen scream, his eyes rolled up into his head, his arms shook like he had a seizure.

"You okay, Paddy?" I called over my shoulder.

"Do you think my insurance will cover two broken noses in the same week?"

If he could joke, he was okay. "How's your head?"

"You kidding me? I'll match a McCree hard head to this guy's knuckles any day, but I'm having trouble seeing because of the pain from this nose. Take a look."

Using the ATV's headlights for illumination, I used snow to clear away the blood. His nose was off kilter again and streaming blood. Otherwise, he only had some minor scrapes and bruises. While keeping an eye on our attacker I went through the how-many-fingers routine with Paddy. No concussion. "This is going to hurt," I said. "I'm going to pack your nose with snow to stop the bleeding."

Paddy yowled in anguish during my ministrations. I wasn't cut out to be a doctor: I hated causing Paddy pain, even though I knew what I was doing would lessen future complications. Of course, most doctors don't work on their own kids.

Once his tears stopped he asked, "Now what do we do with this jerk?"

"No way can we take him with us. I'll tie his hands behind him with the elastic thingie from the waist of his jacket. Then we'll take his shoes and socks to make it hard for him to travel."

Paddy paced to ease his pain. "I could whack him on the head with the rifle. That would keep him put for a while." At my glowered disapproval he added, "It was just an idea."

I patted the guy down and found no other weapons or identification. After flipping him face down, I secured his hands behind his back and flipped him back.

From his eyes, I could tell he was in shock. His spasms had stopped but he moaned low, like a cow with indigestion. Paddy sat on his chest while I removed his shoes and socks. Pulling off the last sock, I accidentally scratched him. His foot showed no reaction.

Molten rock filled my stomach.

I pinched the foot. The other foot. Right leg. Left leg. Right arm and he finally flinched.

I spewed last night's dinner like an exploding volcano. Acid burned up my throat and left a vitriolic taste in my mouth.

"What?" Paddy asked.

"Oh my God." I heaved a second time. "I broke his back. He's paralyzed." His running away was not an issue. I rinsed my mouth with snow. Once I stopped shaking, I put his socks and shoes back on as gently as I could. "We need to leave right now." I said to Paddy's back.

Paddy said, "You'll have to drive. I can't see very well. Another ATV's somewhere nearby. I can hear it."

I forced myself to look at the guy on the ground. "We'll bring help as soon as we can."

He stared at the bluing sky and said nothing.

* * *

Boss shifted from foot to foot, needing to pee something fierce. TV cops on stakeout drink endless coffee and never have to go. This wasn't TV and pressure was building. Sure as shoot pull down a zipper and someone would arrive at the intersection.

For a time, when the wind was right, Boss caught a whisper of ATVs, but for the last half an hour had heard nothing more than trees clicking their upper branches together, castanets in the breeze. *Enough already.* Boss turned from the wind to avoid any unpleasantness and was readjusting the zipper when the weak buzz of an engine came from somewhere up the A Grade. Boss rested the gun barrel on the top of a large flat rock, released the safety, and put the gun into full automatic mode. Dawn would arrive in half an hour so visibility was improving, but it wasn't like anyone could really see anything. At least the rain had finally stopped. Boss peered through the scope and listened as the motor grew steadily louder.

Headlights appeared, running fast down the road. Boss treated the light like a sprinting deer, adjusted for its speed and gave a long burst. One headlight shattered and the vehicle jerked right and left before slowing to a stop. The remaining headlight glowed like a Cyclops. *Cripes, I forgot to replace the darn earplugs. I can't hear a thing.*

Boss thought about hosing it down a second time but spotted no movement. From this distance, it looked like one body was crumpled onto the handlebars and a second flung backwards over the back rack. Boss trotted around in a victory dance, sounding like some TV version of Indian warriors.

Bartelle had forced himself to go to bed by eleven thirty on Monday night and surprised himself by catching five hours of sleep. The case was his for three more hours, until the scheduled conference with the FBI, DEA, ICE—the Immigrations and Customs Enforcement arm of Homeland Security—and God only knew who else would horn in on this mess. Then the power scramble would begin and, with all those initials involved, the chances of the Iron County Sheriff's office retaining control were about zero.

Tex—who had taken a shine to the new nickname—plunked into the chair, pushed a fresh mug of coffee in Bartelle's direction, and tossed a couple packs of blue sweetener across the desk.

"Give me the short version," Bartelle said, "and save the details for the official report." He dumped the chemicals into his coffee, realized Tex had not brought a spoon, and stirred the brew with his finger. "Hot. Hot. Hot." He sucked the finger until the tingling stopped. "Who killed who?"

"Three of Owen's buddies died near the intersection of Shank Lake and Lukes Road. We think it was probably one shooter, based on where we found casings. Ballistics will confirm. Owen's other two friends were killed at a barricade they had set up near the edge of McCree's property. Casings there are from a different caliber weapon. Those match the shells in the gun we found strapped to the ATV in the woods next to the guy with the spider tattoo. He died from a stab wound to the chest.

"I got to give the state crime lab boys in Marquette credit, they are all over this. They just called in a preliminary analysis: the single fingerprint on that rifle belongs to a William Bell—Spiderman."

"So Spiderman killed the two guys and someone else killed the first three?" Bartelle asked.

"We found Spiderman-type shells of the same caliber on the road near the driveway to McCree's little log cabin, so looks like he killed Owen's two guards, fired after the McCrees, and then chased them. Then the McCrees ambushed him in the woods."

Bartelle blew on the coffee and took a slug, felt the warmth slide all the way to his stomach. "Fingerprints on the knife?"

Tex shook his head. "Handle was wiped clean on Spiderman's shirt. There's something else weird: one of the ATVs is missing. Each of Owen's guys brought his own, and we know where all but one of them is."

Bartelle motioned with his hands, asking for more.

"So there has to be three of them—at least. Someone drove away in the missing ATV—someone different from whoever got Spiderman's truck stuck in the mud on Bone Lake Road since there were no ATV tracks in that area. The truck VIN, which sported stolen tags, gave us Bell's name. We pulled his license and the photo matched the stiff. Once we had the name, the lab pulled his prints from the state's records to do the preliminary match. Back to the truck: we can follow its tracks the nine, ten miles from McCree's place. And we only got one set of footprints walking away from the mud wallow."

"Prints in the truck?" Bartelle asked.

"Lots. Gonna take the latent print boys time for those."

"So at least three perps, two of whom got away."

"So far." Tex stretched his arms above his head. "We lost the trail of the truck driver in a swampy area a ways from the truck. We got tracking dogs coming in. Maybe we'll luck out and find the guy has a nearby camp."

"But you don't think so?" Bartelle finished his coffee. Last caffeine this morning or he'd start twitching.

"Anyone with a nearby camp would know not to travel Bone Lake Road after the frost starts coming out. It's a sink hole."

"Think about it," Bartelle said. "These are the same jerks we pull from the lakes each year 'cause they're sure the ice is thick enough to drive their trucks on. It's early spring. He might have thought he could make it."

Tex stood up and paced the room. "We're missing something and I don't think a hundred federales descending on us Northwoods doofuses are going to turn it up. Spiderman was from downstate and had an old record, but he's been clean the last decade. His weapon was top notch, fully automatic. It doesn't look like killing a lot of people caused these guys a lick of concern. It's like the U.P. has become the US–Mexico border."

"Like a drug war? That could explain the DEA's involvement. Sure would be nice if they'd told us something before . . ." Bartelle leaned back in his chair and went into his head-scratching routine. "Are you saying you think McCree is involved somehow? Could he be financing a drug deal?"

"I don't know what I'm saying." Tex flopped back into the chair, which squeaked in protest. "Except we're missing something big. What do you want me to do next? Yesterday, the lab sent the results from the burnt cabin. I can review them or—"

"I don't give a darn about that stuff. I want to nail the missing killers. Work on the weapons. Get all the ballistics right and tell me what kind of gun we're missing. Let me know first thing if the trackers come up with something. Push the state lab on the latents from the truck."

Tex got up to go. "Yes, Sir."

"Wait. I'm about to interview McCree. Has anyone backtracked his movements?"

"It's like he said: they kept the ATV off the main roads and followed a succession of logging roads, skidder trails, and even did some cross-country travel to get around locked gates and such until they hit Tracy Creek Road, which they took to US 141. Couldn't track them once they hit pavement, but it's not too far from there to the gas station in Covington where they made the phone call and waited for us to pick them up."

"Why didn't they go directly to Amasa?" Bartelle asked.

"Claims they heard another ATV heading down the A Grade so they went the other way. I gotta say Sarge, I'll bet the coroner determines McCree did break Spiderman's back, and the guy either didn't want to live a cripple or he didn't want to go back to jail. Who knows? He shoves the knife high into his chest cavity and gets a major artery."

"Why not just slit his throat?'

"You know most suicides don't cut through clothing?" Tex said. "This guy unzipped his jacket, unbuttoned his shirt, and pushed up his undershirt to get to bare skin."

"You sure McCree—the father, that is—doesn't know that fact too?" Bartelle glanced at his watch. "Nothing to say he didn't make it look like a suicide. That Cincinnati homicide lieutenant told us he's killed up close and personal."

"I know you had to arrest him and his kid, just in case, but—"

"Actually, jail is the only place I can be sure McCree is safe, and it allows us to stick a guard outside his kid's hospital room. If they did it, we got 'em locked up. If they didn't, at least they're protected. It'll be the DA's call."

"Sweet. That's why *you're* wearing the stripes. Anyway, I didn't see anything at the various crime scenes to contradict anything McCree said, except he mentioned hearing a burst of gunfire not too long after they had ambushed the Spider guy. We can't match that with anything. At least not yet. I kinda think McCree's on the up and up. He's too nice to have done this."

"Everyone said the same thing about Bernie Madoff."

Twenty-Seven

BEFORE BREAKFAST, A DEPUTY ESCORTED me from my cell in the Iron County jail, where I had spent the night, past the monitoring station and into the interrogation room: drab concrete walls, drab carpeting, four drab chairs arranged around a drab table. This room could depress Little Mary Sunshine. All that was missing was the one-way mirror, although it was equipped with a camera hanging from the ceiling, and I'm sure it was wired for sound. "Coffee?" he asked.

"I appreciate the offer, but I'm fine, thanks. You know anything about how my son is doing?"

"Sorry." He shut the door behind him. I waited a long time before my first interrogators showed up, my mind wrapped around Paddy's welfare. ICE marched in. They had names. They had badges. They had attitudes. They played good cop/bad cop.

I had innocence—which isn't everything it's cracked up to be—and silence, which is more powerful than most people imagine.

Bad Cop finished his final tirade with, "If you think we can't make you disappear until you talk, you got another thing coming."

I smiled because I would have said I had 'another think coming.' Ain't language grand?

"I'll wipe that grin off your face," Bad Cop snarled and raised his hand as if to strike me. Good Cop hustled him from the room.

"My partner's right. We can keep you under wraps until you tell us what we need to know," Good Cop said. "We really do need your help. Aren't you a patriot?"

Silence.

He patted a four-inch binder. "We know everything there is to know about you . . . and your family. Your father was a decorated police officer. What would he think about your refusal to help us?"

I would have loved to see what was really in that binder, but his sharing was unlikely. "Since it's been more than an hour and you might have early Alzheimer's, I'll repeat what I said when you first introduced yourselves.

I'll be happy to help in any way I can after I have conferred with my legal counsel. In case you missed it in English class, the word 'after' means the other event comes first. Legal counsel first, talking with—"

"We told you, that Miranda shit doesn't apply to us. People like you make me sick," Good Cop said as he packed the binder into his briefcase. "Think freedom has no cost, and when they're inconvenienced the tiniest little bit, they go crying to the ACLU."

He slammed the door behind him.

Five minutes later, FBI AIC Cooper walked in. Polished shoes, starched white shirt, rep tie, blue pinstriped suit, Hoover haircut. He enthroned himself in the chair opposite me and leaned into the intervening space poking a finger at my nose.

"I heard you're not talking until you get a lawyer. Fine with me, I'll do the talking. Number one: you hung up on me. Number two: you had a bunch of yahoos prevent us from getting to your house. We're filing obstruction of justice charges against them. Depends on you whether we include you in those charges, starting right now."

"I'll be sure to pass on your expressions of contempt to the families who are mourning the deaths of your so-called yahoos. Were you born an asshole or did you have to work at it?"

"You think you're some kind of hot shit, don't you? Listen up, McCree. If you ever mention our agent's name or anything about our agent's operation to anyone other than an authorized Federal Bureau of Investigation agent, we will charge you and your son with various and sundry felonies. Got it, shithead?"

I did not reply.

After a long bit of silence passed between us, AIC Cooper said, "You should convince your equally stubborn son to tell us how he hacked our computers. If he cooperates, we'll consider reducing the additional charges we're filing against him. And if you don't, we'll add you as a co-conspirator."

So Paddy had sufficiently recovered from the rhinoplasty that the doctors had allowed the cops to talk to him. Was he still in the Iron Mountain hospital where the surgery took place or back in Iron County sharing the jail with me?

AIC Cooper blathered on, but I didn't pay attention. I spent the time trying to understand why ICE and the FBI were so antagonistic. I could have as profitably spent my time wondering when the next meteorite would crash into the earth. My mother, while she still spoke, referred to such questions as "imponderables." After I gave up trying to understand their attitudes, I again obsessed about how Paddy was holding up.

Cooper eventually ran out of steam and left with one last shot: "You're on my list until the day you die."

The two DEA agents were real chums by comparison. They asked me if it was alright to look through a ton of photographs of mostly Hispanic-looking men and women. I gave it an honest effort, but didn't recognize anyone. They left without threats—or thank-yous.

A new sheriff's deputy escorted me to my cell. "Do you know where my son is?" I asked.

"We're not allowed to talk to one inmate about another . . ." He paused for what I took as an internal debate and then continued. "My son? I'd want to know. I'll see what I can do."

BOSS HADN'T FELT THIS SORE since losing a bull-riding dare in college. Everything hurt. Dragging that damned ATV off the road and hiding it deep in the woods with Digger's body was bad. He should have known better than to drive down the road, especially with a bundle attached to the back rack that in poor light looked like a passenger. No way Boss could have walked the twenty-five miles home after getting the truck stuck in the mud on Bone Lake Road. Damned lucky the camp near Four Corners Boss chose to hide out at until darkness had a bonus: parked in the woodshed so flimsy a child could have broken in was a fueled-up ATV with a key sitting in the ignition. Even so, it was midnight by the time Boss got home after burying the clothes and the rifle in a shallow pit carved from the frozen earth on land Hematite National Bank owned.

Fortunately, Boss's first appointment was the noon Tuesday prayer meeting at the church. The only topic of discussion was the horrific attack up in the woods. Two of the congregation's own were among the dead. Boss damn near lost it after a deputy's wife reported the girl hadn't even been at the cabin. No one knew where she was. Boss covered the shock by leading a fervent prayer for all the local families.

After the meeting, the pastor's wife pulled Boss aside. "Where were you last night? I tried to get hold of you to organize the deacons to take care of meals for the two families. You always do a good job."

"Traveling," Boss muttered. "Didn't get home until real late."

"I left you several messages," the witch continued. "I was worried that maybe with your cancer, you'd taken a turn for the worse. How are you feeling? You look worn out."

One more comment about my health, and I'll wear myself out kicking you from here to kingdom come. "Sorry. By the time I heard them, I assumed you had contacted one of the other deacons."

"Well, I was sure you'd get back to me . . ."

Boss glared at her; she faded to quiet with a flutter of helpless hands. Was no one capable of doing anything right? Did Boss have to do everything? Boss sighed, "I'll take care of it this afternoon. Have the funerals been set yet?"

"There was talk about a single combined funeral, but the priest insisted on a mass and our folks don't want that . . ." The pastor's wife gave Boss's arm a tender squeeze. "These are terrible times. Bless you. Bless you, for all your good work." She scurried off.

Boss watched the little ferret disappear. Terrible times indeed. It was hard to understand what Pastor saw in the woman. Maybe she was a tornado in the sack.

Boss grabbed a pad of paper, wrote the two dead guys' names on the top with a vertical line separating them, and scribbled the days of the week down the left with slots for lunch and dinner. Best way to fill in this chart was to appeal directly to the women of the church. Since several of them were related to local law enforcement, a little face-to-face social conversation should draw out whatever the cops knew.

Before starting the rounds, Boss needed to cancel several afternoon meetings at the bank and grab one of those energy drinks so popular with the kids.

Time to do some more good work for God and Country.

NO ONE DISPUTES THE FACT that a few citizens of Crystal Falls stole the court papers from Iron River in 1887. Three years later an election of dubious integrity determined Crystal Falls, and not Iron River, would be the county seat. Given the shaky foundation of justice, I wasn't surprised that the Iron County Courthouse, built of quarried stone, looked directly down the main business street of Crystal Falls and showed Iron River its backside.

An underground tunnel led from the jail to the courthouse, where we took an elevator to the second floor. I entered the courtroom through a set of double wooden doors. With its high ceilings and multitudinous windows, the radiators clacked in their effort to warm the room. The sheriff's deputy steered me to the jury room where I met my new lawyer. Irene Frankle hailed from Traverse City, six plus hours away from Crystal Falls.

"Thanks for coming," I said. "I know it's far for you, but I couldn't think of anyone to call except Leroy Patterson . . . you know, since I had used him in Cincinnati? I thought he could find someone local."

She waited until I settled into my chair before taking her seat. Dressed in a gray checked skirt and jacket, starched white blouse with a colorful scarf, sensible low heels, her most striking feature was the silver dreadlocks. They ran halfway down her back, each one tipped with a string of colored beads that clicked like rosary beads every time she moved. "Leroy and I go back a long, long way. He spoke highly of you, and he knew I'm bored to death in retirement. Now let's discuss what's going to happen this morning."

WE HAD ONLY A FEW minutes before the court clerk called my name. Still shackled, I shuffled past the railing and up two steps. Irene and I took our places at the left-hand table facing the bench. The county prosecutor, a WASP in every sense of the word, sat at the right-hand bench with a pile of folders in front of him and cast a series of side-glances at Irene. I was willing to bet the courtroom had never seen the likes of her, and internally I smiled. The bald judge bent over the papers the prosecutor had given to the clerk, who had passed them to the judge.

The judge informed me of the charges: open murder, various classes of assault, riding an off-road vehicle without a helmet, riding an off-road vehicle on a paved road, operating an off-road vehicle with an unhelmeted passenger. "In Michigan," Irene whispered, "open murder means the jury decides between first and second degree murder."

"How do you plead?"

Irene said, "Not guilty to the open murder and assault charges, Your Honor. Not guilty by reason of insanity to the three ORV charges."

The judge furrowed his brow. "Reason of insanity?"

"Yes, Your Honor. The prosecutor must be insane to bring those charges. It makes a mockery of our judicial system. When the newspapers—"

The judge banged his gavel once and the tittering behind us stopped. "Such antics, Ms. Frankle, may be tolerated elsewhere, but not in this court."

"Yes, Your Honor." Irene said with all the contriteness of a kindergartener caught feeding her brussels sprouts to the family dog under the table. She remained standing, but motioned for me to sit down, which I did.

"Something else?" the judge asked.

"Can you imagine a jury around here convicting my client of the ORV charges?" Irene said. "People were shooting at him. Who in their right mind would take the time to put on a helmet? Would you tell your son, when someone was trying to kill him, that he had to walk because it was illegal to ride double? Puh-lease."

I covered my mouth. The judge's eyes twinkled while he tried to hold a stern face. "I'll look forward to your arguments—at the proper time. Am I clear, Ms. Frankle, or will you be making a donation to the county because of a contempt charge?"

"Crystal clear." She took her time sitting down.

The judge set the preliminary hearing a week hence. The proceedings turned to bail. Not surprisingly, the prosecutor insisted I was a grave flight risk and the court should deny bail. We, of course, thought personal recognizance was sufficient. The judge decided a million dollars would split the difference.

I whispered to Irene, "As long as Paddy's isn't any higher, I won't need a bail bondsman. I can cover it all with mutual funds."

She dipped her head to show she understood. "Excuse me, Your Honor," Irene said after the judge dismissed us. "Could the prosecutor inform us when he plans to hold the arraignment for Mr. McCree's son? Assuming the charges are the same, we are going to have the same issues— other than the issue of insanity—regarding bail. I'd like to start arranging for the release of both my clients."

The judge glared his disapproval of her sneaking in the word insanity, then directed his gaze at the prosecutor. "Is there some reason you are separating these cases?"

"The son may not be released from the hospital early enough to get to court today."

"I don't understand, Your Honor," Irene said. "I was at the hospital two hours ago talking with my client. The doctor told me he could release young Mr. McCree whenever the county provided the necessary forms." She gave the prosecutor her brightest smile.

The prosecutor flushed. "I'll have to check, Your Honor."

The judge leaned forward and peered over his half glasses. "Good idea. I'll expect an answer."

ORANGE WAS NOT MCCREE'S COLOR. "Could you please unshackle him?" Bartelle asked the sheriff's deputy standing outside the interview room.

"We'll be monitoring the room if you need us," the deputy said and shut the door, leaving Bartelle and McCree sitting on opposite sides of the table.

"Where to start?" Bartelle mused.

"The beginning is usually a good place," McCree said.

Bartelle felt a smile crinkle his face. Totally inappropriate, since there was nothing to smile about. "Fair enough. I owe you an apology. If I had trusted you from the beginning, maybe we both wouldn't be in this room." He swept his arm to encompass the room from corner to corner. "Your boss at Criminal Investigations Group, Robert Rand, called today." Bartelle watched McCree and saw a quick widening of his eyes—he hadn't known. "He offered me the complete resources of CIG. If you ever need a character witness, he'd be a good one."

"Let me guess: you're stuck being Mr. Nice Guy to offset Special-Agent-in-Charge Cooper's sparkling personality?"

"Caught me. He does have the personality of a chunk of magnetite. ICE, the FBI, and the DEA are sorting out the power struggle right now. While it's still my case, can we talk, or do you need your lawyer?"

"She's with Paddy, but she told me I could discuss anything prior to the most recent attack. We're as anxious to get to the bottom of this as anyone."

"So why not talk with any of the other agencies?"

"That was before I met with counsel. Besides, they were more interested in telling me how tough they were than understanding what happened."

Bartelle kept a smile off his face. "In response to the request we placed on the radio, we got a call," he flicked open his pocket notebook and rifled through the pages, "from a Mrs. Rita Pirhonen at the Laughing Loon. She happens to be next-door neighbor to my aunt. She said you and your son paid her a visit over the weekend?"

"What have you learned about my son?"

"He's still in a lot of pain, but he's going to be fine."

"Not what I meant," McCree said, his voice filled with exasperation. "What have the Feds told you about his background?"

Bartelle didn't understand the frustration he heard and thought the question odd. After reflection he didn't see any reason not to answer. "Seamus Patrick McCree goes by his middle name. No arrests or warrants prior to yesterday. One of the founding members of a company called LT2P Network Solutions located in Evanston, Illinois. You sit on their board. Earlier this year, it rejected an acquisition offer from IBM, which would have made the founders all rich. He lives in Chicago with some woman whose name I do not remember. Was there something specific you were going for?"

McCree closed his eyes, scrunched his mouth to the left, drummed his fingers on the metal table. "They tell you what LT2P does?" Bartelle shook his head. "They test computer network security, primarily for banks. They make big bucks trying to hack into banks' computers. You can imagine IBM would not want to buy them if they weren't successful."

Bartelle considered the information. "This relates to your conversation with Mrs. Pirhonen?"

McCree raised his eyebrows.

Bartelle considered the hinted implications. He scraped his chair onto its two hind legs, the sound echoing off the harsh white walls, and crooked his arm over his head to scratch his ear. "I think we can work out something your counsel will find satisfactory."

Twenty-Eight

BOSS WATCHED THE ACTIVITY IN the president's office with growing concern. Sergeant Bartelle, holding a piece of paper in his hand, had marched into that office five minutes after the bank's doors opened Wednesday morning. A mop-haired kid from IT soon followed with a fistful of computer paper. Two minutes after that, Bartelle left with the computer paper under his arm and a smile plastered on his face. The kid remained inside.

Checking the president's calendar on Outlook, Boss could see he had canceled a meeting with one of the bank's troubled logging firms in order to make room for Bartelle, which meant it was important. What was Bartelle looking for at the bank? Boss went through every step of the operation. There were no connections between Hematite Bank and the militia. Boss stood and paced the room while listening to "Telephone Time." Some caller was speculating about the week's killings. No news.

In the middle of a step, it hit Boss: the only nexus with the bank was the extra account used to pay the cell phone bill registered in Mrs. Pirhonen's name. Boss willed the kid to leave the office. A minute later, he did. Boss did a fake saunter to the president's office and closed the door with a rattle that shook the walls.

"What the hell did Bartelle want?" Boss demanded.

The president waved to a seat in front of his desk. "Hello, Mother, it's wonderful to see you today. Won't you make yourself comfortable?"

Boss hated her son treating her with orchestrated politeness. She still owned a majority of the shares. She had a right to know. Boss shot him a look only a mother could give. "Well?"

"He had a court order to obtain all the information we had on one account. I can't imagine what for. As near as I can tell, the account was only used to pay a cell phone bill every month. Cash deposits covered the bill. The average balance was only ten bucks. I shudder to think how much money it cost us to maintain that account, especially since the account holder has other accounts with us. I don't know why this one wasn't linked to those. While Sergeant Bartelle was here, we checked the depositor's other accounts: she rarely withdraws cash and never on the same day as the deposits. Very peculiar. I've asked IT to determine which employee opened the account so we can get to the bottom of this."

He spun the papers around and pushed them to her side of the desk.

Of course she knew what she would be looking at, but made a show of flipping through the pages. Each one felt heavy as a stone tablet. She knew they would eventually discover a now-retired employee had opened the account for Mrs. Pirhonen. Once a month, the same retiree recorded a cash deposit for the account. "Mrs. Pirhonen is a resident at the Laughing Loon," Boss said. "She seems to have lucid days and some . . ." She waggled her hand to emphasize the not-so-lucid days. "I've been up at the Loon to talk to her about some investment opportunities. I don't believe I've seen her in the bank in years. You said it pays a phone bill? Maybe one of her family members keeps the account live. You know how things can get screwed up with families and older relatives." Boss shook her head at the sadness of the elderly starting to lose it.

Her son pulled the file back to his side of the desk. "I'll have someone check into this and see if we can't merge it with one of her other accounts." He checked his watch. "We've got those Sunset Hills developers coming in to try to renegotiate their loan, and with this morning's folderol, I'm running behind."

Boss took the hint. It was time to strategize. Bartelle had done a lot of work in a short time if he had come up with the bank account. They obviously discovered the phone number after Jimmie's death—how no longer mattered—and got the information from the phone company. If they subpoenaed the phone company they could also get all the numbers Boss had called or received using Mrs. Pirhonen's phone. It had been good while it lasted. Boss needed to alert her militia contact to destroy his phone, and when she got to camp, she needed to get rid of Mrs. Pirhonen's.

Boss settled into her office chair and turned off the constant chatter of "Telephone Time" to consider the ramifications of this latest news. The firewall she had constructed between various components of the plan was doing its job. Contact with the biochemist had only been through email, and she couldn't see any reason to change the scheduled delivery from Sunday at Da Yooper Tourist Trap in Ishpeming. What she needed were some throwaway phones. A smile twitched her face.

* * *

Wausau, Wisconsin was three hours away. No one knew her there, and most people in these parts thought of traveling to Green Bay before they would consider heading to Wausau. On the outskirts of town she spotted a Mom-and-Pop store for one of the phone companies. By way of explanation, she mentioned to the kid tending the counter—hardly looked professional with studs in both nostrils and purple hair—something about purchasing throwaways for each of her six grandkids. At a nearby park, Boss used one to leave a message for her militia contact in the Mitten, telling him to pitch his phone and call her on the second of her six phones. She left the first phone sitting on a picnic table for whomever happened to find it.

With the third phone, she called the facilities manager at the Laughing Loon. She told him a sob story about the plumbing firm they used getting a big job at the "Soo" that had to start exactly on April 1. They would have to refuse it unless they could reschedule the Laughing Loon for an earlier date because, after all, the deal with the Laughing Loon came first.

The manager couldn't be more accommodating, especially after Boss mentioned a 10% discount for his inconvenience. He never asked why she was doing the calling. The manager confirmed the new appointment for eight in the morning, in exactly seven days.

Boss disposed of that phone at a McDonald's in Rhinelander. *Money well spent. Yes siree, Bob.*

I had expected Paddy and I would be released on bail sometime late Thursday or early Friday since it would take that long to provide the combined two-million-dollar security, so I wasn't surprised when the sheriff's deputy came for me Thursday afternoon. I was surprised, however, when we ended up in the courthouse. Paddy and Irene Frankle were sitting in the first row of courtroom benches, heads together in whispered conversation. Paddy's legs were also free of restraints.

I sat on Frankle's other side. My orange did not clash with her severe charcoal suit, but it rioted with the batik scarf she wore over her dreads. "What's up?" I asked. The guard took the bench behind me.

"All rise," the clerk intoned as the judge stepped from behind the black fabric screen. I peeked at the clock—four forty-one p.m.

The actors in the drama of the State of Michigan against Seamus Anselm McCree and Seamus Patrick McCree took their places on center stage. The assistant prosecutor, a young woman with sloped shoulders and strands of honey-colored hair escaping the clip at the nape of her neck, rose and reported they wished to drop all charges against each of the defendants. In a television show, this would have been a dramatic scene with crowds of reporters rushing to text in their story. Here, the judge looked up from the papers the clerk had placed in front of him and in a monotone said, "Please share with the court the reasons for the prosecutor's sudden reversal of himself."

Without a glance in our direction the assistant prosecutor fell on her sword while trying mightily to justify the original decision. Police had discovered yet another body with the missing ATV. At this time, there was insufficient evidence.

I tuned out the rest of what she said. *Who else had died?*

We traded orange garb for the clothes we were arrested in, and after Irene paid our $12 booking fee and $30-per-day room and board, we were free men. "Let's grab a bite to eat at Generations," she said. "We have a couple of things to discuss."

It felt good to walk without shackles shortening my stride and clinking at every step. The day was unseasonably warm with temperatures in the upper forties. I pointed my face to the sun and soaked in the rays on the two-block walk down Superior Avenue to the restaurant. We settled into a booth, Paddy and I on one side, Irene on the other. Half the patrons wore their Sunday best. It struck me they must have come here from a memorial service. My mouth dried up and tasted like I had eaten ash.

After we ordered a pizza to share, Irene said, "The police have released your house as a crime scene. After we eat, I can run you up there."

"Not going to work," I said. "It's mud season. Nothing but four-wheelers will get in."

"Your ATVs are still evidence, not to mention the issues of riding double and not wearing helmets." Her shoulders gave a little bounce. "I was so looking forward to defending against those ATV charges."

"There's an ATV dealer in Iron Mountain," I said. "Too late to call tonight, but I'd bet for the right price they'll rent us two ATVs, helmets, so we're all nice and legal, and bring them to us tomorrow."

"Sounds like a plan," Irene said. "Then what happens?"

"Then the cops show up," a voice said from behind me, "and spoil the party."

BARTELLE WATCHED ATTORNEY IRENE FRANKLE'S face become granite; her eyes flashed ferocity and she ripped the scarf off her head as though preparing for battle.

"Easy, Counselor," Bartelle said. "We come in peace. We're even willing to break bread together, if you'll have us. Slide over?"

The McCrees moved in and Tex sat beside Patrick. Frankle took her cue from Seamus and made room for Bartelle. He removed his hat and stuck it next to him on the seat. The waitress added two glasses of water and extra silverware. After determining they had ordered pizza, Bartelle ordered another one.

"Not grilled cheese?" McCree asked.

"Different restaurant," Bartelle said, sipped water, felt it cool his mouth and throat, quenching his thirst and calming his nerves. "Okay, I realize right now we're about as welcome as a skunk at a picnic, but let me tell you why we tracked you down. I'm hoping, with you not officially being suspects, we might pick your brains."

McCree pulled the left side of his face into a squint. Bartelle saw Frankle catch his look. She said, "Not officially suspects and not suspects are hardly the same thing. Numerous federal officers have threatened each of the McCrees. Despite that, they have given full and complete statements about what they know. What more do you want, Sergeant Bartelle?"

"I'll be honest," Bartelle said and wanted to kick himself since any time he heard those words from a suspect, he was sure they were about to lie. "As of this second, the FBI is the lead and AIC Cooper isn't much interested in any local input. Tex and I have been impressed with you two and we thought you might have some ideas. So here we are." He pointed to Tex and all eyes focused on him as he drained the glass of water.

"No more DEA?" Seamus asked.

Tex snorted derision. "DEA packed their bags. The only drugs found anywhere were those in the gas tank of Brett Aho's snow machine, which everyone agrees Jimmie Heitzmann probably planted since no self-respecting drug ring would wrap them in a leaky bag. DEA's working this area with a state police taskforce on other stuff. They have no interest in the murders."

"And those fine gentlemen from ICE?" Seamus asked.

Bartelle cleared his throat. "Right now in the background, but still very much interested. Look, Brett Aho and Jimmie Heitzmann were soldiers. Same thing with the two guys who came up from the Mitten to try to take you out. We know they're militia. Everything on them they bought in Iron Mountain in the last week, 'cept the guns. Those were stolen from an armory six years ago. The FBI executed a warrant on all known militia officers and their meeting places in Michigan and came up with squat."

Frankle shook her head and the tinkle of her hair beads caused Bartelle to stop. "Why are you sharing this information with my clients?"

"Because I want them to know I think Seamus stepped into the middle of something really big and really bad when he rescued Jane Doe. Because I think someone evil believes Seamus knows more than he does, and I am concerned said evil person or persons are not going to stop trying to kill him. Because the sheriff's department does not have the resources to protect them. Because I hope to convince both McCrees to leave town tonight. I hope legal counsel will add her esteemed opinion to my own for her clients' wellbeing."

Seamus cleared his throat and got everyone's attention. "Are there any funerals still left?"

Bartelle knew he meant for the five men killed protecting him. "The last one is tomorrow morning."

"I don't exactly have the clothes for a funeral, but I want to attend unless, given the town's mood, you think that would be unwise."

"The surrounding area is naturally in shock," Bartelle said. "But you know, up here we're used to disasters. They lost a lot more than five men in some of the mining accidents a generation or two ago. And just a few years back, we dealt with the tragedy of two cars full of drunk high schoolers playing chicken and meeting head-on. I don't guess anyone will much care what you wear to the church as long as it's not orange."

"And," Paddy said, "since my car and clothes and—I am so screwed if I don't get it soon, my *laptop*—are all up at camp, I'll attend the funerals with Dad."

"It would be a nice gesture," Bartelle said. "The outside media has already left town, and the local paper's not going to bother you. Here come the pizzas. Since you're going to stick around, we'll talk tomorrow after the service. Changing subjects, you guys Cincinnati Reds fans?"

Bartelle's ploy succeeded and conversation turned to the prospects of the Reds, Brewers, Twins, and Tigers in the coming baseball season.

He was glad to learn Frankle was heading downstate in the morning. Since neither McCree had thought to grab a wallet when they were attacked, and the county was no longer responsible for providing a room with barred door and windows, the lawyer would front them for a motel room. Bartelle agreed to arrange for someone to pick them up and take them to the funeral, and he'd arrange transportation to their camp to collect their stuff.

Once Bartelle and Tex were in a squad car, Tex asked, "You didn't really want them to leave, did you?"

Bartelle stopped himself from scratching his head. "Oh, hell no. I'm not a hundred percent convinced they're not involved—not so much the son, but the father. I want him where I can see him."

Twenty-Nine

BOSS WAS DAMNED TIRED OF funerals. This was the last one, but it would be the longest since it involved the Catholic mass for the dead or whatever they called it. Catholic services took forever, and she never knew when she was supposed to kneel or sit or stand. Her knees ached at every change. And she hated the smell of incense—made her want to sneeze. She led her son and daughter-in-law to a pew in the back where she had a good view of the congregation, and not many would notice if she nodded off during the sermon. She was amusing herself flipping pages in the Bible, trying to remember which extra books the Catholics included compared to her Protestant version. The pre-service buzz in the church went up a notch, and she raised her head.

Owen Lyndstrom, dressed in a suit no less, ushered in Seamus McCree and his son. She had heard at breakfast about their release from jail, and she realized it made sense for them to come. Although you would have thought they could have worn some decent clothes. Cops had attended all the funerals, and she was sure they were watching the crowd. She didn't want to stand out as the only one watching father and son. A quick glance around her allayed her fears. Every eye followed Owen as he brought them down and introduced them to the deceased's family before settling into a pew halfway up on the other side of the aisle.

Throughout the service, she snuck glances at the McCrees. The father knew his way around a Catholic service. Had no problem with the ups and downs and mumbled responses. The son, who looked like he'd lost a ten-rounder to Muhammad Ali, was as clueless as she was. Even with the kid's broken nose and swollen face, you could see the family resemblance: same height, same build, even the same walk. Boss had the feeling lots of curious people were going to talk to them after the service, which would allow her to question them without being obvious.

Now if this damned service would just get done.

* * *

KNOWING WHAT TO SAY TO a grieving family has never been my strong suit, and this was worse since their deaths rested heavily on my actions. The father of six children, the husband to his wife, the son to his mother, the brother to his siblings, the former altar boy of this church had died protecting me, someone he had never met. What words could I say to justify this loss? I mumbled my way through the condolences, grateful to Owen for making the introductions. No one expressed anger at Paddy or me; each family member thanked us for being there.

As I let the Requiem Mass wash over me, I recalled the shock of my own father's funeral. Our parish church overflowed with uniforms paying respect to one of their own killed in the line of duty. I don't recall a single thing anyone said to me that day and was surprised to discover hot tears now streaming down my cheeks. I wiped them away with the heels of my hands.

Without thought, I responded to the ritual. While I rejected the doctrine, I understood the power of a congregation: voices ranging from deep bass to boy soprano, mouthing words in unison to force my focus from myself toward something larger. I watched the six children sitting in front of me, aged late teenager to toddler—heads in a row of descending height. I could do nothing to replace their father, but I had the resources to at least help all the families financially. During the homily, I came up with the idea of setting up trust funds for the children. I'd need advice about the psychology around how to do that without seeming in any way to imply the families or community couldn't take care of their own.

Immediately following the service, Owen scooted off to attend the burial. My son the extrovert struck up a conversation with the woman who'd sat next to him, which left me alone with my thoughts as we slowly worked our way toward the exit. The entryway was blocked and, in the muddle, the people in front of us stopped to confab. As I waited, a middle-aged man bumped my arm. He apologized, and then recognition dawned on his face.

"You must be Mr. McCree," he said. "What a terrible tragedy. I'm Sam Maki. This is my wife, Jeanne, and my mother, K.C.—stands for Kathryn Cynthia. No one has called her Kathryn since she socked someone in the eye at age four."

"Sam," the mother said with a look of annoyance, "loves to tell that story. Don't you, Sam?"

I recognized the Maki's names. He was president of the Hematite bank and his mother was Chair of the Board. The previous year the Makis had been interested in selling out and I had performed due diligence on Hematite for one of my clients.

We shook hands all around and I said to Mr. Maki, "You might be able to help me with setting up some kind of memorial fund for the families. I don't know what that exactly means . . ."

"Understood," he said. "And I'm sure done the right way it will be useful and appreciated. It is still early days. When you have a better idea what you have in mind, you should talk to my mother. She's the bank's chair, but she's also the one most experienced with trusts, investments, structured settlements, annuities. That sort of thing. We all call her *the Boss*." He patted his mother's arm. "Right, Mom?"

"Please, call me K.C.—Boss sounds so imposing. I'll be glad to assist however I can. We attend the Presbyterian Church in town and helped that girl you rescued back . . . what . . . five, six weeks ago? We took up a collection of clothes for her. Whatever happened to her? Did she finally regain her memory?"

We had agreed we could not disclose who Agent Pendergast was, but we had not discussed how to describe her departure. To make my temporary confusion worse, I couldn't remember for the life of me what her assumed name was. When in doubt, make a lie sound convincing by mixing the lie with truths people can easily confirm. "Last I heard, she flew to Chicago."

"Did she find out who she was?" K.C asked. The crush in front of us eased and her son and daughter-in-law excused themselves to visit with someone I did not recognize.

Paddy jumped in before I spoke. "Her first name was Bethany. I think she didn't tell us more about herself because she was afraid Dad would change his mind and come after her for all her medical bills. That's not how my father operates, but how would she know? I got the feeling she was visiting friends in Chicago, but I could be mistaken."

"What," K.C. asked, "was she doing in this area? And why was she wandering around in the woods near you?"

Paddy and I shared a look, and I said, "No clue, but she knew the guy they found in Long Lake—not the snowmobiler, the other one. What was his name, Paddy?"

"Brandon, I think."

"They were staying at a camp somewhere nearby."

"I heard they tied some concrete blocks to him," K.C. said. "It's just awful what's happened. I'm surprised the police didn't insist she stay in the area until they clear everything up."

"You know more about it than I do," I said. "Speaking of the police, here comes Sergeant Bartelle now."

K.C. turned from me and offered Bartelle a big smile. "Lon, how nice of you to come to the funerals. We were just talking about that foundling— Bethany is her name? We were hoping she fully recovered her memory and wondered what became of her."

Bartelle pretended to slap her hand. "Now Mrs. Maki, you know I can't talk about active investigations, but I can assure you we're getting closer."

Bartelle extracted them from the clutches of the senior Mrs. Maki, one of the county's most effective interrogators and worst gossips. Once they were out of earshot, Seamus said, "Thanks for rescuing us. Before Niki left, we never thought to get our story straight about what we could say about her, but I don't think we gave anything away."

Bartelle had them go through the conversation and then burst their bubble. "And how did she get on the plane with no identification?"

The McCrees looked at each other, with "oh, shit" expressions.

Bartelle flicked his key fob and unlocked his personal car. "Don't worry about it. We all should have thought of it earlier. K.C. Maki rivals Owen Lyndstrom for having an ear to the ground. There were so many witnesses when we fished Brandon Newhouse out of Long Lake, I'm sure she heard about Agent Pendergast—er, Niki— or was she back to Bethany?— whoever she was—identifying him. Owen gave me a key to his place. He'll meet us there and make sure you get to your camp." He flashed the key. "I have a proposition."

"Gee," Patrick said, "Dad's been propositioned by cops before, but I never have."

"Get in, Paddy," Seamus said, "And let's listen to what the man has to say."

Despite practicing his speech, Bartelle's words tumbled out. "I told you Robert Rand, your boss at CIG, offered all their resources. I spoke with him again—yesterday—I mean last night. So, the sheriff agreed to sign a contract with CIG—I didn't realize CIG never takes money for its work. Anyway, you, Seamus, can work with me under the auspices of CIG's contract. And Patrick, I have in my briefcase a form Rand faxed to sign you up as a CIG employee—minimum wage, I'm afraid—but it will allow you to also work with me under the CIG contract. Everything's nice and legal."

"It would help," Seamus said, "if you told us what you want us to do."

"Of course," Bartelle smacked the back of his own head, "I was so worried about the legalities, I forgot the main point. I've seen Patrick work magic with computers. We can't do anything illegal—" He glanced in the rearview mirror to gauge Patrick's expression; it was neutral. "Nothing illegal, but we can get court orders if we need them. I'm off track again. We've gotten a mass of electronic data from the court orders on the phones, and we don't have the skills in our office to get through it quickly. I suspect Patrick does."

"Probably," Patrick said, "I'd have to see exactly what you've got in mind. And Dad?"

"We got the records from Hematite Bank. They seem willing to help us understand them, but they could also be leading me by the nose and I'd never know. Your father would. Plus, in trying to track down who owned the property where Niki and Brandon stayed, we've run into a Colorado corporation I can't track down."

"To summarize, then," Seamus said. "You want our brains, not our good looks, which is a good thing in your case, Paddy, because you still look like crap."

"And the horse you rode in on, Dad." To Bartelle he replied, "I'm game, and I know my old man is. Dad's always said the best defense is a great offense, and we need to find whoever tried to kill us."

Seamus emitted a grating sound, and Bartelle's brief feeling of relief faded. "Paddy's observation is spot on," he said. "The only thing jail had going for it was I didn't have to worry about somebody coming to gun us down, which is probably why you had us arrested in the first place, although the county prosecutor didn't get the joke."

Bartelle felt heat rise to his face, but kept his mouth shut until he knew where McCree was going. McCree glanced at his son.

"Have you thought about how you can try to protect us without endangering anyone? So many people have been killed . . ."

"CIG expressed the same concern, Seamus. I think we can best discuss it after we get to Owen's." With a crack of thunder, the skies opened up. Bartelle flicked the wipers on high. "Hope this stays rain and doesn't turn to sleet."

Seamus nodded assent; Patrick looked out the window. Bartelle hoped they would consider the surprise awaiting them at Owen's a good one.

BOSS SAT IN THE CAMP recliner, sipped straight bourbon, and crushed out the half-smoked cigarette. Damn things didn't even taste good, whereas bourbon was like wood smoke—a little sip engaged scent and taste receptors, providing fine memories; too much overwhelmed everything. After all the funerals, shutting down seemed advantageous. The worst part of attending the funerals, she decided, was pantyhose. If she had her brief stint as a women's libber to do over, she'd lobby hard for burning panty hose instead of bras. It's easy to get rid of bras when you're young and everything up top is perky; now she found them comfortable and couldn't imagine hanging loose without one, but pantyhose was something else. With nice-looking pantsuits, not too much required pantyhose these days, but weddings and funerals were still formal affairs.

She found her conversation with Seamus McCree unsatisfactory. The girl's name was Bethany Palmer. She needed a photo ID card to fly. To get one, Bethany needed to prove her identity to the authorities. So Bartelle knew who she was and where she was from.

Boss checked with a friend who worked for the airlines in Iron Mountain and confirmed Bethany Palmer did fly to Chicago. Her friend had found no record of Bethany Palmer flying out of Chicago that day or since; of course, since Bethany hadn't checked any baggage, she could have taken another airline and her source wouldn't know.

After fuming at the dead end while draining the better part of a fifth of bourbon, she came to the upside of the situation: it required her to think about her motives in trying to finish off Bethany Palmer and Seamus McCree. Tying up loose ends was only a good thing if it didn't unroll another skein of yarn. She had structured all contacts around hiring the wolf biologists and renting the cabin to go through Brett—although he was unaware of it and now it was too late for him to care. Trying to tidy up all the loose ends connecting her to Brett Aho, the scientists, and the cabin was an error on two accounts.

From a practical standpoint, it didn't matter what Bethany Palmer had told Seamus McCree or Sergeant Bartelle or the world because she didn't know anything to tell him. Furthermore, if anyone had seen Boss in the woods after the Mitten Men disaster, the cops would already have visited her. Once she got rid of the remaining cell phones, the only person who could implicate her was the head of the downstate militia and he had already proven, through a stretch of jail time, that he could keep his mouth shut.

The second count against her was she had been vengeful. *Vengeance is mine, saith the Lord. On that, she needed to reflect further.*

She downed the rest of the bourbon in a gulp and waited until the burn settled from her throat to her stomach before retrieving the ancient laptop. On the way back to the recliner, she pulled the first beer of the afternoon from the fridge and downed it while the computer booted up and connected to the internet. One email:

Sunday meeting confirmed.

She whooped at the news, which soon became a coughing jag so bad it rocked the single-wide as she staggered to catch her breath. Amazing she didn't hack her lung onto the floor. She toasted the news with a second beer and then retrieved Mrs. Pirhonen's cell phone and those remaining from her Wisconsin purchase. What was she going to do with them? If it was later in spring, she could stick a canoe into a nearby lake and dump them in, but if anyone saw her on the water now, it would surely raise suspicions. With the effort it took her to get home from the ambush, she didn't feel like she had the strength to bury a cigarette butt in the nearly frozen soil, let alone all those phones. It had been almost impossible to get rid of her clothes that night. Fact was, if she hadn't stolen that ATV, she would never have gotten home. She used two hands to crinkle the beer can and tossed it into the sink, where it rattled around before rimming out and landing on the floor.

The idea arrived in a burst, and she wondered why she hadn't thought of it earlier, especially since she had simply left two phones in Wisconsin. In less than two days, she would pick up the magic potion in Ishpeming. She could throw the phones away somewhere between here and there. If someone found them and used one, so much the better; it would lead the cops on a fine wild goose chase. She put on a pair of dishwashing gloves, took the cell phones apart and carefully cleaned every surface that could contain a fingerprint. She stored the now-cleansed phones in freezer bags.

She plopped into the recliner with the last of the six-pack and returned to reflecting on revenge. It had been un-Christian and flat out wrong. A lesser person might have blamed it on unclear thinking caused by the lung cancer. She would have none of that self-justification. Nope, her sinful thoughts had caused the deaths of Spider and Digger—plus, she supposed, the five locals—of course, their own stupidity did play a major role in their demise.

She didn't have long enough to atone for two deaths, let alone seven, so it didn't much matter. The best she could do was turn the other cheek to McCree and let bygones be bygones.

Unless he got in the way, in which case she'd squash him like a bug. She placed the empty beer can on the floor and tromped it.

THIRTY

I HAD BEEN TO OWEN'S place only a couple of times. Fortunately for the rest of the residents in the Amasa area, he lived at the end of a long driveway, which made a sweeping curve before coming to the house. Following the curve, we arrived at what had once been a clearing but now stored the remains of uncountable cars, trucks, tractors, and logging equipment, all awaiting resurrection in the Second Coming.

Rain drummed on the car's roof. We pulled off the driveway between what I guessed to be the remains of a Model A Ford and a useable trailer with a disemboweled tractor chained to its bed. Bartelle drove his car close to the front of the house to shorten our walk. Unlike the yard, the house was in immaculate condition. We hustled three abreast up the deck stairs. The door opened and Abigail Hancock, holding a newspaper above her head, walked out.

Bartelle continued up the steps. I stopped, and my quick turn toward Paddy stopped him as well, "Did you know about this?"

He hustled to Abigail and gave her a hug. "Have you come to save my father's ass again?"

"From the looks of it," she said, "you need it more than he does. Get inside before you catch pneumonia. This bodyguard doesn't carry umbrellas."

Her words jarred me into forward movement, but my walk was slow as I tried to understand my feelings. I had last seen her two and a half months ago snowmobiling away, her arms encircling Owen's waist. As the weeks passed, I became more and more convinced she had left me for good. I thought my penance in the wilderness had cauterized the wound. One glimpse of her ripped off the scab and the internal bleeding began again.

Paddy and Bartelle entered the house. I could gauge nothing from Abigail's eyes, which despite the rain were hidden behind mirrored glasses. It may have been my imagination, but I thought the corners of her mouth curled into the slightest hint of a smile. I could not guess its meaning. From my position standing below her, her long legs appeared even longer than I knew they were, and she looked taller than her five feet nine inches. Bulky clothes hid her form, but I still had her shape memorized. She spun around and went inside leaving the door open and me standing in the rain. Once inside, I received a second surprise: Agent Pendergast stood in the far corner of the living room taking in the scene. Abigail was leaning against a wall—as though she had gone to the closest thing to a neutral corner. Bartelle closed the door behind me. "Surprised?" he asked.

Paddy pointed toward Pendergast. "Who are you and what are you doing here?"

"Today, I'm Ashley Pendergast on medical leave of absence from the Federal Bureau of Investigation and temporarily hired by Criminal Investigations Group to assist the Iron County Sheriff's Department in a number of related investigations."

"What's Cooper think?" I asked, still looking at Abigail.

"Cooper thinks I'm sulking at home because he pulled a quick one and had his lap-doctor put me on medical leave. Owen has graciously agreed to allow me to stay here, where it is unlikely AIC Cooper or anyone else will see me. Your Robert Rand arranged for Abigail's reassignment to provide external protection should either of you boys need to leave Owen's lovely establishment." She asked Abigail. "How did I do?"

"Fine as far as it went," Abigail said. "Robert Rand's orders to me were that I was not to let either of, and I quote, 'those ovacaput McCrees with no more sense than a mycoplasma' out of my sight. You know Robert. He won't use a cussword or a contraction but he sure knows how to deliver a highfalutin putdown."

Bartelle still held the door handle. I wasn't sure if it was to prevent my escape or execute an exit himself. Pendergast took the bait Abigail had floated. "For those of us not smart enough to decode Mr. Rand's diss . . .?"

Paddy said, "Ovacaput is concatenated Latin for egg-headed. Myco-plasma are members of the smallest group of bacteria."

"And concatenated?" Bartelle asked.

Paddy continued, "Linking together in a series. Ova for egg. Caput for head. Hence, Robert's Latin concatenation for egghead."

"Enough already," I said. "Let's back up a few steps." I faced Bartelle. "Last I knew, the Feds had grabbed the investigation and pushed you out."

"The FBI, DEA, and ICE couldn't agree on how to proceed. ICE pulled their trump card and grabbed the brass ring. The FBI didn't fold and the pissing match went up to the Director of Homeland Security and the Attorney General.

"About then, your sometime-employer, Criminal Investigations Group in the form of Robert Rand—is there anybody in law enforcement he doesn't know? Anyway, he contacted the director of the state police and found out the state's only role was assisting the Iron County Sheriff's Department and we were currently sidelined. He then contacted the attorney general and gave the AG leverage to use with Homeland Security. The president—you didn't know you were so important, did you?—decided he wanted to slap down the internecine warfare between the two departments and gave the murder investigations back to Iron County. The sheriff, who is a politician first and sheriff second, was smart enough to duck. Yours truly didn't."

"Which," I said, "leaves me wondering what is going on that even the president cares."

"You once asked me," Agent Pendergast said, "if the FBI has people inside the Michigan militias. We do, and they believe the militia is planning a large-scale attack, which they expect to generate large amounts of money. The source hasn't pinned down when or where, but the timing is very soon. The federal agencies are charged with preventing whatever the militia is planning. No president wants another Oklahoma City bombing on his watch."

"And," Bartelle added, "the two guys from downstate were both militia guys. Current thinking is that Agent Pendergast was the target."

"Because?" I asked. "Strike that. Because she's the one that escaped from the camp. Did forensics turn up anything useful at the camp? Who owns the camp? Never mind. Cut to the chase, why are we all here?"

All eyes focused on Bartelle. "Rand wrangled a special deal, which allows Iron County to use the National Security Agency's quick response system for any subpoenas, wire taps, *et cetera*. He convinced everyone that by allowing us to pursue the killers, we might end up providing the rest of them information about their national attack concerns. The NSA's already helping us out."

"Let me guess," Paddy threw in. "Rand specifically required my Dad's involvement since something wonky is going on at Hematite Bank."

Bartelle squirmed a little before answering. "Actually, he said he had given up on your father. He suggested I recruit you for your computer skills, Patrick."

Abigail offered one of her bubbly laughs and it sent a pleasurable shiver down my back. "Don't you believe it," she said. "Robert Rand knows all and sees all. He hasn't given up on Seamus. He's been looking for a way to get your father back in the fold and what better way than to engage his only begotten son. You can trust Rand with your life, but he is a conniving son of a . . . gun."

I smiled as the mere mention of Robert Rand had the effect of cleaning up Abigail's language.

Abigail continued: "Per Robert: Seamus has an innate talent for getting involved with people who want to kill him. I'm supposed to keep him alive as long as he stays up here. Same goes for you, Paddy, so you see, Robert was sure Seamus would stay."

Which left me wondering what her orders or desires were if I left the U.P. "And what about you, Agent Pendergast?" Paddy asked.

"After I got benched, I gave Bartelle a call to let him know how to contact me. Yesterday, he told me his plan and asked if I wanted in. Here I am. Please everyone call me Ashley or Pendergast. The agent part is on medical leave—maybe permanent leave if Cooper discovers I'm here."

"So," I said, "do we have a plan?"

"This rain will soon turn to snow," Bartelle said. "In a few hours, the woods roads will freeze again. Owen will take you to your camp to bring out whatever you need. I've got to get to headquarters and let everyone know CIG and you two are officially on board . . . or am I jumping the gun?"

Paddy and I shared understanding looks. "We're good," I said.

"But I can't do anything until I get my computer," Paddy said.

"Do you have 3G service for your computer?" Bartelle asked. "Verizon's got a tower in Amasa. Or there's a free hotspot here you can pick up with Wi-Fi. Until we get you to your dad's camp, Owen's got a computer he keeps for the grandkids. I'll get you the computerized files relating to the monitored phone calls at the same time I bring Seamus everything we have from Hematite Bank. Should have them to you after dinner sometime. Mr. Maki has agreed to meet us tomorrow early afternoon. It'll be right after the Saturday closing, but he'll make sure his IT guy is there."

"And the security forces?" I asked.

Pendergast answered. "I'm on nightshift since Abigail needs to be available during the day to accompany you guys on the outside. I think we were about to set up security?" She looked at Abigail, who agreed.

Bartelle left to collect the files. Abigail and Pendergast put on rain slickers and took several duffle bags of stuff outside to secure the perimeter. Owen arrived, the rain having curtailed whatever work he was doing.

My mind was a turmoil of competing concerns. Bartelle had not told Paddy and me everything he knew about the case, of that I was sure. It might be a lack of trust—despite Rand vouching for me, there was no way to rule out the possibility I was involved with whatever was really going on. It might be natural police caution to keep things close to his vest. Or it could be some unstated rules Homeland Security or the FBI had insisted upon. Compartmentalized thinking had caused the various intelligence agencies to miss the clues to prevent 9/11. Yet the tsunami of state department material revealed by WikiLeaks demonstrated the downside of allowing too many people access to information. You might as well let everyone know, which was what WikiLeaks had done.

Then there was the awkwardness of staying in the same place with Abigail and Pendergast. They seemed to be working well together, but . . .

There was nothing I could do until Bartelle delivered the files, so when Paddy gave up trying to use Owen's computer, declaring it an historical artifact, I challenged Paddy and Owen to a game of cribbage. By dinnertime, Paddy had cleaned Owen and me out of a combined two dollars and forty-eight cents. Owen, whom I discovered did not like losing at cribbage, paid his share of the damages in pennies.

OWEN WOKE ME AT TWO a.m. for the trip to camp, and I came up swinging. "Next time," Owen said after avoiding my flailing arms, "I'm usin a stick. No wonder women leave you."

Pendergast sat in front with Owen behind the wheel; Paddy and I crammed into the backseat of Owen's truck. Six inches of untracked snow on the ground gave everyone comfort that no one had preceded us into the woods.

At camp, Pendergast checked the house and cabin to make sure everything was secure. I packed my truck with what I would need until mud season was over. Paddy made several trips to the cabin to collect all his belongings and tossed them into his car. We caravanned out on the return trip. Pendergast again rode shotgun with Owen, who led us out on the theory that if one of us got stuck he could pull us out.

At Owen's, Paddy grabbed my arm and held me back from following the other two into the house.

"I've been thinking," he said.

"Glad the bucks for college did some good," I said.

"Good one, Dad. I'll have to remember it. The Amasa Wi-Fi is insecure, and I'm not sure it's a good idea. Even with my laptop, it's going to be slower than evolution. LT2P has an important sales meeting Monday that I really should lead. Plus, at home, I've got a superfat pipe and—"

"Meaning?"

"Sorry," he said. "Way more bandwidth and I've got the right tools."

"So you're heading out?"

"It's a bit crowded at Owen's. Besides, without me tagging along, it might give you and Abigail some *alone time*. It was a bit frosty around the dinner table."

"Yeah, I was thinking about wearing a parka to breakfast. Speaking of which, when did Abigail take you to the range?"

"Cindy was working on an investigation into some shady characters. After your experience in Cincinnati, I wanted to know how to shoot, so I called her up not too long after she lef—after she returned from here."

"And?"

"And she took me to the range a bunch of times until she thought I was good to go on pistols and rifles. Then she helped me buy a Sig like hers."

My son, a gun owner. It wasn't something we had ever talked about, but I never imagined I would see the day. I understood better than anyone the overwhelming compulsion to protect loved ones, but I still believed guns in a house were more dangerous than valuable. I needed to know his reasoning. Somehow, though, what seemed more pressing was finding out if they had talked about me, but I couldn't ask. I had always made it a point to never talk to Paddy about his mother or our disagreements. He had followed suit and rarely mentioned her. He obviously figured the same philosophy applied to Abigail. Despite my desire for answers, I knew he was right.

"I'll be in Evanston for a late breakfast," Paddy said. "I know I'm supposed to report to Bartelle, but I'll let you know if I find anything."

As his taillights faded, my chest hollowed out. The pressure of the emptiness inside threatened to crack me wide open. For me it's easier being the leaver than being the one left behind, but that hadn't been how things had gone recently. I had even forgotten to tell Paddy "I love you," before he left.

Owen returned to bed and his snores threatened to raise the roof. There was no way I could go back to sleep. To paper over the void caused by Paddy's departure, I spread the bank's records on the dining room table. Pendergast rocked on the porch, a low thump announcing each dip forward.

I called Bartelle as early as I dared. "Is there a reason we can't meet with Hematite as soon as they open up?"

"What did you find?"

"Do you know how long they keep their security tapes?"

"What did you find?"

"Last month, on the twenty-seventh, the same day interest was credited to Mrs. Pirhonen's account, someone deposited thirty-eight bucks well after closing. I know it was after closing because the deposit was recorded *after* the interest credit."

From down the line, I heard a scratching pen. "So what?"

I tamped down my exasperation at his inability to actually answer my question. He was trained to ask questions and not give answers. *I shouldn't hold it against him.* "Bank accounting systems are structured so the interest credit is the last transaction of the day. Traditional banking is all about interest spreads and float. I'm off topic. The point is someone made an entry late at night—someone who has afterhours access to a teller machine and knows how to work it. If the inside video is still around, we can see who it is. Otherwise, we've got some work to do."

"You're suggesting someone at the bank was involved with the killings? Seems hard to fathom."

"Bartelle, you didn't become a sergeant based on easy. Call Maki and tell him we're coming now, and tell him to have that day's security tapes ready if they haven't been overwritten."

"Mr. Maki has a meeting in Marquette in the morning, which is the reason our meeting is in the afternoon. Is that all you've got?"

"So you're saying we're SOL on an earlier meeting. If they don't have that security tape, we're going to need to know who has access to the bank when it's closed and who works late at the end of the month. Make sure Maki knows. Gotta be some IT guys running the month-end programs. Also, who specifically worked that day? Someone could have hidden in a bathroom or something until everyone left."

"Got it. Anything else?" After my silence he added, "Not to put the pressure on you, but NSA is saying militia email and phone traffic has increased substantially."

THIRTY-ONE

BARTELLE HAD NEVER WORKED WITH a bodyguard before. Abigail drove her own armored car and he and McCree sat in the back like tycoons. They arrived at Hematite's main branch five minutes early. Exactly at the appointed time, Sam Maki led them to a conference room. Abigail took an "at ease" position outside the conference room.

"Is she armed?" Maki asked. "We have rules . . ."

Bartelle shut the door behind them. "Did you find the security tape?"

Maki shook his head. "They're on an eight-day cycle. If you can tell me what you're looking for, maybe I can save you some time."

Bartelle motioned for everyone to sit down. He remained standing to remind Maki who was in charge. "Thanks for your offer, Mr. Maki. Here's the issue in a nutshell: we're interested in the account of Mrs. Pirhonen's we discussed the last time I was here. All the deposits were in cash, which is a bit unusual, and if Seamus correctly understood the information you provided, all the transactions were handled by the same teller." With a rustle of paper, he spread the computer printouts in front of Maki and tapped the teller codes circled in red. "Who is this teller?" He took the seat next to Maki.

Maki phoned his head IT guy, who kept him on hold for less than a minute. Maki listened to the answer and said, "Impossible." His voice rose in anger. "She retired at the end of the year." He nodded, obviously agreeing with what he was hearing. "Do that now, please. We'll get back to you with any other questions. No, wait. First change the password and then do a search to determine what other transactions Doris supposedly entered since she retired. Good, let me know."

He set the phone down and spun his chair to face us. "Doris Stanchina retired December thirty-first. Someone signed into the system using her password. You didn't ask, but the codes also show that all the transactions occurred in this building. You heard me tell Kenny to change the password and run a list of any other transactions Doris supposedly entered after the end of the year."

"Did she have a key to the building?" Bartelle asked.

"Of course. She was the head teller. But I know she turned it in because she gave it to me." He opened his desk drawer and extracted a keychain. "A few years ago, we changed our key system to these. They can't be copied."

The answer led directly to the second question on the list Seamus had given Bartelle on their way to the meeting. "Who else has keys?"

"More people than you might think," Maki answered. "All our senior officers, the head teller, some people in IT, our maintenance staff, the outside cleaners. There may be others I'm not coming up with off the top of my head." He made a note on the pad of paper in front of him. "I can find out, and if for some reason I can't, I guess it's time to change the locks. What else?"

"Who of those people know how to use the teller systems?" Bartelle asked. "Logging in, making a deposit, that kind of stuff." Bartelle watched closely for any tells. Maki's eyes clicked right—retrieving information.

"Our head teller, of course. The VP of operations. I'm pretty sure our marketing VP worked summers in high school and college as a teller, so he probably knows."

Bartelle recorded their names.

McCree had been leaning back in his chair, fingers locked behind his head. Now he placed both forearms on the table and asked, "What about your head of IT? Does he know how to use the teller systems? And could he, or anyone in IT, modify the codes after the fact?"

Sam Maki opened his eyes wide. "You don't think . . . ?"

McCree resumed leaning back. "All I have are questions. Does he know how to use the teller systems?"

"Kenny might have picked up enough information helping the tellers solve problems. He does reset the passwords. I guess you already know that, but—"

The telephone interrupted with a long and two shorts, like a D in Morse code. Maki swiveled around and answered it with, "Kenny, what you got? . . . only those? . . . no other tellers? Thanks."

He settled the handset into its cradle and turned around. "The only transactions with Doris Stanchina's code since the beginning of the year are the ones you found. He also checked to see if any other teller who left last year had any transactions for this year, and they didn't. You've got me wondering if I can trust Kenny. Prior to you guys showing up, I would have said, 'unquestionably,' but now . . ."

Bartelle began working on his head under his right ear. With the stress of these murders, he'd rubbed the spot raw and wasn't sure if rubbing felt good or hurt, but it didn't matter because he couldn't stop. He gave McCree a quick eyebrow waggle to indicate he should ask his questions now.

"I'm a director of a firm with expertise in banking computer systems: LT2P. They can sign a confidentiality agreement and run an independent analysis to make sure Kenny is telling you the truth."

"What can they do without his knowing?" Maki asked.

McCree explained how LT2P worked and got Maki to call Patrick McCree while they were there. Bartelle couldn't understand much, listening to only half of the conversation, but before it concluded, an assistant brought Maki a signed nondisclosure agreement faxed from LT2P. He scrawled his name on a contract calling for one dollar in compensation.

Bartelle hid his smile. *Talk about letting the camel's nose under the tent.* Of course, what McCree had just done to the bank wasn't much different than what he'd done to McCree.

BARTELLE HAULED ME TO DORIS Stanchina's home after we grabbed a bite to eat. Abigail remained on the Crystal Falls bungalow's front porch taking in the view of distant hills.

Doris settled us onto chairs in her living room. Everything was neatly in its place and nothing was newer than twenty years old. The smell of fresh apple pie filled the air.

Bartelle again led the questioning. No, she had not been back in the bank since her retirement. She banked using the drive-through, but saw her friends who still worked there at church, the high school football games, around town. Yes, it was possible someone else knew her password; she had taped it to the bottom of her pencil holder. Well no, she wasn't sure whether Kenny from IT knew enough to operate the teller machines; she had never seen him try. Yes, there was one person not on the list of people Sam Maki had given us who had a key and could use the teller system: Sam Maki himself.

When Maki's father died three years ago, his mother temporarily ran the bank until she convinced Sam to return home to take it over. Did we know they had a controlling stock interest? I said I did.

Sam went through a year's training before becoming the president. As head teller, Doris had trained him in teller operations. Afterwards, he had spent two months working in all the branches, getting to know employees and how to interact with the banking public. He was an excellent teller. He also spent time in marketing, human resources, financial services where his mother was the tutor, and she couldn't remember what else. A fine young man. The bank and the city were lucky to have him.

Would we like a piece of her fresh-baked pie; it should be cool enough. Before Bartelle could say anything, I accepted for us. The aroma had been working on me since we walked in the door. Besides, I had a feeling that the new information about Sam Maki meant dinner was going to be late.

She served it with a slice of sharp cheddar. Only the good manners my mother taught me prevented me from begging for a second slice.

ON THE WAY TO BARTELLE'S office, he and I agreed to spend the rest of the afternoon uncovering as much as we could about Sam Maki and Hematite National Bank before we interviewed Maki again. I'd take the Hematite material since in a former life I had been a bank analyst; he'd dig out the skinny on Maki. Paddy was presumably sifting through the bank's computer systems.

"Anything I can do?" Abigail asked as she walked us into the sheriff's office. "We'll give you a call to pick him up," Bartelle tilted his head in my direction. Abigail turned on her heel and left. I had the feeling that if she could have slammed the door, she would have. "She was Secret Service, you know," I said. "She might have been—"

"Not in her contract. Let's get to work."

Several hours later over take-out pizza, we compared notes. My research confirmed my recollections of the work I had performed for All-American Bancorp the previous autumn while they considered acquiring Hematite. The FDIC was not likely to shut down Hematite, but the bank wasn't in great shape either. It had issued a number of bad real estate mortgages and had several unsound business loans. The family controlled 62% of the common stock, with Sam's mother's holding a 51% majority stake. To conserve capital, they had eliminated their dividend, which severely affected the Maki family finances.

After Sam Maki's father died, many thought the family would sell to a larger bank. I was not able to determine if the family found no takers—the bank I was doing work for decided not to place a bid—or the offers they received weren't what they hoped for.

"Sam Maki didn't want to come back," Bartelle said. "His mother made him. What we have is good background, but no smoking gun. He's been clean as an adult, with the exception of one arrest in college for DUI. My federal associates did unlock his juvenile file. His father was commander of the local militia during the nineties. Not a nutcase like the guy who claimed the Oklahoma City bombing was the Japanese retaliating for the subway sarin attack deaths. But active.

"Returning to Sam Maki: the Feds raided the Maki's hunting camp while Sam was in high school. The only thing illegal they found was the kid's stash of weed. They concluded the son was also involved with the militia thing. For example, they found training tapes on which he appeared. Someone local brought those two militia boys up from the Mitten to take you out."

"And you're wondering if he inherited more than the presidency of his father's bank."

Bartelle broke into a grin. "It crossed my mind. The Fed's militia source isn't in a position to know who the U.P. players are. I'm surprised we haven't heard from your son yet."

"He was supposed to call—" I pulled my cell phone from my pocket. "Hard to get me if I don't turn the damn thing on."

For the first time, Bartelle produced a belly laugh loud enough to register on nearby tectonic devices.

Paddy blasted me for my stupidity. "Fine, so we agree," I said. "I'm an idiot when it comes to cell phones. What have you got?"

"If anyone in Hematite's IT department is messing with the files, they're better than us. We found no traces of any electronic changes after the transactions occurred. I checked every teller ID. Absolutely the only squirrelly transactions relate to Mrs. Pirhonen's spurious account. The sole purpose of that account was to pay the phone bill without letting anyone like us determine who controlled the phone. I spent the rest of the time cross-checking that phone's outgoing and incoming phone numbers. I can't find a single instance where one of those numbers contacted another one."

"I could hear the good news faster and leave the dead ends for later," I said.

"Fine. One of the numbers, which was located in Hamtramck, was only used in contact with Mrs. Pirhonen's purloined cell phone until three days ago when it received a phone call from a different number. And here's the interesting part: the different number was newly listed that day—in fact, less than fifteen minutes before the call was made."

"So someone ditched the old phone and bought a new one."

"It gets better," Paddy said. "Whoever bought that new phone bought five others in Wausau, all prepaid throwaways. I checked those numbers as well. One made one other call and one received a call from—get this— another brand new cell phone account in Hamtramck. Dad, it is scary how fast these Homeland Security guys and their NSA friends can get search warrants. They tell me if any of those eight phones is used—"

"Eight?"

"Yeah, Dad. The six bought in Wausau, the new one bought in Hamtramck and a cell phone registered to one M. Mouse, who buys minutes for the phone at WalMart. All I can tell you about the last one is the call came to a Crystal Falls cell tower. Anyway, if anyone uses any of those phones, these guys will know, and know what is said, and probably be able to figure out exactly where the phone is. They promised to give Sergeant Bartelle transcripts for anything related to his investigation." He cleared his throat.

I felt a tingle of concern as my neck tightened.

"You know, Dad. Next time a government guy threatens to take you out of circulation if you don't cooperate, take it as a serious threat."

"Great work, Paddy. Anything else to do on your end?"

"Have you considered leaving? I know Abigail's a great bodyguard . . . forget I said anything."

"Forgotten. Love you, Paddy."

"Love you too, Dad."

Before I shut off the cell phone, I saw I had voicemail. I decided not to discover how many times Paddy had called. I briefed Bartelle and concluded, "Sam Maki has become a person of interest, wouldn't you say?

We should determine where he was Wednesday afternoon at the time someone acquired those phones. Of course, even if he has an alibi, someone else could have bought the phones for him."

"True," Bartelle said. "And whoever it is used at least the first of those prepaid phones. What's sticking in my craw is why Maki didn't mention he could get into the teller system. Was he so willing to have us check the computer systems because he knew there was nothing there other than what we had already found? What better way to throw us off track than appear to be helpful? He's a damned fine liar, if he's the one."

"You got enough for search warrants for those throwaway phones?"

"I'd like to hold off until we talk with him again. Thinking out loud: if we interview him on Monday, his administrative assistant will be there and one of us can chat her up while the other talks to Maki. Maybe I'll have a search warrant in hand to check his office for the phones. We can have people simultaneously check his house, his car, his camp and anywhere else we can think of. Frankly, I'm too tired to make a good decision right now. Let's call it a day and get together tomorrow."

I was exhausted too but was a bit miffed at Bartelle putting off what we could do today. I meant to hold my tongue in my back molars to forestall speaking my mind. Instead, I bit it—my tongue, not my mind. I don't know how brains work, but with the sharp pain my thoughts returned to Abigail and me. We needed to talk, and sooner was better than later.

Abigail pulled up and I went to sit in the front seat. "It's safer in the back," Abigail said. "And right now all I'm interested in is your safety."

That effectively ended any consideration I had about talking about us. I got into the back. The air conditioning wasn't on, but it sure felt like it was. I pulled my head into my coat, closed my eyes, and rested against the window.

After a few minutes of silence she asked what we had learned. "Nothing I want to talk about," I said.

In response, the car accelerated.

THIRTY-TWO

PENDERGAST AWOKE TO ABIGAIL STORMING into the bedroom they shared. "Don't ask me," Abigail snarled. "Ask him." She inclined her head toward the living room.

Pendergast exhaled an audible sigh to show her displeasure and left Abigail pounding her pillow. "Time for the nightshift," she said to McCree. "Tell me what happened."

Pendergast thought Seamus was going to reject her request. He looked between her and Owen and finally said, "How about we take a walk. I've been cooped up inside all day."

She took the hint about not saying anything in front of Owen. The downside of everyone staying at Owen's was if anyone said anything interesting, it would be on the county grapevine before the sentence was complete. As she donned her winter gear, she wondered if they could intentionally use Owen to feed something to the masses. From the corner of her eye, she kept Seamus in view. He paced in a short oval as though he were a spinning top.

"Let's walk the perimeter," she said. "I can pretend I'm doing something useful."

"I take it you think you aren't?" Seamus held the door open and they walked outside.

Sweet of him; the world resting on his shoulder, yet he was concerned about her. What a far cry from working with AIC Cooper. She started to take his hand and flashed to Abigail. She wasn't going to get into the middle of whatever was going on there. If she were Abigail, she would have changed the sleeping arrangements and the hell with Owen's sensibilities. Of course, she wasn't Abigail. She needed to find safer ground.

"I'm a *prima donna*," she said. "I prefer center stage. Instead, I'm parked in right field hoping a grounder gets through the infield."

"You play ball?" he asked.

"Softball. Full ride to UCLA. I played second base on three national championship teams. The FBI liked that competitive nature and hired me. I'm not so sure Cooper currently considers it a positive attribute."

"Well, I am in the middle of it and I don't feel like I'm doing anything. At least you have an excuse." He faced her directly. "You know, if Cooper does kill your career, tons of places would hire you in a flash."

"Name one."

"CIG. Why do you think Rand put you on their payroll? Have you remembered anything else from your stay at the camp with Brett Aho and your supposed coworker, Brandon?"

"Nope."

"Speaking of Brandon, I never heard the results of his autopsy."

She had hoped the question wouldn't come up. "You'll have to ask Bartelle. So what did you guys learn today?"

McCree stopped and she walked a couple more steps, hoping to pull him along. He didn't budge, so she retreated. "What?"

"I am so damn tired of being treated as though I can't keep a secret—not that a cause of death should be such a damn big secret. Keep walking your perimeter, Agent Pendergast. I can find my own way back to the house."

She thought she felt the earth tremble as Seamus tromped off.

Anger steamed off him and she couldn't blame him. It wasn't her rule, and it wasn't even Bartelle's. NSA wanted that information locked up, and screwing with them wasn't worth the cost. She completed her circuit and returned to the house, where she plunked down on the rocker.

As near as she could figure, Bartelle was using McCree's banking expertise, while at the same time monitoring his activities. Prudent, but stupid. She had argued they should tell McCree everything they knew, but Bartelle had shut her down. It wasn't her place to slip McCree the information. Maybe she'd argue the issue one more time with Bartelle.

Feeling better about her decision, she popped up from the rocker and went inside. Owen was sharpening chainsaw chains. "Where's Seamus?" she asked.

Owen looked up from his work. "Warn't he with you?"

BOSS WOKE UP EARLY, NEEDING to pee, but feeling as excited as a kid on Christmas morning. Like that kid, she had to wait to get her present. The pastor preached something insipid about how if we weren't true to ourselves, every day was a personal Ides of March. She could see the point, but preferred the fire and brimstone sermons of the Baptist church she had grown up in. She slipped into a reverie about how so much had changed since she was a kid. Nowadays, parents negotiated with their children instead of smacking them if they misbehaved. She could still hear the slap of her father's belt as it welted her butt. She'd never whipped her son, but her hand had buzzed after a few spankings. Kids used to look up to schoolteachers—of course teachers used to wear dresses and ties, didn't come to work in jeans. *We all used to look up to lawyers and politicians too. Hell, doctors made house visits.*

How had it all gone so wrong, with everybody looking out only for number one? That's why she had joined the militia with her husband. That's why, as her dying legacy, she had figured out how to fund it. That's why her son might be blood family, but the militia was her real family.

The congregation rose to sing the last hymn, returning her to the present. Boss spent the requisite time in chitchat, made her excuses for not joining folks for lunch, and headed to Da Yooper Tourist Trap, where everything went smooth as silk. The chemist stored the magic potion in a five-gallon container like Boss had used at camp before she got running water. She placed the container in the well of her passenger seat so it wouldn't spill.

Before leaving, Boss used the restroom and left one of the throwaway phones in the ladies' room towel bin, making sure to hold it with toilet paper so she didn't leave any fingerprints after she had done such a meticulous job of cleaning it. The second phone she left outside the BP station at Koski Korners. The rest she pitched in the woods, one each from the three bridges she crossed between Republic and Amasa. She saved Mrs. Pirhonen's phone for last—why she wasn't sure, maybe because it had treated her so well.

During the rest of the trip home, she went through a mental checklist of all the steps taken and her remaining exposure. All communications with biologists Brandon Newhouse and Bethany Palmer would trace back to Brett Aho. The only person they had seen was Brett, and Brett was dead. Brett had contacted her only through Mrs. Pirhonen's cell phone and the cops had hit a dead end tracking down who paid for the phone. She might possibly come under suspicion, but there would be no proof. Whenever she made the afterhours deposits in Mrs. Pirhonen's account, she'd destroyed the security tapes.

A guy who lived in Colorado owned the camp Brett rented. The guy had a mortgage with Hematite National Bank. Perhaps another tiny circumstantial piece of evidence, but only if the guy happened to remember they had discussed the camp—but everyone talked about their camps.

The cops were convinced Jimmie Heitzmann killed Brett. Jimmie had contacted her only in person at her camp or through the Pirhonen cell phone. No one had ever seen him there, and he wouldn't be telling any tales. If Jimmie had broken the rules and written anything down, the cops would have already been knocking at her door. All dead ends for the cops.

Maybe the chemist at Da Yooper Trap had watched her in a mirror, but what could he tell? Her basic size? She wore camo? Big deal; every third person wore camo. She had covered her hair with a floppy fishing hat. He had arrived after her and left before. They might find him after the deed was done, but then it would be too late.

Only the Hamtramck militia connection remained open. She did need to let him know to lay low and not use his cell phone. If he talked, he'd be a marked man. Once he got to prison, he'd come out in a pine box. Years ago, they had agreed to use each other's local weekly paper as a last-ditch warning system if either one of them became toxic. Unfortunately, the *Hamtramck Citizen* had folded after seventy-five years in business and they hadn't gotten around to another solution. *It's the minor things that trip you up.* She would have to risk making a phone call.

At the trailer she wiped the new container to remove fingerprints and stored it with the gas and diesel containers in the pole barn. Sixty-four hours and then she could put the magic potion to good use.

IN THE MORNING, I RETURNED to the crackle and smell of frying bacon.

"Just in time for breakfast," Owen shouted. He was wearing his funeral outfit, which probably doubled as Sunday church clothes. An apron declaring him the world's best grandpa covered his pressed shirt. The apron suggested a side of Owen I would like to see.

"How you want your eggs?" Owen shouted at me.

"Owen," I shouted. "You forgot to turn on your ears." I tapped both my ears.

He reached beneath the apron into his shirt pocket and found the switch. After a moment's adjustment he spoke in a normal volume. "They're both out lookin for you. You shoulda seen the cat fight when they discovered you was gone. Heard tell you was talkin to Doris Stanchina yesterday. Sweet woman. Did she give you a piece of pie? She makes the finest . . ."

Abigail entered the house and stamped the snow off her shoes. She pulled off a wool watch cap and her brunette tresses tumbled down. I tuned Owen out and tensed for the assault.

"The mighty warrior returns," she said. "Owen, that smells splendid. Could you please fry a couple for me?" She crooked her finger at me. "How about we step outside for a sec."

Although spoken softly, I took it as a command. She waited until we were both outside. "Mind telling me what that was about?"

"I was pissed. I did what I do when I'm pissed and don't want to hurt anyone. I walked away. I'm back. No harm, no foul. Why didn't you ever contact me after you left?"

She jabbed me in the chest. "Because *you* told me not to. *You* needed your space to think about everything. *You* needed your wilderness experience. *You* needed to recover from your self-perceived failure to protect me when I was shot at your home. Because, damn it, *you* pushed *me* away." She teared up. "I can't tell you how many times I wrote letters and tore them up because I didn't want to interfere with your healing. All I could hope was you still wanted me and you'd figure it out."

I retreated a step, dumbfounded. This was not how I remembered her departure at all.

"This time you walked away from the professional me. I trusted you and . . ." Tears trickled from under her shades. "Women want to talk things out, Seamus. Men want to think them through, which is fine up to a point, but then you have to share your thoughts. We had been constant companions for six months, but you could never get to the second stage, could you?

"It's like we were the Blue Nile and the White Nile—together but separate." She demonstrated with her hands. "At your camp, without any outside influences, we became less, not more, just as the Nile starts to evaporate in its run to the sea because there are so few tributaries."

She shoved her shades in a pocket and wiped her eyes with her hands. "And look at you . . . you've evaporated. You're all skin and bones."

She stomped her heel hard enough for the porch floor to shake my legs. "Here we are again: I'm doing all the talking. Damn it. Your turn, Seamus. What's going on? And why don't you start with, why didn't you call me back when I left you messages while I was driving up here?"

"What messages?"

"Where's your cell phone?" She stormed off to retrieve it from the room Owen had assigned me. I stood rooted in place until she returned. "Just once I wish you would recognize cell phones as two-way communication devices. But why would you, since you don't know what two-way communication means? They're not only for you to call someone. Other people call you because they want to talk with you."

She thrust the phone at me. "You have six messages. See how you do this? One is from Robert Rand—remember him? He's your employer. Two are from me, and three are from your son. Oh, Seamus, what am I going to do with you?" She jammed the phone into my hand. "Never mind, you're Pendergast's problem now."

"Meaning?"

"Meaning Rand pulled me."

"But it wasn't your fault."

"You think? Oh, crap, I forgot to let Pendergast know you showed up." She left me shivering on the porch.

I listened to the messages. All six ended with the same request: could I please call as soon as possible?

Talk about feeling like a piece of garbage.

Pendergast returned before I had screwed up my courage to go inside. She mumbled as she went past me, "We need to talk."

Owen left to go to church. Breakfast was silent, after which Abigail went into the women's bedroom and returned with a bag.

Pendergast asked, "How can I get all your electronic ears to you?"

"If Seamus is still alive he can send them back. If not?" She shrugged. "Ball's in your court, Mr. McCree."

"You're really leaving?" I asked.

"I always said you were the intuitive sort," Abigail closed the door behind her.

THIRTY-THREE

Normally Boss took breakfast in town, but something told her this morning she should hang around camp. Good thing. She met Bartelle and McCree at the door of the single-wide and didn't have to feign shock as they handed her a search warrant. Before she let them in, she slowly read it to give herself time to recover from sweaty palms and a racing heart. They were looking for cell phones: Mrs. Pirhonen's and six with 715 area codes, and the fifty-caliber rifle. Good thing she had dispatched the cell phones the day before. The rifle was buried on Hematite Bank's foreclosed property with the clothes she had worn that awful night.

She ushered them in. "Looks legal to me, but what do I know, other than you're wasting your time? I won't bother asking why you're searching here. I'm sure you won't tell me. Can I get you boys some coffee?" She had expected the cops would look at her, but probably not until after her death. What would they find? The militia material she'd blame on her husband. They could probably recover emails from the laptop. What would she say if they asked about the new five-gallon container with the magic potion? Nothing. The search warrant didn't cover it. To present a happy face, she visualized deer hunting with her father. Those were such good times.

Bartelle and McCree began in the kitchen and opened every drawer, every cupboard, tapped the floor for false bottoms, pulled out the refrigerator. Next came the living room and bathroom. In the bedroom, they discovered the militia material and the false bottom drawer, but she had already emptied it. Since it didn't fit their search warrant, they couldn't spend too much time with the militia stuff, but she decided to spin it anyway.

From the doorway she said, "Frank's stuff, my late husband. He spent all his free time here, and I haven't wanted to throw out anything of his. I know it's kind of silly. It's been three years, but this is the place where I still feel his presence."

They mumbled understanding while poking under the bed, feeling under the mattress. Boss asked, "Looks like you're almost done in here, you want me to unlock the outbuildings?"

"Give us the keys," Bartelle said. "We'd prefer you to stay inside."

"How about when you're done here, I lock up this place and unlock all the outbuildings? Then you won't need me here, and I can get some work done in town. You'll lock them up when you're finished?"

"We'll have to do your truck next, but it sounds like a plan," Bartelle said.

After they finished inside, she locked the door behind them. McCree crawled underneath the single-wide and she led Bartelle to the old latrine and various sheds and unlocked everything to his satisfaction. "Just snap them shut." she said.

Bartelle searched the truck, which was totally clean, and wished her a great day.

Not today, she thought, but two days from now will be special.

BARTELLE AND I WATCHED MRS. Maki leave. "She seemed nervous," I said. "Especially as we looked at the militia stuff."

"Well, we already knew her husband was a commander in their heyday."

"Any indication she was involved?"

"It was a macho outfit. I'm not even sure women were allowed. I can understand not throwing stuff away, though. My Aunt Angelica still keeps a Hudson Bay wool shirt my uncle wore. She claims to use it on cold nights, but I think she still wants something to remind her of him all these years later."

"So you think she was telling the truth?"

He left my question unanswered and we continued our search. We found no cell phones and no fifty-caliber rifles in any of the structures. Tacked on the back side of a woodshed were two pelts. "Those aren't—"

"Not wolf," Bartelle said, "Coyote. Look at the ears: they're pointed, not rounded. He touched the nose. "And a coyote's muzzle is also more pointed than a wolf's. Don't try to judge by overall size. A young wolf can be smaller than a grown coyote. Huh?" He stepped closer to the pelts. "Look at these holes."

One had two holes; the other had six. Half the holes were round, the other half jagged. "Okay," I said. "They were shot from the right and the bullets exited their left side. What else am I supposed to see?"

"The bullets punched through the coyotes so they were shot with a high-powered gun. Not surprising, but the interesting thing is the pelt with the six holes. Bing, bing, bing. The coyote didn't stand there after getting shot once for the hunter to do it a second and third time."

"A three-shot burst," I said.

"Bingo, just like the ones used to kill those guys at your place."

Bartelle's cell phone rang with a "God Bless America" tune. The state troopers who had searched Sam Maki's home and office found nothing of interest. We spent the rest of the daylight hours scouring Mrs. Maki's forty acres. In the first five minutes, we found the coyote remains, well picked over by scavengers. Otherwise, our search was fruitless. As dark gathered and a light mist began to fall, Bartelle took me to Owen's.

Bartelle pulled up next to Owen's rusted iron menagerie and clunked the car into park before it had completely stopped. "I'm pretty much flat out of ideas. Maybe we'll get lucky and someone will use one of those phones."

"I've been meaning to ask you," I said. "What was it that killed Brandon Newhouse?"

Bartelle looked at me sharply, shifted his gaze to the car roof, and shrugged once. "Pneumonia."

"That kills one theory I was working on. You going to ask Mrs. Maki about the coyotes?"

"It's about all we've got unless someone uses those phones. And Seamus, stay put tonight. Just because you lucked out when you walked into Amasa to the Rusty Sawblade doesn't mean it will happen again. Who knows what might have happened if you hadn't found that guy who poured your foundation and he let you crash on his couch. Walking around alone is crazy right now and I don't want to attend any more funerals."

It felt like a cheap shot. It also felt like I deserved it.

TUESDAY MORNING, THE SMELL OF bacon filled the house as Owen served another artery-clogging breakfast. We sat in our assigned seats, boys on one side, Pendergast on the other next to the empty place where Abigail should have been if I hadn't been so damn stupid. I had tossed and turned all night. Tossing because I was missing something crucial in the investigation. Turning because I had screwed up my personal life. Again.

I knew the best way to come up with missing investigation pieces was to take a break from the problem and let my unconscious work. Unfortunately, my unconscious seemed clueless about my personal life.

"Owen," Pendergast said, "I'm taking Seamus to meet Sergeant Bartelle. I notice you're low on veggies and fruits. Anything in particular you want me to get at the store?"

"What do you mean?" I said. "You can't leave here."

"And you need protection." She resumed eating, as though she had already won the argument. She shrugged, then added: "Besides, lying around all day watching TV isn't my idea of fun. I'd rather be out and about."

I put my fork down. "Rand must not think I do since he ordered Abigail away instead of just chewing me out. There's no reason for you to cross AIC Cooper. It's one thing watching Owen's and my backs while we're sleeping. It's something else if you shove your involvement under his nose."

"Abigail lied to you. Rand didn't order her to protect you. She twisted his arm to let her. That whole line with ovacaput—she made it up. You're an idiot if you don't know she loves you."

"And you know this because?"

"We talked. Something you should try."

I pointed a fork at Owen, who was shoveling in food as though he was eating by himself. "What do you think?"

"Before I got these choppers fixed up, all I could eat was soft stuff." He pulled the dentures from his mouth, studied them like Hamlet contemplating the skull, and then returned them to their proper place. "I got so sick of overripe bananers and pears and mushy vegetables, once they fixed me up I swore off that stuff and, despite what they say on TV, I cain't eat no apples. I can do corn on the cob, but that ain't in season. If you're wantin somethin different, that wouldn't make me no nevermind. I tolerated them soups Seamus made when I'd bring him his supplies. Still got more home fries if you want 'em."

I rubbed my forehead with both hands, trying to make sense of this conversation. "I won't permit you to screw up your life, Agent Pendergast."

"And who made you God?" She kicked me under the table with a socked foot. "This is the twenty-first century, McCree. People get to make their own choices. For better or for worse. Besides . . ." She kicked me again, but this time gently. "You can't drive unless I return your gas cap."

"Gas cap?"

"Yep. One of the things they taught me at Quantico. Within a mile your engine will shut down because without your gas cap the pressure in the engine is all wrong."

"You was in the Marines?" Owen asked.

"You took my gas cap?" I asked.

She smiled at Owen. "The FBI has their training at Quantico." She exaggerated her smile for me. "I wasn't about to have you drive off without me."

Owen cleared his throat. "Don't play checkers with that one. While you're in town, Seamus, you call on them window fellas. Your replacement windows should be in. If we get one last cold spell to freeze the roads, they might get them in before spring. Otherwise, you're lookin at May. How long you fixin to stay?"

"I know we're an inconvenience—"

"That ain't why I'm askin. If I didn't want you here, you'd come back from town and find your stuff on the porch and the door locked. I was wonderin if I should invite the grandkids over for some of their Easter vacation."

"I couldn't possibly impose on you so long," I said. "That's nearly a month away."

"Are you thick in the skull? There's nothin—" Owen slammed his fist on the table, rattling the plates and spilling Pendergast's coffee. His face turned dark purple. "Nothin more important than gettin these people. You can stay here until Christmas as long as you and Bartelle are still lookin at those killins. We lost five fine people, and there ain't nothin I wouldn't do to bring them back. But since I cain't, the next best thing is to string up the polecat that done it."

I mumbled appreciation and forced down scrambled egg, which had now lost its flavor. I wondered if we were making progress.

Pendergast handed me the gas cap after she climbed into the passenger seat.

"I know I can never outlast your quiet," Pendergast said after we reached paved road. "I'm not going to even try. You got both barrels of the shotgun this morning between Owen and me. Not that you didn't deserve it." She gave my thigh a friendly, but not too friendly, pat.

"I'm sorry if our time together got in the way of you and Abigail. She and I talked a lot while you were AWOL. Listen up, Seamus. The woman is crazy in love with you. I'm not saying you two should get hitched, buy a two-story ranch in the suburbs and have two point five kids—well one point five, you've already got Patrick and he's great. You would be a fool if you don't crawl on your knees down to Chicago and make up with her. Besides, you're stupid if you don't realize you love her as much as she loves you."

My jaw ached from clenching my teeth while she talked. I didn't want to be lectured to, but it was justified. Probably.

"I've watched you long enough to know you won't start crawling south until you're done up here. So what did you and Bartelle find with your search warrants? Oh, and in case you were thinking of dumping me, I'm taking permanent possession of your gas cap."

She gave my upper arm a friendly punch and stuck out her hand. "Friends?"

"Either that or I need to drive your side of the car into a tree," I said.

THIRTY-FOUR

Pendergast sat in the office by herself plodding through case files while Bartelle and McCree interviewed Sam Maki. She saw no burning bushes, heard no heralding angels. As soon as the guys returned, she pounced, "Get anything?"

McCree shook his head. "He claimed he was asleep with his wife the night of the killings at my place. Where else would anyone be? He's now hired Paddy's firm to do a complete security analysis of their systems. He sure seemed seriously angry about someone screwing with their software security."

"The man," Bartelle said, "has brass balls. Or isn't our guy. He claims he resigned from the militia as a sophomore in college. Showed me a letter from his father ripping him a new one for deserting the cause. Would you have kept that letter?"

McCree leaned his head back and howled with laughter. "Well, it would be great cover for a moment such as this."

"Yeah right," Bartelle said. "He knew nothing about the coyotes. Only hunts partridge and deer with business colleagues. Never owned a fifty-caliber gun. I verified his alibi for when the phones were purchased down in Wausau.

"Oh, and speaking about those phones, yesterday I got a call from a local Wausau officer who stopped by the store to inquire about the phone sale. The clerk remembered the sale to a late middle-aged white woman. Couldn't remember much else and there's no security tape. The clerk was only twenty and put the buyer's age between forty-five and sixty-five. The girl didn't think it would help to work with a police artist, but thought she might recognize the woman if we had a picture."

Pendergast asked McCree, "What's your *gut* tell you?"

"Sam Maki is either a great actor or we're barking up the wrong tree. Of course, I've been fooled by great actors before. I say the word, 'bodyguard,' what comes to mind? A big strapping hulk of a guy, right? Abigail fights that image all the time because she's not male and, while she's not small, she's also not an Amazon. She often says she's more effective because people don't think she is a bodyguard."

Pendergast witnessed Bartelle crook his arm over his head and start scratching away. She figured he was equally clueless about McCree's point. "And . . ." She gestured to indicate she wanted more.

"It's those coyote pelts. They've kept bothering me and—remember the Feds running over each other trying to figure out how the militia was using the camp that burned down to fund operations? The DEA was convinced they were bringing in drugs from Canada. AFT thought they were smuggling firearms, and Homeland Security suspected they were tied into terrorists. All of them were getting intel from the NSA, but each saw what they wanted to see. What do you think about when someone mentions a militia outfit? A bunch of guys. Assume Sam Maki has been telling the truth all along. Who first ran the bank after his father died?"

"His mother, K.C. Maki," Bartelle said.

"Right, and it's a banking family. I'll lay dollars to donuts she knows how to run the teller machines. Maybe she worked in the bank as a teller when she was young. Where did we find the old militia information? Her camp. Where did we find the coyotes with the three-burst kill pattern? Her camp. There's money involved here somewhere and what does she do for the bank? Personal investments and financial planning. Why couldn't she be the link to everything? Her husband dies and she runs the bank until she can get Sonny up to speed. Maybe she also took over the militia operations from her husband?

"In fact," McCree slapped his forehead so hard it showed white before turning red. "Who guaranteed the viatical settlement payments? Hematite Bank. Who at Hematite is responsible for personal finances? K.C. Maki. Remember what I said about your aunt's policy?"

Bartelle stopped scratching, leaned forward. "You think the militia is going to storm the Laughing Loon and kill all the geezers? That's crazy."

"What," Pendergast asked, "are you two talking about?"

"First things first," Bartelle said. He flipped through his notes and phoned Doris Stanchina. McCree waved Pendergast quiet while Bartelle asked Doris about K.C. Maki.

After listening to the answers, Bartelle pursed his lips and raised his eyebrows. "So Mrs. Maki filled in whenever anyone called in sick?" Bartelle asked. "No reason to apologize for forgetting about her. We didn't think to ask either."

Bartelle replaced the receiver. "You know everyone's nickname for her is 'Boss.'"

"Even her son introduced her to me that way," McCree said.

"How about," Pendergast said "you fax a picture of Mrs. Maki to the phone clerk in Wausau. See if she can identify her. There's a recent picture in the *Iron County Reporter* of her giving me clothes at the hospital. If she's the one, so much for Christian charity!"

Bartelle got the administrative assistant to take care of the details and checked Kathryn Cynthia Maki for a record—all she had accumulated were a few speeding tickets.

"Is there a way to protect the Laughing Loon?" McCree asked after giving Pendergast the viatical details.

Pendergast joined Bartelle in head shaking. "He's got no evidence, Seamus. The best he can do is put a tail on Mrs. Maki. Even if this is her play, it's hard to see her leading the raid. It would come in the middle of the night, just like they tried at your place."

"Crap," spat McCree like a forty-five going off. "Then get her phone records and see if there's a link anywhere."

"We got nothing we can go to a judge with," Bartelle said. "We can't use the militia stuff we found at her camp or the coyote pelts. Even if we could, it's still not near enough."

"Yeah, but the NSA people don't seem to need much of any reason. I'll call Paddy and have him see what they'll say."

BOSS LET HERSELF INTO THE church through the side door off the alley. Taking the darkened stairway to the basement, she ran a gloved hand along the concrete block wall, following its rough edges to the central religious education room. She slipped inside and, using her fingers like spider legs, found the phone hanging on the wall, placed there years ago so the teachers could call nine-one-one without having to leave the room in case a child got hurt. Now, of course, everyone had cell phones.

The number pad lit at her touch, making it easy to dial in the dark. Voicemail answered; she whispered to disguise her voice, "Destroy that phone. No contact at all. The cops are all over this, but after tomorrow morning they'll be too late." Less than ten seconds, she thought. The cops won't be able to trace her call. Only one more link left to destroy, and no time like the present to do it.

At camp she set up the old Inspiron laptop and deleted all the emails from both the inbox and sent folder. Experts could retrieve things from the hard drive unless you used special erasing software, which she didn't have. What she did have was a sledgehammer, and she took great joy in pulverizing the machine. She collected the pieces and put them into a black plastic bag.

A dozen miles away, she threw the bag into a dumpster kept near the Florence Natural and Wild Rivers Interpretative Center picnic grounds. The effort of screeching the lid up pushed her into a coughing jag, which took forever to stop. It was worth the effort, though. The Wisconsin DNR would be more worried about litter than tying this to any investigation across state lines.

Despite the constant pain, she was jubilant. The plan would work. The only thing left to do was apply the five gallons of magic potion the next morning.

PADDY CALLED BACK MUCH QUICKER than even I expected.

"Not yet," he answered to my question regarding access to K.C. Maki's phone records. "Someone just called the Hamtramck cell phone and left a message. The call came from the Presbyterian Church in Crystal Falls two minutes ago. I quote, 'Destroy that phone. No contact at all. The cops are all over this, but after tomorrow morning they'll be too late.'"

"That's it?"

"Yeah, but given the analysis of calls I've done so far, the chances are ninety-nine out of one hundred Mrs. Pirhonen's cell phone was used to order up those two guys from Hamtramck."

"How do you know?"

He cleared his throat. "Remember, NSA's probably monitoring me too. The other thing you should know is that two of the six Wisconsin prepaids have been used. ICE already checked the people out. They appear to be just regular people who found the phones in Marquette County. I'm afraid someone got wise and ditched all the phones. I'll let you know when I have something more."

Bartelle called the Crystal Falls police to have someone run to the church. A minute later the answer came back: it was empty and locked. They would contact the church sexton.

Next, he ordered Tex to meet us at the church. The church sexton greeted us at the main entrance. He had no idea how many people had keys. "Too many, but no one listens to me," he said.

Tex dusted doorknobs, phones in the office, and the phone downstairs. "Too many prints," he kept muttering under his breath.

Outside and away from the sexton's hearing, Bartelle told Tex to start with the prints from the phones. First thing, check them against K.C. Maki." Tex raised one eyebrow, a trick I had never mastered.

"She got prints on file?" Tex asked.

"I'll bet," I said. "She had to be fingerprinted for her NASD exams."

"NA what?" Bartelle asked.

"National Association of Securities Dealers. If she's giving advice or selling annuities, she needs to have passed some of their exams. They require your fingerprints. Broker/dealers need to get the Criminal History Record Information from the FBI." I laughed at myself. "I know, too much information. The point is: her prints are on file somewhere."

"If the sheriff's department took them, they're in Michigan's database," Tex said. "The whole thing is automated. If I'm only trying to match her, we'll know later today."

"Just to be on the safe side," Bartelle said. "Check her son as well. Sam Maki."

With a roar of stressed engine, Tex laid rubber like a teenager on a hot date leaving us breathing burnt rubber.

After tomorrow morning they'll be too late. I had to make Bartelle understand those words from the phone message were a ticking clock and that not acting might seal the fate of those who had signed the viatical settlements.

"Let's make a quick stop at the Laughing Loon," I said. "I don't remember the name of the company buying those policies, and we can ask your aunt who the salesman—or, if my guess is right—saleswoman was."

After a moment's hesitation, Bartelle said, "I'll give her a call."

"It's just around the corner. Pendergast can cool her heels in your office for another ten minutes. I've found talking to someone in person is preferable to the phone." I could see the indecision in his eyes. "Please," I pleaded. "Ten minutes."

Bartelle rubbed his eyes with the heels of his hands. "Ten minutes. Max. Maybe when we get back Tex will have something on the prints."

BARTELLE SIGNED THEM IN AT the Laughing Loon and led the way to his aunt's room. "Just a second," she called from the back after Bartelle rapped on the door.

She wheeled out in her chair; a huge smile lit her face when she saw Bartelle, who made the introductions. "Seamus McCree, this is my aunt, Mrs. Angelica Ricci."

"Isn't this the man who looked at my viatical settlement?" At Bartelle's nod, she continued. "Everyone who signed the deal had their checks clear, so I decided if some fool wanted to pay more than they should for the investment, I'd be darned if I wouldn't let them. I took the money and laddered a few CDs since interest rates are lousy. That way, if rates go up, I won't be locked in forever."

"Laddered CDs?" Bartelle asked.

"It means," McCree said, "she bought several certificates of deposit with different maturity dates, and she'll roll them over as they come due. Sounds like a good plan to me. I don't recall the name of the company making the viatical settlements."

"Slips my mind too," Mrs. Ricci said. "K.C. Maki made the sale. You know her, don't you, Lon?"

Bartelle and McCree traded sideways looks and Bartelle asked if she still had the papers available. She pulled them from a drawer. Bartelle wrote the name in his notebook: Freedom Settlements of Michigan, LLC.

"What's the big interest all of a sudden?" Mrs. Ricci asked. "You didn't make a math error did you, young man?"

McCree gave her a charming smile. "No, ma'am. How do you like living here? I ask because at some point I'll need to find something similar for my mother."

She chattered on with a little encouragement from McCree, and Bartelle checked his watch, wondering where he was going with his questions, especially when his aunt's biggest complaints were that they kept the rooms too hot and the hot water too cold. He caught on after McCree said, "It's nice they take you on trips. Do you have any in the near future?"

"Oh yes!" she said. "And you know it just came up. Twice a year they try to get as many of us as possible to go to the casino. They make a big deal of it. Serve us a free lunch. Give us five bucks for the slots. We usually have at least two busloads. Normally, it's in April or May and again in October or November, but this year it's pushed up to tomorrow. They must have gotten a better deal."

"Tomorrow?" Alarm filled Bartelle. McCree's supposition just gained traction. "You going?" He heard the anxiety in his voice.

"Of course." She soundlessly laughed and clapped her hands together. "Those old folks play the slots, but I usually do pretty well at blackjack and craps. Do you know the house has the biggest margin on the slots?"

Bartelle stood up. "Sounds like fun," he said. "I'll look forward to hearing all about it. Mr. McCree and I have a few other things to check on the investigation." He leaned down and kissed her cheek. "You take care now and don't bust the casino."

I TAGGED ALONG AS BARTELLE tracked down the Laughing Loon's manager, a thin wisp of a man sporting a comb-over that fooled no one except himself. His voice was whiny, but I was only half paying attention to their conversation. I was plotting how to uncover the ownership of Freedom Settlements of Michigan, LLC and wondering who was behind it.

Bartelle determined the Laughing Loon was using the tour bus company they had always used for the casino trip. They were going to the same casino. The tour bus operator supplied the drivers; Laughing Loon provided the attendants to help the residents on and off the buses. They also used two specialized vans for those with wheelchairs.

"Really, officer, there's nothing unusual about this. We do it twice a year, timed for the HVAC guys doing system maintenance. They need to shut down the furnace and test the air conditioning. Depending on how long it takes, some of the rooms can get cool—not dangerously so—but some older people find it uncomfortable."

"But some people don't go on the trip?" Bartelle said.

"Sure. They're too ill or can't be easily moved. For example, one lady had a recent hip replacement and she's too fragile to go. We bring those left behind to our day room, which we heat with electric heaters for the duration. You haven't told me what this is all about."

Bartelle ignored the implied question and got contact information for the transport company and casino. We left Laughing Loon at a fast walk. Once safely in Bartelle's car he said, "Are you thinking what I'm thinking?" While talking to the manager, Bartelle had presented a calm exterior with the exception of a nervous tic in his left eye. Now the stress showed all over his face.

"What are you going to do?"

"I'm open to ideas. Should I cancel their trip?"

"Maybe you should let it go forward, but introduce a bunch of safeguards. Sounded like two buses and two vans. Can you add a guard to each, get the vehicles inspected before they leave the company's lot— brakes, fluids, bombs—that sort of thing. Maybe even replace the drivers? If you shut it down, they may change plans and end up mowing everyone down in their beds some night. They've shown they're not averse to killing people. Of course, that may be their plan anyway. Not my call, though, and thank God."

"Point taken. Above a sergeant's pay grade, too."

"Why don't we try to shake up K.C. Maki? Without giving any specifics, let her know we're onto her scheme. Then put on a tail. Maybe she'll call it off or lead us to someone. What have we got to lose? I also want to try to track down who owns Freedom Settlements of Michigan. Maybe we can get a lead that way."

Something niggled at the back of my brain, but I couldn't work it into the light. Bartelle called the sheriff and brought him up to speed. When the conversation concluded, Bartelle motioned to me to follow him. "Let's see if we can rattle Mrs. Maki."

Thirty-Five

BOSS SAW THEM WALK IN the bank's door and head directly toward her office. She picked up the phone and dialed her home number. She conversed with her answering machine, letting Bartelle and McCree hear her give such noncommittal information as "uh-huh" and "I can see how that would work," and "Tell me a little more about that." All the while, she worked to control her bouncing knee. She looked up, gave them the "just a minute" sign and motioned to the chairs in front of her desk.

Once she calmed her leg she signed off the phone call, promising she'd get back to the other party in a day or two. Putting on her brightest smile, she asked, "What can I do for you gentlemen today?"

She expected Bartelle to take the lead and damn near crapped her pants when McCree opened the conversation with, "I hear they call you Boss. Well, Boss, the biggest mistake you made was not killing me. Too late now. I figured out your scheme, and I guarantee this: not one penny from the life insurance proceeds will be paid if those people at the Laughing Loon die in some collective tragedy." He rose partly from his chair as though he was going to vault the desk. "Mark my words, in days or maybe even hours, your life is over. O-V-E-R."

She felt Bartelle's eyes focused on her until McCree started his spelling lesson. Then he reached up and pulled McCree down to his seat, but said nothing.

Boss's mind raced to frame an answer. The threat on her life was nothing. Cancer was going to beat justice. Whatever else, she must protect the plan. She chose righteous anger as her weapon. "Who are you to come into my office and accuse me of . . . of . . . whatever it is you are accusing me of?" She sounded a bit strained to herself, and the words didn't come out as she had intended them. "You may leave right now."

McCree smiled, like he had won some battle.

Bartelle cleared his throat. "We hoped not to have to take you to the jail to talk. We thought it would be easier for you here. Maybe we should close the door?"

Now she got it: bad cop/good cop—even though McCree wasn't one. Bartelle reached behind him and closed the door. The harsh click startled her back to the present.

"We know you stole the phone from Mrs. Pirhonen," McCree said. "And you manipulated the bank's records so it would look like she kept paying the phone bill. Nice setup. And those calls you made right before those two guys from the militia came to the woods and killed five of your neighbors? Wouldn't surprise me if your lawyer doesn't go for a change in venue."

"Now, Seamus," Bartelle said. "We didn't come here to badger her. We wanted to give her a chance to tell us how she got involved in this whole mess. It's probably something her husband sucked her into and she didn't know the details until it was too late. I'm sure we can find some way to smooth this over for one of the county's leading citizens."

McCree's face reddened in anger and Boss thought he might spit at her. Instead he poked his finger at Bartelle. "I'll tell you this," he yelled. "If one more person dies, it is all on her head." He jabbed his finger in her direction and she rocked back in her chair. "I know you can't arrest her yet, but as soon as the clerk verifies she's the one who bought all those phones in Wausau—" He abruptly rose, knocking his chair backwards and leaned over the desk. "You made a big mistake calling Hamtramck again. We're checking prints on the phone you used at the Presbyterian Church."

Boss tamped down fear, surprised anything could still make her afraid. She knew she had a glazed look because she felt as though someone had taken a bat and smacked her on the head. How had they figured out everything? Somehow she managed to say, "If you have specific questions, perhaps I can help you, but I'm really confused by what you're saying."

Bartelle again took charge in his soft, comforting voice, asking once more about Mrs. Pirhonen's phone—she denied having anything to do with it. She thought about having her lawyer present for this questioning, but decided she was better off feigning innocence and stonewalling. She reminded herself: despite what McCree claimed, nothing had really changed. They had nothing solid and could have nothing unless someone talked, and they had yet to mention any names. She relaxed in her chair and, like a wily trout, ignored the lures Bartelle cast in front of her.

Remember, she told herself, get through tomorrow and everything will take care of itself.

OWEN GOT CRUSTY ON ME after I complimented him on the wholesome dinner he had concocted with the fresh ingredients we provided. "Just don't get used to it," he said. "So spill the beans. What's goin on at the Laughin Loon?"

"You tell us," Pendergast said.

"Heard tell there's a big scare about takin the residents to the casino tomorrow. They replaced all the bus drivers with retired cops, and off-duties are ridin shotgun."

"I helped Bartelle with that," Pendergast said. "It's amazing how many police officers or retired cops up here are licensed to drive buses."

Owen snorted. "You usually need two or three jobs around here just to make it. Anyone retirin from a government job keeps workin at somethin else."

"Well," Pendergast said between bites, "Bartelle already got the buses inspected—all clean—and they're under guard. The DNR's going to cover them from the air."

"I hear tell the cops wanted the Loonies to cancel the trip, but I didn't hear nothin about who's supposed to be plannin this ambush. What if it's a roadside bomb type deal?"

"I'm sure they considered all the risks," I said. "While Pendergast was arranging security, I traced who owns the company that bought the insurance policies from folks at the Laughing Loon. I found a spaghetti bowl of interlocking corporations, which ultimately end up being owned by a private foreign corporation."

"Which, I'll bet," Pendergast added, "is located in one of those fine upstanding countries where secrecy is the biggest business."

"Bingo. This is so elaborate it must be set up to launder money."

Owen yanked out his dentures and wiped them with a finger. "Dad-burn seed hurts like a sumbitch root canal." With dentures back in place he asked, "What's all this about dry cleanin money? You know who the baddies are?"

"Sure do, Owen," I said. "But we can't talk about it, so mum's the word."

"You can count on me," he said. "'Bout time I get to the senior center for bingo." After Owen left, Pendergast asked why I told Owen we had a suspect.

"He'll tell everyone at bingo, they'll tell their families, and by tomorrow morning everyone should know. Maybe then they'll think twice about whatever they planned. The whole idea is to catch them before they do anything, right?"

"I see your point. While Bartelle guards the caravan tomorrow, I thought I'd look through the files one more time. Want to join me?"

"Bartelle say I could look at the files?"

She flashed a smile. "I'm sorry. The tree frogs are so loud tonight, I didn't hear what you asked."

BOSS NOTICED THE TAIL FOLLOWING her up Rock Crusher Road to camp and wondered when it had started. She pulled into the driveway and parked behind the single-wide, retrieved the five-gallon container of magic potion and placed it in the passenger footwell. Once inside the trailer, she brewed a pot of coffee.

After pouring steaming coffee into a thermos, she grabbed a pint carton of half and half and a nearly full bottle of whiskey and walked down to the road. Sure enough, parked up the road a piece, pointed toward town, was the unmarked Iron County Sheriff's car. Those antennas give them away. She walked up to the driver's window, and the surprised young man lowered it.

"I'd invite you in, but I'm sure you aren't allowed. I don't know how long your shift is, so I brought you coffee." She handed him the thermos. "Half and half?" She held up the whiskey bottle. "Or something a bit stronger? I can get some sugar if you want it sweet."

He tried to return the thermos. "I can't take these, Mrs. Maki."

"Oh, you're going to need them because I'm not going out tonight and don't have to leave until noon tomorrow." The last was a patent lie, but best to set expectations early.

"Please, Mrs. Maki, I can't accept this."

"Well, if you need to use the facilities, come right in. The door won't be locked and I'm a heavy sleeper, so I'll never know. You have a good evening now." She collected her offerings and returned to the single-wide.

Now what the hell was she going to do? If it weren't for the five gallons of stuff, she could slip out the back and walk to town, but she needed the potion and she needed a few plumbing tools. The cop car was pointed toward town. She could escape in her truck going the other way, but there'd be a BOLO on her before she made it to the first turn. She'd planted the seed about her sticking around; she either needed to figure out how to get past him with the car, or rig up some method of carrying the potion and the tools if she walked. That wouldn't be practical—someone would see her.

The rough woods road running from her property onto the adjacent state land was her last chance. If she could make it through without getting stuck and without the cop noticing she was gone, then she had a few hours before they would miss her.

She returned to the cop and he rolled down his window. "Ma'am?"

"I decided to take a little ATV ride. I thought maybe I should tell you so you didn't get worried. I expect to be gone less than an hour. I'll let you know when I get back?"

She wished she could capture a picture of the kid's face. He had no clue what to do and would have to call it in. By then she'd be gone and about the time they had their undies all in a wad, she'd report back.

Good thing she had checked the woods. She had to clear two downed trees from a late-winter storm. She returned from her scouting mission to find the unmarked car had company: an Iron County vehicle towing a trailer with an ATV. She reported in, again offered coffee and/or whiskey, gave them a convincing yawn and a realistic hacking spell. Minutes later, she was asleep.

SHE HAD BEEN A BIT rankled when, for her last birthday, Sam unilaterally replaced her well-used F-150 with a Lexus RX hybrid. Yes, it was fuel efficient. Yes, it was reliable—the point the kids emphasized in their birthday note. Yes, the bank was wooing a Lexus dealership to settle in Crystal Falls. Yes, its ground clearance was acceptable at a touch under seven inches. But what she really appreciated right now was its silent start.

Not until she was several hundred yards away from the single-wide on the two-track to the state land did the gas engine engage. The cop was unlikely to hear it or attribute it to her.

Expecting the buses and vans to leave at nine a.m., she had given them an extra half hour and arrived at the Laughing Loon at nine-thirty a.m. with tools and container in hand. The cops were all gone except for the rent-a-cop manning a makeshift barricade in the driveway.

She lowered her window, smiled at a face she knew, but wasn't coming up with the name. "Problem?" she yelled over his radio blaring "Telephone Time."

"Not hardly, Mrs. Maki. I'm supposed to get everyone to sign in since the receptionist is off to the casino with all the old . . . er, residents." He handed a clipboard through her window. She scrawled an illegible signature on the line and handed it back. "Thanks, ma'am." He waved her on.

What were the chances he would remember her? Well, it would be his word against the cop babysitting her camp, who would swear she never left. She drove past the facility and took the service road around back. As previously agreed with the manager, the bulkhead doors were unlocked. She pried one up with a squeal of disuse and ducked down the stairs to the furnace room carrying the five-gallon can. The manager had done the initial preparation and turned off the furnace to let it cool. It would only take a few minutes to finish her work.

THIRTY-SIX

PENDERGAST AND I OCCUPIED A pin-drop quiet meeting room in the sheriff's office with the various case files stacked on the table. It was depressing to realize each of the ten red folders reflected a death: Brett Aho—believed to have been killed by Jimmie Heitzmann; Jimmie Heitzmann—drowned when his snowmobile broke through Long Lake's ice cover; Brandon Newhouse—weighted down with cement blocks and pulled out of Long Lake with Jimmie Heitzmann; the first militia guy—a suicide; the second militia guy—finally discovered in the woods with the stolen ATV, either accidently shot or purposefully killed to eliminate a witness; and finally, the five locals—gunned down trying to protect me.

The Laughing Loon trip was scheduled to last all day, leaving shortly after breakfast and returning in time for dinner. Bartelle shadowed the caravan from a DNR plane. The sheriff, ensconced in his office, monitored everyone's position. Ahead of the caravan, police blocked road crossings with the same precision as if the president were touring the U.P. At least that was the plan.

Consequently, we would have an uninterrupted day to scrutinize the files. I had forgotten the amount of mind-numbing detail police investigations involved. Because many of the deaths were related, many pages cross-referenced other files. I was convinced Hematite National Bank and one or more Maki were involved, and so I initially focused on them.

After a couple of hours, I decided bouncing from file to file wasn't getting me anywhere. Pendergast's approach was to read each file from beginning to end. She was the trained investigator, so I modeled her behavior. I picked up Brandon Newhouse's file since his death was first. Reading his autopsy report, I came across the first piece of critical new information.

"Hey, Pendergast, why didn't you tell me Brandon died of Legionnaires' disease?"

"State secret. Literally. Homeland Security threatened us all. Technically pneumonia killed him, but Legionnaires' was the proximate cause."

I quickly pulled Brett Aho's and Jimmie Heitzmann's autopsy reports. Each had been tested for Legionnaires' disease and each was clean. I sifted through files until I came to the one with the forensic analysis of my home. The chemical analysis of the samples Tex took showed nothing harmful. Penciled in the margin was a note: "no L.D."

Legionnaires' disease? I folded my hands behind my head, closed my eyes, and leaned back in the chair. My heart was pounding blood so strongly I could feel the pressure in my eardrums. I thought I knew, but I couldn't jump to conclusions.

"Where did you and Brandon go that Brett Aho didn't go?"

She looked up from the file she was reading. "He was pretty much with us all the time."

I shook my head. "Can't be. There had to be someplace. Did he avoid a particular part of the cabin?"

"Nope. You saw: the cabin only had three rooms. Everybody went everywhere."

I pulled Tex's notes on his biological search of my house and read them again. He was concentrating on hot water. The camp Brandon and Pendergast had stayed at had running water, but I couldn't remember seeing a hot water heater. "How did you guys stay clean?"

"Sauna."

"Brett ever use the sauna?"

"What are you thinking?" She closed one file and opened another. "Now you mention it, he said he hated saunas—made him feel all woozy on account of asthma or something. He grabbed showers in town someplace."

"You were guinea pigs."

She gave me a what-the-hell-are-you-talking-about look.

"They intentionally infected you and Brandon with Legionnaires' disease in the sauna. Why else would they be so anxious to capture or kill you? The only person you saw was Brett Aho, and they killed him, so they had to be worried about something you could have told someone."

I whacked myself on the forehead. "It all fits. The Laughing Loon casino trip is today because of furnace maintenance. They're infecting the heating system today. Maybe they already have. We've got to evacuate the Laughing Loon and test their system."

"But you get Legionnaires' disease from air conditioning equipment. The FBI was supposed to check every place Brandon and I went."

"And obviously found nothing or you would have heard. The key to Legionnaires' disease is it needs to be transmitted in an aerosol. Hot water can work just as well. The Laughing Loon has steam heat—essentially the same delivery mechanism for Legionnaires' disease as a camp sauna. They're going to infect the old folks with Legionnaires' disease and collect on the life insurance policies Mrs. Maki bought from the residents. They're betting people treat it as a natural tragedy. Probably spur political investigations and lawsuits and whatnot, but the insurance companies will pay off on the life insurance. Whoever controls the secret account at the end of the corporation ownership chain I tried to follow will make a ton of money."

I paused to make sure I had her full attention. "Wanna bet this is how the militia is planning to fund their arms purchase?"

"No Seamus, you're wrong. Boiling water kills the bacteria that cause Legionnaires' disease. Anything over about a hundred and fifty degrees is enough, and you're talking steam heat."

I felt sure she and Brandon had been guinea pigs, but obviously I was wrong about the sauna. "Must be the air conditioning then."

PENDERGAST DECIDED I *COULD* BE right. I knew convincing the sheriff was beyond my talents and left Pendergast to the task. I phoned Owen instead. He beat me to the Laughing Loon and I wanted to hug him. He was standing talking to some guy blocking the driveway and making people sign in.

"When you called," Owen pointed toward his truck, "you didn't say nothin about what plumbin tools we'd need, so I brung everythin I had."

I was hardly paying attention to Owen's words. *It can't be air conditioning. Each room has its own unit. Those aren't the type that foster Legionnaires'.* Once out of the guard's hearing, I pointed out the problem to Owen.

"The annex with the dining room has central A/C. Got one of them big-sucker units on the roof."

We were back in business.

The manager and assistant manager were on the casino outing, as were most of the other employees. The guy checking us in didn't know where the maintenance man was and didn't know how to contact him. While I signed my name, I tried to read the names of everyone who had signed before me. I didn't recognize any names and several were such scrawls I figured they must be doctors.

We found the access stairs to the annex roof and I led Owen up. We had climbed several stairs when I held out my arm and stopped Owen. "These stairs are dusty." I said.

"Un-huh."

"And," I continued, "we're leaving footprints but there aren't any on the steps ahead of us. Is there another access to the roof?"

"Blamed if I know," he said.

We pushed open the door to the roof and Owen led the way to the cooling tower. "Sorry, Seamus. No one's been on this here roof. We're leavin tracks and there ain't none around the A/C."

Shit. Shit. Shit. "Maybe they don't know steam kills the bacteria. Let's check the furnace."

Clumping down the stairwell to the basement we sounded like two horses released from Noah's Ark. We found the boiler in a small room lit by a bare forty-watt bulb. On the far wall was a red switch, which I flicked off. "I hope that kills the furnace. You know anything about furnaces and stuff?"

"Never seen one this big, but theys all gotta operate about the same way, eh? Heat water to steam and the steam does the rest. Thermostat somewhere to control the furnace."

Using flashlights, Owen checked the furnace while I inspected the boiler. Dust covered everything. "I don't think anyone's been here," I said.

"They don't need to mess with the heatin elements if alls they gonna do is pump in contaminated water. Just drain off enough so's you can replace it. Let's take us a looksee at the boiler intake and drain." He followed the flashlight's cone and pointed. "Nope, dirtier than a dog that's been dustin himself for fleas."

Damn. Damn. Damn. My head ached from the pressure. I was wrong on all accounts, but my twisted stomach told me I was close to being right. *Think, brain. Damn it. Think.*

I closed my eyes and breathed in deeply through my nose. Owen was talking away, but I ignored it. I released the breath to a count of twenty and inhaled. On the third exhale, I had it.

"Where's the hot water heater, Owen?"

He pointed the light toward another corner. "Lookee there on the floor," he said. "Water ain't fully evaporated. And see here." He shined the light on a copper pipe. "This here's wiped clean and everythin else's dusty. Oh, he's good. Your perp pumped in the contaminated stuff through this intake."

Perp? Owen had been watching too many cop shows on cable. "You sure?"

"How I'd do it. You turn off the water, disconnect this here filter—see, there's some more water on the floor here—drain off whatever you need and then use a cheap little electric pump and, bingo, you sucked water from your container into the hot water holdin tank."

"What kind of container are you talking about?"

He waved the flashlight around and found a five-gallon container against the wall. "Somethin like that."

BOSS FIRST HEARD OF THE ruckus at the Laughing Loon from one of the bank's customers. According to that person, health officials had forced evacuation of the Laughing Loon's residents.

A deep sadness overcame her and she wanted to crawl under her desk and curl into a ball. She tried to tell herself all was not lost. Disposing of the Loonies with an "accidental" spread of Legionnaires' disease was a bust. But, having discovered one plot, the authorities might let down their guard. Then it would be up to someone else to bomb the place or raid it and finish the job.

Come on, K.C. You didn't earn the title "Boss" because you give up easily. She stuck her head into her son's office. "I'm not feeling so hot today. I gotta go home and lie down." Involuntarily she started hacking. "I probably won't be in until Monday. I'll reschedule my appointments."

Her son glanced up from the pile of papers covering his desk. "Maybe you should see your doctor. You've been coughing a lot again."

She waved away the idea that it was her lungs. "Might be coming down with something. I'll be fine."

On the way to her camp she stopped at the Jubilee and loaded up on groceries. The devil wanted her to ask the cop following her to help load the supplies into her SUV, but she refrained.

At camp, hidden from the road by her single-wide, she hitched a five-by-eight trailer to her ATV and packed in the supplies. She added billycans of gasoline, a couple thirty packs of beer, and two bottles of Jack Daniels. Using a duffle bag, she collected a few changes of clothes and threw in her revolver.

At dinnertime, she offered the police officer some freshly warmed pie. He refused the dessert and her offer to join her on an ATV jaunt. She washed the dinner dishes and put everything away before driving away on the ATV, again taking the back trail to the state land. From there, she took back roads to the land Hematite owned near the reservoir, where she dug up the canvas sack with the fifty-caliber automatic and two hundred rounds of ammo. She reburied the clothes. By the time she finished, she was huffing and puffing and coughing like an old-time car on its last legs.

She couldn't go faster than about fifteen miles an hour towing the trailer. She met minimal traffic along her route. No one stopped, and with the heavy clothes she wore against the forty-degree temperatures and the helmet with its dark facemask, no one could recognize her. For the last nine miles, she met only a snowshoe hare, halfway through its camouflage transition from white to brown, and two deer.

She slowed at the intersection where she had accidentally killed Digger—or was it Spider?—it all seemed a blur now—no, it was Digger, the fool. The snow and rain had obliterated most tracks and the police had removed whatever yellow crime scene tape they had put up. More likely they had just barricaded the road for a while.

Reaching the junction of Lukes Road and Shank Lake Road, her thoughts returned to the night she had ambushed the three guys. She had done her job. She had always done her job. If only Digger and Spider had done theirs. No use crying over spilt milk, as dear old Mom used to say. In retrospect, given McCree was the one to figure out the plan, her first instinct to take him out had been right.

It took three hours to get there, but it was the perfect spot. She was pleased to see her sources were correct: the cops had released McCree's house and it was no longer festooned by yellow tape. With mud season going full bore she was sure it would be empty, and who would think to look for her there? After parking the ATV and trailer in the pole barn, she busted a glass pane on the door from the deck, reached in, and undid the dead bolt.

Thirty-Seven

The next afternoon, Pendergast and I had a command appearance before the collective inquisition of the FBI and ICE. Bartelle waylaid us before we got to the assigned conference room. "Are we heroes or goats?" I asked.

"Tex confirmed a high level of Legionnaires' disease bacteria in the hot water tank and in the bit of water left in the billycan," Bartelle said. "That makes you heroes. Unfortunately, AIC Cooper has been spitting bullets at the sheriff for hiring CIG, knowing CIG had hired Agent Pendergast." Bartelle gave Pendergast's shoulder a squeeze. "We're all skewered goat's meat for that. Sheriff, bless his heart, didn't back down. Thought you should be prepared. Course we're in our own hot water."

I questioned that statement by furrowing my brow.

"Well, we are. We managed to lose the main suspect. When Mrs. Maki didn't leave for work the day after the fireworks, the on-duty officer knocked on her door. No answer. Her car was there, but her ATV and trailer were gone. Apparently, she told the nightshift officer she was planning an after-dinner ride and he never bothered to check."

Inside the room, the sheriff and Bartelle occupied one corner of the table, ICE another, and AIC Cooper a third. Pendergast and I settled into the empty spots.

Cooper fired the first salvo, telling Pendergast she was now on unpaid administrative leave. She showed more restraint than I would have, only turning red at the news. "Where's Owen Lyndstrom?" Cooper snarled. "He was supposed to be with you."

"He's working and needs the money," I said. "He told me to tell you he didn't know anything more than I did, and if you wanted to talk to him, you could come out after dinner and yap all you want. His words, not mine." I gave the moron my best false smile.

Bartelle confirmed they had searched Boss's home, camp, son's home, had talked to everyone they could think of. "We know she had a couple weeks' worth of supplies with her. We have to consider the possibility that she, her ATV, and trailer were all picked up by a larger enclosed trailer and taken someplace far away."

"The FBI has not been sitting still," Cooper said. "We matched the fingerprints on the inside of the billycan cap to a retired biochemist from the Midland area. We found Legionnaires' disease in his home lab and he's under arrest. Not talking . . . yet." He sent a curious look toward the ICE people, but they looked as relaxed as two guys could be. "You guys?"

"With the help of Patrick McCree and the cooperation of several email service providers, we nailed down evidence linking Maki—the mother—and the biochemist." To Cooper he said, "We'll get it to the FBI by the end of the day."

The second ICE agent smiled at me. A crocodile smile—all teeth and no warmth around his eyes.

"I apologize for getting off on the wrong foot with you, Mr. McCree. The federal government wants to thank you for your valuable assistance in this matter. We do have a few remaining questions. Perhaps Agent Pendergast could excuse us?"

Once we were alone, they wanted to know how I came up with the Legionnaires' disease "scenario." I took them through my thinking process, concluding with the final revelation. "While I was in the basement, I finally remembered that when I washed my hands in Mrs. Pirhonen's room, the hot water was not very hot. At the time I didn't think much of it, but in racking my brain for a solution, I realized management wouldn't want residents to accidentally scald themselves, so they wouldn't have the temperature set very high. The residents took showers—there was no bathtub in Mrs. Pirhonen's room—and that could provide the aerosol mechanism."

I didn't expect applause for my brilliance, but I didn't expect a three-hour grilling either. Apparently, someone considered the timing of my "discovery" of the plan a tad too convenient. They figured it was possible I had been in on the plot all along— maybe was even the mastermind—and had "solved" the crime only after it went south to throw off appearances of my collusion.

Only Owen slept well that night.

The next day officially ushered in spring. To celebrate, we had another cold snap with temperatures diving below zero at night. It matched Cooper's treatment of Pendergast. He wanted her gone. The only way the sheriff could appease the FBI without appearing to cave in was to decide he no longer needed CIG assistance on the cases. Without the CIG buffer, Pendergast had no choice but to leave town.

I again put her on a flight from Iron Mountain to Chicago. They called her flight for the Homeland Security inspection and she said in a serious voice, "I wonder if Cooper cut a deal to make sure I get strip-searched."

"He wouldn't—"

"Joke, Seamus. It was a joke. In all seriousness, I doubt we'll run across each other again. You're a great guy, but if I were you, I'd hurry to Chicago and straighten out your love life. Say goodbye to Patrick for me." She leaned in and gave me a dry peck on the cheek.

In the evening, I met a builder Owen recommended who would undertake rehabilitating my house. We agreed on scope and price. All I needed was to give the insurance company pictures of the damage. The agent didn't want to travel into the "dark beyond," so I decided to borrow Owen's ATV and ride up to my camp Sunday afternoon. I had a camera there.

Once I snapped the pictures, I would have no reason to stay. Bartelle let me know he would still be interested in running stuff past me, but I figured it was more *pro forma* than real. Pendergast was right: I needed to see Abigail. I thought she had permanently benched me, but Pendergast insisted I had earned two strikes, so if I was open and honest, Abigail's next pitch might be a batting practice fastball down the center of the plate.

All I could do was try.

I informed Owen of my plan to take pictures at camp and then leave Monday. He thought I should have a bodyguard. "I cain't go," he said. "My oldest grandkid's got a dance recital. I'll get someone to go with ya."

"No, Owen. K.C. Maki is gone. No one else cares a whit about me. I want to do this myself."

The woods roads were in the worst shape I had ever seen them, never having experienced the depth of mud as frost comes out of the ground. The ATV, with its four-wheel drive, got through without a hitch until I took a swale about three-quarters of a mile from my camp too slowly and became mired. Getting off, I sank to my knees in goop. I pushed. I pulled. I pushed again, slipped, and took an unanticipated mud bath. I didn't get my mouth closed and earned the opportunity to taste the mud. Bland, actually, and a bit crunchy.

I had no choice but to walk to camp, grab the come-a-long and chain, and schlep back to extract the ATV. With each step I felt the squish of mud in my boots. Eventually I spit out most of the gunk in my mouth. The socks I could throw away; the boots would clean up once they dried; I'd use lake water and brush my teeth at camp.

This would, of course, provide Owen with gossip fodder. I owed him at least that and, smiling at how he would spin the tale, I started enjoying the walk. Too early for black flies, the earliest spring flowers were luxuriating in the brief period of unobstructed sunlight occurring after the ground thaws and before trees sprout enough leaves to block the sun. An early phoebe repeatedly called its name.

With its characteristic *weep-weep-weep* call, a wood duck exploded from a vernal pond beside the road. From the pond's edge, the first spring peepers tried their voices. If I had been into maple sugaring, this would be the time. I slowed my walk, considering whether I should take it up some spring. It would be a lot of work, but I had plenty of sugar maples.

A hint of wood smoke intruded upon my reverie.

I checked the tops of the trees. No breeze, the fire had to be near, unless one of my neighbors down the lake was burning brush. At the driveway to my cabin I looked up to see if someone had broken in. No smoke from the chimney, which was a major relief.

Thirty yards farther I got the first glimpse of the house roof, from which a curl of smoke drifted. Adrenaline kicked in full force and the concept of flight did not cross my mind. Some asshole had broken in to rob the place and had the audacity to light a fire to keep warm while he took his time leaving nothing unsearched.

BOSS SAT IN THE ARMCHAIR with her feet propped on the ottoman. It had taken better than a day to get the house heated because of the high ceilings and the glass pane she'd broken, but McCree had an adequate supply of kindling and wood stored on the screened porch so it was easy to keep the fire stoked.

Unpacking the trailer had winded her beyond anything she had experienced. She had never done hard manual labor, but thought she had gained a true understanding of the expression, "bone tired." As with most true understandings, this one had come too late for her to put it to much use. The day after she arrived, she couldn't do more than feed the fire and sleep.

Boss wasn't even interested in drinking—the booze had no taste and she no longer liked the warm glow in her stomach. The doctor's calendar said she still had time, yet not wanting to drink convinced her it wouldn't be long. Which, to her surprise, didn't much bother her. She was ready and, with that first realization, came an epiphany of sorts: she was not angry at McCree. She forgave him for doing what he thought was right.

Could he forgive her? She had only been doing what she thought was a moral imperative to wrench the country away from the politicians and return it to the people. Just like if you are planting a crop, you need to till the soil; similarly, the best way to give the country a fresh start was to wipe out much of the current government. Fresh elections would plant new seeds. Everything about this objective required money—a lot of money.

By the second full day, a bit of energy returned, but with it more pain. She had not eaten the day before. She went to light the gas stove and the igniters didn't work. She laughed at herself, the sound echoing in the empty house. Of course they didn't work, the electricity was turned off. She rooted around in the mud room and came up with one of those things you used to light recalcitrant grills—what were they called?

Using a flashlight, she surveyed McCree's library in the basement. It was all nonfiction and much of it liberal bullshit, but she did find an interesting read on the wolves and moose of Isle Royale. Mostly she slept or looked out the windows to the lake. A pair of bald eagles cavorted all day, trading ear-piercing calls. It was time for a new generation.

On the third day she found pads of paper and pens in McCree's study. She decided she needed to write to her son and daughter-in-law. She had expected to have a long sit-down conversation to help them understand her reasons—even if they didn't like them. Now it was best for her to write them down while she still had time.

Sunday, she listened to two church services on the wind-up radio McCree had. To her surprise, she found the message from the Catholic mass more to the point. From the death of winter comes the promise of spring, the priest intoned. Although she had not succeeded, with those words she convinced herself a phoenix would arise from the ashes of her failure.

The fire was burning low; she needed to bring in some more wood. She opened the French door onto the porch, loaded an armful of wood, and was surprised to hear someone yell, "Get the fuck out of my house!"

THIRTY-EIGHT

FRUSTRATION BUILDS ON FRUSTRATION AND, unless we find a way to sublimate, it comes out in anger—or so I think I recall from my minor in psychology so many years ago. Anger at whom or what depends on our personalities. My first thought was to charge inside my house and kick the intruder all the way to Amasa, where I would call the police and press every possible charge.

Anger brought me boiling over the hill at a run. Even as I topped the hill between my cabin and house, two competing thoughts fought for control. First, there might be—indeed, there probably was—more than one person in my house. Second, most Yoopers, especially those committing crimes in the backwoods, were armed. I was not. I had again ignored Owen's advice and come into the woods with only my wits. More accurately, only half of them.

I stopped behind a large maple tree and caught my breath and senses. Anger was not going to make me think more clearly, so I set it aside. My injured leg still throbbed with pain. I did not want to get into a shootout. Much as I loved reading his books, I did not want to become Lee Child's Jack Reacher, for whom violence and killing were justified in a good cause and engendered no internal turmoil. Unless it became a last resort—or to protect Paddy—I needed another way.

I was under no obligation to handle this myself. So said my rational side. I actually took several steps toward the nearest year-round camp on Deer Lake where I could get a ride to Amasa. Then a different part of my brain took control. By the time I made it to Deer Lake, got to Amasa, corralled the police, and returned, hours would have passed and the burglars would be long gone. The police would want a description of the criminals and I'd have nothing.

I hadn't spotted a vehicle in the driveway. Keeping the pole barn between me and the house, I jogged to the rear of the pole barn, and pushed in the OSB covering the broken window. Inside were an unknown ATV and trailer. If they were going for a quick grab, wouldn't they have parked close to the ramp for easy loading?

The trailer would have a license plate. Jimmie Heitzmann had accessed my pole barn through the rear window, and I hadn't heard him until he tried to firebomb us. One other thing Jimmie had done was to steal the keys to my vehicles. My turn.

I levered myself through the window, making a lot more racket than I had intended. If whoever was inside the house heard the noise, I'd be trapped with no quick escape. I waited until I could hear something other than the pounding of my heart, tiptoed to the back of the trailer, and memorized the plate number. I pocketed the key, which, in true Yooper style, was in the ignition. Now at least we had equal transportation. Only one helmet sat on the seat. Looked like the burglar was a solo act. As long as I was in the garage, I might as well get the tools I needed to extract my ATV from the mud. I tossed the come-a-long and a chain out the rear window.

Having the plate number, logic said the thing to do was beat a retreat, free my ATV from the mud and ride for help. Of course if the plate was stolen, just like the plate had been on Spider's truck, the number was worthless. I didn't have binoculars like Jimmie Heitzmann had used to spy on me, but I figured I could at least try to get a description of the guy before leaving.

I stayed hidden on the hill and spent a fruitless thirty minutes waiting to see movement in the house. Limited to peering through the unbroken backside windows, I saw and heard nothing. Normally, I might try to look into the side of the house facing the vernal pond, but OSB covered those windows. The opposite side had the screened porch making it tough to see all the way into the house. The lakeside windows provided a viable option. I could slip around the porch, staying far enough in the woods in case anyone was on it, and find a safe place to observe through the wall of windows.

I was most of the way around the house when someone came out the French door from the great room onto the screened porch. I dropped to my knees, landing on a rock I hadn't seen. I went through a mental litany of cuss words in every language I knew while crawling backwards to the protection of a too-thin birch. The person groaned as they loaded their arms with split wood for the fire.

As the person walked toward the interior door, I realized it was K.C. Maki. Without thinking I stood and yelled, "Get the fuck out of my house!"

She dropped the wood in a crash and stared at me. "Why Mr. McCree, this is an unexpected surprise. You alone? Of course you are. Why don't you come in and we'll have us some conversation? I brought whiskey and beer, and I noticed you have some nice-looking wines in your basement. I'd recommend the Laughing Stock. Those Canadians sure have a sense of humor, eh? Course I don't know anything about wine, I just like the label."

Her mocking tone had me clenching my teeth. "You can't escape. I've taken your ATV key."

She laughed and waved her upraised hands in mock surrender. "Oh, my goodness, what shall I do? What shall I do? I didn't come here to escape, Seamus. May I call you that? I do wish you would call me K.C." She started another laugh, which changed to a fierce coughing fit. It might have been an opportunity to rush her, except I was too far away from either the deck steps or the porch ramp.

Once she stopped hacking, she leaned against a four-by-four post as though to get support. I had watched many a killdeer feign broken wings to gradually lead me away from their nests. "You can call me K.C." was not going to con me.

"I'm dying of lung cancer. It won't be long. In a true cause, whenever one soldier falls, another rises to take his, or in my case, her, place. You could leave and get your friends. Then, in one grand last stand, I'd feel compelled to defend myself with the rifle and ammunition I brought. But really, what's the point if I kill one or two or three of you and you kill me? Nothing changes."

"So you admit hiring two guys to come here to kill me?"

She gazed toward the porch as though asking for guidance. "I'm not planning on playing twenty questions, Seamus. I would truly love to sit over a drink or two and have a civilized conversation. Here's what I'm going to do: I'm going to put this wood back—seems like I won't need it now. I'm going to dress more warmly and sit on one of the chairs on the deck with my bottle of whiskey. We'll talk."

She began to cough, which stopped after she slammed her foot down. "If you have a long gun, I'll be an easy target. You got yourself a pistol, you need to be a better shot, 'cause I'm not letting you get close enough to

Taser me and take me in. Nor will you get close enough to rush me. I was born free and I'm going to die free. I will not have you or anyone else put me in a cage."

I contemplated my response while she restacked the wood. Before I decided what to say, she had gone inside. Whatever I had expected, this was not it. I had her ATV key, so she was not going anywhere. I could free my ATV from the mud and notify Bartelle. Or take hers. Any scenario involving Bartelle would end in her death—and maybe some others'. If she died, she would cheat all those who needed the catharsis her trial would provide.

I needed to play for time; I needed to keep her alive. Maybe I could get her to drink enough to pass out. Of course, maybe she was going for her rifle to try to gun me down. I used her absence to sneak closer to the house and burrow behind a large hemlock growing on the mound of a nurse tree. I would be safe there, and I had no doubt that even with a gimpy leg I could outrun her if she tried to get to me.

Five minutes later, she came out shivering in bra and panties, carrying an armful of clothes. She pirouetted. "I'm proving I have nothing hidden." She pulled out the pockets on the pants and shirt before pulling them on, following the same routine to show there was nothing up her sleeve or in her socks or under her hat. "This is all I've got." She waved a pistol above her head. "And this." She held aloft what was probably a whiskey bottle. "No ice. No nothing. You show me the same, and I'll let you go into the basement and get whatever wine you want and we can have ourselves a little down-home chat. Otherwise, we'll have to converse from here to there."

"You tried to kill me too many times for me to trust you with a pistol in your hand," I said. Since she brought out whiskey instead of a rifle, getting her inebriated was still my half-baked plan to allow me to eventually rush and subdue her.

She held the whiskey bottle to her lips and tipped it up. She took three large glugs before setting the bottle down. I wondered if she had filled it with water.

"I want you to know that I forgive you," she said.

"Forgive me? For what?"

"For ruining everything I had planned as my sendoff gift to the nation. But I have to say—" She tilted the bottle back and chug-a-lugged another three swallows. "I have to say, once I forgave you, I became much calmer inside. I'm sure that's what Jesus had in mind. Do you forgive me?"

She did not slur her words. Anyone who could belt straight whiskey as she was ostensibly doing would have to consume a fair piece of the bottle before showing its effects. "I haven't given it any thought," I began, but I realized I had actually thought about it and, no, I could not forgive and forget. Maybe it's in the Irish genes to remember longer than we should. I was better at physically turning the other cheek than at forgiving. "If you've done what I believe you've done, then I don't think I can forgive you for the deaths of so many."

"Every righteous war has cost innocent lives. Think of how many families lost fathers and brothers in our Revolutionary War. Look at the hundreds of thousands of lives we lost putting down our Southern Rebellion. Were they justified?"

What could I say to that? While disgusted that she compared her actions to these events, I was curious how she rationalized things. Perhaps she would reveal details of the plot that could help law enforcement. I chose not to interrupt.

"Thomas Jefferson wrote to Jimmie Madison about the necessity of rebellions." She closed her eyes. Was she falling asleep mid-thought? Moments later she stood and, eyes still closed, recited Jefferson's words:

I hold it that a little rebellion now and then is a good thing, and as necessary in the political world as storms in the physical . . . It is a medicine necessary for the sound health of government.

She opened her eyes and put on an expression that seemed to ask if I had a comment. Knowing time was on my side, I chose continued silence.

She sat down. "Deep down, I'm a libertarian—not one of those crazy libertarians who don't think government should even exist. We need a strong government to deal with other countries. We need one for disasters. We even need one to take care of those who can't take care of themselves. Let me ask you this . . ." She downed another healthy glug of liquor.

"In Lincoln's Gettysburg address, he proclaimed that government of the people, by the people, and for the people would not perish. But it has. Don't you agree that we are now a government of the corporations, by the corporations, and for the corporations?"

"Pretty much," I said.

"And I'll tell you what you'll do about it—not a bloody damn thing.

You're the kind who'll vote Democratic or Republican and think you might make a difference. It doesn't matter one bit. They're both owned by the big corporations. The people need to know freedom again."

"And I suppose killing helpless seniors at the Laughing Loon was going to bring back their freedom?"

Another slug of whiskey. "Their families didn't care enough about them to take them into their homes like we used to do. Think of them as superannuated soldiers giving their lives for you." She shrugged, hacked once, and continued. "If that doesn't work, think of them as the flotsam and jetsam of modern society. We need to bring down the entire federal government. All three branches at the same time. That takes money. Don't you think it's poetic justice that insurance companies would have paid for killing them all?"

What were they going to do, buy a cruise missile and take out the president? And Congress, the Joint Chiefs, and the Supreme Court Justices all at the next State of the Union address? "To be honest," I said. "I think it's crazy."

"I felt the same way at your age. Now, it's something—" She tipped the bottle, drank deeply, and then began to cough. She slammed the bottle on the table and doubled over in the coughing.

A film reel of the church service and the six fatherless children played in my head. They needed a villain to juxtapose with their hero father. I scrambled up and ran toward her. Fully expecting her to take a shot at me, I hoped her racking cough would leave her weak enough to spoil her aim. I lasered in on her, forcing my other senses to allow me to avoid trees and boulders. At the bottom of the steps, I lost sight of her, but could still hear her continue to turn herself inside out with coughing. I crested the stairs and launched myself across the deck. That's when she pulled the trigger.

EPILOGUE

MY NAME IS PATRICK MCCREE. If my father brainwashed you, it's all right if you think of me as "Paddy." He can't speak for himself, so I'm taking over the wrap-up report. Of the various law enforcement agencies, in my opinion, the Iron County Sheriff's Department and the Michigan State Police came out looking the best. In the investigations that followed, none of their officers were criticized, and their cooperation was lauded as a model for other agencies to follow.

The FBI has not released their internal investigation, but both Agent Ashley Pendergast—whom I still call Niki as our private joke—and AIC Cooper were put on administrative leave. Cooper quit and took a job with a corporation. Frankly, I couldn't care less what he's doing as long as we never cross paths again. Niki was reinstated but, since bureaucracies aren't usually fond of independent thinkers, they shunted her to some outpost office in Mississippi. Robert Rand heard about that and offered her a job with CIG. I've kept in touch with her, and in her latest email she said she's sticking it out and learning to like grits.

The chemist who cultivated the *Legionella pneumophila* and prepared the mixture that Boss used to try to kill the Laughing Loon residents pleaded guilty and is residing in an unnamed federal secure facility. Niki kept her promise and briefed Cindy Nelson, my investigative reporter girlfriend, about the entire operation. Cindy vowed to protect Niki and not publish anything until she could get independent confirmation, which has so far been impossible because Homeland Security kept a news blackout on the entire affair. Cindy's Freedom of Information Act request produced material so heavily redacted only the prepositions remained. As far as I can tell, there have been no additional arrests.

The Laughing Loon itself is back in operation with a new owner, new facilities operation manager, and a clean bill of health. Mrs. Ricci reports by text message that the residents are delighted to be back in their rooms, and she and Mrs. Pirhonen are now very close friends. None of them knows the true reason for the residents' evacuation or what was wrong with the heating and plumbing systems.

I don't know who spoke with Owen Lyndstrom, but someone convinced him not to talk about his role in this affair, and in fact, he can keep a secret. He's still a U.P. grapevine regular and with the new computer Dad gave him as a thank-you gift for housing all of us, I've shown him how to automatically keep track of his relatives and friends on several social networks. If it's raining, he's on his computer; if it's not, he's outside making ends meet.

WIKB's funeral report took several days before announcing the death of Kathryn Cynthia "K.C." Maki, survived by her son, Samuel, daughter-in-law, Jeanne, and predeceased by her husband of nearly forty years, Frank. Funeral arrangements were private. Owen tells me she was cremated, but not before her brain was donated to science. Sam Maki resigned the presidency of Hematite National Bank and gave his shares and the ones he inherited from his mother to a charity he created to support victims of violence throughout the Upper Peninsula. I understand he and his wife moved downstate, where he is teaching business math at a community college as an adjunct professor.

I followed Dad's wishes and set up trust accounts to assure all six children of the man murdered guarding my father have the financial means to attend college or trade school. It turns out two of the other murdered men had families also in need of financial assistance, and I found ways to accomplish that as well. Since the stock Sam Maki donated to the charity would take some time to liquidate, I contributed $500,000 of Dad's funds for use as the charity's seed money. I managed everything anonymously, although I'm sure Owen has figured it out by now.

The day after K.C. Maki shot herself on Dad's front deck, he showed up at my office. His taxi waited long enough for him to hand me two things. The first document was a notarized power of attorney authorizing me to handle his finances and legal matters until such time as he revoked the powers. The second was a notarized statement about what happened at his camp the day of Maki's death.

After he had finally extracted his ATV from the mud hole—I asked why he hadn't just taken Boss's ATV. He figured he needed to get his ATV sooner or later, so why not then—anyway, he drove out of the woods, phoned Sergeant Lon Bartelle, and informed him of the events. He paid one of Owen's friends to take him to Milwaukee, where he drew up the legal documents and bought a train ticket to Chicago. He taxied from the station to Evanston to see me and then to Abigail Hancock's apartment in the city. They were gone for the better part of a week. Abigail returned alone. They had talked, she said, really communicated, and had an agreement about their relationship. I didn't figure my power of attorney covered relationships, so I left it at that.

She would not tell me where she left my father, or where he was going, or when I might hear from him. A week or so later, I received an invitation to a private message board. I was about to delete it as spam when I saw the subject heading requested an initial password of "Nessie." In the body of the message it said that if I had not accepted the invitation by midnight, the password would change to "Snuffleupagus."

When I signed into the board, he had left a single message, "Heading to New England. Your grandmother wants to talk."

Thank you for reading this story. If you've enjoyed *Cabin Fever*, I would appreciate your writing a short review and posting it at your favorite online retailer.

The story continues:

Starting on the next page you can read the first two chapters of *Doubtful Relations* . . .

ONE

Momentum, obligation, and a speck of hope pulled me down the Masonic Hall stairwell and out the door. On the back stoop, I reread the text message. *Good News. Call ASAP Urgent.* The more I considered it, the more I was not reassured at nine thirty on a Friday night by the juxtaposition of "good news" with "urgent."

"Happy June first," Karen Miller, my real estate agent, said once we connected. "We've received a full-price offer on your house. It comes with a few conditions. Naturally. Inspection, which we know will be fine."

Her tone struck me as overly cheery. I caught myself chewing my inner cheek. "You're telling me the good stuff. What's urgent?"

"That's the Seamus McCree I appreciate. Always to the point. The buyer insists on meeting you face-to-face. I have absolutely no clue why, and I don't think her broker does either. Makes me nervous."

I wasn't nervous; the worst that could happen was I didn't sell my house to this buyer, which wasn't a change from the current situation. The unusual request made me suspicious. I had never heard of such a thing. Why did the buyer need to see me? What could she want to talk about that only I could answer? Was she someone looking for the inside skinny on the shootings that had occurred there? My son's partner, an investigative journalist, might pull such a stunt to get access to a story—but the shootings were three years ago.

Thinking about that night still gave me the willies. "Aha!" I said and chuckled. "This has all the earmarks of a surprise party. Paddy hinted he was contemplating doing something special for my birthday, but it's a month and a half past. Did he put you up to this?"

"I've never met your son."

"He knows our schedule, so he knows we're in Ohio, only a half day from Cincy. It would be just like him to cook up something like this. You didn't answer my question. He could arrange something without you two actually meeting."

She laughed. "Sounds like fun, but no, I'm not part of some master family conspiracy. Buyer's name is Beth Cunningham from the East Coast. Seems motivated. Wants closing in thirty days. I pretended to object and let them persuade me."

Something about the name tweaked a nerve. I tried to chase it down focusing on my East Coast days, but came up empty. "She's in town?"

"Leaves midday Sunday, which is not much of a window, but if you're only a half day away Lady Luck is on our side. Can you do it?"

"We were planning a leisurely drive down to Mom's next gig in Nashville. That's not until next weekend." All I'd need to do was change some motel reservations. "Tomorrow afternoon?"

"Saturday is perfect. I've already notified the two previous prospects—"

"I need to get back upstairs for Mom's finale. Tell me a time and we'll be there."

"Four thirty. By then I'll know how serious the other prospects are, which will determine our negotiating strategy."

"Tomorrow then." Maybe Lady Luck *was* going my way. This trip with Mom would be complete in another month. She was doing well enough that I could get her permanently situated in Boston and begin getting my own life in order. With Mom settled and shucking the millstone of the Cincinnati house, I could decide where I wanted to live when I didn't want to be at my camp in Michigan's Upper Peninsula. I squeaked open the outside door and, feeling energized, hustled up the concrete steps, my footsteps echoing from the plaster walls and ceiling. I muscled the fire door open and heard chanting.

"Tru-dy. Tru-dy. Tru-dy."

I eyed the scene from the far corner of the auditorium. The chanting reverberated in the spacious room with its fifteen-foot ceiling and hardwood floor. To my left, the bar area was doing a brisk business. Most of the cheering crowd sat in folding chairs ordered to provide access from right, left, and center aisles. Mom beamed from her position on the low stage at the front.

Standing next to her was her most recent victim, a mid-thirties guy with more ink on him than *The Sunday Times Magazine.* A chalkboard stage right indicated she had polished the guy off with her third dart of the throw, a double seventeen, reaching the required 501 score on the dot.

I do not understand how a woman in her seventies can inspire largely male audiences to love her even as she beats the stuffing out of the local darts players. Wherever we went, and in the last three months we had traveled all around New England, upstate New York, Pennsylvania, and now Ohio, the same thing happened. Excusing my way through the chanting crowd, trying not to interfere with the exchange of crumpled bills settling side bets, I parked myself against the center of the back wall and waited for my mother to call me to the stage.

She quieted the crowd and, as was her routine, challenged the last player to a match in which she'd throw lefty. She neglected to mention that she's ambidextrous. After winning with her left hand, she beat the guy a third time employing unusual techniques: hiking her darts, throwing them over her shoulder, standing on one leg, sitting, or doing whatever came into her mind.

We were set for her finale. She introduced the blindfolded challenge with a speech. Alone on the stage, she spoke into the microphone so softly people leaned forward to hear her. She told the story of my father's death—a cop killed on duty when I was young. She spoke of her struggles to get her children through college, and how once I had graduated she had retreated to silence for more than two decades. Two years ago she resumed limited verbal communications and now you couldn't shut her up—the crowd always laughed at the line.

I was unprepared the first time she made her speech, and bawled. Partly because she spoke of my father's death. Partly because she exposed her vulnerabilities to a crowd of strangers, something I could no more do than don a cape and fly like Superman. It had taken me a while, but I could now listen to her story without getting teary.

That night, no one talked, no one moved, no one even drank their beer while she spoke of loss and redemption. Applause pulled me from woolgathering about what tomorrow would bring. I should have been focusing on the task at hand, steadying myself instead of worrying myself into what was quickly becoming a throbbing headache. Not good, and no time for a pain reliever. Mom waited for the applause to die down before she spoke.

"I have one final proposition for you tonight. A small wager, should you choose to participate. But first, I need to accessorize."

On cue, the emcee came on stage and tied a bandanna across Mom's eyes. She tapped the microphone with her finger and at the sound the audience settled. "Give me five darts and I'll bet I can hit the bull's eye."

The crowd's murmur swelled. Mom raised her hand and they quieted. "I'll throw an exploratory dart. My son, Seamus—oh, Shay-mus, where are you?"

Her singsong calling of my name was my cue. I ambled down the middle aisle to polite applause. Once on stage, I gave her a hug.

"This is my son, Seamus. He's available and a good catch if anyone's interested. He has all his own teeth, his hair is natural, although I don't like seeing the gray—makes me feel old. He's six foot two, weighs one eighty-five. He's nearsighted, which accounts for the specs, but ladies, he has the nicest baby blues you have ever seen."

Knowing this was coming, I held my hands up in a "why me?" expression that got a laugh.

"I'll throw a practice dart and Seamus will tell me where it lands. Then I have five more darts to hit the bull's eye. Wouldn't you say the probabilities are against me? Despite that, I'll give you even odds. That's fair, right? Should I be fortunate enough to win, I'll donate my winnings to a charity Seamus helped set up to assist victims of violent crimes and their families. Because of its nonprofit status—and Seamus warns me to say this is in no way tax advice—you should endorse your checks directly to the charity to qualify for a tax deduction. If you don't have a check, we're high tech and have a smartphone credit card reader. If I lose, I hope you will be generous in donating my money to tonight's local charity. The most I ever lost was five thousand bucks. I hope you'll do me proud. Questions?"

A guy with a flushed face and prodigious beer belly yelled, "How do we know you're not cheating?"

Mom put her hands at the sides of her face and mimed a shocked expression. "My goodness. What a world we live in when people don't trust a little old gray-haired widow of a policeman. Sir, why don't you come up and check the blindfold? While he's doing that, could someone record the bets?"

The emcee hopped off the stage and noted wagers on a pad. To a mixture of hoots and claps, the doubting Thomas worked his way forward. He tried to boost himself onto the stage, but his protruding belly struck the edge. Failing a second time, and accompanied by cheers and jeers, he mounted by the side steps.

He made a big show of checking the blindfold, the darts, the dartboard, and frisking me. The audience got into his act and applauded his final bow.

The emcee gave me the thumbs up indicating he had finished collecting the bets. I took the microphone from Mom, led her to the oche—the shooting line—where I stood behind her and aligned her in front of the board exactly parallel to the line. I stepped away and she rearranged herself into her throwing stance, stepping back with her left foot, bringing in her right heel and placing most of her weight over her right foot.

This first dart was a reflection of how well I had pointed her. I held my breath, each heartbeat tapping behind my eyes. A big miss was on me. Once she settled her stance, she wasted no time and zipped a dart that thunked into the board outside the scoring circle between the one and four of the fourteen and a bit higher than halfway up the numbers. My shoulders dropped, relaxing on my exhale. Holding the microphone near my mouth so the audience could hear, I reported the dart's position to her.

She and I, (because I found myself mirroring her breathing), inhaled deeply and let it out. During the exhale she released the next dart. It stuck in the thirteen pie slice, two-thirds of the way between the outer double circle and the inner triple circle. Mom nodded understanding of my description of the dart's location. She made a minor adjustment in her feet placement, breathed in and out, and fired again.

"Nine spot, one-quarter inch out," I said and retrieved her three darts. "Two down and three to go. No pressure, Mom." The spectators, who had moved from their seats to stand close to the stage, nervously giggled at my remark.

"Easy for you to say," Mom retorted, "It's not your money on the line."

The remark received a big laugh, despite the reality that it *was* my money. Why should facts get in the way of theater?

She inhaled and released her breath, apparently did not feel centered, and repeated the process. The dart struck the outer green bull's eye. The audience exclaimed a collective shout of glee. She had picked their pockets and they cheered her.

"Green" I announced into the microphone.

Mom held out her hand, and I gave her the mic. Keeping her back to the audience she raised the mic high over her head to request quiet and, as if they were well-trained first graders, they stopped talking. "Wait. Wait," Mom said. "I didn't mean the *green*. I meant the *red* bull's eye."

The crowd shouted their disagreement. Some restarted the "Tru-dy" chant. Mom handed me the microphone and held up a hand for silence.

After a longer time, she got it. She'd made them believers. They wanted Mom to win their money, and now she was refusing them that privilege.

Part of me was proud of her uncompromising spirit. The headache part of me wanted her to declare victory so I could crash at the hotel.

She made a big show of settling in while I described exactly where in the green the dart had landed. Her movement was all upper body; Mom's feet had not shifted a micrometer from where she had thrown the last dart. A number of Catholics in the crowd now grasped the crosses hung around their necks for good luck. The beer-belly guy was actually kissing his silver crucifix. Mom took a clearing breath before she launched the fourth dart into the center red bull's eye.

The crowd roared its approval. Those close enough slapped their hands on the stage. Others rhythmically stomped their feet on the hardwood floor. "Tru-dy. Tru-dy. Tru-dy."

While I helped Mom remove the bandanna, I wished tomorrow would go as well as tonight, and I'd have my house sold.

Two

"**Such a lovely old brick** house," my mother said as I pulled into my Cincinnati driveway. "It looks even nicer than your pictures. Tell me again why you want to sell?"

Workmen had sandblasted the brick, removing more than a century of accumulated city soot along with the recent fire damage. The wood trim was resplendent in its painted-lady colors. Good-looking wasn't the issue. "Because Abigail was shot here. Because I ended up killing a guy here. Because the bad guys tried to burn down the place." My stomach roiled at the recitation.

"You should smudge the house and get rid of the bad vibes."

"Been there. Done that. Didn't work. Come on, Mom, let me introduce you to my agent."

We exited my ancient Infiniti G-20 and met Karen Miller at her Lexus. She brought a finger to her lips and motioned for us to walk with her. Three city lots down, she stopped. "Sorry for the skulduggery, but I didn't want the competition to overhear us." She offered an aristocratic hand to Mom. "You must be Seamus's mother."

Mom pulled Karen into a big hug. "My son's told me so many nice things about you. Thank you so much for helping him."

Karen's eyes became all pupil, but she hugged Mom right back. My agent's unflappability was a quality I appreciated. Hug over, she faced me. "The couple I told you had an appointment earlier today? I'll eat my hat if we don't get an offer from them. The wife really gave the husband the what for because he hadn't let her make an offer last month. I finally had to push them from the house so they didn't bump into your prospective buyer. We might be able to play the couple off against the offer in hand."

"No," I said. "This Beth Cunningham person made a good-faith, full-priced offer. Let's try to get the couple to make a contingent offer in case this falls through." I inclined my head toward the house. "Anything I should know before I talk with Ms. Cunningham?"

"Be your normal charming self. Are you feeling okay? You look a little . . ."

Shaky, I thought. I said, "I'll be fine." With the likelihood of a second offer, my concerns about screwing up this one lessened. I attributed my parched mouth to the challenges of the house itself. The sooner this was over, the better. "Showtime. Shall we?"

Before I could enter the house Mrs. Keenan yelled, "Alice! Alice, come back here." I turned in time to catch Alice, my next-door neighbor's pampered golden retriever, before she barreled into me. She buried her nose in my crotch while I rubbed her ears. "Belly rub?"

She flopped on her back, her tail sweeping the sidewalk. I squatted down and rubbed her chest and belly. "Okay, Alice." I gave her a couple of solid pats. "I have something I need to do. Go to your mother before you get me in trouble." Alice rose to her feet, gave herself a good shake, and trotted off, grinning as only goldens can do.

Mom: "Friend of yours?"

Karen: "I love golden retrievers, but their hair . . ." She checked her clothes for offending Alice hair.

Me: "I owe Alice and Mrs. Keenan a lot."

Mom: "It won't bother anything if I walk around, will it?"

Karen steered us by the elbow to encourage us toward the house. "You've never been here before, Mrs. McCree?"

I wondered how Mom would spin her decades-long institutionalization at Sugarbush that had prevented her from ever visiting me.

"Trudy—please. I'm embarrassed to say this is my first trip west of the Appalachians. I'm so glad Seamus thought of this idea to combine my passion for darts with seeing the country."

Karen's sales smile appeared. "Darts is such a . . . unique game."

"I grew up living above a bar and it impressed the boys when I beat them."

Karen was still shooing us toward the house. I delayed one final time, pointed at the plantings in front of the house. "Don't those lilies of the valley look nice? Usually they're squashed from the newspaper guy's bad tosses."

The buyer's agent met us in the entryway. Whereas Karen was tailored suits, leather attachés, and heels made for comfort, this guy needed his mother to dress him. His getup included scuffed shoes, mismatched socks, a bulge where his wallet stuck out of his back pants pocket. His top half combined a short-sleeved checked shirt whose buttons strained to control his stomach with a too-wide paisley tie. No briefcase for him, he carried a sheaf of papers in one hand and cheater glasses in the other. He reeked of incompetence and I wondered if the buyer wanted a private chat because she didn't trust her agent to represent her interests.

Karen made introductions. Mom commented on the ten-foot high ceilings and the bold colors I had chosen for the first floor. She decided to start her tour on the third floor and work her way down. Watching her climb the main staircase, I recalled the beautifully carved newels and balusters the fire had eaten. My heart sank. Such old-world craftsmanship was irreplaceable.

The artisans I'd hired had done a nice job rebuilding the house while maintaining its Victorian character, but it wasn't the house I had bought, the house I had once loved. My possessions had either burned in the fire or been ruined by water damage. To make the house more presentable I had rented furniture. A whiff of sawdust and paint still hung in the air underlying the fragrance of the fresh-cut flowers Karen had placed in vases around the house. With a will of its own, my gaze slid from yellow tea roses to the foyer floor where I had killed a man.

As though it had just happened instead of occurring over three years ago, I had a vision of Lt. Hastings, the head of Cincinnati's homicide unit and a personal friend, pointing to the head of the outlined body on the floor. "Seamus stood over him and fired shot after shot after shot while Abbott lay helpless on his back. Ka-pow. Ka-pow. Ka-pow. Ka-pow. Ka-pow. KA-POW."

I shivered remembering the percussive way she had pronounced those ka-pows. Hard as I tried, I could not remember the actual incident, but the memory of Hastings' demonstration accosted me in nightmares and now daymares. Already feeling wobbly, I didn't dare look into the dining room, afraid it would produce visions of Abigail lying nearly dead in a pool of blood. I had replaced all the oak flooring to eliminate any physical sign of the event. Unfortunately, I had found no way to refurbish the floorboards of my memory.

Could I ask the buyer to meet me outside on the porch? Beads of sweat formed on my forehead. With luck this was the last time I had to walk into this house.

"Mr. McCree?"

The question mark in the other realtor's voice broke through my reflection.

"I know this is unusual, and I appreciate your flexibility. Beth is waiting for you in the kitchen."

I edged past the agents, who headed for neutral corners. Approaching the dark passageway between the pantry and the back staircase, I realized this Beth person had closed the kitchen door. Even though it was my house, it didn't feel right to burst in unannounced on the soon-to-be-owner. I hesitated and put my ear to the door. Nothing.

I gave the new solid six-panel door a quick double tap, realized it was insufficient, and knocked loudly. Still nothing. I opened the door and peered in.

She was looking out the window over the sink into the backyard. Her shoulders hunched in on themselves. She held her legs stiffly, as though they would collapse if she gave them permission to relax. Her clothes exuded wealth, but hung limply off her thin frame. My impression was of great sadness, but I might have been projecting my feelings about the house onto her.

Not sure how to proceed, I entered the room and said, "Um, you wanted to see me?"

Twirling fast as a shot-putter, she faced me. "I need your help, Seamus."

It was Lizzie. My ex-wife.

Author's Note

This book is a work of fiction. People familiar with the Upper Peninsula of Michigan will recognize many towns, streets, businesses, and geographical references. I have used all of them in a fictional way to serve the needs of the story. I have also taken the liberty of creating new businesses, roads, and geographical features.

While conducting research for this story, I spent several days in the Iron County Courthouse watching the proceedings brought before the Honorable C. Joseph Schwedler, Chief Judge. He and the Court Administrator, Lori Ann Willman, were kind enough to answer my questions between court sessions. Neither one ever hinted even a stone could have figured out the answers to some of my questions. Hal Arenstein of Cincinnati gave me an insider's look at criminal law from a defense attorney's perspective. As any lawyer reading this story will tell you, it is not a legal procedural, as I have taken a number of liberties with court proceedings.

Similarly, this story is not a police procedural. Sgt. Wade Cross of the Iron County Sheriff's Office and D/Sgt. Jay M. Peterson of the Michigan State Police crime lab in Marquette, Michigan took personal time to help me understand the investigation process. Iron County Sheriff Mark Valesano provided me an insider's view of the county jail. The shortcomings of the fictional Sgt. Bartelle should in no way reflect on the officers or conduct of any of Michigan's various police forces, for which I have high regard.

Cathy Sonnenberg and Kaye George of my Guppy chapter of Sisters in Crime critique group provided excellent insight on areas for improvement in an early draft of this work. I also received very helpful suggestions from my beta readers: E.B. Davis, Dottie Caster, Dave and Rita Stull, Marcia Eckstein, and Mary Kellogg.

A special thanks to Barking Rain Press in the person of Sheri Gormley, who again agreed to help bring the story to life. And a ginormous thanks to my editor, Julie Spergel. She not only saved me from howlers such as having people drive automobiles that were not available to them and attending doctor appointments in the middle of a weekend, she sorted through my sometimes idiosyncratic grammar and wording choices to help make the manuscript sing.

As with my earlier publications, Jan Rubens has been my first reader and my last reader; but if there are any errors left, they are all mine. Right, honey?

James M. Jackson
Amasa, Michigan

James M. Jackson authors the Seamus McCree series.

Jim has also published an acclaimed book on contract bridge, One Trick at a Time: How to start winning at bridge.

He calls the deep woods of Michigan's Upper Peninsula home. You can find out more about Jim or sign up for his newsletter at his website, https://jamesmjackson.com.